AGENDA INDISCRIMINATE

A Leap of Justice

―――――――――∽∞∽―――――――――

By

PETER HARPER

Copyright © Peter Harper 2021
This book is sold subject to the condition that it shall not, by way of trade or otherwise, be lent, resold, hired out, or otherwise circulated without the publisher's prior consent in any form of binding or cover other than that in which it is published and without a similar condition including this condition being imposed on the subsequent publisher.
The moral right of Peter Harper has been asserted.
ISBN-13: 9798522356538

This is a work of fiction. Names, characters, businesses, organizations, places, events and incidents either are the product of the author's imagination or are used fictitiously. Any resemblance to actual persons, living or dead, events, or locales is entirely coincidental.

By the same author:

Cascade

Death of a Lie

AUTHOR'S NOTE

Agenda Indiscriminate is a stand-alone novel.
However, the background to the Lend-Lease B-25 plane,
mentioned in the Prologue, can be found in *Death of a Lie*
– as can the fictitious West African country, 'Séroulé',
occasionally referred to in the latter stages of *Agenda Indiscriminate*.

Additional note

FMLN is a political party in the Republic of El Salvador
(*Farabundo Martí Liberación Nacional*)

ACKNOWLEDGEMENTS

Special thanks to the Roque Dalton Foundation, El Salvador,
(*Roque Dalton Fundación y Archivo*)
for permission to quote from the poem 'Todos'
and to
UCA Editores, El Salvador, publishers of *Patria Exacta*,
for permission to quote from the poem 'Exact Homeland'
by Oswaldo Escobar Velado

Daylight Thrillers
www.ricochet-universal.com

"Any intelligent fool can make things bigger, more complex, and more violent. It takes a touch of genius – and a lot of courage to move in the opposite direction."
E.F. Schumacher, author of Small Is Beautiful

"There are many things that can only be seen through eyes that have cried."
Óscar Romero

CONTENTS

AUTHOR'S NOTE i
ACKNOWLEDGEMENTS iii
PROLOGUE 1
PART 1 FRACTURED 13
    CHAPTER 1 13
    CHAPTER 2 26
    CHAPTER 3 39
    CHAPTER 4 45
    CHAPTER 5 53
    CHAPTER 6 70
PART 2 TREASON 81
    CHAPTER 7 81
    CHAPTER 8 91
    CHAPTER 9 100
    CHAPTER 10 108
    CHAPTER 11 121
    CHAPTER 12 131
    CHAPTER 13 137
    CHAPTER 14 144
    CHAPTER 15 151
    CHAPTER 16 158
    CHAPTER 17 164
    CHAPTER 18 175
    CHAPTER 19 187
    CHAPTER 20 194
    CHAPTER 21 206
    CHAPTER 22 212
    CHAPTER 23 226
    CHAPTER 24 236
    CHAPTER 25 251
    CHAPTER 26 264
    CHAPTER 27 274

PART 3 RETRIBUTION 282
    CHAPTER 28..282
    CHAPTER 29..288
    CHAPTER 30..294
    CHAPTER 31..301
    CHAPTER 32..308

PROLOGUE

Manhattan, New York Even when he stayed over in Santa Monica with its wall-to-wall sunshine, theatres, art galleries and legendary restaurants, there was nowhere Joshua Waldo preferred to be than at his brownstone on East 81st Street. Its interior design wasn't lavish by any standards. In fact, one might have expected the president of Loran Communications to dwell in architectural splendour around the corner on Fifth Avenue, with stunning views of Central Park. But no, Waldo had never been one for over-indulgence when it came to bricks and mortar, often confounding his peers and competitors who could never quite size him up. And now, having just racked-up eighty-seven years, he was, by his own admittance, a worn-out relic, biding his time for the inevitable.

That was how he'd felt last week, and the week before that. In point of fact, for the past couple of years, if the truth be told. Until, that is, four days ago when a couriered document came into his possession, its impact having reawakened this media 'dinosaur'. Ahead of him now, staring straight at him, was the endgame for which Loran Communications had perhaps been built to deliver. The cost didn't matter. Hell no, for he was about to go to war – a war like no other. Until now, he'd questioned whether he had the grit to see it through. But then, as can happen on occasion to a nagging dilemma, fate intervened – in this instance, like a sword slicing open a vale with a swift, well-defined downward stroke.

Waldo leaned back from his desk and the microfilm projector, taking with him the envelope from the courier. Judging by the labels on the outside, coupled with the anonymous note within, the package had begun its journey in Romania.

Discovered in the wreckage of a Lend-Lease B-25 that came down in Timișoara, Romania, in 1944. With each and every crisis now unfolding and gaining momentum, the material contained within can no longer be ignored.

Good luck!

Obviously, he'd cross-checked the scant facts in the introductory note and could now confirm that a Lend-Lease B-25 Mitchell had indeed crashed on the outskirts of Timișoara in 1944, having departed Gore Field Airbase in Montana, refuelling at Ernest Harmon in Newfoundland and again at RAF Ballyhalbert, Northern Ireland. From the single photograph he'd managed to unearth on the Web, he imagined that, unless they'd parachuted from the plane, the Soviet aircrew had died instantly since the wreckage lay strewn across a couple of smallholdings, the buildings of which appeared to have remained miraculously intact.

Aside from the note, the envelope included several sheets of photocopied paper covered in code. It was a relatively simple code to decipher, a combination of Polybius and Playfair Squares, the information more or less mirroring what was on the microfilm. The contents of the envelope merely confirmed what he already knew: the extent of the Agenda. But it had inspired the cogs to turn, and four days later they were still turning.

Waldo reached for the current *International Filmmakers' Directory* on the side table next to him, and opened it at the point where a folded piece of plain paper protruded. He ran his finger past the biographical passage where it mentioned that Rafael Maqui had begun his life in El Salvador before stowing away with his mother on a voyage via Panama to the Port of Tilbury. He was twelve years old, although the accompanying asterisk and footnote stated that his age could not be precisely determined.

Films: Shorts – The Fearful Night *(act.) 2007;* Despatch *(unfinished) 2008;* Damage *2008;* The Fisherman *(act.) 2009. Features* – Tomorrow Calling *(co-dir. with A. Selden; UK) 2010;* The Unforgivable Reprieve *(act.; UK/Fr.) 2012;* Loki's Amendment *(UK) 2014;* Gift-Wrapped and Loaded *(act.; UK/Fr./It.) 2015;* Rose *(UK) 2018;* A Song for Nemesis *(UK/Ger.) 2020;* The Short Straw *(UK) 2022. Documentaries* – Murderous Distraction? *2017;* Rainbow Obscure *2019*

He closed the book, just as a couple of knocks came on his study door.

'Anna?' he called.

The door swung open and in came his 'treasure', Anna Sangster: domestic and social fixer – a slender, fragile-looking yet infinitely energised woman in her mid-sixties. 'You had your nap, Joshua? I'm not fussing.'

Waldo chuckled and then dipped his hand back and forth. 'Not sure. Too much happening in the grey cells. But I'm fine.'

'Something more for you to chew on,' said Anna. 'He's just called back. Lena Rudbeck's giving a charity concert down in El Salvador. Something she does every year, apparently. Rafael said if all goes well, it'll be Tuesday when they arrive in Santa Monica.'

'He sounded enthusiastic?'

'Intrigued, I got from his tone.'

Waldo smiled quietly. 'I guess that's the reaction we should expect at this stage.' He sank deeper into the armchair. 'Know what? I might try for those forty winks now, Anna.'

* * *

Two months later: Brighton, 13:29 hrs. Guy Brooker saw the commotion from his room, two floors up on the cramped suburban street. The two boys ran out together from a side alley and almost knocked over the postman, who swore at the pair of them. The taller of the two boys threw up a V-sign in response while his pal whooped and then followed suit. Brooker turned to the dresser with its chipped mirror and reached for his mobile phone. The face that stared back at him through wintry grey eyes under tangled black hair looked older than his thirty-four years, the cheeks sallow and sunken. He went back to the window, took the SIM card from the phone and ground it to nothing against the stone ledge.

Just as the breeze blew away the particles of silicone, he glanced over his shoulder at the knock on the door.

'I have a letter for you, Mr Brooker. Are you there?'

Ocean View B&B's somewhat chubby landlady tried to peer into the room as she handed over the envelope, but Brooker swiftly closed the door in her face. She muttered something under her breath before her footsteps faded down the corridor.

He tore open the envelope.

HOLBARTH ACADEMY PRESENTS

LENA RUDBECK

Supported by PROTIUS

… … … *Zone-H* … … …

7:15 pm

The date had been stamped on the back of the ticket, Friday – this very day. He took the last cigarette from the duty-free packet on the dresser and picked up the gun from the chair in the corner of the room. It had the name *Zigana* on it, with *C45* emblazoned in silver along its muzzle. He swung it around, pointing it at a picture pinned to the wall of a flaxen-haired girl standing in front of a microphone.

Brooker grinned and gritted his teeth. 'No more days left for you, girl. Only hours, cos you *tortured* me. I told you. Why didn't you listen? Why didn't you *stop*!'

Putting the cigarette in the corner of his mouth, he wedged the Turkish handgun in his waistband, tugged the zip up on his fleece jacket and vacated the guest house. Seeing the keys to the premises in his hand, he chucked them into a lopsided laurel bush and left the gate wide open.

* * *

Later that day, much of which he'd spent drinking cans of lager on a bench in Queen's Park, Guy Brooker caught a train to London, arriving at Victoria on the tail end of the rush hour. While following a steady stream of commuters down an escalator to the Underground, he deftly switched the Zigana to an inside pocket just as a train approached the southbound platform. Shouldering his way through a barrage of passengers, he snatched a seat alongside an elderly West Indian lady, her left arm drawn up in a sling. The woman clutched her canvas handbag and jerked her head away from him, as if he'd given her an electric shock. As he disembarked at Stockwell, he caught sight of the woman wrinkling her nose and flapping her hand theatrically in front of herself.

Brooker bought a packet of cigarettes from a kiosk and chain-smoked his way through the drizzle along the Clapham Road towards the Oval Cricket Ground, before joining a restless audience at the Holbarth Academy, a concrete monstrosity formerly known as the Sapphire during its days as the first multiscreen cinema south of the river. The support band had ended their gig by the time Brooker arrived; a shimmering blue mist presently drifting across the stage, accompanied by a succession of vibrant chords that resonated around the auditorium.

Lena Rudbeck made her entrance by means of a trapdoor, working her trademark Ibanez guitar through the overture to *Midnight Surrender*. A roar went up from the four-thousand strong audience, followed by whistles of approval. The drummer's hands shifted to an explosive blur above the percussion as the flaxen-haired singer crossed the stage to join her bass guitarist.

Brooker turned to leave the auditorium, moving through a fire exit into a long corridor. He passed an Asian-looking girl who was crying, her male companion holding her hand while muttering words of solace. An unusually wide door in the distance displayed the words STRICTLY NO ADMITTANCE. Brooker picked up his pace, crashing his hand onto the door's push-release bar. Ahead of him, two burly security guards positioned above a row of steps halted their chitchat.

'Hey, buddy!' shouted the one on the left. 'Where d'you think you're going?'

Brooker pulled the gun.

'*Jesus!*' gasped the guard opposite.

The gun kicked up as Brooker shot him in the thigh, the startling report blending into *Midnight Surrender*. The guard went down with a twisted face and his astonished colleague didn't hesitate to raise his hands.

'Don't...don't do it.' His voice was a near squeal, eyes bulging. 'I got kids!'

Brooker kept the gun on him before peeling off into a separate, narrower corridor. More steps, and another door. He struck the release bar and the door flew open. He felt himself floating, his feral eyes seeing an array of technicians frantically abandoning various pieces of equipment that blocked his path onto the stage. He kicked an amplifier aside – and then caught sight of her, radiant like a sunlit fountain.

Lena Rudbeck happened to step back from the microphone at the precise moment Brooker appeared from the wings. She gave a double-take, her face scarcely having the time to switch from bewilderment to horror before the first bullet struck her shoulder. The impact threw her like a rag doll to the floor. Brooker immediately strode over to her and fired another three shots into her torso and neck. Then he pulled away, only to gaze down at what his broken mind had ordered him to do.

Screams spread rapidly through the audience, people scrambling towards exit points that rapidly became choked by the volume of bodies fleeing the auditorium. Directly behind Brooker, a couple of backing vocalists and other members of the band vanished into the wings, the exception being the bass player, who daringly flung his Rickenbacker at Brooker.

The guitar struck Brooker on the chest and upper arm. He lost his footing and the Zigana tumbled from his grasp. He quickly scooped it back up, swept his straggly hair from his face and aimed at the base player. The gun wavered, Brooker screaming an obscenity at the petrified musician, who stood like a mannequin in a wash of pale-yellow light.

Brooker stared directly into the frenzied auditorium, rivulets of sweat running down his face. He'd seen it before, in his illuminative dreams – the completion of the task: a blur of red mist from the violent detonation spewing itself across the stage and over Lena Rudbeck's inert body. From that point on, he would own her, and do so for eternity – the fusion of blood on blood.

Brooker screamed again to drain and purify his soul for the journey ahead of him. With a final surge of adrenaline, he raised the Zigana to his head and readily jerked his index finger against the hair-trigger.

* * *

Pimlico, 20:37 hrs. Rafael Maqui left the ringing telephone to switch over to the answering machine, closed the door to the backroom behind him and handed his principal cameraman a memory stick. 'Better I don't send it electronically,' he said, moving into the kitchen. 'Could be construed as sensitive by some, I suppose.'

'Not the entire screenplay, then?' Marc Fauré's accent was heavily French, its tone conjuring red wine flowing over gravel.

'I'm still waiting for the speech penned by Joshua Waldo. Much of the related material rests between the lines, the key characters that we'll be targeting yet to be named.' Rafael poured a couple of beers. 'Take your time. No urgency.'

Marc slipped the memory stick into an inside pocket of his duffel coat. 'I'll take a look at it over the weekend. You'd still prefer it to be a documentary?'

'Keeps crossing my mind, I have to say.' Rafael fed the Budweiser bottles into the waste compartment under the sink unit. 'But you know how it is, the moneyman has the final say. If we do it right, I figure it'll receive a wider audience. So, I guess Waldo has a point.'

'What about a sabbatical after this one?' Marc took a swig of beer. 'I'd like to get out to Nepal, do some trekking. It struck me the other day we've been almost as prolific as Fassbinder.' He took another swig. 'How about it? A sabbatical?'

Rafael sat at the table, only vaguely aware of what Marc was saying. The phone call prior to whatever message had just been left on the answering machine had put him on edge. He just hadn't expected it. Although, on reflection, perhaps that wasn't quite true.

'You disapprove?' said Marc.

Rafael looked up. 'Sorry?'

'Taking a sabbatical?'

'Oh, that.' Rafael struggled to put the call out of his mind. 'No, I agree. Hell, we deserve time off.' He drove a hand through his tousled hair and reminded himself to visit a barber. 'By the way, we want to make an announcement this evening – Lena and myself. You'll need to bring Susan over.'

'Announcement?'

'All in good time. Just the closest of friends arriving after the concert.'

'Intriguing.' Marc came and sat at the table. 'You seem distracted. Something to do with this announcement?'

Rafael toyed with a pencil. Up until ten minutes ago, it had been a perfect day. The most perfect day of his life – without question. He returned the pencil to the table. 'Before you arrived, I had a call from El Salvador.'

Marc noticeably stiffened and held his beer an inch or so from his lips. 'Oh, yes?'

'It's developed into a desperate situation. There's a rumour that the *Mara Salvatrucha* – in other words MS-13 – is set to join forces with the 18th Street gang against the government. I can't quite believe it myself. Up until now the gangs have hated each other. Fact is, I've been asked to go out there. Maybe I really could be of some use. Who knows?'

'No way.' Marc put down his glass and squared his shoulders. 'Look, we're all deeply sympathetic. The situation's dire – horrifically so. But contractual obligations aside, if you don't come back, you're going to wreck lives over here.' He hardened his stare to the point of glacial. 'Right? I mean, Lena, just to start with, for Christ's sake!'

Rafael nodded quietly and finished his beer, Marc's inevitable perspective already working away at settling his dilemma. 'The call caught me out,' he confessed, leaving the table and swilling out his glass. 'Threw me, emotionally.'

'Of course. But you can still be an effective voice from London.' Marc took a disposable lighter from his coat pocket and lit a Gauloise. 'As for this minute, are we going to leave to catch the last half of the concert, or what?'

'They're having some fun, by all accounts – the last gig of the tour.' Rafael glanced at his watch. 'Might as well head on over. I'll just go upstairs.' He left the kitchen to change his shoes, hearing Marc's mobile phone emit its saxophone ringtone. He was finding it hard to keep a lid on the 'declaration' he and Lena intended to spring on their friends after the concert. Just a few hours more, he told himself, reaching the bedroom. And then...well, one hell of a celebration!

Rafael tied the laces on a pair of sneakers and went back down into the hallway. Marc seemed different; he noticed it immediately. No two ways about it, in fact – ashen and vague-looking. Rafael clapped a hand on his shoulder. 'Hey, don't fret about it, *mon ami*.' He was surprised that the mere mention of the phone call had affected Marc so profoundly. 'I'm not going to Salvador.' He took his keys from the kitchen table and started to set the alarm in the cupboard under the stairs.

Marc steadied himself, putting a hand on a wall, his eyes avoiding Rafael. 'Jeff,' he muttered weakly. 'He's...he's just called. They're taking Lena to St Thomas' Hospital.'

Rafael swung away from the alarm panel. 'Hospital? Whatever for?'

Marc shook his head and stared down at the chenille rug he happened to be standing on. 'I-I don't know. I mean...'

Bewildered, Rafael crossed the hallway and seized his arm. 'Marc, tell me.'

'We've got to go there. To the hospital. Jeff said something about a guy with a gun.'

'*A gun?*'

Lena's been shot…that's what Jeff said. She's been shot.'

'Shot?' Rafael felt his chest drop to the floor. 'But, Marc—'

Marc freed himself. 'Come on, Rafael. We'll use my car. We've got to hurry.'

'But where? How? At the concert? What the hell are you *saying*?'

Marc opened the door. '*Merde!* They're here already. Come on!'

Rafael went over to Marc, horrified by what he saw. His mouth became parched as journalists and paparazzi poured into the street from all directions – some arriving on motorbikes, others by car, the scale of the incident all too apparent.

I've got to reach her! Rafael told himself. He remembered to close the door, his hands shaking while a part of him considered whether what was happening could all be explained away as a macabre dream. But as he stepped onto the pavement, he found himself focusing on a sterile plaster, wrapped partially around a hand clutching a Dictaphone. The plaster, its edges frayed and with a slight stain, seemed to trigger a sense of outright panic in him. He could see Marc's car across the street and he started to shoulder his way through the barrage of questions and jostling cameras, his hands clenched into fists and ready to lash out before he realised Marc was no longer at his side. Anxious, he turned his head, and caught sight of him listening with a look of dismay to a bearded journalist they both knew.

'What's going on?' demanded Rafael as he strode over to them. 'What's happened to her?' His eyes locked onto the journalist. 'Tell me!'

The journalist exchanged an uneasy glance with Marc. 'It's not good, Rafael. Not good at all.'

'But she's okay? Right? Lena *is* okay?'

Marc grabbed Rafael's arm. 'This is too much. We have to get away from here.'

Rafael swiped a camera out of his way and turned on the journalist. 'What did you just tell him? What did you tell Marc?'

'Rafael, we'll go back inside,' intercepted Marc. 'This isn't the place—'

'I want to know what he said to you!'

'She…' For a second Marc looked at Rafael's crazed eyes. 'I'm so sorry…' His voice began to crack as tears rolled down his face, glistening against the digital flashes. He raised a hand to Rafael's ear as though to mask what he had to say from the invasive microphones. 'Lena…Lena's left us. The hospital, they couldn't…they just couldn't save her, Rafael.'

Rafael felt himself go blank inside, as if his vital organs had been switched off. He tried to say Lena's name, as if saying her name would put everything back together. But then a camera flashed, a sheet of silvery-white lightning that cut into his eyes. His legs buckled and he felt himself falling away from Marc, the shouting around him fading swiftly into oblivion.

PART 1

FRACTURED

CHAPTER 1

Departamento de Chalatenango, El Salvador

'Rafael!' cried a damaged voice from a jagged outcrop of rock.

Rafael wedged his back against a tree, frantic. Having virtually annihilated the MS-13 cell, the one who'd fled had evidently taken the decision to pick up their trail. He looked across his shoulder, his guide some thirty metres away and out of sight.

'Your condition?' he hollered. 'Give me your condition, damn it!'

'I'm down. Leaking bad—'

A torrent of gunfire came at them and seemed to shake the ground, squirts of dust moving off into the skyline.

'Javier?' Rafael's scared eyes flashed across the sweltering lowland. 'Javier – I can't locate him!'

'He's in the trees. One-fifty metres, max. I'm out.'

Rafael struggled with trembling fingers to feed fifteen bullets onto a stripper clip to replenish the Kalashnikov's magazine. Once spent, he had little with which to protect himself other than a borrowed machete. But did he truly care? He laid the worn machine-gun between his outstretched legs, the temptation altogether more rational, more *coherent*, than ever before.

'Rafael,' called Javier, 'what are you doing?'

'I'm thinking...' Rafael shut his eyes against the searing sun.

'*Thinking?* Shit, I need you over here!'

Rafael figured that on balance it would be a selfish act. Although he could make it appear it wasn't his choice – the gunman wiping him out. Just a split second, that's all it would take. A single breath, out there in the open. But if he quit this lousy wreck of a world, his guide would be captured, hideously humiliated, and then shot. No two ways about it.

'*Rafael?*'

He wiped the sweat from his brow, and managed to gouge a small rock out of the parched earth. 'I'm working on it...'

Another burst of gunfire came at them, the salvo crackling through the air and splintering bark like shrapnel from surrounding trees.

'Son of a bitch!' Javier raged. 'You've got to do something, Rafael. My rifle's jammed. He hit that too!'

Rafael was barely listening. He snatched a breath and threw the rock at a cluster of barbed bushes as a diversion – as if he were tossing a piece of equipment to a previously unsighted compañero. The bushes rustled and, sure enough, gunfire erupted. He rolled out from his cover, already firing into the densely wooded area in the far distance. He aimed low and then zigzagged his way further up into the canopy before ducking back behind the outcrop of rock, unaware that his right side was fractionally exposed.

'Javier, what do you reckon?' he hollered.

Silence.

'Javier?'

A stream of gunfire tore back through the stillness, and it was as if a thunderbolt had blown apart his arm. Rafael cried out and dropped from his knees onto his shoulder, struggling to breathe, his lungs semi-paralysed by shock...

...before all the suppressed outrage in him finally broke loose. He seized the Kalashnikov with his left hand and manoeuvred it awkwardly to return the gunfire. The sound of silence came and went, his own voice pleading with whatever to take his last breath as his head spun under a molten sky.

* * *

Against the volcanic terrain, the makeshift sled finally disintegrated beyond repair, just as they came to a ceiba tree with huge buttress roots on an otherwise desolate ridge. Rafael threw the rope down into the dust. Javier's bloodied legs were grotesque enough, but it was the wound to his chest and the crimson smear on his lips that concerned him more. Rafael propped his guide up against the tree. Javier's eyes flickered open. He was dazed but able to shoot Rafael a look of intuitive gratitude before passing out again.

Rafael squatted and took another look at the wound to his forearm: an ugly fusion of congealed blood and puckered flesh. He still imagined the gunman to have been attached to the MS-13 cell rather than some 18th Street rogue squad. To have these two gangs in El Salvador was a heartbreak of a tragedy. He blamed it on erroneous decision-making from the Pentagon, way back in the 1970s, and the civil war that erupted as a consequence of the pervasive paranoia that left-wing ideology was sweeping up from the south into Central America. But it went deeper than that – a whole lot deeper, the strings being pulled behind the scenes by so-called 'presidential advisers' whose agenda was more deadly than anything any president or dictator could possibly envisage or implement.

The swelling had now reached his hand. Rafael leaned against the ceiba's smooth trunk as Javier's head lolled onto his shoulder. How far were they from the village? A couple of kilometres at most, perhaps. If they could find a vehicle of some description... Rafael almost laughed at himself. He was in a state of delirium, for God's sake. In the midst of such poverty, it would be a sensation to find transport of any kind in these hills other than perhaps a haggard-looking mule!

Javier stirred. 'Rafael...' His eerie rasp was horribly distant as if it were already halfway into the next world. 'Take me to a field of corn. The silent ones will lead the way.'

Rafael's fingers touched a stone, which he seized and threw at a bush that was managing to survive in the scorched environment. 'It's the village we need,' he told Javier tersely. He wasn't in the mood for mindless talk, regardless of whether his guide had taken leave of his senses. 'Nothing's changed.'

Javier's leathery face lightened, until he started to choke on the blood in his throat. He part swallowed and part spat it out. 'Forget the village. The Good Shepherd couldn't put me back together. Admit it.'

Rafael wiped his brow, the heat more intolerable than ever. Even the birds had fallen silent. He found himself staring at the dash of blood Javier had brought up as an insect moved towards it, the cycle of life showing itself to be as monstrous as it was relentless.

'I'll tell you this...' Javier held the wound to his chest. 'The ring tied to my neck is worth many dollars. If we don't reach...reach the corn, you can take it. But if we find some corn, the ring goes into the earth with me. What you say?'

'I say go to hell!' snapped Rafael. 'For Christ's sake...' He dropped his head into his hands, the absurdity of life dragging him down into a pit of constant outrage and despair.

Javier chuckled up another dash of blood. 'You break my heart.'

Rafael looked across at him: it was surreal that Javier could be so blasé. 'You're certifiable,' he said. 'I'm telling you.'

'You don't say…'

Drained to the bone, Rafael struggled to haul Javier up onto his shoulder, managing it on the second attempt. '*Definitely* certifiable.'

* * *

The maize had been planted on a terrace behind the ridge from the ceiba tree, and Rafael was surprised by the crop's vitality, given the arid earth in which it was expected to survive. He knelt beside Javier and moistened his lips with the thimbleful of water he had left.

'Because of what happened to Lena, you wanted to die this time, Rafael,' uttered Javier, straight from nowhere. 'The pictures…the pictures and the risks you took prove I speak the truth. But it's not an issue this way. You're the only one out of us who can make the film.' He looked away. 'Thirsty… Talk too much. My problem.'

Rafael caught hold of Javier's ragged collar and had to stop himself from shaking him. 'Listen to me, damn it! Just *listen* to me. Keep talking. I'll get help. I'll fix things. The village can't be far away.'

'It's about…about faith, *mi amigo*,' Javier said through clenched teeth. 'Live each day with faith, and liberty will grace this world. This miracle… Rafael?'

Rafael reached for his guide's hand, dreading the moment when its flesh grew cold. *If there is a God…* he told himself.

'The corn, Rafael…' Javier persevered against the mess trickling across his jaw. 'Protect the corn.'

* * *

The blistering sun quickly dried the blood on Javier's empty face.

Rafael struggled to let go of the calloused hand. Putting aside profound memories that erupted haphazardly across his mind's eye, he cut a head of corn with his machete and folded Javier's blunt fingers around it. Then he realised he wanted to make the sign of the cross.

'Ask the spirit world to guide me, *mi querido amigo*. It is my wish. My only wish.'

Rafael wiped away his tears as a verse from *Todos* by the revolutionary poet, Roque Dalton, deepened the shadow that had cast itself across his existence.

To be a Salvadorean is to be half-dead.
That which still moves
Is that half of life they left us
And as all of us are the half-dead
The murderers presume not only that they are alive
But also immortal
But they too are half-dead
Living only by halves...

Rafael rarely smoked, but seeing the squashed packet of cigarettes at Javier's side made him light one – all the while looking around himself, primal instincts beginning to rise above his grieving. Having abandoned his own rifle with its discharged ammunition, he now needed to re-arm himself for it was well known that *bandidos* roamed this brutal landscape of volcanic rock and seared earth.

* * *

The settlement lay in a shallow valley some distance from the cornfield. Rafael wiped the dust from his lips as he shuffled between seemingly deserted shacks with ill-fitting doors and rooftops, much of the materials used in their construction likely to have been scavenged. Then, quite suddenly, he heard voices coming from a concrete structure that had its precarious shutters wide open. He ventured inside and found a place where staple goods such as powdered milk, beans, cooking oil and rice could be purchased – as well as alcohol. He looked further around the poky lean-to. The basic seating area was almost deserted, although he had the feeling there were more than two pairs of eyes upon him – this stranger who, without any warning, had appeared in their midst. He knew what they were thinking: that he was an omen – an ill omen. And they were right; the news he had for them was wretched enough.

He sat down quietly at a table next to an archway with flaking blue paint. A couple of hens in the adjoining yard pecked at the bare earth while a cockerel hesitantly approached and then retreated from a mongrel dog dozing in the midday heat. Way beyond were the mountains he had traversed for the past couple of days. It hit him then, like a dull thump in his solar plexus that made him want to retch, that he wasn't ever going to see Javier again. He looked down at the blood on his shirt, the blood of the dead and of the living. Well, he felt dead too. It would be perfect to be just that. Such indulgence!

He shook his head, irritated by his self-pity. After all, everyone was in some fix or another, even the peasant several tables away who sipped his beer slowly, methodically, like an automaton in a shop window.

To be a Salvadorean is to be half-dead.
That which still moves
Is that half of life they left us…

'You are wounded.'

Rafael glanced up from the table, startled by the interruption. He'd been vaguely aware of the girl, making *pupusas* or whatever from a bowl of cornmeal while chatting occasionally to the elderly campesino, but he hadn't taken any notice of her looks. What he saw now as she came and stood over him was a rather inquisitive face, the whiteness of her teeth against her dark skin and black hair luminous by way of contrast.

'I will take care of it,' she said, unfolding her arms. 'So long as you are nothing to do with MS-13 or 18th Street. If you are, then you can go to hell.'

Rafael raised a hand as he fought to contain his mood. 'Three beers, then you take care of it.'

The girl hesitated. 'Do you have money?'

'I'm thirsty.'

'I can get you water. Water would be better for you if you are thirsty.'

'I want beer. And a rifle. I need a rifle.'

The girl swung away, a distinct air of defiance about her.

'Hey, you!' flared Rafael. He started to stand, his legs a little shaky. 'What are you doing? A simple request.'

She looked over her shoulder. 'We are not a charity. I will fix your wound and give you water. That is all we can afford to do.'

From a doorway behind her, a man moved towards the counter. His face was gaunt, with pouches of wizened flesh beneath the narrow eyes that were now fixed on Rafael.

'I am José Roldós, the owner of this store. What is it you want from us?' His tone was neither hostile nor convivial.

'A rifle,' insisted Rafael, running a sleeve over the feverish sweat on his brow.

From under the counter, the owner produced a 9mm Colt pistol. 'It's all I can offer you.' He handed it over. 'My rifle stays with me.'

Rafael examined the gun briefly. It felt chunky in his grasp, and in that same instant he was reminded of the Zigana handgun and the Holbarth Academy. If *only* he'd attended the concert. He might just have set eyes on the madman before he made his deadly entrance onto the stage… He put the gun down on the table. 'And if it's not stretching you too much, three beers. I'll pay you back another day, five times the amount owed. For now, you can take my wristwatch, worth seventy dollars – minimum. Is that acceptable?'

The owner gave the girl a business-like glance. 'Senica, three beers for our guest.' He turned back. 'There is no need for your wristwatch, señor. What news?'

Rafael waited for the girl to serve him before speaking – noticing for the first time a faded portrait of El Salvador's most celebrated archbishop, Óscar Romero, pinned to an adjoining wall. His assassination, with all the hallmarks of having been directed by the junta government at the time, had very nearly demolished with a single blow the campesinos' morale and consequently their uprising against the ruling oligarchy. Now there was an altogether different civil war: the battle to make El Salvador an anarchistic state.

'For you, it's not good,' Rafael told the owner. 'The rumour persists that both gangs have joined forces, totally set on corrupting the government into what they want it to be. MS-13, in particular, are causing havoc by taking money from whoever has it – from companies, stores, even a church in Cuscatlán. I've heard 18th Street intend to hit on Sensuntepeque.' Using his left hand, he sipped some beer. It wasn't chilled; the settlement equipped with intermittent electricity at best. 'How many of you are there?'

'Ninety-three.' The owner shrugged his skinny shoulders. 'Maybe ninety-four by the morning. It would be just Antonia's luck.'

'Then I suggest you follow the Lempa to Honduras, and that you leave tonight. From this point, you can only be ten kilometres from the border at the most. If 18th Street head down from Chalatenango to Sensuntepeque they're certain to follow this valley. You'll be directly in their path. They'll take everything they can from you, including your lives – just for kicks. I'm telling you.'

The owner seemed to stand to attention. 'No, no, no! Absolutely not. We'll fight the pigs.' His haunted face twitched, either from a touch of insanity or desperation to protect his fragile livelihood. 'I tell you, señor, we will fight them. Fight them all the way!'

The elderly campesino across the room looked up. He finished his beer, only to revert to his impassive state.

'You're daydreaming.' Rafael wiped his feverish brow. 'You cannot even produce a rifle for me.'

'We have rifles here and there, but none to spare. I tell you, I fought alongside the FMLN all those years ago. We can do it again!'

Rafael pointed a finger. 'If you know what's best for you, you'll make your way to the border with Honduras. Now, do as I say and be *sensible*. You need to think of the women!'

With those final irrefutable words, the exchange ended. Rafael watched the owner retreat, head down, through the doorway from where he had emerged. Well, he had concerns of his own. Like whether he wanted to return to London. The fact was, he didn't. Pure and simple. There was nothing left for him, not there. Not anywhere.

He started to fish out a piece of paper from the breast pocket on his chequered shirt: remnants of an email attachment – now with smears of blood obliterating much of the middle section. He glared down at it, as though the words were of immense significance to him.

I'm taking you back eight hundred years, to Lake Baikal, not so far north of what is now the border between Mongolia and Russia. The tribe, or sect, for want of another word, living there was headed by Rieten Keta, a one-time confidant to Khubilia, grandson of Genghis Khan. Keta saw Europe as the key to achieving global power and organised an expedition to investigate the possibility of conquest.

But Rieten Keta died en route, apparently from septicaemia. Salaniri Rikuin, Keta's nephew, took control of the expedition once the brotherhood reached France, where it became clear that the Knights Templars had unprecedented power and were generally regarded as being pioneers of international banking...

Rafael skipped past the crimson stain.

...promoting the concept of an inheritance tax in Britain (one of the wealthiest countries in the world at that time) which, coupled with two world wars, effectively wiped out any threat from the aristocracy. What followed next was the banner-headline: 'stabilisation through globalisation', initially taken up by the political and economic branches of academia, before politicians the world over found themselves producing a rash of treaties and alliances. Attractive, maybe, but under the circumstances a ruse by the Council of the Faithful Brethren to gain universal power.

Details to follow via courier.

Warmest regards to you both, Joshua

Rafael carefully refolded the attachment. 'Another beer,' he said abruptly, without looking up.

The girl complied with his request, and as she did so he was too distracted by the corpse he'd left in the foothills to catch whatever it was she muttered as she turned away.

...You wanted to die this time, Rafael, Javier was telling him. *The pictures and the risks you took prove I speak the truth. But it's not an issue this way. You're the only one of us who can make the film.*

He slipped the attachment back into his shirt pocket, drank from the bottle and pushed it across the table. 'Another.'

The girl swung around. Rafael presumed she was going to pass by and tend to the elderly campesino until she stopped right beside him, her eyes wild with indignation as her hand flew from nowhere. Rafael tried to dodge it, but it glanced off his jaw.

'Don't give yourself the satisfaction of thinking you can intimidate me.' She drew back her hand. 'Like I said, you can go to hell!'

Rafael straightened up and watched her strut to the counter before his gaze switched to the campesino as he stood up from his chair.

The campesino ignored Rafael.

'Senica, clean and dress his wound,' he told the girl quietly. 'Despite his lack of respect, he's not one of them.'

The girl shrugged her shoulders and went behind the counter. 'He can apologise.' She waved a finger. 'It'll cost him nothing. This is my home.'

The campesino hesitated, as if he wanted to say something more, perhaps impart a few words to soothe her. But then the girl left the lean-to through the doorway from which the owner had appeared. The man unexpectedly went over to Rafael.

'Where did you leave him?'

Rafael looked up at the campesino's steady eyes. 'Leave him?'

The campesino gestured at his shirt. 'If all this blood had come from you, you wouldn't be here now.'

Rafael stared at the bottle in his hand. 'Up in the cornfield.' He carried on staring, as if searching for imperfections in the coloured glass. 'He was a good man. Make whatever you do to him decent.'

'And the others?'

'It was just the one. We dealt with the rest of the cell earlier. I took him out in some woods over to the east.'

The campesino said nothing more and left the store.

Rafael put the bottle down on the shabby table and found himself focusing on the gun. *Just pick it up and put it against your head*, goaded a voice. *Pull the trigger and...all that you feel now will be gone. Forever.*

The girl reappeared and brought the final beer over to him.

'I don't need it,' Rafael told her. He hunched forward, swallowing hard against the sudden wave of nausea. He caught hold of the table.

'And I apologise. I guess I've been discourteous. Rotten day, really, you know?'

Senica stood still for a moment, watching him. She took the bottle back to the counter. 'Let me see to your wound. But first, you must wash yourself.'

Rafael hauled himself up from the chair, his head clearing. Taking the gun with him, he followed the girl through the archway and into the yard where, to the right, stood a robust concrete tub.

'You're not going to tell me your name?' she said.

'Rafael.' He caught his breath, referred pain starting to shoot into his hand. He struggled to remove his shirt, the sleeve sticking to his arm. The flesh stung viciously as he peeled the material away, as if someone were aiming a blowtorch at it. He threw the shirt down and met her uncertain eyes. 'Just Rafael. That's all you need to know.'

CHAPTER 2

Alongside the tub, in the shade, with a sheet covering his nakedness, Rafael watched the girl slosh what he guessed – prayed – to be virtually pure alcohol over a long-bladed knife to sterilise the 'instrument' from infectious substances. Then, without a moment's warning, she poked the tip of the blade into the wound and he nearly threw her away from him, the invisible blowtorch akin to acid striking tissue, nerve endings and bone.

'Could have been a ricochet.' Senica spoke as if she were just passing the time of day with him. 'What do you think?'

'I didn't realise you were going to set about it like that, that's what I think! Dear God…' Rafael bit his lip. 'Give me some of that firewater.'

She handed him the bottle and he took a swig – and straightaway wished he hadn't, the liquid searing his throat. 'Which one of you makes this moonshine?' he wheezed, pulling a face.

'José, my uncle. The owner of the store. The one who gave you the gun. It's *aguardiente*. You like it?'

'When my voice recovers, I'll let you know.' Rafael gave her back the bottle.

'It's his pride and joy.' She mopped up the blood from his forearm. 'Before you leave, I'll prepare balsam resin for you to use as an antiseptic.' She poured *aguardiente* over a separate knife and delicately began to work both knives together. 'I could really do with a pair of forceps,' she murmured, her concentration palpable. 'You mustn't move. I'm nearly done…'

Rafael watched with his mouth drawn back as, with a degree of teasing from the girl, the bullet slid out from under the bruised tissue. The relief from seeing the foreign body, nearly a couple of centimetres in length, was besieged by the fierce pain drilling through his elbow and into his shoulder.

Senica seemed to read his scepticism. 'It'll hurt for a while. We're not designed to accept bullets. Do you want it for a memento?'

He shook his head and tried to relax his facial muscles.

'Can't say I blame you.' She threw the bullet into some undergrowth beyond the yard and wiped her hands.

'Are you going to stitch it?' rasped Rafael.

'I've searched for my equipment. It's not where I usually keep it.'

Rafael found himself thanking fate for small mercies. 'What next?' he said, almost cheerfully.

'I'm hoping our loyal friend, the bandage, will be sufficient. Keep your arm crooked and upright to quieten the flow of blood.'

Her tender touch as she bound the wound with linen brought him a measure of shame over his behaviour on entering the store. He knew these people lived impossible lives – a far cry from his comfortable existence in London.

'Rest your elbow on the ground.'

Rafael kept his forearm upright. 'Okay?'

'Perfect. Where were you making for when this happened?'

'A rendezvous of sorts, which never happened. At least, not in the way that was intended. Now I'm heading for San Miguel.'

Senica tied off the bandage and quietly moved aside the *aguardiente* and knives. She sat on a wooden box next to him. 'I don't know quite how you got this. I'm now convinced you're not a member of 18th Street or MS-13. I can only presume you are working against them in some way, perhaps on behalf of the government. It's not my business. Even so, I want to say something to you.'

Rafael turned his head from the lazy blue sky to meet her eyes, intense in their gaze.

'You are brave, yes,' Senica said. 'My gut feeling tells me this to be true. But you cannot win. The gringos in the north are sending weapons down through Mexico and Guatemala, straight into the hands of both gangs. I tell you, Rafael, on this matter I speak the truth to you.'

Rafael nodded. There was no denying that Washington appeared to be turning a blind eye to weaponry 'misdirection'. Nevertheless… 'But that is, I have to say, a superficial explanation. It goes far deeper…it's a slow-release global coup d'état we're faced with. You have to look at the planet, not just the country.'

Senica put her head back and narrowed her brown eyes. '*Global coup d'état*? What are you saying?'

'It doesn't matter.'

'But I'm interested to hear your opinion,' she persisted.

'It's complex, to say the least.' Rafael glanced back at her. 'To be honest, I'm quite exhausted.'

'Of course. Sorry.'

'Don't be sorry. You've done me a massive favour. I'm guessing you're a student, visiting your family.'

Senica stared at him with an initial display of suspicion, which then thawed towards curiosity. She flicked her hair back from her shoulders. 'You flatter me.'

'I do?'

'I long to be a student, but it's impossible. I could not afford the fee. None of us could. Not here. Take a look at our clothes and the patched-up buildings we live in. If it weren't for the landowner west of the hills, we would live with even greater difficulty.'

'Your parents are living here with you?'

Senica straightened his forearm, so that it remained upright. 'My father got himself addicted to alcohol. One day, he picked a fight with someone armed with a machete. He lasted a couple of days, and that was it. The end of him. As for my mother, she met another man and made a new life for herself – in Mexico, by all accounts. She left me with my uncle, her brother.'

'The owner of this store?'

'José's not a well man. He joined the FMLN in his teens and fought in the Civil War. He was captured, tortured – and whatever they did to him broke him. He's never truly recovered. He never will. I'm convinced of this.'

Rafael took his hand from his brow and gazed back into the serene blue sky, before giving her a sideways glance. He found the girl's integrity somewhat therapeutic after the events of the past three months. 'To make amends for my behaviour earlier when—'

'It really doesn't matter.' She got to her feet. 'You were in a bad way. I get that.'

'Listen to me... I have books in San Miguel that might interest you. It's your call, entirely up to you.'

Senica hesitated, her brown eyes wary once again. She started to move away. Then, over her shoulder, she said, 'I need to get you some leeches.'

* * *

Senica put Rafael's stained clothes into the concrete tub to soak and left the store with a glass jar, an excitable voice calling out to her suddenly from across the dusty street.

'Senica! Senica! Where are you going?'

Senica sighed; she had wanted to be alone with her thoughts. The boy, orphaned at only a few months old, lived with her at the store and although very dear to her, he had a habit of making himself a perfect nuisance.

'To the hills!' she called back.

'To see Sancho?'

'Yes.'

Jorge ran across the street and fell into step alongside her, his shirt a size too big for him while his patched trousers barely covered his shins. 'Where's the soldier? I've heard that he's wounded.'

'I don't want him disturbed.'

'Was he shot by MS-13, or 18th Street?'

'I've no idea.'

'Have you got the bullet? Can I have it for my collection?'

'I threw it away. That's what he wanted.'

They turned onto the track that led to the hills.

Jorge looked up at her. 'Is he a FMLN fighter?'

Senica clenched her hands. 'There are no FMLN fighters these days,' she all but snapped, feeling her life to be hopeless. Trivial, even. Why did this person have to say that he thought she was a student? She craved like nothing else on earth to be a student – of medicine. Given the primitive environment, he should have had more sense than to assume such a thing!

'Has he got a machine-gun?' persisted Jorge.

In a flash, Senica seized Jorge's arm, recalling all too vividly the ludicrous bravado of the boy's father and the trouble it caused. 'Guns kill people. I've told you that before. So just stop thinking about them!'

When she let go, Jorge gave her a shrug. 'Okay, okay...' He

tapped a stone in front of them. 'Are you leaving with the others for the border?'

'Yes.'

'I'm staying with Sancho.'

'Stop talking nonsense.'

'I'm *not* talking nonsense!' Jorge kicked the stone off the path. 'He'll be wanting it from you. That's what I reckon.'

Senica rolled her eyes heavenwards, wondering as she often did whether Maya spirits had sent Jorge to test her patience. 'Is this a guessing game?' she asked dully.

'The soldier, he'll be wanting some pushy-pushy with you.'

'Some—' She didn't know how she managed it, but she stopped herself from striking the boy. She lowered her hand. 'Who taught you to speak like that?' Now she was more hurt and disappointed than incensed by the remark.

'Roldán,' Jorge answered smugly. 'And I bet I'm right. You wait and see!'

Senica caught hold of his arm and this time looked him straight in the eye. 'Then let me tell you something, don't you ever be so disrespectful towards me – or any woman, or girls of your own age – ever again in your life.' She pushed his arm away from her.

Jorge gazed down at the ground, his right shoe toying awkwardly with another stone, a heavy look about him. 'I...I didn't mean anything bad,' he said quietly.

Senica gave the boy some slack. She loathed to see him miserable. 'I'm sure you didn't. But what I've just told you is very important. We are all suffering. Dreadful things are happening to women across this land, if not the wider world. When you grow older, you will understand this. But for now, you take my word.'

The journey continued in silence. It seemed to Senica that the older boy, Roldán, was intent on violating Jorge's childhood, and that Jorge was fast becoming a lost cause. Roldán's mother, Carmela, was an intimate friend and no matter how awkward it might be, she was going to have to mention her concern to her. Sooner, rather than later.

They reached the cornfield and Senica saw that the maize was almost ready to be harvested, the leaves having lost their luscious shine. She looked across the steady incline, to focus on a ridge where, slightly out of view, stood her favourite tree – a ceiba, the most sacred tree of the Maya. Sometimes, she would read in the shade beneath its sturdy boughs, or lie back and watch the clouds at play above the handsome, interlaced canopy. She didn't want to believe this life had in any way been cruel to her, but occasionally her resolve would crumble and she would cry a little – until she felt the ceiba's assertive roots shake the ground and rise up from the Underworld to cradle her, the wisdom of her forefathers resonating across the skies, reinforcing her with the necessary self-discipline to manage the store, keep José well, and Jorge out of trouble.

She could see Sancho in the far corner, working over some earth with a spade. She guessed what he might be doing and didn't want the boy to witness it.

'Wait here,' she said firmly.

'Why?' Jorge was evidently perplexed. 'Are you going to talk to Sancho about me?'

Senica started to leave the boy. 'Just wait here, that's all you need to do.' She made her way towards what she suspected was a body and imagined the state of it, recalling the blood on Rafael's clothes. It explained why he had initially been in such a foul mood. She was perfectly aware that the depth of mystery surrounding him both unnerved and fascinated her. An educated man. But what a curious accent!

'Did he give you a name?' Sancho called over, his dark oily eyes watching Senica.

'No, not at all.' Senica joined him. 'Did he tell you about this when I went to check on José?'

'It was a hunch, so I asked him where he'd left the body.'

'He must be with the government.'

Sancho shrugged and glanced at the covered-over grave. 'This one's something of a street fighter.' He brought his gaze back to her. 'He has scars, one of them from a bullet, the other three cast by a blade.'

'I'm guessing Rafael tried to reach the village with him,' decided Senica, before an abrupt movement caught her eye. 'Jorge, I thought I told you to wait for us!'

Jorge gave her critical glare a wide berth. 'The corn is part of my education,' he said, his tone confident. 'You told me that.'

'And so is listening to and obeying your elders. Why must you give me so many headaches?'

Jorge scuffed the dusty earth at the side of the mound with his right shoe. After a moment, he looked up at Sancho with one eye shutting out the sun. 'What are you making, Sancho? Can you please tell me?'

The campesino drove the spade into the earth and moved away from the grave. Senica and the boy followed.

'When you return from the border,' Sancho told Jorge, 'we will discuss the question together. But for now, you keep out of trouble. Understood?'

'Of course, Sancho. You know me.'

'Oh, indeed…' Sancho muttered. Clearly he was not taken in by Jorge's fixed smile. 'They're getting ready to leave, then?' he asked Senica.

Senica responded with little more than a nod, having decided on a different arrangement for herself. 'I need two leeches to reduce the risk of fever and to prevent his blood from clotting.'

Sancho glanced at Jorge. 'Go to the swamp in the hollow by those trees and find Senica a leech. If you're feeling clever, you'll find two for her.'

The boy took the glass jar from Senica and ran off. 'I'll find three!' he shouted.

Senica turned from watching Jorge. 'I have come here to ask you to leave with the others,' she told Sancho directly. 'It will not be for long. Perhaps when the moon is full it will be safe to return.'

Sancho chewed on a cocoa leaf, rejecting the notion with a flick of his bony hand.

'But what if 18th Street get hold of you on their way to Sensuntepeque? Our visitor believes gang members will follow this valley, that they are mere hours away.'

'They are not country people,' he assured her. 'It would take any one of them many a full moon to step on my shadow. They will take to the road.'

'And if there are roadblocks?'

Again, Sancho dismissed her concern with his hand.

Senica bit her lip, annoyed by his nonchalant obstinacy. Although, truth be told, if he were dragged away from these hills he would likely die from shock.

'I'm leaving for San Miguel,' she said. She wrapped her arm around Sancho's, enjoying the sudden breeze on her face and in her hair. 'He says there are books there that might interest me. If they are going for free, it's an opportunity I cannot afford to miss. By the time I've collected them, it should be safe enough to return. For the moment, I'm not mentioning any of this to Jorge. The last thing we need is for him to throw a fit.'

As they neared the path leading to the village, Senica allowed her thoughts to broaden. She wanted Sancho's opinion on Rafael. 'Such a strange accent…'

'Our visitor?'

'Yes.'

'He's lived outside the country,' Sancho remarked matter-of-factly. 'That would explain his accent.'

'But where, Sancho? I've met people from Guatemala and Honduras. He speaks quite differently to them.'

'Further afield, in my opinion. Didn't you notice how often he wiped his brow?'

'I took that to be the beginning of a fever.'

'Fever or not, he is not used to this heat. That aside,' Sancho warned as they watched Jorge leave the stream, 'he's likely to be involved with the government. You should not ask him too many questions.'

'I've found two!' Jorge yelled. When he reached them, he held up the glass jar. The brown-backed leeches looked to be quite docile. 'There!'

Senica put her hand on his shoulder. 'At last you have managed to do something useful today.' She turned to Sancho, her decisive embrace conveying both affection and respect.

'My thoughts are with you,' she said, sensing her voice about to tremble. She turned quickly away and, though tempted, didn't look back.

* * *

The sudden clatter gave Rafael a jolt. His eyes flashed open, just as his left hand fumbled for the gun under the sheet.

Senica had returned to the yard, a boy at her side who had

evidently kicked over an empty oil can. He righted it and then followed her as she came towards him.

'How are you feeling?' Senica asked.

Rafael let go of the gun and took a cigarette from a crumpled packet her uncle had given him. 'It aches, but that's all,' he said. The sight of the urchin next to her evoked memories of his own childhood in El Salvador when, by the age of eight, he had become an expert in foraging and recycling as he and his mother moved from one town to another.

Senica turned to the boy. 'Jorge, give me the leeches.'

Jorge tried shaking the leeches from the jar while lifting his gaze. 'Have you got a machine-gun?' he asked Rafael directly. 'Will you please tell me. I will be most interested to know—'

Senica snatched the jar from Jorge. 'What have I *told* you about guns?' she shouted. 'Hey?'

'I just want to know if he has a machine-gun.'

'He hasn't a machine-gun, all right? So there's your answer.' Senica reached for one of the knives she had used to extract the bullet.

Rafael watched her movements nervously.

'It's better I pierce the skin for them,' Senica explained. Holding the blade as though it were a pencil, she deftly nicked his arm both above and below the wound. 'These books…' she said. 'In what way will they interest me? I mean, what are they about?'

'History, mainly – only from a different perspective. One that you don't get to see so easily, in more ways than one.' He turned away, fed up with the sight of blood. 'If you want, we can be in San Miguel by midday tomorrow, and I'll give you the money I owe your uncle for the beers and hospitality.'

Jorge shot to his feet. 'No!' He came towards them from the tree stump he had been sitting on, staring wildly at Rafael. 'Senica stays with me. I'm taking her to the border. We're leaving with the others tonight.'

Senica smeared the bead of blood above the wound on Rafael's arm and held the second leech to it. 'If he's giving me books,' she told Jorge, 'then I must collect—'

'What do you want stupid books for?' argued the boy. 'It's a trick!'

'Don't be silly.'

'I'm coming with you – I'm coming with you to San Miguel.'

'Absolutely not,' Senica said. 'You will go with José.'

Suddenly tearful, Jorge looked away. 'What is there left for me if the *Mara Salvatrucha* get hold of you and finish you?'

It came to Rafael to take the pair of them with him, but it wasn't hard to draw the conclusion that the boy was something of a challenge, and he just wasn't in any frame of mind to go along with it. Besides, there was talk of checkpoints being set up around San Miguel in an attempt to ensnare gang members, which could complicate matters on an altogether separate level. Any hint of bravado from the boy and they would likely be interrogated, which might just result in brutality – psychological or physical, or both. The leech finally took to him, and he watched as Senica reached for Jorge's hands.

'I'll be fine,' she told the boy gently. 'Now, go and help Sancho's brother. Felipe is old, he will need your help to make certain he understands the situation.'

* * *

When Senica left the yard to prepare herself for the journey into San Miguel, Rafael started to wonder whether Javier's grave had already been dug. If he had, in fact, been buried.

Because of what happened to Lena, you wanted to die this time, Rafael.

Javier. He needed to inform people of his fate.

Rafael rolled onto his side, careful not to disturb the leeches. He felt restless, seeing himself back in London. Nail varnish remover and cotton wool, he reflected as he recalled what forensic tests had found on the Zigana handgun. Evidently, before the lunatic got hold of the weapon it had been cleaned, all previous fingerprints removed. But why use nail varnish remover and cotton wool? He pictured a woman sitting at a dressing table, calmly taking her prints off the gun…

CHAPTER 3

He watched her in the mirror as she came into the en suite: her ocean-blue eyes and flaxen hair, her gentle manner. He imagined her just there, smiling serenely across at him as she cradled their firstborn, and savoured the apparition while he finished shaving.

'You seem happy, Rafael,' Lena remarked. She wrapped her peach bathrobe around herself and sat on the wicker stool by the door. 'Lots of humming.'

He put the razor back in the cabinet. It fell off the shelf and tumbled into the washbasin. He was all fingers and thumbs. He decided he'd ask her now. He dried himself off and brought her to her feet, relishing her curiosity.

'Someone gorgeous passed by me in the mirror this morning.' He kissed her cheek, his hand in her hair. 'I'm telling you, Lena, you wouldn't believe how gorgeous. Like a Nordic goddess rising out of Lake Mälaren — Freyja herself, or one of her daughters. Hnoss or Gersemi, perhaps. That's how it struck me. I couldn't believe my good fortune.'

Lena laughed quietly — a low yet spirited resonance that reflected the warmth in her eyes. She inclined her head, watching him closely as she lifted a finger to his chin. 'And you look like a mystery to me,' she said. 'Have you done something that requires my forgiveness? Surely not.'

'I was wondering — just wondering, you understand — how serious you might be about getting off the road?'

'Touring, you mean?'

'Yes.'

'Very.' She kissed the side of his mouth, her lips lingering. 'It's not the same as it was. It used to be fun.' She came into his arms and kissed him again. 'Perhaps it's the endless bureaucracy. Or perhaps the truth is I'm getting old...'

'Or that we should get married.'

Lena flashed him a double-take, eyes wide open. 'What?'

He hesitated, uncertain how he should interpret her startled reaction. He looked down at the towel in his hand and found some words. 'I realise the aesthetics are hardly appropriate for such a proposal, but I simply can't hold out any longer. It's been driving me crazy.'

Lena stepped back from him and felt behind herself for the stool. 'You're kidding me?'

'When it comes to our future?'

'My God, Rafael. I wasn't expecting this!'

He reached for her hands, his tone resolute. 'Let's get married, Lena. It has to be the right thing for us to do. That's how it feels. It's been this way inside of me for months.' He brought her hand to his lips and kissed her ring finger. 'I'm going to get down on one knee.'

Quite suddenly Lena stopped him, leaping from the stool and into his arms. 'I don't need any of that.' She ran her hands through his hair, eyes glistening. 'I'm ready for it, too. A thousand yeses, my darling. And a thousand more!'

Light-headed with relief, he nevertheless held her face. 'I need to kiss you...' He fought to take his time, tasting her, her mouth passionate before Lena delicately rubbed her semi-naked thigh against his groin. The manoeuvre caught his breath.

'How can there ever be another moment quite like this?' he said. He encouraged her robe to slip away from her shoulders. 'I have everything I've ever wanted, here in my arms.'

Lena touched and then kissed his lips. 'You'll have me cry, and I don't want to cry.'

* * *

Over breakfast, Lena's tangible bliss, disrupted only by moments of fluster, caused him to smile – his contentment absolute.

'I must call Stockholm,' she said. 'Monika will want to know. She's been waiting years for this. And then there's all the arranging to think about!'

Keeping the smile, he spread Marmite on a slice of toast. 'I've a thought or two on that.'

'On what?'

'Arrangements. Couldn't we make it a simple affair? Your mother and a few close friends. It'll be more intimate. Does that disappoint you?'

Lena's blue eyes peered at him over the rim of her coffee cup. By degrees, she lowered the cup – lips slightly apart, eyes perfectly still, until her faintly bemused expression melted into a reflective shrug. 'I suppose not,' she said, before adding gaily, 'It's rather appealing, actually, because I certainly don't want the media putting in an appearance.'

'My sentiments, exactly.'

'That would be awful.' She set her cup down. 'Can I tell Jeff?'

'Sure. Of course.'

'Incidentally, we're having huge fun tonight at the Holbarth Academy, as it's the last gig of the tour. I'm playing bass on a few numbers and Jeff's leading. We're making the switch at some point. So try and arrive for the last half, if you can.'

'I'll be there. Marc's coming over, so we might show up together.'

'Make sure you do. I haven't seen him – or Susan, come to that – for quite a while.'

'Talking of Jeff...is he still clean? No mescaline?'

'Two months now. Can you believe it? It's great. He's put on a little weight since you last saw him, too.'

'He has you to thank for that, getting him off the stuff.'

'Up to a point, perhaps.'

'Don't be modest. I've an idea.'

Lena took her cup to the sideboard and came and sat on his knee, throwing an arm across his shoulders. 'More surprises?'

'After the Academy, why don't we bring a few people back here and share our celebration with them?' He put down his toast to gently brush away a wisp of hair that had fallen across her cheek. 'Keep it a secret till then, yes?'

'I just want to keep my arms around you, despite you reeking of your beloved Marmite!' She kissed his lips, then rested the tip of her nose against his. 'Can I tell you my secret wish, the wish that I've held inside my heart for all the time we've been together?'

'Of course, you can. I must know!'

'I want to marry you at the Ansgar Chapel on Björkö.' She kissed him again quickly. 'There, I've told you!'

He couldn't help but react to her 'secret' with the broadest of grins; the sparsely inhabited island just off Stockholm was where they had first met during the filming of his first feature, Tomorrow Calling. 'Lena...Lena, it's perfect.' He held the side of her face. 'The sooner the better!'

* * *

Later that day, when the driver came to collect Lena to take her to Lambeth and the Holbarth Academy, he drifted from one room to another, half his mind elated by the prospect of children running around his feet, the other half heavily weighed down with Agenda Indiscriminate. Although he had sketched out the screenplay, the task had become a chore, his mind elsewhere – with starting a family, perhaps.

Just then, the telephone rang. He was passing the backroom, and so lifted the receiver in there.

'Hello?'

'Rafael!' There was a sharp burst of static. 'It's Lazaro, Rafael.'

Oh, Christ... His heart sank. He knew exactly what was coming: the excitable tone and the virtual civil war in El Salvador said it all.

'Long time, Lazaro.' His throat was dry and tightening up.

'We need you, Rafael,' roused the voice from Central America. 'You know that, don't you? There's a chance you can do it. Make MS-13 and 18th Street see sense. There's a strong rumour they're ready to join forces against the government. We can't permit that to happen—'

'Lazaro, for God's sake…'

'People in Europe…they must be made aware of our plight. To understand – to protest. Madrid, Lisboa, Roma, Londres…' More static. 'Washington's a waste of time. They goddamn started it. And that buffoon of a president had the affront to call us a shithole of a country!'

He stared out onto the honeysuckle-scented patio: sun shining, birds twittering – paradise, he knew, compared to what Lazaro was seeing. He sat down. 'I have Lena, Lazaro… I don't see how I can make the gangs see sense. I'm telling you.'

'I have a loose contact with an influential figure in MS-13. He loves films – the kind of films you make. It could just work—'

'How the hell can it work?' he all but shouted back at the caller. 'There are too many of them. Too many who have no prospects other than to slaughter and pillage!'

'Shallow graves have been discovered in Sensuntepeque,' Lazaro went on, more excitable than ever. 'Their throats cut. The people they quietly take off the streets to drain their bank accounts we're not seeing again, Rafael. I've witnessed it myself...'

His dilemma was unbearable. How could he abandon his own flesh and blood – and Salvadoreans were that to him. Flesh and blood. His heart ached constantly with the suffering these people had endured over the years, from way beyond Washington's paranoia over communism sweeping up from the south, triggering the most brutal of civil wars when it supported the right-wing oligarchy – El Salvador's ruling elite. The oligarchy's mantra: 'Keep the peasants in chains at all costs!'

'…Our brothers and sisters, Rafael,' persevered the caller. 'Our sisters are being raped in terrible, unspeakable ways. For our brothers, the gangs seem to have found new tort—'

'Stop!' Tears burned in Rafael's eyes. *I know what's happening. We've seen it before, remember? It's always the same!*'

'It seems far worse. We're convinced there's CIA involvement — how else can these gangs get hold of so much weaponry?'

'I need to speak to Lena—'

'Javier's leaving for Santa Ana this evening. He'll meet you there, so better to enter via Guatemala.'

'I'll call you back tomorrow.'

'The number's changed.'

'Give it to me,' Rafael reacted tersely, knowing he should somehow have curtailed the call seconds after he'd picked up the receiver. He scribbled the number down. 'I'll call you back. And if I come out, no longer than a fortnight, Lazaro.'

He stood up. The sun still shone but dark clouds had now gathered in his mind.

Our brothers and sisters, Rafael. Our sisters are being raped in terrible, unspeakable ways. For our brothers, they seem to have found new tortures…

Lazaro knew such words would reach into him!

The doorbell chimed.

He looked at his watch. It had to be Marc. He left the backroom and crossed the hallway to the front door, his mood thoroughly morose.

CHAPTER 4

'Rafael...'

He stifled a cry of anguish as his mind stumbled back into the present, the dream so vivid he could still feel the warmth of Lena's embrace and even visualise, in perfect detail, the vibrant joy in her eyes when he kissed her before she left in the taxi for the Holbarth Academy.

He looked across the yard as Senica came towards him in jeans and a green jacket, a rifle in each hand. 'We must be on our way,' she told him. 'They've started to leave for the border.' She looked up at the clear night sky, a dome of stars and a quarter-moon over by their destination: San Miguel. 'With luck, we'll keep this cool air until dawn.'

Rafael turned the sheet aside and left the mat. Given the rudimentary setting and that it was dark, he doubted she was bothered by his nakedness. 'Where's Jorge?' he asked over his shoulder.

Senica averted her gaze. 'Helping Roldán ready the mules to carry the old ones.'

'You've said farewell to him?'

'Yes.'

'How did he take it?'

'Calmly, oddly enough. Your clothes are over by the tub.'

Rafael trod carefully as he crossed the uneven yard. 'So, how did you get to be called Senica?' he asked curiously. 'It's not Spanish, by my reckoning, so is it Mayan?'

Senica laid down the rifles and sat on the tree stump. 'Father Rodríquez, who lives on the way to Chalatenango, once told me that my mother went to see him over some issue and noticed a book he had by a scholar called Seneca. My mother could hardly read, but she liked the look of the name on the cover. Do you know this scholar? This Seneca?'

'He was around during the time of Christ – a tutor to Nero.'

'And this Nero was an emperor, and he forced Seneca to commit suicide?'

'Yes, I believe he did.'

'Why?'

'I'm not altogether sure.'

'My mother asked Father Rodríquez to change the spelling, mind you.'

Rafael took his trousers from a branch. 'She did?'

'When she heard Seneca was a man, she asked Father Rodriquez to make the name feminine, so he changed the *e* in the middle to an *i*, and pronounced it Sen*ee*ca.'

'It's a nice name, that much she did give you.' Rafael waved his chinos. 'Absolutely dry,' he said, amazed. 'Feel good, too.'

'You must rely on machines to do all that where you come from.'

He noted her inquisitive tone, inevitable as it was. 'You're right. Usually I do.'

Her uncle, José Roldós, weaved his way through the archway, plainly quite drunk. 'Senica,' he slurred softly, 'I'm making my way now.'

Putting on his shirt, Rafael wondered how the man expected to cross the River Lempa in such a state without falling in.

'My thoughts will be with you, José.' Senica left the tree stump.

'Hopefully, 18th Street will have passed through this valley in a matter of days and then we can all return safely. Until then, if Jorge gets up to mischief, you must be firm. I'll be having words with that Roldán, I can tell you!'

'He's gone on ahead,' José said. 'We're going by the cornfield.'

'Good,' agreed Senica. 'Sancho will make him wise to what's happening and give him strength.'

Rafael felt José's eyes follow him as he moved away from the tub to join them.

José tilted his head towards Senica. 'She is my treasure.' His voice was very quiet and settled but nevertheless had a dark edge to it. 'The child I never had. You understand what I'm saying?'

Rafael struggled to fasten his trousers and then held out his hand. 'Of course.'

'So, you will return her to me without a scratch – without a blemish?'

'I will.'

José glanced at the proffered hand, and dismissed it. 'When you came here, I said to myself…this man is trouble—'

'José!' Senica looked aghast. 'You can't say that. Not now.'

José lifted a hand to calm his niece, his bloodshot eyes levelled at Rafael. 'But as I stand here, a speck of dust in this world where deceit and arrogance march side by side, I see that you are a decent man. You fight for the campesino. An honourable cause.'

They chanced a handshake, awkwardly to begin with since Rafael could only offer José his left hand.

'A decent man, I tell you!' José repeated robustly, swaying a little as he moved away and beckoned the mongrel dog to tag along.

Senica looked at Rafael, her brown eyes anxious. 'Please understand, the situation's very difficult for him. He tries so hard.'

Despite the wretched pain in his arm, the bond between the girl and her uncle and their fragile existence tugged at Rafael's heartstrings. 'There will surely be better times ahead,' he said, perfectly aware his optimistic note fluttered precariously in the light breeze.

* * *

They had barely covered a couple of kilometres when Rafael sensed they were being trailed. For the most part they had walked in silence, and in that silence he was certain he'd heard the occasional tap of a stone across the uneven track. Javier had mentioned on more than one occasion that *bandidos* roamed the area, loyal to no one but themselves.

Without a second thought, Rafael caught Senica's wrist and felt her stiffen. 'Sorry,' he whispered. 'I need to check out what's going on behind us.' He ushered her towards a ditch that was barely discernible in the moonlight.

Sure enough, as they crouched there, a figure came into view – a rifle slung over the left shoulder. But it was the white bag swaying from the right hand that puzzled Rafael. Why white? Anything but luminous white.

And then it dawned on him, just as Senica scrambled out of the ditch and tore after the individual.

'You!' she screamed.

Jorge swung around.

'You liar. You filthy little liar!' Senica promptly swiped the boy's jaw with the back of her hand. 'José must be out of his mind with worry, thanks to you!'

Jorge put down the carrier bag 'I told Roldán to tell him where I was going. I'm not stupid. I keep telling you that!'

Rafael swore at the racket they were making, certain it was echoing across the valley. He climbed out of the ditch. '*Enough*, the pair of you.'

Senica circled the boy. 'Where did you find this rifle?' she demanded. 'Who did you steal it from? Give it to me!'

Jorge backed away. 'No. It's mine.'

'No, it's not.' Senica made a grab for the M16, until Jorge bit her arm in the scuffle and won it back.

'You girl!' retaliated Senica. 'Only girls bite.' She turned to Rafael. 'Take the rifle from him. He cannot be trusted with it.'

'I'll knock your heads together if the pair of you don't cut it out,' Rafael warned. 'They must be able to hear you in Honduras.'

'No one takes this from me,' countered Jorge. 'I'm going to have a go at MS-13 with it.' He held the rifle tightly to his chest. 'Roldán told me about the screams when they took her.'

'"Took her"?' Senica looked perplexed. 'What do you—?' Suddenly her eyes flared wide open. 'He had no business to!' she retorted, clenching her hands. 'No business at all. Sancho was the one who was to tell you what happened that night, and no one other than Sancho.'

'They would have raped her first,' Jorge persisted. 'I know what it means, I know what happens! Roldán told me.'

Rafael noticed Senica flinch, and in the stunned silence that followed it was as though the boy's words had crushed her in some way. She looked up at the stars, as if trying desperately to compose herself. He speculated what might have happened on the night in question. Had MS-13 entered the village – by chance, or for retribution?

'A month ago, you had little to say.' Senica's voice was faint and shaky. 'You were like that for days. Was it then when Roldán told—?'

'And he showed me pictures of bodies lying on a rubbish tip near San Salvador.' Jorge stepped closer to her. 'Is that where they left my family? On some rubbish tip?'

Senica glanced at Rafael, as if seeking his support. 'Can I put something to you?' She turned back to Jorge. 'Will you listen to me?'

Jorge gave her a reluctant nod, his wariness palpable.

Rafael backed away. It was uncanny, as if he was experiencing a sense of *déjà vu*. Thirty years ago, it could have been himself on this same track being lectured by his mother. He lit the last of José's cigarettes and watched Senica address the boy.

'You learn fast, Jorge,' she conceded gently. 'We both know that. And believe me, I can't wait for the day to come when I can respect you, learn from you. But before that can happen, you need to convince me you are capable of recognising wisdom when it presents itself to you. Violence is stupid. A simple fact, Jorge. Violence can make an orphan, can cause untold despair, and much more besides.' She turned to Rafael. 'Do I speak the truth?'

Rafael retreated from an image of the cargo ship that had brought him to England as a stowaway, his mother face down in front of him in the ship's hold with her neck broken. 'Yes,' he replied, but he'd hardly heard a word.

Jorge glanced indifferently at Rafael. 'The way you talk, you're from the city. So, what do you know?'

'I thought you agreed to listen,' Senica intervened.

Jorge lowered the rifle from his chest.

Senica pointed at it. 'Who did you steal it from?'

'Felipe,' muttered Jorge.

'When?'

'A few days before Sancho planted the corn.'

'Have you used it?'

'Yes… But only a little. By the Lempa, where we used to sit together.' Jorge squared his shoulders. 'I'm quite good. I think I have some of Farabundo Martí's blood in my—'

'If Farabundo Martí were alive today,' snapped Senica, 'he would be offended to hear his name mentioned in such a matter as this. Understand me, Jorge…*offended.*' She turned her attention to the carrier bag. 'What have you in there?'

'Bullets for the magazine.'

'And that is all?'

'Yes. Can I come with you?'

'You bit my arm!'

Jorge looked down at his battered shoes, one shoelace replaced by twine. 'I'm sorry… I wish I hadn't. It was wrong.' He peered up at her with puppy-like eyes. 'Can I come with you now? Please.'

'Oh, why don't you ask Rafael,' countered Senica. 'I've had enough of you for one day. And I'm not altogether sure whether I should believe your apology. You might be able to sweet-talk José – even Sancho – but not me. And don't you ever forget that!' She walked away, leaving Rafael stuck with the boy.

Jorge watched her until she was out of earshot. 'Senica's a girl,' he said in a feverish whisper. 'She'll fiddle about with her hair and stuff like that. What good's that to you against *bandidos*? And there's lots of them around here, Rafael. I know about these things. You're going to need me.'

Tired, irritated and full of pain, Rafael prodded a thumb against his chest. '*I'll* be the judge of whether or not I need you.'

'Of course, Rafael. Of course. I just want you to know that I'm—'

'And you show some respect to Senica. Right?'

'Oh, yes, Rafael,' improvised Jorge. 'It's important we do that. That's why I'm here. To help you protect her. See? We've got to protect Senica.'

Rafael lifted a finger. 'Don't push it.'

'Push what?'

Rafael turned away. 'Give me a minute,' he said bluntly, 'then join us.'

'A minute? Why?'

'Never mind why,' Rafael said over his shoulder. 'Just do as I say. Which is the way it's going to be from now on.'

Senica was standing further down the track. Her eyes looked puffy; clearly she'd been crying. 'He adores you,' Rafael said, knowing it to be true.

'That's not the point. He has to learn to do as he's told and understand that he can't just roam about the place endangering lives – including his own.' She looked behind them. 'What's he doing now?'

'I told him to give me a minute. What happened to his parents?'

Senica switched the rifle she was carrying to her left hand, flexed her fingers and took a deep breath. 'Twelve years ago, Jago, his father, had a gambling disagreement with members of MS-13 in Sensuntepeque. It wasn't long before they showed up at the village with other members of the gang. We already had wind of what was likely to happen. Jorge was given to Sancho, who took him up into the hills. Jago and Carmen were about to leave when they came for him. The gang set fire to some of our homes, and…' She looked away. 'They did things to us.'

The last few words were barely audible, and Rafael was left to imagine the rest. It sickened him to the pit of his stomach to think that someone might have assaulted this resilient good-natured girl beside him.

He glanced over his shoulder to see Jorge catching up with them. 'He's certainly a live wire, isn't he?' He smiled, wanting to draw Senica away from the dark place to which recall had taken her. '*Selling fridges to Eskimos* comes to mind for some reason.'

CHAPTER 5

A sudden metallic click caused Rafael to jump. He swung his head around, only to see the boy deftly re-engage the magazine forward of the trigger-guard on the stolen rifle.

'Hey, Rafael!' Jorge called excitedly. 'Now I'll show you how good I am.'

Rafael rubbed the remnants of a restless slumber from his eyes, the three of them having slept in the open under a pink-tufted maquilishuat tree. 'Where's Senica?' he asked, leaning on one elbow.

'Gone to wash herself or something. You know what girls are like!' Jorge shook the rifle with confident aggression. 'Point to something for me to hit.'

Rafael gazed across the cocoa plantation at an array of derelict-looking outbuildings. Javier had organised the safe house and they had left the place together. But all he could picture now was his guide rotting away in a cornfield. He ran his fingers through his hair in an attempt to tidy himself up and looked at the boy. 'We're not taking the rifles with us. We're leaving them here.'

Jorge's jaw dropped. He stopped polishing the rifle with his shirt sleeve. 'And how will you – *we* – protect Senica? You talk shit!'

Rafael jumped to his feet, his sense of desolation throwing him out of control. 'You've just about crossed the line with me! I'm telling you. No more warnings!' He moved closer to the boy. 'Now, you apologise, or I'll leave you here…leave you here for you to rot in your own goddamned insolence.'

Jorge shifted his gaze, choosing defiance.

Enraged, Rafael grabbed the boy's arm. 'Apologise, you son of a bitch!'

A moment of shock seemed to pass between them. Rafael looked away, unable to meet Jorge's eyes for it felt as though he had just defiled the boy's mother. And if Lena could see him now, what would she think? That he was unfit to have children? Swearing at a child. What next? The notion that he was disintegrating into a full-blown breakdown scared the hell out of him – his fingertips clawing at a cliff face with nothing but jagged rocks and squally seas below.

'I shouldn't have said that.' He faced the boy and saw Senica in the distance, walking towards them. 'I just shouldn't have said it. All right?'

Jorge brought his gaze back to Rafael, one eye shutting out the early morning sun. 'I think we should keep the rifles, Rafael,' he ventured, clearly bolstered by the apology. 'I've got lots of bullets.'

Senica stepped over an irrigation pipe. 'I have some fruit.' She pointed over to her right. 'And if you two want to freshen up there's a shallow stream the other side of those trees.' She handed them each a barely ripened orange before taking a blue ribbon from her jeans and tying her hair into a ponytail. While peeling her orange, she said, 'Jorge, I think you should go and wash.'

'I washed yesterday,' he answered back.

'I'm not talking about yesterday. I'm talking about today.'

'It's only just started.'

'There might not be another opportunity.'

'If I keep washing all the time it's going to wear out my skin,' whined Jorge. 'I've told you that before.'

'What nonsense.'

'Roldán's got a blotch on his neck where he was washed too hard.'

Senica sighed and rolled her eyes. 'That's a *birth*mark, silly!'

Struggling to tuck in his shirt with his left hand, Rafael wondered what he'd let himself in for. The omens didn't look good, not by a long shot. He'd heard that a couple of neighbourhoods in San Miguel were on the verge of lawlessness, and what with the boy plainly coming across as a heap of trouble…

Senica turned to him, as though suddenly aware of his presence. 'Your arm, Rafael, how is it?'

He was unsure what to do with the orange, since he had no appetite. Finally, so as not to offend her, he made an attempt to peel it using his teeth. 'I doubt it's strong enough to change gear, so you'll have to learn to do so when I get the car.'

Jorge lurched forward, wide-eyed. 'What about me? I'll be good at doing that!'

While Senica checked his arm, Rafael pointed in the direction of the irrigation pipe. 'We'll see… But right now, I want you to take the rifles and leave them in the long grass over there.'

'And when you've done that you can go and wash yourself,' added Senica.

Rafael cast another glance at the outbuildings in the distance, and then at Senica as she took away the stained bandage to replace it with a fresh dressing. 'I need you to follow the line of trees until you come to a track,' he said. 'Don't move from there. It'll take me about fifteen minutes.'

* * *

Rafael quietly entered a leafy grove, where he scanned the farmhouse and the area around him for signs of unwanted activity. Using his feet and his uninjured arm, he cleared away several fencing posts from a balsam tree, and finally a partially corroded sheet of corrugated steel. He found what he was looking for in the excavated hollow and came out of the grove, shaking the remainder of the soil from the knapsack.

The aging Ford was where he had left it, in a shed that housed agricultural equipment, above which daylight breached the darkness through fissures in the dilapidated roof. Rafael set to work, taking a change of clothes and shoes from the knapsack. After a moment of unwieldiness, he managed to raise the Ford's bonnet. Resting it on his shoulder, he positioned the stay and checked the water level – until an unexpected creak over by the double doors made him dive for the floor.

He struggled to pull José's handgun from his waistband, Javier's voice all at once with him. *While looking for advantages over your opponent, remember to breathe – and as sweetly as a crocodile!*

Rafael breathed, the side door opening hesitantly. He watched from under the car as the broad shadow of the intruder showed itself in the shaft of light that pierced the gloom.

'Señor? Are you there, señor? Is it you?'

Rafael sighed and privately cursed the man. He felt wetness underneath the clean bandage and assumed that the abrupt manoeuvre had disturbed the wound.

The overweight man waddled towards him. 'Señor, you must not visit me again.' His brow glistened with sweat.

Rafael returned to checking the fluid levels on the Ford. 'And why is that?'

The farmer gazed at the antiquated machinery as if afraid to meet Rafael's eyes. 'I received a visit from two men only yesterday. They…they asked questions.'

'About the car?'

'I told them it was my brother's. He's no longer with us, you understand.'

Rafael sat in the seat and turned the key. The battery held just enough voltage to fire the engine. Something was finally going his way. 'Open the main doors for me.'

Eagerly, the farmer did so. Rafael backed the car out and resumed the conversation while he revved the engine to charge the battery.

'So, where's the problem?' he asked, not that he particularly cared. He was through with any future government-backed 'assignments' concerning MS-13. There was no one he would trust with his life more than Javier.

'They had a bad look about them,' blurted the farmer. 'When I was younger, such a look didn't trouble me, but now I have a wife and three children – all of them girls. They said that if they found I had links with the "enemy" – meaning the government – they would deal with me in an unpleasant way. Can you imagine!'

'MS-13, or 18th Street?'

'What's the difference, señor? One of them had several tattoos. He looked like a gang member to me.'

Rafael doubted the farmer's tale of woe, but accepted his fear. There was more to be had in way of extortion in the cities than the countryside. Had he been visited by MS-13 or 18th Street, rather than issue him with a warning they would have robbed him to nothing and raped his daughters and wife. Then most likely have killed the lot of them and burnt the place to the ground – just for the thrill of it, if nothing else. He crossed his left arm over himself and knocked the gearshift out of reverse. 'There's ammunition and three rifles in the far corner of the plantation,' he told the farmer, 'close to the irrigation pipe. They'll be collected at some point. As for the clothes in the shed, dispose of them.'

The farmer seized upon his words as if he'd been offered a chest of gold coins. 'I will do that, señor. I'm telling you, I will do that!'

Rafael nodded and pulled away. He skirted the grove and joined the track, and as he drove over a slight crest he saw Senica and the boy emerge from the plantation in the distance. Relieved not to find them arguing, he came to a stop and waited for Senica to open the nearside rear door – Jorge having already clambered in beside him to put a white-knuckled hand on the gearshift.

'Show me what I have to do with this, Rafael!'

* * *

Senica found Rafael to be more intriguing than ever. The black jeans and pale blue shirt were definitely of high quality, the stitching perfectly placed. And the cut of the shirt against his swarthy complexion made him look rather appealing. She leaned forward. 'How did you get the car? The change of clothes? They're yours, right?'

Rafael negotiated a sharp bend on the track, the camber dropping away at a precarious angle. 'Now bring the stick down,' he told the boy.

Jorge yanked the gearshift.

'That's fourth. I want to go back to second…'

Another yank, cogs grating ominously.

'Just a minute!' Rafael wiped his brow. 'Give me a chance to press the clutch down.'

'I'm doing really well, aren't I, Rafael?' Jorge glanced over his shoulder at Senica. 'Wait till I tell Roldán about all this. About me having driven a car all the way to San Miguel. He'll go mad!'

Senica leaned forward again. 'Are you connected to the government in some way?' she asked Rafael directly. 'What is your position?'

More grating on the gears as they made it back up into third.

'Do you own this car?' persisted Senica.

Rafael pulled up suddenly in a pile of dust alongside a stretch of water, as remote as it was stagnant. He stared back at her through the rear-view mirror. 'How I got the car and change of clothes is my business. It has nothing to do with you.'

'Oh, yes, it most certainly does.' She wasn't fazed by his defiant glare. 'I'm responsible for Jorge. It's down to me to see that no harm comes to him.'

'That's wrong,' butted in Jorge, 'I'm—'

'Shut up, Jorge,' warned Senica.

'But I'm the one who has to protect—'

'Jorge, why is it I'm hearing your voice all the time?' Senica felt her irritation rise – notably towards Rafael over his constant evasiveness. 'You shouldn't be here at all!' she added pointedly. 'And I still haven't forgiven you for biting my arm. It was a terrible thing to do.' She settled into the seat and, with calculated coolness, waited for Rafael to answer her questions.

* * *

Rafael turned off the ignition and gazed at the potholed track ahead of them. She was right: the boy shouldn't be here. And neither should she. He shouldn't have asked her to leave with him for San Miguel. A big mistake. He wondered why he'd asked her, why he'd used the books as an excuse. Something to do with loneliness, perhaps. No, not 'perhaps'. Definitely. Loneliness, anger and despair. He was goddamned howling beyond description inside with it all. He had enjoyed her company back at the village, he couldn't deny that – but now she was a bloody nuisance.

'No harm came to the campesino back there,' he told her flatly. 'I didn't threaten him.'

'You'd better not have. He happens to be a friend of José's, and has offered work to us in the past. And this car belongs to you?'

'Yes.' Rafael thought it strange she hadn't mentioned the farmer before. 'You should have told me you knew him.'

'I don't have to tell you everything, particularly when you are being so evasive with me. For all I know you could be in with MS-13.'

'That's absurd.'

'Okay. 18th Street, then.'

'I repeat…absurd.'

'Absurdity has become a way of life for the campesino. You should know that.' Senica folded her arms. 'In what way are you linked to the government? What is it that's expected of you?'

Rafael looked back at the rear-view mirror. He owed her an explanation, he supposed. If only he could sort himself out, get a balance. Difficult that, when you're loaded to the gills with resentment. Or was it self-pity? He couldn't tell. He started to climb out of the car. 'Jorge, wait here.'

'Where are you going?' Jorge's hand was still attached to the gearshift, as if it had become an extension of his anatomy.

Rafael walked over to the stagnant pool of water. The stench of rotting vegetation filled his nostrils, adding fuel to the anger already inside him. Salvadoreans deserved better than this, he told himself for the umpteenth time. So much for the United Nations. But then he knew why; hostages to debt were the order of the day. National governments, environment, gift of life… Everything and everyone, hostages to trillions of dollars of debt. The veiled takeover into global government and servitude!

He turned to face Senica, who had followed him. 'In recent years, when I have time on my hands, I take photographs.'

'Of what?'

'Mainly, the aftermath of what Washington assisted in wreaking on this country during the Civil War, resulting in present-day issues such as the horrors of gang warfare. The pictures I take, to answer your next question, go to an agency in Europe, and from there to authors writing on the plight of Central America.'

'Newspapers?'

'When it suits them.'

'So, you're a journalist?'

He shrugged. 'Loosely speaking. On occasion.'

Senica tucked her hands into the pockets of her jeans and gazed with him across the Lempa valley at the hydroelectric *15 de Septiembre* dam, named after Independence Day. 'And now? You have taken pictures of this…civil war, shall we say? That's what it amounts to, you have to agree…two gangs attempting to corrupt and dismantle a legitimate government.'

'I came here for a different reason this time.'

'I see…' She paused. 'You know, Sancho warned me not to ask you too many questions. He felt that you had connections with the government.'

Rafael smiled without humour. 'A wise man, that Sancho.'

'I suppose. Well, yes, he is. Of course, he is. Can I ask…do you think the government can resolve the situation?'

He looked down at the ground. 'I'm not overly optimistic. I don't see how anyone of us can be at the moment. We are locked into this cycle – a global cycle.'

'Global cycle? There you go again! What exactly do you mean, Rafael, by *global*?'

'Simply that there are people in this world who have a vested interest in maintaining fear and debt – and that the mindless discord continues unabated.'

Senica shook her head. 'I can't live with such pessimism. The UN...' She seized his arm. 'The UN will help us. I know they will. Sancho doesn't believe it, but I do. They have to help us, to put right a wrong that the gringos inflicted on us.'

Rafael began to sense a complex soul behind those brown, and for the most part inquisitive, eyes. She had endeavoured to educate herself and was probably very brave, not to mention practical – capable of removing a bullet. He regretted thinking of her as a nuisance, once again grateful for her company.

Senica withdrew her hand from his arm, as if embarrassed by her knee-jerk reaction in response to his negativity. 'If you say there's no hope, why risk your life doing whatever it is you came out here to do?' Her eyes met his. 'You see, Rafael, you don't really believe there's no hope for us.'

The pool of water with its lumpy slime reminded Rafael too much of death. He started back towards the car. 'That's all you need to know,' he said.

* * *

An hour later, they arrived in San Miguel. Rafael turned out of the traffic into a neighbourhood that had seen better days and parked the car, having spared the gearbox further abuse by successfully using the gearshift himself.

'There's someone I need to talk to about Javier,' he told Senica. 'In the meantime...' He took Jorge's grubby fingers off the hazard-warning switch. 'Just stay here and don't draw attention to yourselves.'

Rafael left them and made his way towards a paved square with an austere-looking chapel at the far end. It was flanked by stalls that were now deserted but by dawn would be a hive of activity. In the far distance, several kilometres away, towered the majestic

Chaparrastique volcano, which on rare occasions disgorged ash over the city. This, though, Rafael told himself, was hardly the time for sight-seeing as his attention locked onto a couple of heavily tattooed men sitting outside a bar. MS-13, he figured, and ogres of the highest order, their menacing presence maintaining the fear that hung over parts of San Miguel like doomsday itself.

He passed them by and turned smartly into a cobbled street. The wall to his left displayed graffiti that had defied an attempt to erase the words:

Revolution or Death
It is the daily cry
It is the slogan of the people
It is the destiny of all

He'd seen the slogan countless times, in documentaries and articles describing the Civil War over forty years ago. Alongside Guatemala, its neighbour and steadfast ally, this potentially paradisiac land – a land he was perfectly prepared to shed blood for – caused him to literally weep on occasion, its poverty and organised crime foisted upon the nation by external forces. It was here, though, in his beloved El Salvador, with its immeasurable courage, dramatic landscapes and fine poets, where he categorically wanted to settle, as opposed to Europe – a continent that, to some extent because of what happened to Lena, had started to feel increasingly alien to him.

Finally he arrived at the entrance to a tumbledown warehouse in a deserted alleyway, the weathered door secured by a chunky padlock. Taking a key from his pocket, he stepped inside. The dense aroma of coffee beans combined with hessian made him sneeze. He rubbed his nose with the back of his hand, a feeble lightbulb guiding him between a mound of sacks and a wooden wheelbarrow that would have looked equally at home in an English cottage garden. He had visited the warehouse several times in the past. On the first occasion, he had only just met Lena, at a time when her career had been boosted by an invitation to support the celebrated rock band, Coup d'État, in South Africa. So, with Lena on tour, he'd decided to make a ten-minute flick on the legacy of deprivation from when both El Salvador and Guatemala had effectively become buffer zones between right- and left-wing ideologies – the Soviet Union, for its part, keen to take advantage of Mexico's newly discovered oil fields. His supervisor at the Wymarke International Film School in London had helped cover the cost of the flight. No sooner, though, had he arrived in his homeland than he came into contact with Lazaro Dueñas, who'd asked him to concentrate his efforts not on the past but on covering the present warfare between the gangs of MS-13 and 18th Street. The following day he was given a Pentax and an assortment of lenses before being introduced to his guide, whose appearance and manner resembled that of a brawler. That evening they'd got drunk, Lazaro and Javier keen to know all about England and what English people thought of El Salvador and its gangs.

Rafael pulled himself together and returned the key to his pocket, suddenly a shade concerned that he'd left Senica and Jorge alone in an unfamiliar city. He figured Senica was reasonably streetwise, but that the boy was capable – *perfectly* capable – of being lippy, unaware of the likely consequences.

He climbed a narrow stairway to reach Lazaro Dueñas's humble living-quarters, and called his name.

'Rafael? In here,' came a cordial voice from across the corridor.

The kitchen looked as though it had been a meeting point for several poltergeists, with plates and cutlery scattered throughout. Rafael stepped towards Lazaro, sitting at the table while bathing his feet in a steel bowl.

'Where's Reina?' Rafael asked.

Lazaro smiled, his blunt features making him in some curious way resemble the legendary Che Guevara. He cast a hand across the cluttered table. 'Because of this, you ask?'

Rafael nodded, sat on a stool and watched as Lazaro's face turned towards contempt.

'They picked up her brother last week.' Lazaro shook his head and heaved a hefty sigh. 'There's no hope for Leoncio. He was too involved against both gangs and their apparent unification.'

'And Reina?'

'She's in Sesori with her mother and younger brothers.' Lazaro pointed with his thumb over his shoulder. 'Take a beer from the cooler.'

Rafael threaded his way through the clutter towards an archaic-looking refrigerator. 'I…I too have rotten news,' he said awkwardly.

'What can any of us expect these days!' Lazaro snorted. He dried his feet with a cloth. 'We are born to suffer, it seems. Only fantasists believe otherwise.'

Rafael handed Lazaro a can of beer and found himself tongue-tied. He looked out of the dusty window onto the street below. A campesina was hawking bananas, her clothes virtual rags.

'You okay, Rafael?' came Lazaro's voice. 'What sort of news? I've heard 18th Street slit the throats of six campesinos because they refused to be drug mules. Bastards.'

Rafael left the window to sit at the table. 'Javier. He…he died yesterday.'

Lazaro gawped, his hand holding the cloth motionless. '¡Mierda! How?'

Rafael hunched forward. 'We were stung. When the government contacted you to set up the meet with MS-13, you don't think by any chance there was some kind of interception?'

Lazaro was quick to shake his head. 'Absolutely not. The minister I was dealing with was close to my father in the war. He has a very distinct voice, a slight lisp to it. I'll prove it in a moment. And the wire used was perfectly safe. No one could have listened in to the coded conversation we had. But what happened to you and Javier?'

'Basically, the so-called meet quickly turned sour.' Rafael was curious to know what information Lazaro had come by. 'I have my suspicions that the sub-commander never left Sensuntepeque for the meet. Nevertheless, we engaged with the cell. Five of them. Heavily armed. Straightaway, they wanted to take our weapons and for us to walk in front of them. About fifty metres and some rocky terrain separated us at this point while we negotiated. Javier refused point blank that we give up our weapons and insisted we would trail them to the meet. The negotiations went on for several minutes, Javier refusing to budge. Then, suddenly, before we knew it, we came under fire.' Rafael snatched a swig of beer, his hands trembling slightly at the recollection. 'Javier took out four, while another must have initially fled, before deciding to double back. Later in the day, he sighted us and hit Javier. If it hadn't been for Javier's rule to keep to a minimum of sixty paces apart while on the move, he would have taken us both out. So, I was left to finish the scout, more by luck than skill. He was well camouflaged.'

Lazaro sat perfectly still with his arms folded on the table and his head bowed. Rafael was quite aware that he and Javier had had their differences, and that they tolerated each other for no other reason than the shared desire to make the gangs see common sense and act on it. Javier, it was fair to say, on occasion seemed to relish in tormenting people. Although irritating, it had been nothing more than a harmless by-product of his mischievous ways. Unfortunately,

Lazaro, always the sensitive one, could never accept this and had once pulled a gun on Javier.

'You say you have news for me?' Rafael asked.

Lazaro's head jerked upwards, as if he were snapping out of a daydream. 'Hard to believe, maybe, but apparently Joaquín Hernández has apologised. He sent word to the minister this morning. You already know Hernández is a big fan of your films. And the minister says Hernández still wants to meet you. What do you think of that?'

'Interesting, I guess,' agreed Rafael, 'but I'm going to have to put any such encounter on hold for now. I've urgent business in London to deal with.' He noticed the disappointment on Lazaro's face, fully aware of what he was likely to be thinking: what could be more important than attempting to fix El Salvador for the better? 'I really can't put it off any longer, Lazaro. The producer is well into his eighties. I've already pushed my luck with him by coming out here. He's also financing the screenplay.'

'I get that,' said Lazaro. 'We're grateful, truly…'

For the umpteenth time, Rafael found himself drifting back to the previous day and the firefight with MS-13 up in the hills overlooking Chalatenango. 'You know, Lazaro, I feel envy towards the one I took out. In all honesty, I simply wish it had been me torn from existence rather than him – or Javier.'

Lazaro lifted his head. 'Because of Lena?'

'Yes. I suppose so. Definitely, in fact. I feel completely unmoored, and I hate the feeling because it takes me back to my childhood. A childhood of just drifting from town to town with my mother before boarding the ship as stowaways in Panama. Lena was so much to me, a kind of catalyst from which came refuge and inspiration. Especially refuge.'

Lazaro cleared his throat and straightened himself in his chair. 'Have there been any developments?'

'I haven't been in touch with the detective in charge. I find it difficult to talk about what happened with people I'm not familiar with.' Rafael took a swig of beer. 'But I've been kind of wondering why the gun had been wiped with nail varnish remover and cotton wool.'

'The provider of the gun wouldn't want his prints on it, would he?' Lazaro ventured while emptying the bowl of water. 'Chances are he's probably on record with the police.' He made a start on lifting the plates and cutlery out of the tarnished sink.

Rafael finished his beer. 'Reluctant as I am to return to the UK, I need a favour from you. Someone to take a girl and a young boy back to their village in a few days' time.'

Lazaro looked over his shoulder. 'Where is it?'

'Not far from Los Henriquez. I picked up a strong rumour that a sizable posse of 18th Street are heading out of Chalatenango down to Sensuntepeque. They're likely to follow the valley where the settlement rests. With luck they'll miss it, but to be on the safe side I told the residents to head for the border. About ten kilometres at the most.'

Lazaro dried his hands on his patched-up trousers and went to the refrigerator, which had started to buzz softly. 'Not a problem.' He extracted a couple of beers. 'I'll take them back myself, in fact. It'll give me the opportunity to visit Reina in Sesori.' He offered Rafael another beer, and then looked him in the eye. 'I tried with Javier. You know that, don't you, Rafael? I really tried to understand him.'

The remark caught Rafael by surprise, although he probably should have seen it coming. 'When we first met,' he said quietly but firmly, 'you told me his heart was in the right place. And you were right to say that, Lazaro.' He pulled back the tab on the can of beer: 'So, I tell you this…you never failed to understand Javier where it mattered. Now, let's salute the man.'

CHAPTER 6

The apartment, above a dingy-looking haberdashery a couple of blocks from Lazaro's warehouse, held little in the way of furniture and ornaments. Maroon tiles ran the length of the living-room floor and two solitary paintings adorned the white walls. One depicted a featureless volcanic landscape, the other a mountain stream. The latter marginally appealed to Senica, but if the paintings were anything to go by, then Rafael's taste in art was thoroughly bland. She pondered this further as Jorge veered towards the television set. The apartment's nondescript tone was either deliberate or suggested that it was rarely occupied.

'Show me how to make it work, Rafael!' Jorge scrutinised the set, examining it from all angles. 'Has it got a film machine with it? Tell me it has. Tell me!'

Senica looked on while Rafael explained the remote control to an enthralled Jorge, startled by the way they suddenly resembled father and son sharing a moment together. She sensed her eyes about to well up as she reminded herself that a technically-minded father figure was what Jorge so desperately needed, to lessen the chance of him becoming an 18th Street gang member and target MS-13 for taking his parents – God forbid.

'Put something funny on, Rafael,' Jorge insisted. 'I want to watch something funny.'

While Jorge became absorbed in Charlie Chaplin's *Modern Times*, Senica followed Rafael into the kitchenette.

'This is your place?' she enquired politely.

'Yes.'

The refrigerator needed defrosting, the cans of beer barely visible. She watched Rafael chip away the ice with a serrated carving knife, noticing – not for the first time – that his jaw was tense to the point of him virtually grinding his teeth. Again, she recalled Sancho's warning in the cornfield not to ask too many questions, but she couldn't help herself.

'There's something going on with you, isn't there?' She took the blue ribbon from her ponytail, letting her hair tumble down her back, then shook her head, sat on a stool and folded her arms. 'You're grieving over Javier, I get that. But there's a whole lot more besides, isn't there? I mean, you're kind…but there's a lot of anger inside you. A lot of resentment. That's what I think.'

The knife skidded on the ice. Rafael cursed. 'You think I'm interested in what you think?'

Senica looked straight down at the floor. So clumsy, she told herself. Stupid! 'It's your business. I'm sorry. I didn't mean any harm.'

Rafael extracted a can of beer and heaved a sigh. 'Hell, it's me who should be apologising. Not that it's much of an excuse, but I guess I'm tired and, to be honest, still in some pain.' He gave her a smile and handed her the beer. 'If it hadn't been for you, my arm would be well and truly infected by now.'

Senica liked his smile. A wholesome, perceptive smile that made her feel safe and relatively content in his company. She wished he would smile more often. 'I think it's fair to say I shouldn't intrude,' she said.

Rafael opened a can for himself, the gas escaping with a lively hiss.

'Whatever, I'm in debt to you. Now I'm going to shower. Feel free to do whatever you want.'

Senica sipped some beer and leant on the worktop. It hadn't really struck her until now. Or maybe it had, subconsciously – she couldn't be sure, what with the upset of having to leave the village and Jorge's unexpected reappearance – but she found Rafael to be quite good-looking with his strong, well-defined features and dark eyebrows that she wanted to reach out and touch. She had a thing about eyebrows. His hair was a bit scruffy, but a trim would put that right. And a shave. He needed a shave. She hated stubble. Apart from giving the impression of neglect, it was horrible to kiss, like it would always sting her lips…

She clamped her eyes shut. *Whatever* was she thinking? He was probably taken, anyway – with kids, even. Besides, as far-fetched as the idea seemed, given that she'd received no formal education, had no money, had lost her DUI card and hadn't bothered to re-register herself with the authorities, not to mention the fact that she was now half a moon away from her twenty-sixth birthday – or possibly her twenty-seventh – she still wanted to try and find a way to study medicine. That was her goal, and a man was the last thing she needed cluttering up her life.

There was *something* oddly familiar about Rafael, though. She couldn't quite pinpoint where she'd seen him before – or someone similar to him – but imagined it must have been when she'd lived for a time in San Vicente. Or maybe she hadn't actually seen him, but a picture of him? A picture in a newspaper or magazine, perhaps? She wasn't sure. The sensation felt weirdly distant on the one hand, yet immediate on the other. She took another sip of beer before curiosity got the better of her. Taking advantage of Rafael's temporary absence, she entered the living room to take a look around.

'This film's boring,' Jorge told her without turning his head from the screen. 'It must be really old. It's not even in colour! I'm going to try another.'

Senica glanced over her shoulder while picking up a magazine with a camera on its cover. 'Jorge, don't break anything,' she said. 'Remember, we're guests.'

Jorge leaned towards the DVD player. 'I know what to do. He showed me. The thing comes out of the machine by itself. It's like magic. Like the one Roldán's father found in Chalatenango.'

Thieved more like, Senica told herself while returning the magazine. She went to another shelf beside a window that overlooked an overgrown yard with several domestic appliances rusting away in a corner. Frustratingly, the few books on the shelf were in a foreign language – even the atlas. Was it French? She loved the 'exotic' sound of French. It felt as sensual to her ear as silk was to her skin. When she could afford the bus fare to take her into Chalatenango, she liked to visit the library to look at the atlases. Very often they would enthral her with dreams set in far-off places, releasing her from the horrors that were tearing her country apart. Her favourite dream was walking carefree through the streets of Paris, occasionally accompanied by an imaginary French lover. More often than not, though, she preferred to be alone, a summer's breeze playing with her hair. Returning to the stool in the kitchen, she balanced the atlas on her knees and took another sip of beer.

Jorge rushed up to her. 'Senica, take a look at this!'

'I'm busy. What is it?'

'Rafael. I think it's him on the telephone.'

'Telephone?'

'Television.'

'Don't be silly.'

'I'm not.'

She opened the atlas. 'Go back and take a proper look.'

Jorge tugged her arm. 'It's him.' Another tug. 'I'm telling you!'

When he tugged her arm for a third time, Senica gave up. With a terse sigh, she followed him back into the living room and cast a glance at the television set – and thought her legs were going to collapse from under her.

'It looks like him, doesn't it?' said Jorge, fiddling with the volume. 'And she's quite pretty for a white girl. What are they doing?'

Senica took her hand from her mouth and moved closer to the screen. 'They' were holding hands with smiling black children, a woman's voice serving as the narrator. And yes, the girl was pretty. Flaxen-haired, svelte, blue-eyed – and Senica recognised her as being enormously talented. During her stay in San Vicente, someone had once mentioned to her that Lena Rudbeck's partner was a Salvadorean film director and had shown her a picture of the couple…

…and now here she was, standing in *their* apartment.

* * *

Rafael put on a clean shirt and jeans. He needed to call Rory Foster, find out whether the detective was any closer to identifying the madman who murdered Lena. The name he'd given the landlady at the Ocean View guest house – Guy Brooker – had clearly been false. She'd claimed he spoke with a slight northern accent but wasn't completely sure since he'd barely spoken a word to her. By now, though, the detective must have unearthed enough evidence to be well on the way to identifying the monster. If not, then he was going to make a complaint to the detective's superior. Closure was never going to happen, but to ascertain the killer's identity might just lessen his wretched insomnia.

With a degree of awkwardness, he sat in the chair by the window and eased on a pair of patterned socks, before a faint knock on the door made him look up.

'Yes?' he answered.

'Can I come in?' Senica's voice seemed uncharacteristically timid.

'Sure.' He watched her enter the room, holding a glass of water. As an afterthought, she went back and closed the door, her hair briefly swirling around her shoulders.

'It was quite a shock…' Senica avoided his eyes as she hovered by the foot of the bed. 'Quite a shock.'

In the silence between them, Rafael could hear *Rainbow Obscure*, a documentary on the dire plight of Yemen he had made with Lena. There and then, he wished he'd never shown the boy how to use the player, surprised that he'd taken it all in so comprehensively.

Senica withdrew the rim of the glass from her chin and tilted her head towards the living room. 'Jorge found a DVD with you on it.' She perched herself on the edge of the bed. 'I…I really don't know much about you, I'm ashamed to say. I'd like to know more. It's not often someone like me gets to meet a film director, is it? You must have led an interesting life.'

Although her curiosity came as no surprise, Rafael knew it would ultimately lead to Lena. And that concerned him, because he wasn't sure whether he wanted – or indeed was strong enough – to talk about her to this relative stranger without breaking down.

'There's nothing unique about me, Senica.' He tried to find an angle to put her off. 'Rather the opposite, actually.'

'I would like to be given the opportunity to make up my own mind about that.'

Rafael looked at his hands. Just like the boy, an answer for everything! 'What do you want to know?' he asked dully.

Senica picked up on his tone. 'Rafael, that's hardly fair. You asked me quite a few questions about myself. I must be so boring in comparison.'

'Don't be ridiculous.' He leaned further into the chair, watching her, becoming more conscious of the fact that she had very little by way of Spanish blood, her Mayan physical charm, if anything, oriental-looking. He shifted his gaze from the tiny birthmark to the left of her nose that fascinated him, sensing that he might have been staring.

'Where do I start?' He shrugged. 'Before leaving El Salvador, we moved around for much of the time, my mother and myself. Obviously, I asked her where my father was, but she merely said he'd passed over, and that the spirit world had summoned her to take me to Europe because the hardship throughout much of Central America was never going to go away. Maybe she was half crazy, but either she or the spirits were right about that.'

Senica leaned forward, as if keen to catch his every word. 'What age were you when you left El Salvador?'

Rafael started to think it odd that she hadn't mentioned Lena. Presumably she had recognised her on the DVD. Lena had been something of a hit in El Salvador, having referred to the tiny country in several of her songs. 'Around ten,' he said, trying to keep his eyes off the cute birthmark. 'Hard to say for sure. It took a while to reach Panama, where we stowed away on a container ship. Throughout the voyage to England, when it came to food at least, we'd never had it so good. The cargo in the ship's hold consisted of tinned fish, corned beef and fruit. Fresh water was something of an issue until, a couple of days after we'd set sail, I came across a disused shower room. I was asleep when we docked. I believe it was then that my mother lost her balance and fell. The fall broke her neck.'

Senica gasped, placing a hand on her breastbone. 'Oh, Rafael…that's awful! That such a journey should end in that way! It must have been horrible for you.' She crossed her legs and supported the glass on her knee. 'What happened to you in England? Who looked after you?'

Despite the burning ache in his arm, Rafael tied the laces on his trainer-styled shoes. 'I was handed over to foster parents. They were pleasant enough, and in fact helped me to obtain dual citizenship, which obviously I came to appreciate in later years. But I soon became bored living with them. I wasn't used to staying in one place. I made my way over to France and met a guy called Marc Fauré. Later on, we started to make films together, Marc being the cameraman and associate scriptwriter.'

'I imagine you to have been a little like Jorge,' smiled Senica. 'You know…up to all things. But tell me, where's Lena? In England? I've heard her music, mainly when I lived in St Vicente. It's nice. Sometimes mellow, sometimes rock.'

Rafael found himself looking out of the window, a blood-spattered body on a stretcher at St Thomas' Hospital replacing the armoured vehicle cruising through the street below. He recalled stroking her hair, wanting only to lift her up into his arms and take her back to the house they shared in Cambridge Street, to put her to bed, kiss her brow and pray with all his might for a miracle, for resurrection itself.

'Someone blasted her life away three months ago,' he said, his tone mechanical while he doggedly held himself together. 'At a concert.'

Senica stared straight back at him, eyes thrown wide open. 'What are you saying? Some…someone killed her?'

'You never read about it or saw it on television?'

'No.' She put her glass down on the bedside cabinet. 'I can't believe what you're telling me. I'm so sorry. I had no idea... They have the person?'

'He killed himself, there and then. Incredible.'

'Oh, Rafael...' Senica grimaced and shook her head. 'I slapped your face!'

He raised a hand. 'Don't beat yourself up. I deserved it. We both know that.'

'You'd just lost Javier.'

'Even so—'

'And now you give me this awful news about Lena... I feel out of place!'

'Out of place?'

'Of course, I do,' insisted Senica, spreading her hands and becoming altogether animated and Latin. 'Not only are you a filmmaker in Europe, but you were also Lena Rudbeck's partner and now you're telling me she has been murdered – at a concert she was giving! It's such a shock to me. I mean, with this sudden knowledge I'm surprised you bothered to ask me here. I'm grateful for the books you are giving me...'

'I've thought about that, too,' admitted Rafael. 'About why I asked you to come with me to San Miguel. All I can say is this: that, set against Lena's murder, there's something therapeutic about you. Your courage, your integrity, in such adversity.' He laid his throbbing arm across his knee, a blotch of dried blood visible on the bandage. 'I'm leaving for Europe tomorrow. A colleague of mine will take you to your village. Should difficulties arise, then you must return to this apartment until a safe passage can be guaranteed.'

'I have to get to Uncle José, but thanks.' She watched him for a moment before leaving the bed to kneel in front of him. 'Can I ask you, Rafael…do you believe there is a hereafter, a spirit world?'

'A spirit world?' Rafael found himself taken aback by the directness of her question. But then he shrugged. 'When Lena was taken from me, I wanted to believe it to be true. Though I have to say, it all feels a shade far-fetched. Do you believe there are spirits in the hills around the village?'

'Most of us do. Mayan spirits, mainly. That's what we believe… Promise me something, Rafael. When you leave tomorrow, remember these words. It was Mayan spirits, in my opinion, that brought us together – for a reason.' She gave him a quiet smile and put a hand on his knee. 'Unfortunately, I've really no idea what that reason might be. Although, I have to say, it feels important. I suppose by saying that I'm opening myself up for you to regard me as being completely off the wall!'

Rafael touched her hand, all at once wanting to share her belief in a hereafter. 'I'm hardly likely to forget you…your signature is on my arm.'

'And now you're going to take it to Europe. Surreal for me to know that. But it would have been neater if I could have put in a couple of stitches.'

'I'll wear the scar with pride.'

He met her eyes, and then perhaps the same thought ran through them both like an electric shock, for Senica swiftly withdrew her hand, as if embarrassed by their unexpected physical proximity.

She sat on the bed, first crossing her legs and then uncrossing them. Finally, she finished off the glass of water.

Rafael sensed her awkwardness while he busied himself looking for his watch. 'I'm starving,' he said.

'Yes, me too.' It was as if Senica had been searching for something to say herself to break the silence. She turned to look at him. 'We've only had an orange each today.'

'There's a café around the corner. There's nothing much in the cupboards here.' He found his watch under a shirt on the bed. 'We can go there now, get something to eat and bring back a few beers.'

'That would be nice.'

Rafael looked over his shoulder, just as they were leaving the room. 'Remind me to give you those books.'

Senica held his gaze. 'Absolutely, I will. I love books.'

They went into the living room to find Jorge all but wearing the television set, his chair mere centimetres from the screen.

PART 2

TREASON

CHAPTER 7

The guidebook in Raoul Cregan's hand informed him that the castle in the hazy distance had been the scene of a battle with US troops in 1847. Now a museum but back then a military academy, six cadets had died defending the school. Raoul craned his neck another inch and glimpsed what he took to be the monument Los Niños Héroes – the six white columns honouring the event rising like plumes of ocean spray above the treetops.

The panorama from his suite at the Salamanca Hotel took in much of Chapultepec Park, with its castle, boating lake, botanical gardens and a leafy section of Avenue Paseo de la Reforma. Naturally, he would have preferred to have left Mexico City the previous evening to be at his desk in London, having successfully acquired the Embajador publishing group, but Erika had persuaded him to stop over, complaining that they didn't spend enough time together as a family. It was all such a damn nuisance.

Raoul drove a hand through his prematurely greying hair and glanced down at the busy avenue, the multi-coloured dots that swept along it having no idea – *absolutely* no idea – of the Council of the Faithful Brethren's existence or its ability to conjure up war or insurmountable debt, to maximise on the bungling of famines and exoduses by the satellite governments, and so forth. Eight centuries earlier, through exceptional cunning, the Council had appropriated the innovative financial systems of the Knights Templars and had exploited them to full effect.

'Raoul?'

He turned from the window. His wife had wrapped a towel around her reddish-blonde hair. Raoul wished she wouldn't do that after she'd taken a shower. It made her look common, like one of those imbecilic dots in the avenue below.

'You're taking Adam to the zoo, as we agreed, right?'

'If I must.' He didn't bother to look back at her.

Erika strode over to a jade-tinted glass coffee table. She lit a cigarette and blew the smoke at the ceiling in a flurry of palpable annoyance.

'He's your son, Raoul. It really would help if you showed more interest.'

Raoul tossed the guidebook into an armchair. 'How long are you going to be at the museum?'

Erika shrugged and tightened her robe around herself as if she were applying a layer of armour. 'As long as it takes.'

'Haven't you an approximate idea?'

'Not really, no. Could be a couple of hours, could be longer. You know how interested I am in anthropology.'

'I thought you wanted us to be together?'

'Adam would only become bored.' She drank some juice and came back across the room, her crimson robe swirling around her shapely legs. 'He's seen a kite he would like. It's in a shop window by the entrance to the park. We saw it yesterday, when you were at the meeting. But the shop was closed.'

'He's got a kite at home.' It seemed to Raoul that Erika was mollycoddling the boy – giving in to whatever took his fancy. 'He should be doing more in the way of studying, reading books—'

'He's only eight, for heaven's sake!' She stubbed out the remainder of the cigarette. 'I'm not in the mood to have a fight with you, Raoul. Okay?'

'Who said anything about a fight?' Raoul lifted his hands, goading her to answer him. Then something caught his eye.

They turned together. Adam stood quietly in the doorway, lips apart, a bewildered look about him.

Erika went and tucked his shirt into his shorts. 'Adam, darling, your father's taking you to the park.' She fussed some more with his appearance. 'You can buy the kite we saw yesterday. You remember the shop?'

The boy didn't look at his father. 'Yes, Mummy. Can't you come? Please.'

Erika tidied a wisp of hair that had fallen across the boy's brow. 'I want you to have some time with your father. And when you come back, I want to hear all about the animals you've seen.' She stood back and, apparently satisfied with her son's appearance, gave Raoul a cursory glance. 'I'll see you later,' she said dismissively.

Raoul took a deep breath as his wife all but slammed the bedroom door shut.

Bitch. He reached for his cotton jacket.

* * *

Adam pointed in excitement. 'There it is!'

The lights changed and Raoul crossed the road with a firm grip on his son's hand, guiding him through the menacing pollution towards the entrance to the park.

'That's the shop with the kite!'

'You're not having it!' Raoul snapped at once.

The boy looked up at him, shocked. 'But Mummy—'

Raoul yanked the boy's arm. 'Now, look…listen to me. She's your mother – and you call her Mother. I've told you before. You *don't* call her Mummy. It's pathetic to call her Mummy. It shows disrespect.'

'But she likes—'

'Don't answer me back!'

They skirted the lake in silence before following an avenue of giant cypress trees that led to the zoo. Despite his father's mood, Adam gazed in awe at the animals, particularly the giant pandas, next to a rather pensive-looking arctic wolf. Then, quite unexpectedly, they came upon a baby giraffe. Adam smiled as it frolicked about before accidentally bumping into its mother, who looked down at her offspring with an expression suggesting forbearance.

Like the arctic wolf, Raoul was lost in thought as he trailed behind his son between the various enclosures. He wondered if Erika's erratic behaviour had anything to do with her hormones and whether another child might help to quieten things down. He felt himself shake his head. One child was enough, as far as he was concerned. Its gender male, fortunately. But the fact remained that his wife was becoming all that he had feared she would become, a loose cannon primed with defiance, making divorce itself risky. Left unguarded, she might try and humiliate him in some unforeseen way in front of his peers. Such retribution could quite easily wreck his chances of an already belated – by his reckoning – succession to the inner sanctum of the Council of the Faithful Brethren, with which his father and grandfather had been closely associated throughout their lifetimes.

They emerged from the zoo by the boating lake, the shimmering sun creating jewel-like ripples that drifted lazily into the far distance. Adam pointed. 'Look. Can we do that? Can we go in a boat?'

'In a moment,' Raoul responded vaguely, taking a Samsung phone from his pocket. He had bought it back in London, opting for the pay-as-you-go set-up, giving a false name on the registration slip. 'I need to speak to someone first.'

They sat on a bench and Raoul made the call.

'Yeah? Who is it?'

Raoul winced, finding the guttural voice with its West Midlands dialect irritatingly lethargic and wholly unprofessional. 'It's your client speaking. Anything to report?'

'Few bits an' pieces.'

'Have you anything more on Liam Fenney?' Raoul asked impatiently, drumming his fingers on the bench.

'Cracked up, didn't he. Dunno why. Tryin' to find out. Joshua Waldo got him into a nuthouse in Santa Monica.'

'What's his history?'

'Liam Fenney, you mean?'

Raoul felt his temper rising. 'Of course I mean Liam Fenney. I'm hardly likely to mean Joshua Waldo, am I?'

'Hey – now look, mate, just cut the attitude. Everythin' will be sweet. Okay? You have to be patient in this game. Right?'

'Now you listen to me,' interjected Raoul, 'I'm paying you handsomely, and right now you're looking out onto East 81st Street. Your next client, at a guess, will have you poking around in rubbish bins and the rest of it. So, I suggest you answer my question. Agreed?'

'And what was the question?'

'*Fenney!* Liam Fenney. What's he done in the past?'

'He's army. I've already stated that.'

'Well, tell it to me again.'

'The Bill Browns.'

'The what?'

'Grenadier Guards. He's working for Joshua Waldo now. Sure of it. When he got out of the nuthouse, he visited 81st Street.'

'Any idea why?'

'Nope. Stayed there about an hour before Jake followed him to Kennedy. He took a flight to dear ol' Heathrow.'

Raoul felt a twinge of concern. 'And who might Jake be?'

'My assistant. Haven't got ruddy wings, you know. I'm trainin' him up. D'you want anyone taken out?'

'Taken out?'

'Bumped off.'

Raoul contained his astonishment, reminding himself that he was dealing with a useful idiot who could still provide him with the information he so desperately needed. 'No, I don't. Anyone else been visiting Joshua Waldo?' He went back to drumming his fingers on the seat – until it dawned on him that germs might have been left there by previous occupants. 'Like Rafael Maqui, for instance?'

'Nope, not him. Just the usual, mate. I've sent photos to the PO box.'

'Call me if there are any developments. Straightaway. Regardless of time of day. And, incidentally, I'm not your *mate*. Bear that in mind in future.'

Raoul put the phone back in his pocket and gazed beyond the boating lake at the forest surrounding the castle. Where could Maqui be these days? Why hadn't he visited Joshua Waldo? It was at least three months now. He could only assume he was still somewhere in El Salvador, perhaps filming an introduction or whatever, using the country's rampant gang warfare and poverty as a case in point. He looked up. Adam was nowhere in sight.

Raoul stood up and cast a frantic glance around himself. A group of rowdy men to his left kicked a football. Then he saw Adam – and he couldn't believe his eyes. His head pounding, he cut straight across the makeshift football pitch to the campesina holding an infant to her chest.

Raoul jerked his son away from the startled girl. 'What the hell do you think you're doing?' he shouted at the boy.

'She kept pointing at the baby's mouth,' Adam answered tentatively. 'I...I was giving her some of my pocket money. The baby needs food.'

'You don't give these people money. You don't give *anyone* money. Do I make myself clear?'

Adam stood pale-faced, taking short breaths. He looked down at his shoes, and then clenched his hands.

'Do I make myself clear?' Raoul repeated. 'Answer me!'

'No!' Adam shouted back, retreating. 'I hate you. Hate you!'

The shock on his father's face seemed to shore up the boy's courage.

'You hurt Mummy. You upset her. I *hate* you!'

The boy ran off. Raoul felt his jacket being tugged, the girl pointing vigorously at her open mouth with its assortment of broken and rotten teeth. He pushed her off and went after his son, keeping up a stride whilst at the same time trying not to draw attention to himself. The boy was making for the lake and Raoul cut back across the football pitch. Dismissing a shirtless player shouting what sounded like an obscenity as the ball flew over his head, he kept his eye on Adam, who hesitated while looking in the direction of the castle. He stayed in the boy's blind spot, sweeping up behind him to clap a hand on his shoulder. Adam spun around, and cowered immediately.

'Don't hit me!' he cried. 'I didn't mean it... I'm sorry. I'm sorry, Father.'

Raoul released his grip and caught his breath, and then noticed a blotch on the boy's shorts. He was mortified. The heir to the Sarron News Agency had actually wet himself!

A shrill came from his jacket pocket. He flicked open the mobile phone. 'Yes,' he snapped.

'You're not going to believe this. He's only turned up, hasn't he?'

'I'm not a psychic. Who's turned up and where?'

'Rafael Maqui, for crying out loud! On East 81st.'

'You're kidd—'

'True as I'm standing here. He's just gone inside.'

Raoul's mood changed completely; now he found himself positively cheerful. 'That's excellent news. Keep me posted. I want to know how long he's there and where he goes after he leaves. You hear me?'

'Loud and clear.'

Raoul put the phone back in his jacket pocket and looked at his son, who was still sobbing. An idea came into his head. Besides, he didn't think he could take another of Erika's tantrums.

'It's all right, Adam,' he said soothingly. 'Tell you what, let's buy that kite. But first we must find you some shorts. Don't be embarrassed. Careless of me to have frightened you like that.'

'I'm sorry, Father,' Adam mumbled.

'Don't worry.' They started to walk away from the lake. 'When we get your new shorts, your mother will ask what's happened to the ones you were wearing earlier. We'll say you tore them on a boat. Right?'

'Yes, Father.'

Raoul reached for his son's hand. 'There's something else, Adam…'

The boy looked up.

'It's your mother… She's not well. Not at all well.'

'Has she got a cold?'

'More than that, I'm afraid.' They left the park and Raoul had to raise his voice to be heard above the traffic. 'She's very tired, so she gets easily upset. We don't want to say anything that might make her unhappy. Understood?'

'Yes, Father. Can we buy her a present?'

'Well done!' praised Raoul, relieved. The boy was getting the gist to mention only the 'tear' on his shorts. 'That's a good idea.'

'When will she get better?'

'We can only pray, Adam. That's all we can do.' Raoul put a reassuring hand on his son's shoulder and cast his mind back to the phone call with the private investigator who, he suspected, and indeed hoped, was acting *very* privately – operating much of the time outside the law. Had he opted for a legitimate company, with all its law-abiding restrictions, then he felt he could never have stated the name 'Joshua Waldo' without eyebrows being raised – hence the somewhat odious individual the Internet had presented him with after whittling down a shortlist of potential candidates.

D'you want anyone taken out?

It might be advantageous to simply eliminate Rafael Maqui, in the process wrecking any immediate threat to the Council from Joshua Waldo and Loran Communications. He called back the number.

'Yeah?'

'Say… Say Maqui needed to be…removed.'

'Eliminated, you're saying?'

Raoul patted his brow with a handkerchief. 'Kind of thing, yes.'

'Jake'll do it.'

'What would I be looking at, cost-wise?'

'He'll do it for fifteen. Eight-k upfront. Cos I'm training him up, you won't get a better deal. For that category of target, others will ask upwards of eighty-k.'

Raoul ignored the substantial discrepancy within the sales pitch. 'You wouldn't do it yourself?'

'Touch of Parkinson's. Crosshairs wobble about. Jake'll sort it. Nice and clean.'

Raoul became aware of how surreal a moment it was to be walking along Avenue Paseo de la Reforma with his son and deciding on whether to deliver a death sentence. He was desperate to become a member of the Brethren's Inner Council, something neither his father or grandfather had achieved. In a sense, he supposed he was conducting his own initiative-come-initiation test. With the evidence he now had of Joshua Waldo's relationship with Rafael Maqui, it seemed obvious to him that an attack was imminent—

'You there, mate?'

Raoul winced at the man's brashness, took an intake of breath and calmed himself against his audacious strategy. 'Just do it,' he said. 'The money will be deposited as before.' Ending the call, he thought fifteen thousand pounds was ridiculously cheap. There again, depending on how this 'Jake' fellow went about it, it might be just a few minutes' work.

He pocketed the mobile phone with a growing sense he had made the right decision. His peers would surely applaud his foresight and the efficient manner in which he had terminated the threat. A seat within the Council was virtually guaranteed.

He turned to his son. 'Right, Adam, let's find that present for your mother.'

CHAPTER 8

The lobby in which Rafael stood on Manhattan's East 81st Street was dominated by an Enzo Plazzotta figurine, not by way of size but by its feminine elegance and, more specifically, the rather sensual lips that were ever so slightly parted, emphasising the look of wonder in her eyes. Rafael continued his tour of the lobby. A Willem de Kooning, with the suggestion of each garish smear, twist and turn having been applied to the canvas amidst a frenzied seizure, caused him to reflect on how many mouths its monetary value would feed. Recently, he'd found himself making such comparisons to the point that he now preferred to avoid those who owned excessive material wealth, suspecting exploitation had likely played a part in their so-called achievements. But Joshua Waldo was an exception, his scheme, meticulously assembled piece by piece, being unequivocally humanitarian.

'Sorry to keep you waiting, Rafael,' came a voice from behind him.

He looked over his shoulder to see Joshua's assistant-cum-confidante, Anna Sangster.

'I was calling through the grocery order,' explained Anna.

Rafael appreciated her embrace: the flight up from Central America had been lonely as hell. Although they had met briefly in California, he still found it difficult to fathom Anna's age. Her vibrant features and agile mannerisms gave the impression she was in her mid-fifties, but it was her wizened hands that made him wonder whether she was much older.

'We've been thinking of you,' Anna said.

Rafael took off his woollen trench coat. 'I kind of felt you had. Thanks.'

Anna wiped a tear away from the corner of her eye with a turquoise tissue. 'You're coping?' she asked, tucking the tissue back into her sleeve.

Rafael couldn't help himself and sighed. 'It comes in waves, Anna. The desolation – the reality of it all.' Then, something of a smile. 'Thank heavens for Joshua, I guess. And filmmaking.'

Anna took his coat. 'For what it's worth, I think you're being remarkably brave.' She moved across the lobby to the coat stand. 'Hungry?'

'Maybe later.'

'Leave it to me.' She glanced at the robust door ahead of them. 'He's in there. Been like a bear with a sore head. Good luck!'

* * *

Rafael extended his injured arm and made the greeting as brief but as polite as possible. His own frailty, however, hardly matched that of Joshua Waldo's, and it occurred to him that the president of Loran Communications might have had a mild stroke since he'd last set eyes on him. He didn't like to ask, fearing that his hunch was entirely accurate. Or, God forbid, that something more terminal was taking shape.

'Why not sit down?' Rafael suggested, his tone betraying his concern.

Joshua Waldo waved a dismissive hand. 'Don't start shoving me around the way Anna does,' he growled. 'She's driving me bananas. Fussing all the time. An old man desires peace from the fairer sex, not perpetual chastisement.'

Rafael was reassured by the coltish glint in Joshua's watery-blue eyes. 'Anna has my sympathy. So there.'

Joshua muttered 'humbug' just loud enough for it to be amusing and leaned into an armchair beside the open fire. 'I've been mad with you... Guess I shouldn't have been.' His fleshy face was noticeably rueful as he pointed vaguely at the chair opposite. 'Callous of me.'

'You had reason to be upset,' Rafael replied simply. 'I'm here now. Let's just leave it at that.' He sat in the cushioned armchair to which he'd been directed, careful not to jar his right arm. 'So, fill me in on what's new.'

Joshua shook his head and heaved a hefty sigh that seemed befitting of his once towering build. 'Industrial espionage, or whatever...that's what's been going on. This place was wired.'

'Wired?'

'Bugged. This very room and my study.'

'I know what you mean, but—'

'I happened to discover two hidden microphones, each the size of a thimble.'

'But just a moment,' Rafael interjected, 'microphones the size of a thimble sounds distinctly amateurish to me. Industrial espionage these days would consist of apparatus far more discreet. The size of a pinhead in comparison.'

'If not industrial espionage, then who would have planted them and for what purpose? The production? Are the Council of the Faithful Brethren already in the know about the blow we're about to deliver against them? God's sake!'

'I don't see how,' said Rafael, feeling Joshua's concern. This was a one-shot opportunity in more ways than one. Once Joshua Waldo left this world, there simply wouldn't be a media outlet daring enough to take on such an undertaking as *Agenda Indiscriminate* for fear of ruination by the Council. 'Security from my end, Joshua, is still as tight as it can be. Before what happened to Lena, I'd made a start on contacting technicians to warn them that I'd be needing them, but none of them to date has received a draft of the screenplay apart from my lead cameraman, Marc Fauré.'

'You haven't been in touch with him?'

'No, not yet.' Rafael's sudden restlessness took him to a window that overlooked a rain-swept cityscape, shades of autumn in the form of golden-yellow maple leaves scattered along its pavements. 'Why do you ask? Surely you're not implying—'

'Of course not.' Joshua fiddled with a cheroot. He reached for a match but didn't strike it. 'There's been an incident…in Cambridge Street, London.'

Rafael jerked his head away from the window. 'What kind of an incident?'

'We were too late.'

Rafael left the window, anxious. 'There's been a fire, or something?'

'No, no, no. Not a fire.'

'What, then?'

'A break-in. That's what we think.' Joshua lit the cheroot. 'After your disappearing act, Marc and I took it upon ourselves to protect your property. Liam Fenney, who I'll come to, called me to say the safe in the kitchen's been interfered with. In fact, it's empty, according to Liam.'

Rafael wasn't wholly taken aback, because he knew it was nothing to do with the screenplay. A raid for souvenirs – nothing more sinister than that. The outrage he felt was more akin, he imagined, to finding the grave of a loved one desecrated.

'Something else, too…' Joshua turned his gaze from the fire back towards Rafael. 'Three pieces from my Ming collection in Santa Monica were taken three weeks ago. The most valuable pieces. Talk about professional…'

Rafael recalled the collection. Although he was no expert, it had certainly looked impressive.

'Over fifty years I've been collecting it,' grumbled Joshua, as if to himself. 'But as for Cambridge Street…were they looking for the script?'

Rafael was quick to shake his head. 'They wouldn't have found anything, Joshua. Despite my disturbed state, I had the presence of mind to clean up before I left for El Salvador.'

'Clean up? How do you mean?'

'I wouldn't write a screenplay of this sensitivity on a PC that's connected to the outside world. The laptop I used is stripped down to nothing more than a word processor. Granted, the screenplay's on three sticks. You have one, Marc and myself the other two. I wiped the file from the laptop before leaving. The memory sticks we have are heavily encrypted. Mine is hidden from sight in the spare bedroom in Cambridge Street. As you know, the names in the screenplay are presently fictitious and, of course, the speech has yet to be handed over by your good self. If by the remotest of chances someone came across the screenplay in its present format, it would simply resemble a run-of-the-mill thriller.'

Joshua gazed at the tip of his cheroot for several seconds before tapping off the ash. 'But if discovered in its present format – as you put it – someone directly linked to the Council of the Faithful Brethren would surely latch onto what we're up to? Someone like my European counterpart, Raoul Cregan, say?'

'Agreed. But there's no way anyone from the Council has seen the screenplay. How could they have done?'

'Then why these incidents all of a sudden, Rafael? The break-in…the hidden microphones…the theft of the Ming collection – although, I suppose we can discount the latter. But Cambridge Street and the microphones?' Joshua made his way with a slight shuffle towards a decanter of whisky. 'Your more recent films have been controversial, that's why I approached you. I recognised that we were in the same vein, politically. It's fair to say that I was ahead of you, because of my age and that I've met some of those in the Council – notably, of course, Raoul Cregan, since he is the chairman of the Sarron News Agency over in London.' He handed Rafael a glass before hesitating. 'What if he, for whatever reason, decided to put some gumshoe onto me, and that gumshoe saw you arrive in Santa Monica with Lena? Or even arrive here, this very afternoon? Wouldn't you start to think twice about what was going on if you were Cregan – or anyone from the Council of the Faithful Brethren?'

'I probably would,' admitted Rafael. 'But I simply can't believe this to be the case. I'm all but convinced Cambridge Street was a raid for souvenirs. They'll go for a fortune, guaranteed – any of Lena's possessions now she's no longer with us. That's the world we're living in.'

Joshua nodded quietly and leaned back into the armchair. 'Six months, Rafael. No longer.'

So, not a stroke, Rafael gauged, *but definitely something terminal!* He started to wonder how the hell he was going to redraft, film, edit and screen the picture within twenty-four weeks – or near as, damn it. 'And that's a fact?' he said tersely, hearing his sense of alarm soak into his voice.

'According to those in the know.'

'I'm sorry.'

'It's the drugs that get you in the end, of course. In the meantime, it's a balancing act. Pharmaceutical harmonisation.' Joshua took a near gulp from his glass. 'You'll like Liam Fenney. Conscientious, in his own way. He's secured an apartment for you in Holland Park, if you choose not to use Cambridge Street.' He met Rafael's eyes directly. 'Might be wise not to, in fact. Call me paranoid, but you never know. It would give me peace of mind, put it that way.'

Rafael sampled the whisky. Glenmorangie was just about his favourite, and whatever it was Joshua had poured him wasn't far off it. 'I'll take up your offer, Joshua. Living in Pimlico would likely be a distraction... Talking of Sarron, I read on the plane coming up from Salvador that Cregan's acquired Embajador.'

Joshua chuckled. 'Ironic, really. Embajador was started by my father. It was one of three publishing concerns I sold in the eighties to raise finance to get my hands on Loran Communications.'

'What's Raoul Cregan like when you meet him in the flesh? In the pictures I've seen of him, he looks hard-nosed and decidedly cruel.'

Joshua shrugged. 'It's probably the image he prefers to project. The hard-nosed aspect. He has a charming wife, Erika, and a son around eight or nine years old. Cregan's a schmuck, that's all there is to it.'

'Something of an evil despot, I'd say.'

Joshua made no further comment, and instead quietly topped up their glasses.

Rafael watched him settle back in the armchair, his mind made up. 'I'm on the next flight out. New York's not the place for me right now.'

Joshua glanced at a framed photograph on a side table of himself when he was middle-aged, standing next to a young woman with a quiet smile at what appeared to be a ski resort. 'I know what it's like, to a certain degree,' he remarked softly, 'though the manner in which they were taken from us was quite different, of course. At least I had some warning, time to prepare myself.'

Rafael followed Joshua's gaze, the wound to his arm beginning to itch. A healthy sign, he imagined. 'The epitome of screen presence,' he said softly. 'She never ventured into films?'

'No, just the boards. On occasion Broadway. Being a movie star never appealed to her.'

There had been a daughter, Rafael recalled from his initial research into Loran Communications and its president when he'd first been approached to write the screenplay. Jemima had died suddenly from a cerebral haemorrhage, although Joshua had never mentioned a word about her to him. Just his wife, Sarah.

'Do you believe we are reunited with the ones we hold dear?' asked Joshua, as if on cue.

Rafael turned from the picture, struck by the question. He recalled Senica, sitting on the bed in his apartment in San Miguel. *Can I ask you, Rafael, do you believe there is a hereafter, a spirit world?* He put his glass down on the side table. 'I never gave it much thought until recently.' He stood, ready to leave. 'But suddenly nothing about this life makes sense to me, unless I believe I will see Lena again.'

* * *

Inside his oak-panelled study with its mellow wrap-around lighting, Joshua picked up a photograph of a sun-kissed face with flowing mousy hair. A perfect image of a carefree child. He touched the silver frame and smiled as he leaned into an armchair.

'We've got the right man. Know that, Jemima?' His smile resurfaced. 'Course you do.'

He wiped the sudden tear from his fleshy cheek and brought the portrait of his daughter to his chest. Would the Council of the Faithful Brethren fragment or implode in some way, once they'd been exposed and named? As for the United Nations, he wanted the political and economic branches of academia to rise up and speak with one voice within the organisation under a state of emergency, where credit and fiscal policies would be addressed, to enable equality to regenerate and flourish unabated.

With something of a boyish smile on his otherwise worn face, Joshua closed his eyes.

The right man, he repeated, before resting his head against a cushion and falling asleep.

CHAPTER 9

With the remainder of the previous day spent in a tearful state in a shabby and barely tolerable motel close to Kennedy Airport, Rafael waited impatiently for the evening traffic to clear on the Bayswater Road.

'How far are we?' he asked the black-cab driver.

''Bout a mile, down on the right. Worse than Bangkok, eh?'

Rafael paid the fare outside the Czech Embassy, crossed the road and eventually came to Norland Square, which he'd driven past many times and which he now realised included an acre or so of trees and shrubs encompassing a tennis court. He moved away from the railings and found the number he was looking for: a creamy, three-storey Regency-styled building. He pressed the bell-push without a name card and waited…and waited some more. Then he heard a buzz, followed by a metallic click and presumed someone had disengaged the lock from the relevant apartment. He put his hand on the tarnished knocker just as the door swung open.

Rafael found himself staring at an individual who had something of a chiselled face, with a streak of scar tissue across the left side of his jaw.

'I'm Liam. Liam Fenney.' A hurried smile, and just a hint of an Irish accent. 'And you're Rafael, for sure.'

Rafael climbed the step. 'Correct.' Combined with the brawny physique, he found the scar intimidating and wondered how the hell Joshua Waldo had got to know the man?

Liam stood back from the door to make room. 'We're up on the top floor.'

They shook hands, and Rafael smelt tobacco on Liam's breath. He followed Joshua's 'minder', or whatever his job description happened to be, towards a polished stairway. *We're up on the top floor.* No way! He needed privacy, for God's sake. Privacy to curse aloud, bawl his eyes out, punch the walls from frustration or fury. If this character had taken up residence at this location then he would head straight over to Cambridge Street, regardless of the tortuous stream of memories that doing so would likely entail.

They arrived at a carpeted platform – as opposed to a landing, per se. Liam opened the door to the apartment. 'I've brought over some belongings from Cambridge Street. It was hard to know what you might need.'

Rafael took an immediate dislike to the ornate furniture as he emerged from the abrupt hallway into the spacious living room. He was a minimalist at heart: clean-cut lines, functional. Stark, Lena would say – and that it probably had something to do with his nomadic childhood.

Liam handed him a set of keys. 'The larger one lets you into the communal garden out in the square.'

'Where are you staying?' Rafael asked, holding his breath.

'Pimlico.'

Rafael looked up from the keys, surprised. 'Cambridge Street?'

Liam nodded and rubbed the scar on his jaw as if he wanted it to vanish. 'If you approve? Marc Fauré gave me the key at Joshua's request after the break-in. I imagine they tried contacting you first.'

Rafael found himself focusing on the scar. The slightly ragged welt suggested it had been badly attended to and that it had happened recently: months rather than years. 'I was under the impression you'd be tracking my shadow non-stop?'

'Depends on whether you're marked. No proof as yet, it seems.'

'How badly did the thieves mess up the house?'

'Amateurs, at a guess,' shrugged Liam. 'Nothing broken, though. They didn't shit anywhere. Still plenty of ornaments on the shelves. They got into the safe. It might have been just one person. Hard to say. Much inside it – the safe, I mean?'

'Lena's passport and some cash, as I recall.'

'It's empty now, for sure.' Liam reached for his coat on the settee. 'They left the pair of laptops. They're on the desk over there. Marc Fauré was keeping a daily check on the house, up until I arrived. We think he might have disturbed them in the nick of time and they sneaked out when he checked upstairs.'

Rafael crossed the room to the twin pedestal desk and looked out of the window. It was a good view: Holland Park Avenue itself, if he happened to crane his neck. And yet it was obscene: a month's rent undoubtedly able to sustain a campesino and his extended family for a year, at least. His gaze returned to the square itself. 'I can't make up my mind if this square's Regency, or Georgian.'

'Neither.'

Rafael turned from the window. 'Neither?'

'I bumped into the guy in the apartment below. It's Victorian – early 1840s. Built on a racecourse, apparently. That's what he said.'

'Interesting. Would never have guessed.' Rafael leaned into an armchair and took a packet of Delta cigarettes from a trouser pocket. 'Want a smoke?' he asked, recalling the waft of tobacco in the entrance.

Liam declined and put on his overcoat.

'If you happen to be carrying a firearm, Liam, get rid of it. Conceal it some place, but not Cambridge Street.'

'The old man wants it this way. You'll have to take it up with him.'

Rafael shook his head; his mind already made up on the flight out of New York. 'Joshua hasn't a choice on this one.' He lit the cigarette using a match. 'And he knows it. Shooters have a habit of complicating situations, that's the reality…' He tailed off, for out of nowhere he recalled the conversation he'd had with Lazaro at his warehouse. Liam was now over by the door, about to leave. Rafael got to his feet and cut across the room. 'I want to ask you a question.'

Liam straightened, his eyes hesitant, wary. 'What sort of a question?'

'Do you know what they found on the gun? The gun that killed Lena?'

Liam dropped his shoulders and drifted back towards the settee. 'I seem to remember something in the papers about nail varnish remover.'

'That's right. Nail varnish remover. Identified as being part of the Santini Products range, which can only be purchased in the States and parts of Canada.' Rafael went back to the armchair. 'What do you read into that? What do you see?'

'That the gun could have been handed to the lunatic by a woman.'

'And? Anything apart from that?'

Liam cleared his throat and looked down at his shoes. 'Leave it to the police, Rafael,' he advised gently. 'They'll get there. They'll identify him.'

'But maybe the killer was an American, or connected to America in some way.' Rafael was keen for Liam to show a degree of interest. 'The police need to exhibit pictures of him in the papers and on the networks over there. They're not doing that. I should have mentioned it to Joshua. He might be able to do something through

Loran Communications, via Loran News.'

Liam sat on the arm of the settee with a dazed look about him, as if he'd just emerged from a car crash. He lifted his head. 'Don't do this to yourself, Rafael,' he said in a near broken whisper. 'Thinking like this isn't going to help. It'll cut you up, I'm telling you.'

'But I want to know where he got the gun from,' Rafael persisted, despite the abject look Liam was wearing. 'Did he buy it, or did someone give it to him? And why nail varnish remover and cotton wool? Why not methylated spirits and a rag? Why not whisky, for Christ's sake?'

Liam fidgeted for a moment. 'Focus on the film, Rafael.' He stood up, ready to leave. 'I'll assist you in any way I can. That's what I'm here for. Support.'

'The film?' Rafael chuckled sarcastically, shaking his head. 'Focus on the film, you say?' He simply couldn't stop himself, as if Liam had inadvertently stepped on a land mine – charged with blind fury. 'Christ, I lost Lena, my whole world! Not through natural causes, but because of some…some crazy guy. Some bastard—'

'Now look…' Liam pointed a finger. 'That's enough.' He zipped his coat, perspiration starting to show itself across his hairline. He rubbed the scar tissue on his jaw. 'You're tired, Rafael. I can see that.'

Rafael stared at the floor, alarmed by his outburst. Next, he'd be ranting at passers-by on the street. He put out the cigarette. 'I seem to be drowning in self-pity these days.'

'It's not self-pity,' Liam said with unexpected conviction. 'You're grieving. Okay? You don't have to make excuses. Not to me, you don't.' He went over to the door. 'Take a shower, or better still a long soak in the bath. Then try and get some shuteye. I'll call you in the morning.'

* * *

After Liam had left, Rafael leaned forward in the armchair and gazed into the empty fireplace, images of Lena and the maniac who took her life colliding in his mind's eye. If he were a bona fide churchgoer would all this be any easier for him? If he steadfastly believed that God was all-caring? He couldn't see it himself. Not a bit of it! He left the chair and crossed the room to the window, where he found himself watching the cars as they travelled along Holland Park Avenue, their headlights glistening in the downpour. Rational, contented people, going about their business, perhaps setting out to a restaurant for the evening or to watch a movie. *Good luck to you!* he silently cried. *Ride the dream while you can.*

He threw the curtains together and sat at the desk, only to see Lena telling her mother over the phone that they were going to be married. And after the call, she had rushed up to him in the kitchen. *Our marriage, at the Ansgar Chapel on Björkö!*

He clutched his head and shut his eyes, seeing Javier. *Because of Lena you wanted to die this time, Rafael. The pictures and the risks you took prove I speak the truth. But it's not an issue this way. You're the only one out of us who can make the film.*

He ran a sleeve over his tears. And then Senica, the girl who had nothing, and yet radiated an inner serenity – perhaps born out of acceptance. *There's something going on with you, isn't there? You're grieving over Javier. I get that. But there's a whole lot more besides, isn't there? I mean, you're kind, but there's a lot of anger inside you, a lot of resentment. That's what I think.*

Rafael left the desk for the bathroom, where he washed his face with cold water.

London… Maybe he should move out. Maybe he should deal with the screenplay somewhere abroad. Italy, France – anywhere but London.

Six months, Rafael. No longer. Joshua Waldo.

He took off his shirt, then very gingerly the bandage. For the first time the wound, encircled by a yellowish bruise, no longer showed any weeping. But as for his soul…

He washed his face again and caught sight of himself in the mirror. He looked terrible, as if he'd picked up a dose of the flu.

Claw your way through it or lose your mind. Do you want to lose your goddamned mind!

In an attempt to offset his mood, he went to take a look around the kitchen, and found on the worktop half a jar of coffee granules presumably left for him by Liam. In the cupboard above the kettle were several cups and a green mug. He chose the mug. At the desk he saw that Liam had left his mobile number. He called it. Like hell did he want to pay a visit to Cambridge Street. He was going to have trust this character.

'Rafael – okay?'

'Convenient to talk?' asked Rafael.

'Sure. I'm in traffic. I'm almost at Cambridge Street. An issue?'

'Not really. Thanks for meeting me here. Appreciate it. Just a small favour…'

'Go ahead.'

'Up in the spare bedroom, there's a memory stick. I tucked it away before I left for Salvador. Just as well I did, what with the break-in. Wondered if you could bring it over tomorrow.'

'No problem. So where is it, exactly?'

'Inside one of the pillowcases on the bed. You'll find it.'

'Leave it with me.'

'Thanks, Liam.' Rafael ended the call and continued to sit at the desk. Strange, but on reflection Liam had been quite abrupt when he mentioned he was drowning in self-pity – as if his remark had touched a profound chord.

It's not self-pity. You're grieving.

The way he'd reacted was as if he had first-hand knowledge – or empathy to some great extent – over the horrid void that felt so excruciatingly physical and to which he now found himself harnessed. Liam was right: it wasn't self-pity; he *was* grieving, for God's sake!

He switched on the PC that was little more than a word processor to avoid it being hacked into, convinced that Liam himself was recovering from a disturbing incident of some description. If so, then by having Liam stay over in London Joshua had, purposely or by chance, strung together a sort of two-man support group.

Time would tell.

CHAPTER 10

Rafael disengaged the memory stick with the redrafted screenplay from the PC and turned his attention to the Acer laptop to log onto the Sarron News Agency website. A Raoul Cregan double would reinforce the despotic speech that was to be at the heart of the film. He located a portrait of the man and sent it to the printer. He felt he'd come into contact with a lookalike recently but he couldn't think where. He'd ask his cameraman, Marc Fauré, when he visited him later in the day. Pulling up *ProtonMail*, he started to delete old emails, one of them with an encrypted attachment from Joshua Waldo. He remembered Lena reading it with him over his shoulder a couple of days before they stayed overnight with Joshua in Santa Monica.

I'm taking you back eight hundred years to Lake Baikal, not so far north of what is now the border between Mongolia and Russia. The tribe, or sect, for want of another word, living there was headed by Rieten Keta, a one-time confidant to Khubilia, grandson of Genghis Khan. Keta saw Europe as the key to achieving global power and organised an expedition to investigate the possibility of conquest. But Rieten Keta died en route, apparently from septicaemia. Salaniri Rikuin, Keta's nephew, took control of the expedition once the brotherhood reached France, where it became clear that the Knights Templars had unprecedented power and were generally regarded as being pioneers of international banking. (Research points to the brotherhood at this stage having never given itself a collective title, but I will refer to it here as simply 'Keta'.)

The brotherhood (of Keta) was fortunate in that the sovereign ruler, Philip IV, was heavily in debt. On the pretext they had crucial information concerning the welfare of his kingdom, Rikuin and his cohorts requested an audience with the king. The upshot of this encounter was that they successfully convinced Philip that the Knights Templars were guilty of corruption and heresy. The king, wasting little time, ordered the arrest of all Templars. From that point on, the brotherhood basically hijacked the entire monetary system generated by the Templars and as a reward for their warnings of heresy received land confiscated from their would-be competitor. Centuries later, the brotherhood offloaded virtually every hectare of real estate it had acquired across Europe, before promoting the concept of an inheritance tax in Britain (one of the wealthiest countries in the world at that time) which, coupled with two world wars, effectively wiped out any threat from the aristocracy. What followed next was the banner-headline: 'stabilisation through globalisation', initially taken up by the political and economic branches of academia, before politicians the world over found themselves producing a rash of treaties and alliances. Attractive, maybe, but under the circumstances a ruse by the Council of the Faithful Brethren to gain universal power.

Details to follow via courier.

Warmest regards to you both, Joshua

Rafael deleted the email, and with it an image of Javier's blood on the copy he'd kept in his shirt pocket in El Salvador. Quite why he had done so, he had absolutely no idea – unless it had something to do with Lena having read the email with him when it arrived in his inbox. That aside, he wondered whether the email had been hacked into and the encrypted text deciphered. He felt himself shake his head; at this stage of the game he still regarded Joshua's suspicions as stemming from fear – which he understood and sympathised with. Time was limited, in more ways than one. His gaze shifted to a framed photograph of his murdered soulmate, which Liam had brought over from Cambridge Street. He'd taken it a couple of years ago and it showed Lena standing amid the ruins of King Arthur's legendary home in North Cornwall, a choppy Atlantic in the background. When Liam handed the photograph over to him, he made the suggestion he should at least visit the house where they had lived together. He dreaded going back to Cambridge Street, knowing that whatever courage he had left would likely desert him, leaving the core of his being entirely out of kilter.

His mobile phone rang. A glance at the screen confirmed it was the call he'd been expecting. *Detective Foster.*

'Hi, Rory.' He left the desk and stood at the rain-spattered window. 'Lousy weather.'

'Chucking it down here. Apologies for breaking the call earlier, something came up. Nothing to do with the case, I'm afraid.'

'So, what's the latest?'

Rafael listened while the detective told him there still hadn't been any known sightings of the murderer prior to him buying a ticket for Victoria at Brighton Railway Station. He then went on to explain, with what sounded to Rafael like contrived optimism, that forensics had examined the killer's body in greater detail, taking samples of bone and lung tissue in the hope they would find mineral deposits compatible with a particular region inside the UK.

'Yesterday, I visited the landlady again,' continued the detective, 'and she's adamant that he had a slight northern accent. Problem is he only mumbled a few words to her—'

'I'm convinced he had some sort of a connection with America,' Rafael interjected, suddenly tired of listening to the detective's spin on the case.

'On what basis?'

'Santini nail varnish remover can only be bought in America and parts of Canada. It was used to clean the gun, presumably to remove the previous owner's prints. To me, that signifies there's likely to be a connection Stateside. We should be putting a picture of him on the networks out there.'

'We tried that when it happened,' countered the detective briskly. 'America, Europe, just about everywhere. No one came forward, apart from the usual cranks.'

Rafael returned to the desk, frustrated by the news – or rather, lack of it. 'Rory, it's coming up to four months now. We have the body, but still no idea who he was or where he came from. What about when he swore moments before he killed himself? Can't that be narrowed down to a particular dialect?'

'Still a mixed bag,' chirped the detective. 'The problem facing the analysts is that it was basically two words of just a few syllables, partially masked by the commotion in the auditorium and distorted further by the state he was in.'

'God's sake...'

'It's that breakthrough, Rafael. It'll happen, I'm sure of it.'

'Let's hope so. Thanks for the call, Rory. Talk to you later.'

Rafael cradled the receiver and put his head in his hands, the extent of the mystery torturing him. If the body could be identified, then perhaps there was a chance he could come to terms with the heartbreak. He looked back at the photograph of Lena. There again, how the hell *do* you come to terms with the murder of one's life partner?

His mobile phone rang again, making him jump.

'Hello?'

'Rafael, it's Liam. I'm just turning into the square.'

'I'm on my way. Two minutes.'

Rafael shut down the laptop, switched off all the lights and grabbed his jacket from the settee.

*   *   *

While Liam drove him across London towards Pimlico and Cambridge Street, Rafael sensed Rory Foster wasn't committed to the case, leaving some underling to do all the legwork. When they first met, Rory mentioned he was a golfing buff, and quite possibly it was on some golf course where he was spending much of his time. He would give it another fortnight, and if Rory hadn't made any progress by then, he figured he ought to speak directly to his superior to see what more could be done.

It wasn't until they reached South Kensington that Rafael noticed Liam was on edge. His fingers drummed the steering wheel whenever they got caught in traffic and he repeatedly rubbed the scar on his jaw. Rafael wondered again how the injury might have happened. A knife-wound in a brawl, perhaps.

'Everything all right, Liam?' he asked with a casual glance. 'This isn't taking up too much of your time?'

'No, no. My suggestion, if you remember.' The lights up ahead changed from red to amber. Liam flustered over the gears, but got first eventually. 'Going to Cambridge Street must be hard for you,' he said, looking away.

'You can say that again.' Rafael gazed forlornly at the Natural History Museum on their left, oblivious on this occasion to its majestic twin towers and overall architectural splendour. 'God only knows—'

'You're not alone, you know,' Liam cut in.

Rafael felt his eyes swivel. 'Sorry?'

'All this business. This grieving. You're not alone.'

'What do you mean?'

The traffic started to move. Liam dropped the handbrake.

'Different circumstances, of course,' he said, switching lanes. 'Murder, all the same. Everything was destroyed. I don't have the home where we lived. Maybe that aspect's a blessing. Could have turned the place into a shrine…sat there all day…become a recluse.'

'Shrine?' Rafael sat up, a shiver coursing the length of his spine. God Almighty, he'd hit the bloody nail on the head with just one word! Rafael took a moment to settle himself. 'But you know that's exactly what scares me about Cambridge Street, Liam, that I might finish up doing just that…building a shrine within its walls and shutting myself off from the outside world.'

'Well, there you go. It can happen, to be sure.' The traffic ground to a halt. Liam knocked the gearshift into neutral and pulled on the handbrake.

'Can you talk to me about it?' Rafael felt a surge of interest that he couldn't quite define. Perhaps Liam's presence afforded an opportunity to confront what he was struggling to come to terms with. 'The other day it even crossed my mind to visit a medium.'

'Not a good idea – not at this stage at any rate. Could mess you right up. Leave you disillusioned and downright miserable. Better just to live with the hope you'll get to see her again.' Liam negotiated Sloane Square, the gears starting to flow once more. 'Her name was Maria, a refugee from Guatemala. When we met, I was on an exercise with the Grenadier Guards in Belize. Well, we had a good time together, and then she got pregnant. Twin boys, as it turned out. Beautiful. Christ, it changed me – mellowed me out, you know? So, I left the army and headed to the village where Maria grew up, eighty kilometres south-east of Guatemala City, close to the border with El Salvador.

'Everything was as sweet as a nut to begin with. And when I say sweet, I mean sweet. Like a fairy tale of sorts, I guess.' He glanced at his passenger – listening intently. 'Hardly any trouble at all in the region. I'm telling you, Rafael, my heart melted to see Maria so happy and at peace with herself. But that changed when the generals decided to flex their muscles. Simultaneously, a flood of weaponry entered the country from the US. Washington apparently drew the conclusion that it was its old adversary – communism dressed up as socialism, sweeping back up from the south. All bullshit. Just the unions asking for a decent wage and an end to exploitation. To this day, I don't know what the true thinking was at the Pentagon. But then I can say that for just about every conflict it instigates – and when you go back through the years, it's instigated a hell of a lot of conflicts, with the UK more often than not taking on the role of a trusty lieutenant.'

'Lena gave a concert with fellow musicians to raise funds for medical supplies to be flown into Guatemala,' Rafael mentioned, sensing he'd found a friend for life in Liam. 'Raised over several million dollars.'

'I remember. But by then I was right out of the loop.' Liam turned off the busy Belgrave Road and took a shortcut through Eccleston Square, his face having reddened slightly. He ran a finger under his shirt collar and adjusted the Peugeot's air-conditioning. 'I got Maria and the boys into a cellar we'd dug out as a precaution. Then I worked alongside the elders, all of us defending as best we could. But the shack took a direct hit. Before I could reach Maria, a rocket grenade detonated inside the building I was using for cover and slammed me unconscious, a piece of metal or glass slashing my jaw.'

Liam found a space and parked up in Cambridge Street. 'To put it bluntly, the village was taken off the map. A couple of days later, I buried my family and crossed the border into your neck of the woods – El Salvador – finding myself roughing it on the outskirts of Santa Ana.'

Rafael glanced at Liam and saw that his brown eyes were watery. It must have taken huge courage to have told his story. 'That's hell,' he sympathised. 'To have so much and then lose it all in a split second because of some imbecile's grotesque decision-making in a faraway land. Sickening!'

'I can say with hand on heart, I had the perfect life, Rafael. Austere in some ways, you might say, but perfect. In fact, it was the simplicity of it all that made it so perfect. Every night we'd sit under the stars after putting the boys to bed. Sometimes, an elder would wander over and share a beer.' Liam bowed his head and gave a drawn-out animated sigh. 'I can never be the same person again. Impossible. My little boys, blown to pieces. And Maria… I feel constantly empty of life inside. A shell of a person, and that's about it. Nothing more than that. I exist, but that's all. The strange thing is, I've now grown comfortable with that feeling.'

Rafael scanned the street hesitantly. The house he had shared with Lena was out of view down on the right. The thought of leaving the car flipped his stomach, as if it had now become his refuge from an emotionally chaotic world beyond. 'I believe I know where you're coming from,' he murmured, grateful for the opportunity to share his brutalised frame of mind. 'But what I'm finding is that whenever I think I might be healing inside – by that I mean coming to some kind of understanding or acceptance – a specific memory or a sudden image jumps out in front of me and…and the rawness of the desolation it generates just hurts so much. Then there are the dreams. When I dream of Lena, it absolutely crucifies me. I'm no good for anything after waking up, sometimes for the entire day.' Rafael took his eyes off the street as he recalled the moment journalists and the paparazzi swarmed all over it. He'd arrived at an idea. 'Are you off the nectar, or what?' he asked.

Liam pulled the key from the ignition. 'It's no longer an issue.'

'Well, I realise this might seem a shade inappropriate, but there's a pub just around the corner. Good food...' Rafael avoided Liam's harsh gaze.

'You can't put it off, Rafael. You've got to go through with it. I didn't open up about Guatemala for nothing. Right?'

'Sure. I appreciate that you did so, Liam. Of course, I do. We're talking Dutch courage here, that's all.'

'All?'

Rafael bit his lip. 'I don't know, maybe. Hard to say. I just need a drink. After all, I've been working bloody hard on the screenplay this past week.'

Liam's gritty expression thawed to the extent that he even cracked a smile. 'All right, come on.'

They walked back towards Sussex Street. Rafael felt the drop in temperature from when they left Norland Square. He looked at the iron-grey sky and thought the drizzle might turn to sleet.

'But Joshua,' he asked, declining the cigarette Liam offered to him, 'how did that come about?'

'A day or so before I crossed the border into El Salvador,' said Liam after lighting a cigarette for himself, 'I came across a cameraman contracted to Loran. He'd got himself into trouble with some local thugs and I sorted it for him. Months later, a journalist from the same network tracked me down to a pub in Ealing that I'd taken to using on a regular basis, as it were. My sister's partner happens to be the publican. The following day, I found myself on a flight to Santa Monica, the big man wishing to thank me personally. A couple of days after that, he booked me into a clinic.'

Inside the Duke of Monmouth, they ordered a couple of pints of Hawkshead ale and occupied a table beside the bay window. Liam took off his coat.

Rafael watched him. 'Liam, you know the reason – or at least, part of the reason – behind that conflict in Guatemala, don't you? Aside from the bullshit that came out of the White House?'

'Joshua tried to explain. At the time it was difficult to get my head around it – or anything else, come to that.' Liam pulled a chair out from the table. 'But it boiled down to some Council of Brethren thing – a bunch of people who for centuries have had it in their heads to basically govern the world. Yes?'

'The Council of the Faithful Brethren, yes.'

'They strike me as being stupid. Clever tacticians, no doubt, but at the end of the day bloody stupid for obvious reasons.'

'Few would dispute that. Conspiracy theorists believe they are inside the United Nations and have been for years.'

'And you?' Liam toyed with a beer mat. 'You think that, too?'

'If I were one of them, one of the Brethren, I'd definitely want to influence its decision-making for the simple reason it extends globally. Some folk already feel it's morphed into a World Government and that now all that's required is the dissolution of nationhood. If at all true, that'll likely be achieved via subliminal prompting to the younger generations, along the lines of nationhood being the cause of all our woes: trade wars, discord and corruption, et cetera, et cetera.'

'But how do you control countries from a single…platform, so to speak?'

'Primarily through debt, and by creating wars – whether trade or military. There's a whole host of applications you can administer to create discontent and division through twists and turns, such as enforced migration.' Rafael put down his glass, curious about Liam's reaction to what he had to say. 'The global debt is now monumental.

It can't possibly be paid off. National governments have, let's face it, become next to useless, with weak or corrupted leaderships. Recall that joker of a president who called El Salvador a shithole of a country, along with several other countries he named?'

'How can I forget it,' said Liam, lifting his glass. 'A total and utter disgrace.'

'I guarantee you, Liam, he was destined for the presidency the moment he entered the election, if not before – because he was capable of doing great damage by way of foreign policy and generating division amongst his own people. Since proven to be the case tenfold.'

Liam nodded and drank some beer. 'Completely unaware that he was assisting the Brethren's policy as regards to the abolition of nationhood, yes?'

'Quite so, despite his speeches to the contrary,' said Rafael. 'I mean, a global overseer or watchdog, supervised by highly regarded academics with a practical perspective in their outlook, isn't a bad idea, but not if it's going to make the switch into a global dictatorship via the deliberate disfigurement and erosion of national identities.' Rafael finished his beer, the knot in the pit of his stomach tightening; he wanted only to fast-forward the next sixty or whatever minutes. He reached for his jacket. 'Okay, Liam, let's do it.'

* * *

The house felt desolate, as if it had never witnessed laughter or music. It didn't feel a part of him. He had become a stranger to it. While Liam made coffee for himself in the kitchen, Rafael kept his hands in his pockets, not wanting to touch or disturb anything as he drifted tentatively down the hallway, going from room to room, accompanied by a sense of composed reluctance. He was fairly certain the thieves had taken Lena's beloved Ibanez guitar from the back room. Nevertheless, despite the disturbing suspicion, he was in fact doing better than he'd predicted. A philosophical approach was how he saw it. It had to be done, and he was doing it.

But that changed the moment he climbed the stairs and arrived at their bedroom, where he immediately became enveloped by an intimate presence. An indefinable scent, but nevertheless *their* scent. He felt he could almost call her name and she would reply. With its pastel décor and furnishings, the bedroom was quite feminine, and he liked that. When Lena first unveiled it to him, he wasn't so sure: his minimalist self would have opted for white walls and a remote control to dim the lights whenever required, making for interesting shades and shadows. But Lena said it would grow on him, and she was right. She called it their womb. Sexual attraction aside, she often remarked that they might just as well have been born twins.

He stood by the bed, hearing only their pillow talk, their laughter, and recalling how Lena would walk with the grace of a ballerina from the en suite. Sometimes, when the mood took him, he would have her in stitches by miming whatever came into his head. Invariably, she would demand an encore.

He picked up her hairbrush from the dresser and carefully, reverently, ran a strand of her flaxen hair between his fingers. Tears spilled down his cheeks. He sat on the bed and put his face in his hands. If there were another world, another life after this one, then what was Lena doing; what was she actually thinking? Was she content? At peace with her surroundings? Were there flowers, rivers, forests, birdsongs? Did she think of her past life? Of him? Was she *waiting* for him, for God's sake?

He sensed a presence and looked up; his frantic hope confirmed as ludicrous on seeing Liam in the doorway.

'How's it going?' Liam asked. 'Or just tell me to butt out.'

Rafael wiped away his tears and reluctantly returned the hairbrush to the dresser, though his eyes refused to let go of it. 'Lena had always said we would have to be married first, before having children. So that morning, the morning of the day it happened, I asked her to marry me. She was so happy.' He managed to drag his eyes away from the brush. 'For my own sanity, I need to put this place on the market – and quickly. Do you think I'm doing the right thing?'

Liam came further into the room. 'You have to ask yourself, will keeping it serve any constructive purpose? It brings memories back to you of the times you shared with Lena, yes. But those memories are already in your mind, and that's all they can ever be…memories.'

Rafael nodded. 'Feels brutal put like that, but there's no denying the logic in your reply.' He took a deep breath and stood up. 'Thanks for getting me over here, Liam. Despite the state of me, it's been a step forward.'

CHAPTER 11

Rafael sensed that the living room in Norland Square was different in some way to how he had left it. But hardly in the mood to be interrogated by Liam, he kept the suspicion to himself and handed him an encrypted memory stick.

'Thanks for doing this, Liam,' he said, still trying to fathom what made the room *appear* different. 'I'm just right out of time to get over to Heathrow. If it weren't for Joshua's mounting paranoia, I would have sent the screenplay electronically.'

'What's the courier's name?' Liam asked.

'Michael. Michael Ramsey. Pleasant enough. Ex USAF. I met him briefly on my first visit to Joshua.'

'I know who you mean.'

'His flight's due in at four o'clock.' Rafael glanced over his shoulder at the desk. 'I get the impression Michael's a kind of handyman for Joshua.'

'From my observations, Michael does a bit of everything,' said Liam. 'Chauffeuring, shopping. Bodyguard, whenever required too, probably. Met him a couple of times. Gave me the impression he could handle himself.' He tucked the memory stick safely away in an inside pocket on his Berghaus fleece jacket. 'I'll give you a call later on. You going to be okay?'

'I'm fine,' nodded Rafael. 'Relieved we did it. I'm putting it on the market, no question.'

Rafael closed the door behind Liam, now perfectly aware that the photograph of Lena on the desk was partially facing the square. He was certain he had positioned it away from the window, not wanting any direct light to reach it. It was pure habit. He sat in the chair and glanced at the portrait of the chairman of the Sarron News Agency, Raoul Cregan, which he'd printed off earlier. Unable to settle, he toured the room, then the bedroom. Apart from the framed photograph of Lena, everything seemed just as he had left it before joining Liam down in the square.

Or was the truth of the matter he'd put the photograph down quickly when Rory Foster called – or perhaps Liam? There again, he couldn't quite remember picking it up in the first place. But he assumed he must have done, and while it surprised him that he hadn't turned it away from the window at some point, it could be that his mind had simply been preoccupied with his imminent visit to Cambridge Street. As clear-cut as that.

He went back into the bedroom, kicked off his shoes and lay on the bed. It had taken all his willpower not to leave with Lena's hairbrush. If Liam hadn't been there, he might well have done. The degree of stability he'd managed to win for himself with Liam's help felt precarious to say the least.

* * *

That evening, with a dreamless respite behind him, Rafael left the Underground at Belsize Park. He flicked up his coat collar to fend off the wintry breeze and made his way down Haverstock Hill. The fact that he'd yet to secure his actors weighed heavily on his mind. The female lead needed to personify someone subtly graceful and, above all, engagingly aloof. Right out there on her own, in fact, on the rim of society – an intriguing off-the-wall loner, as it were, and yet perfectly capable of making profound and succinct statements.

He joined Upper Park Road just as the guttural roar of an engine erupted directly behind him. He turned on his heel; a blaze of headlights locked onto him as if a missile had been launched. Through fright rather than judgement, he vaulted a garden wall and scrambled away from the road before he all but felt the screaming vehicle clout the kerb. Shock punched through his diaphragm and seized his windpipe, leaving him gasping for breath. He had the presence of mind to look up, but the licence plate was indecipherable as the silver car zigzagged violently into the distance, the nearside wing clipping a parked van.

Rafael wiped the thread of saliva from his chin and fought against an urge to throw up. Curtains were being whisked open on both sides of the road, a ghostly wraithlike face with a mop of unruly white hair peering out of a window alongside him. Struggling to his feet, he tried to settle himself. His legs seemed frail and remote from the rest of him as he slid off the garden wall and onto the pavement.

Several yards further on, he leaned against a car. He still felt nauseous. It had happened in an instant – as if in a dream. A cyclist came into view and he moved off so as not to draw attention to himself. He tried to focus his mind, and inevitably recalled the photograph of Lena in Norland Square. *Had* someone casually picked it up while taking a look around? If so, then the directive had hardly come from the Council of the Faithful Brethren, surely? To involve themselves in such skulduggery was simply too grubby for words. Or was it? Rumours still persisted from the last century of poison and the hiring of hitmen being deployed to remove influential individuals who refused to toe the line.

He coughed up some bile burning his throat and scanned the road for signs of the silver car. Nothing, nothing at all. He thought it might have been a Ford. Hard to tell at just a glance under the streetlights. He climbed several steps to stand under a beige Doric porch. Watching the street over his shoulder, he pressed the bell, and the moment the door opened swept past his lead cameraman.

'Did you hear it?' he asked.

Marc Fauré closed the door, his tough features disrupted by confusion. 'Hear what?'

'Bloody idiot up the road lost control of his car.' Rafael wiped the freezing sweat from his brow. 'If I hadn't jumped a wall I'd have been done for. Talk about a close shave!'

'*Merde*,' breathed Marc, running his thumbs up and down his yellow and turquoise striped braces, as if he'd just emerged from the bathroom and was still adjusting matters. 'How far up the road?'

'Fifty yards or so.' Rafael handed over a USB stick and made his way through a maze of tea chests and cardboard boxes towards an armchair. He'd forgotten Marc and his wife, Susan, were in the process of moving out of London. 'He must have been drunk.'

Marc gave his braces a final tweak and veered off towards a mini-bar set in the wall alongside a pair of patio doors. 'And that's exactly what happened?'

'Absolutely what happened. I've got mud over me from the garden.'

'You need to tell Joshua Waldo,' Marc decided, pouring beer. 'He'd want to know.'

Rafael shook his head, his mind already made up. 'Joshua's paranoid enough as it is.' He reached for the glass. 'Marc, I need something stronger. I'll have this afterwards.'

'Then tell Liam.' Marc opened the cabinet within the mini-bar and took out a bottle of Jameson's. 'At least get his opinion. This could be the start of something, what with the subject matter we're dealing with.'

Rafael shifted awkwardly in the armchair. 'Liam's a shade fragile at the moment. We can't afford any risks when it comes to firearms. He was armed when he introduced himself to me. I asked him to drop the idea. Or I should say, Joshua's idea. As much as I'm starting to like Liam, I don't want him living in the same apartment as me, armed to the hilt.'

Marc looked up while handing Rafael a straight whiskey. 'What do you mean by "fragile"?'

'He had an issue in Guatemala. A massive issue, in point of fact.'

'What happened to him?'

Rafael gave a thumbnail sketch.

'Nasty,' Marc agreed.

'He told me in confidence. At least, I presume he did. Tell Susan, by all means, but leave it at that.' Rafael fidgeted in the chair before standing. He couldn't keep still. 'By the way, where is Susan?'

Marc moved aside some books to make room on the settee. 'In Devon, with her aunt Lisa. Said she needed some sea air. You know she's quit teaching?'

'It was on the cards before I left for Salvador.'

'I'm relieved, to be honest. Up all hours, dealing with reports and what have you.'

Rafael paused at the window, the car predictably nowhere in sight. He drew the curtains together. Just someone three sheets to the wind, he told himself. Hopefully. He re-seated himself, finished off the whiskey and felt better for it, grateful to be in one piece – before all at once he felt he had the answer to the question that had been plaguing him for the past week. 'That's it!'

'What, exactly?'

Rafael unfolded the piece of paper he'd taken from the printer. 'Who does this person remind you of?'

'Who is it, first?' Marc asked.

'Raoul Cregan. Chairman of the Sarron News Agency, here in London. Who does he remind you of?'

'I'm trying to think…'

'Go back to a party you had right here – it must have been in March.'

'Susan's thirtieth?'

'Jeff came with a cousin, a saxophonist. Lena wanted him to tour with her, but he was tied up with some band in New Zealand.'

'Which Jeff? The novelist or Lena's bass guitarist?'

'Jeff the guitarist. The guy he brought with him is the spitting image of Raoul Cregan. Cregan's one of them – one of the big shots linked to the Council of the Faithful Brethren. Joshua confirmed it when I saw him the other week on my way back from Central America. I need a double for when we film the speech.'

'His dour expression looks as if it's been carved from granite!' Marc handed back the portrait. 'I can imagine him being a despicable piece of work. Do you want me to call Jeff?'

'If you would. Thanks. It'll save me making the call, which will undoubtedly be emotional.' Rafael refolded the portrait and cast a glance at the tea chests. 'Have you found a buyer for this place?'

'A few hopefuls. Nothing definite.' Marc finished his beer. 'Any decision on Cambridge Street?'

'I'm putting it on the market. It's going to hurt, for sure.' Rafael told Marc of his frustration concerning the investigation into Lena's death. Marc consoled him the best he could, replenished their glasses and made ham, cheese and pickle sandwiches. Rafael was surprised to learn that Susan had a Burmese cousin working for Oxfam in Honduras and that Marc and Susan intended to visit her after the film's release.

Rafael leaned forward in the chair. 'Marc, this is fate. Forget about moving to France. Make it Central America – for the time being, at least. We've never made a film or a documentary in the region. It'll be an adventure. Like starting anew.'

'More like my death!' Marc put down his glass. 'I'm not joking. You're all quite insane out there – machetes flying in all directions. And what with the gangs, too. It's all so different to over here in Europe.'

'I'm still hoping to contact an influential figure in MS-13. Lazaro, an old acquaintance, is trying to set things up. See what can be done.' Glancing at his watch, Rafael left the armchair. 'I'd better head back. Stack of work to do tomorrow. Contacting actors and technicians. Can I leave finalising the camera team, et cetera, with you?'

'It's all in place. Ready to roll, in fact.'

'Music to my ears. One less concern.' Rafael opened the front door and cursorily scanned the street before turning back to Marc. 'Like the braces. Dazzling. Lena gave them to you, right?'

'Last Christmas,' said Marc. 'Eleven Christmases, eleven birthdays. Twenty-two pairs she gave me in total. Do you think you should stay over?'

Rafael glanced back at the street and shook his head. 'I'll be fine. Like I said, so much work to do. I'm hoping he was just plain drunk, or doped up. Probably in some hospital or police station by now.'

* * *

Rafael tried not to stare as he stood on the southbound platform at Belsize Park station. A glance by itself, however, wasn't enough. There was something about the girl's stance that held his attention. The straightness of her back, perhaps, or the detached way she stood gazing at the posters on the wall opposite them. Despite the weather, she hadn't a jacket – just a cream sweater and faded threadbare jeans.

Her hair seemed lighter than when he first noticed her. Above all, she came across as being perfectly aloof, while her profile – showing off high cheekbones – displayed a subtle charm.

The train blasted towards them, the thunderous roar and pursuing vortex of dust leaving Rafael with a queer sense of isolation, reminded by the girl's presence alone how much he missed female companionship in its most intimate form. As the doors hissed shut, he found himself sitting opposite the girl. She averted her gaze, and he did likewise – but not for long, drawn by her Eastern European looks. There was something altogether erotic about her. The fullness of her lips, perhaps, that gave her a generous mouth, set against her pale skin and those high cheekbones.

He started to convince himself that an unknown for the role of Nina would enhance the screenplay's intrigue, and found himself recalling a girl from his past. It took him a moment to bring to mind the part of his life in which she had featured. As for her name… Heidi? He wasn't sure. Strange girl. Strange house, come to that. It was in Putney and consisted of several bedsits. By then, he'd already started living with Lena. It seemed people would come and go on a regular basis, and sometimes when they went it would be to a cell for some offence, or to live on the streets for no apparent reason. Heidi. Lena came to the conclusion that she had a screw loose. Once, he remembered, there was a faint knock on the door. It was Heidi. She explained in a small voice that her electric meter had jammed and that she had no light. Could he help?

The train came into Tottenham Court Road. He left the girl in the carriage and changed to the Central Line, taking his time. Heidi. That *was* her name. He'd struck the meter a couple of times to settle the coins in the congested box, and when the light came on he'd been taken aback. Although Heidi had lived in the house for some time, the room was almost empty. The only possessions visible were a few underclothes and a photograph of an Alsatian on the floor beside the single bed. He couldn't be sure, but he thought she might have told him that the Alsatian had been abandoned and that her sister was looking after it in Germany.

Why was he thinking so much about this, though? Why was he thinking of Heidi? He hadn't thought about her for years.

The train slowed, and he was shocked to discover he had overshot Holland Park. He started to make for the opposite platform at White City, but then found himself seized by an irresistible desire to walk the streets, his imagination keen to draw fresh ideas as it scampered boisterously from scene to scene, character to character.

Outside the station, he kicked a plastic bottle-cap along the pavement, while in his mind's eye he watched an Arriflex camera with Marc at the helm explore a somewhat shabby corridor via a tracking shot before the lens arrived at the principal female's bedsit. The slightly creased photograph of an Alsatian would be black-and-white, and positioned on a scratched and time-worn table, suggesting an atmosphere of woe, a solitary glass and a dripping tap adding the final touches to Nina's immediate backcloth.

He came to a side-street and made out what looked to be an off-licence a short way up on the right. Heidi... It all made so much sense now, the various threads drawing together by degrees. He purchased a half bottle of whisky from the store and twisted the cap, the alcohol warming him against the night's wintry chill.

'Interesting,' he muttered to himself. He started back down the street to re-join Wood Lane before taking another swig. *Interesting*, because the unexpected memory of Heidi was telling him to change the storyline – superficially in one respect, fundamentally in another. What he now had in mind was to make a film within a film, and increase the exposure of the Council of the Faithful Brethren twofold from several perspectives, whilst at the same time avoiding altogether the risk of the picture resembling a documentary.

He found himself sifting through the evening's trail of events. The silver car, his fortunate escape without injury and his eventual visit to Marc Fauré could all be integrated. Although he hadn't acted for some time, it crossed his mind that perhaps he should take on the role of Saúl Majano, and in doing so resolve the problem of looking for a suitable candidate. But for Nina, he wanted an unknown actress. Someone sensitive to the cause, who had the intelligence, the passion and the capability to bring that sensitivity to the screen...

Promise me something, Rafael. When you leave tomorrow, remember these words: It was Mayan spirits, in my opinion, that brought us together – for a reason. Unfortunately, I've really no idea what that reason might be. Although, I have to say, it feels—

'Hey, you, you piece of black shit!'

He hadn't noticed them. They were on the opposite side of the street and heading over towards him – four of them.

'We're cleaning up the streets of you foreign shit.'

'He says it right,' shouted another, wearing a pink and green striped bobble hat. 'We're getting the black shit off the streets and out of our country. *Our* country. You got that, blackie?'

Then, all of them in unison: 'Get the black shit! White man rules! Get the black shit!'

A sudden rush forward, and Rafael knew he hadn't a chance. The bottle flew into the air, his assailants dragging him to the ground before his head struck something cold and unforgiving.

After that, there was nothing.

CHAPTER 12

A traffic accident, Rafael figured, the sound of vehicles speeding past him distinctly audible. Oddly, though, there were no voices, voices of concern, voices asking him questions.

Or could it be that he was near an airport?

His head pounded viciously. And he was cold, bitterly cold, as if he'd been encased in a tomb of ice. But it was the intensity of the jagged pain driving ever deeper into his right leg that finally opened his eyes.

What he saw puzzled him. Since when did it ever snow in El Salvador, apart from the day a freak weather condition hit Chalatenango? When was it? He couldn't remember… He used to know. Everyone in Salvador knew. Cerro El Pital, in the municipality of San Ignacio. But when did it happen? What year?

He wiped away the wetness across his jaw and noticed blood on his hand.

Europe. It snowed in Europe.

Somewhere in France…but not Marseille.

Blood. Not a good sign.

Or London.

It snowed in London.

* * *

A growing sense of vulnerability and disorientation brought him to his feet. He looked around himself, his left leg taking much of his shivering weight. A *TO LET* sign attached to a broken post lay on the ground next to him in the overgrown front garden. He limped out onto the pavement and moved cautiously down the street, fumbling through his pockets. His wallet and mobile phone were missing – as was his watch, he now realised.

He recognised the road he turned into as Wood Lane and wondered why he was so far from Holland Park. People who passed him were taking a wide and cautious berth. He came to a van and adjusted the wing-mirror.

'Oh, shit,' he muttered, and reeled back slightly. He steadied himself and took a closer look; the left side of his face was smeared with blood and dirt. The wound was to his scalp, though mercifully no longer bleeding.

He found a phone booth that hadn't been trashed and made a reverse call charge to Cambridge Street. Without his watch or phone, he was unsure of the time, but judged it to be after midnight.

Liam will be pleased, he thought.

* * *

The snowstorm had worsened, and Liam's face looked just as bad, like thunder and contempt rolled into one. 'I'm disappointed,' he announced before Rafael had even closed the passenger's door. 'There's a chance you could be a target. So, what do you do? You increase the risk by walking the bloody streets at this hour.' And then the smell of whisky must have hit Liam. He thumped the wheel with his fist. 'What's more…drunk!'

Rafael glanced up while he struggled to fasten his seatbelt. 'Do I look drunk? The bottle I was carrying—'

The Peugeot jolted forward as Liam let out the clutch and Rafael nearly struck his head on the doorframe.

'Do you know how to drive this thing? I'm in a bad way as it is!'

Liam snatched second gear. 'There's nothing wrong with my driving,' he retorted, as if Rafael had thrown the gravest of insults at him. 'But I'll tell you what is at fault…your commitment to deal with the film. What if whoever jumped you had wiped you out? I don't know about you, but I owe Joshua. Owe him big time.'

Rafael debated whether he ought to get himself checked over at a hospital. He felt slightly giddy but wasn't sure if it was a consequence of being struck on the head or Liam's twitchy driving. 'Back off with the sermon.' He renewed his effort to locate the seatbelt catch. 'It was a racist attack. They called me a black piece of shit, and all the rest of it. I remember now.'

'You're not black—'

'I'm black so far as racists are concerned. I need your phone.'

'For what?'

'Cancel my cards.'

Liam handed it over. He cursed the weather and increased the speed of the windscreen wipers. 'I reckon I need to get tooled up,' he muttered. They arrived at Shepherd's Bush and Liam struck another glance at his mangled-looking passenger. 'Tooled up, I'm telling you,' he repeated, as if to provoke a reaction. 'Know what I mean?'

Rafael sighed, and wished he hadn't made the call in the first place.

* * *

By the time they arrived at Norland Square, Liam was more or less back to his old self. Rafael took a beer from the refrigerator, just to unwind him that little bit more. He was tempted to take a can for himself, but since he was on a damage limitation exercise opted for a cup of water instead, which reminded him to buy some glasses since there were none in any of the cupboards. He limped back out of the kitchen.

'This girl…' Liam resumed, tossing his overcoat into an armchair. 'The one at the station. She didn't come over to you and start talking?'

'No, no – you misunderstood me.' Rafael handed Liam the can. 'We never spoke.' He leaned gingerly into the settee. The pain in his right leg still stung viciously and he just wanted the day to end. 'She got me thinking, that's all, about using an unknown for the female lead. I was lost in thought, that's probably why I overshot Holland Park.'

Liam sat opposite and hunched forward. 'So, two incidents…' He rotated the can between his hands. 'The question is, are they connected?'

'The wayward car and the assault?'

'Yes.'

'The assault was racist. Basically, kids. They said they were out to clean up the streets of black shit like me. "White man rules", and all that crap.'

'God help us,' muttered Liam. 'Okay. Something of a coincidence, which I'll go along with – for now. So, we're left with Upper Park Road. Question: a drunk driver or something more sinister? I'm inclined to suspect the latter.'

'On what grounds?' Rafael shifted his posture to take the pressure off his right hip, curious now as to whether he had overlooked some detail.

Liam finished his beer and went to the kitchen for another. 'Put it this way, would you use a drunk in a scene like that in one of your films, with one character going to meet another in the same road?'

Rafael looked up at him. 'I doubt it.'

'And why not?' continued Liam, re-seating himself.

'Too coincidental. Or, if you prefer, a ridiculous red herring.'

'Exactly. But you would put a hired gun in the driving seat.' Liam pointed a finger. 'The driver of that car is one hundred per cent foe. Deranged foe, maybe, but foe all the same.'

Rafael reached for the phone on the coffee table, a sudden idea thrusting its way to the surface inside his pounding head. There was still one message – sure enough from Marc. 'That's how he got to know I would be visiting Upper Park Road.'

Liam paused while taking a swig of beer. 'A break-in? Is that what you're saying?'

'I reckon so. I think he picked up the photograph of Lena on the desk over there. I swear to God I had it turned right away from the window to protect it from the light before I joined you in the square. When we came back it was virtually facing the window.' Rafael reached for his glass. 'Marc left the message while I was in the shower this morning – or rather, yesterday morning. This character must have entered the building when we were over in Cambridge Street. Once he got the information from Marc, where and when I was expected to meet him, he only needed to wait for me to arrive.' Rafael hauled himself up from the settee to draw the curtains. 'Part of his job, to look around.'

'For whom? The Council of the Faithful Brethren?'

'I doubt it.'

Liam leaned forward, the light from the shade above them accentuating the scar across his jaw. 'If the Council's as you describe it, these people don't want adverse publicity, which is what this film will give them. If they're suspicious of Joshua, then why not get rid of you? He only has six months or so to live, according to the man himself. They could fix Loran Communications at a later date, if necessary.'

Rafael still considered the possibility of the Council's involvement as remote, and told Liam so. History suggested they would make use of the media and the legal system first, rather than the services of an assassin. After all, they had the perfect opportunity to link him to Lena's murder. Falsified evidence and no bail. 'That's how it works,' he added. 'Retribution usually involves humiliation of one kind or another.'

'There can always be an exception to the rule.'

'Agreed – but I still think it's unlikely. If deliberate, it was clumsy for a pro. The chance of too many witnesses. A damaged car.'

'Then who, and why?'

Rafael shrugged. 'I keep opting in and out of theories. But they just fizzle out as being nonsensical.'

Liam stared at the carpet, chewing his bottom lip. Finally, he heaved a sigh and took another swig of beer. 'I don't know what to bloody think.' He finished off the can. 'But I still say you were targeted by the driver of that car.'

Rafael stood up, carefully. 'Stay over, Liam,' he suggested. 'Use the spare room. We'll talk in the morning. Right now, I need to crash. Excuse the pun.'

Inside the bedroom, Rafael stripped and examined his injuries in front of the cheval mirror. A sizeable bruise had surfaced through the graze across his thigh. Another bruise on his upper arm pointed to the scar from the wound he'd received after Javier was gunned down.

Senica. It still made sense, he told himself while under the shower. Besides, he realised he truly wanted to see her again. Ironically, she felt as mysterious to him now as Heidi had been in that strange house in Putney – only addictively so. It was perhaps her practicality and soulful eloquence above all else that made him want to see her again. The question was, however, how to extract her safely from El Salvador and get her into the UK?

CHAPTER 13

Rafael cast a bleary glance at Liam standing in the doorway. He'd hardly slept. 'Rory Foster?'

'The very same,' said Liam. 'On the landline, right now.'

Rafael eased himself up from the bed and grimaced at the bolt of pain that shot through his right leg. 'Liam, bring the phone in here.'

'The cord's not going to reach, is it?'

'I'll call him on my mobile.'

'You haven't got one. Remember?'

Rafael puffed out his cheeks and sighed. He remembered!

'You can use my mobile, if you have the number.'

'It's on my mobile.'

'Then I'll get him to call my mobile, if you want.'

'No, it's okay.' Rafael started to ease himself off the bed. 'I can't lie here all day.'

Liam must have seen the colourful bruise across Rafael's thigh. He pursed his lips and whistled. 'Bastards sure had a go at you, didn't they?'

Rafael wrapped a towel around his middle and noticed a smudge of dried blood on the pillow. He touched his head lightly and felt the bump. 'I think they jumped me from behind.' He shuffled into the living room and, with another grimace, reached for the receiver. 'Rory?'

'Rafael,' chirped the detective. 'Good news, up to a point.'

'Go ahead.' Rafael switched the phone to speaker for Liam's benefit.

'His name was Stephen Briggs. Seems like he'd been moving around the West Country for several years. A former girlfriend's come forward—'

'It's taken her all this time?' Rafael was incredulous.

'It's to do with the gun. It belonged to her. Or rather to her father, in point of fact.'

'What the hell prevented her from coming forward?'

'Possession of an illegal firearm, basically. Her father's in prison. In America. Sixteen-year stretch for kidnaping and extortion. His daughter visits him on occasion.'

'So, at some point she must have cleaned the Zigana with Santini nail varnish remover and cotton wool, since the product can only be purchased in the States and parts of Canada?'

'She's admitted to that. She wiped her prints off it and sold it to Stephen Briggs. She's confirmed that Briggs was obsessed with Lena.'

'Right…' Rafael winced as he sat on the chair at the desk. 'A lot to take in, Rory – but if only this girl had come forward earlier.'

'She'll likely get a severe reprimand for withholding information and be ordered to do community service. Hasn't brushed up against us before.'

'Okay, Rory, call me if anything more comes to light.' Rafael put the receiver down gently and turned with the stiffness of a cardboard cut-out to face Liam. 'You heard all that?'

Liam drew back the curtains, but so bleak was the day outside it made little impact on the gloom around them. 'Why did he have to go and fire a gun at her, for Christ's sake?'

'The power of infatuation, at a guess. Strange, though…we never had any warning in the way of letters or whatever. He might well have been stalking Lena, for all we know.' Rafael shuffled towards the bedroom. 'I'll get dressed. There's something I need to talk over with you. Better to do it outside, just in case this place is miked up. I also need to fix myself up with a new phone.'

* * *

They sat at a table away from the counter in the Jupiter Café, just around the corner from Holland Park tube station. Rafael grimaced on taking a sip of his coffee. He had never tasted battery acid before, but he felt he'd just come close to doing so.

Liam's disapproval was more forthright. 'Christ, what have they done to this? Straight from the bloody drain, at a guess.' He cleared his throat and leaned forward. 'Anyway, to business.'

Rafael pushed his cup to one side. For the sake of the favour he was going to ask, he made an effort to sit upright and all but heard his skeleton creak as he gingerly changed his posture. 'Go ahead.'

'Well, it's like— Are you okay?'

'Apart from feeling I've been run over by a steamroller, never felt better.'

'Right… Well, it's like this…' Liam tore open yet another sachet of sugar and tipped the contents into his coffee. 'Last night proved one thing – we have a saboteur in the frame. So I need to make a suggestion on Joshua's behalf, as it were. A couple of suggestions, actually. I feel I owe it to him to do so.'

'I understand that, Liam. What do you have in mind?'

Liam put his cup back down. 'This guy disturbs me – the driver of the car last night. I think you should get out of Norland Square, and Marc and Susan should do the same over at Belsize. And while you're at it, change your car.'

Rafael watched as Liam sat back, and realised very little of what he had said had registered with him, his mind thousands of miles away, in Central America.

'I take it we're in agreement on that, then?'

Rafael nodded. 'Makes sense, Liam,' he said off the cuff, spreading his hands. 'Every bit of it.' Now for the fireworks... 'My turn?'

Liam glanced at the window. A road sweeper in a balaclava moved steadily up the pavement towards the café. 'Sure, go ahead,' he said vaguely.

Rafael came to the point, having decided a more subtle approach would be a waste of time. 'I want you to get someone out of El Salvador for me.'

Liam's eyes swivelled straight back to Rafael.

'I'm fairly certain she hasn't been out of the country before.'

'Now, hold on a minute—'

'Liam, you've got to do this for me. If I had the time, I'd do it myself. The fact is I need to make significant changes to the screenplay before next week. Are you with me?'

'You can't be serious. From the way you're talking, I'm judging this person definitely hasn't a passport.'

'Unfortunately, not.'

'Male, female?'

'Female.'

'Speak any English?'

'Not a word.'

'Oh, Christ... Why have I got this phrase *sandwich short of a picnic* inside my head?'

Rafael brought his chair closer to the table, his tone desperate. 'Just hear me out, okay?' He toyed with a spoon. 'I want you to visit Joshua and explain to him what I have in mind. Get Michael Ramsey, the aide who took the script off you at Heathrow, to meet you at the nearest airport to wherever Joshua's presently holed up.'

Liam chewed his bottom lip. 'Some... Well, somewhere in southern Switzerland. Michael boarded an Air France flight bound for Geneva.'

'A village called Cartigny,' Rafael figured aloud. 'It's several kilometres out from Geneva. I was going to meet Joshua there with Lena but there was a change of plan. I want you talking to Joshua by this evening, persuading him that it's crucial Senica comes to Europe, and apart from featuring in the film she would be just the right soulmate for me while making it. Put up a good defence on my behalf. That said, it would take forever to fix her up with a passport, let alone a visa, so to get her out of Salvador we need a forger. Know of one?'

Liam leaned forward, his voice a broken whisper. 'Providing, and I repeat, *providing* Joshua rubber-stamps all this, there's another method. I'll still need to take Ricky, an old army buddy of mine, with me.'

'He's a forger?'

'Yes.'

'Has this person been out that way before?'

'Never. But he's the best of the best when it comes to forging documents.'

'What's the suggestion?'

'It would save time if Ricky didn't have to make up an entire passport and the documents needed as a backup in case questions are asked. I'm in possession of a suitable UK passport, including Home Office papers addressing confirmation of citizenship and various other communications.' Liam moved the sugar bowl to one side and folded his arms. 'When the dirt hit the fan in Guatemala, I got Ricky to forge everything Maria needed to get her into England. As I see it, we would need to change little in the passport itself. Obviously, we'll keep the name as it is.'

'Maria Fenney?' Rafael intoned, hardly believing his ears. 'I figure that would leapfrog a whole heap of obstacles.'

'Precisely.'

Rafael picked up the spoon again and wondered if Liam had overlooked the obvious. 'I don't want to blow away a brilliant idea, but I've just got to make the point that if you use Maria's name, then in a sense you're bringing her back to life. It might set you back, Liam. I'm not going to entertain such a risk.'

'It won't set me back,' assured Liam. 'Quite the opposite. I got…*annoyed*, shall we say, with you last night because, like Joshua, I want to see the reaction when this film hits the screen. What I've learnt from the pair of you has been nothing short of a revelation. Makes more sense to me than any politician ever will. And, obviously, I want to play my part at getting my own back at the shitheads of the Faithful Brethren for what they've done to Central America, via the Pentagon.'

Rafael felt a grin spread across his face for the first time in days. 'Good. I'll give you the address of my contact in San Miguel and all the relevant details on the way to the airport.'

'The girl's name again?'

'Senica.'

'And not a word of English?'

'No. But we can delay her arrival into the UK. Instead of bringing her here, clear it with Joshua to take her to Switzerland. I'll join you over there, probably with Marc since both of us need to fine-tune various aspects of the screenplay with him. While we're there, Senica can learn a little English. In fact, start teaching her the moment you set eyes on her.' Rafael stood up. 'Let's head back for some decent coffee.'

They walked along Holland Park Avenue and, as the square came into view, Liam remarked, 'What are you going to do about reporters, now the killer's been identified? They're going to be over you like a rash, surely?'

Rafael glanced at the slate sky, sensing either sleet or rain. 'After driving you to the airport, I'll get in touch with a journalist I've trusted for years. Once my reaction's been printed, I'll be yesterday's news, simple as that.'

Liam nodded. 'I guess that's how it works.'

Rafael tucked his hands inside the pockets of his jacket, satisfied that, largely due to Liam, he had everything on what appeared to be an even keel. It was now down to Senica. And, just as importantly, she would likely remind him, the guidance of the Mayan spirit world.

CHAPTER 14

The Sarron News Agency's headquarters occupied a resplendent six-storey Georgian building on the corner of Chapel Street with its main entrance adjoining Grosvenor Place. Raoul Cregan's office was on the third floor, with sleet presently slashing against its recently refurbished casement windows. But as he gazed in the direction of Buckingham Palace, Raoul was not watching the hoi polloi scurrying to and fro with disdain or mockery. Nor was he contemplating humiliating a politician, or the prime minister himself, or even a member of the Royal Family – or anything, in fact, that represented the identity of the country. No, today, his mind was preoccupied with Joshua Waldo and Loran Communications.

He left the window, sat at his burnished desk and glanced again at the *Daily Inquirer* headline.

IDENTIFIED: *Rudbeck's killer*

Maqui gives interview

From the bottom drawer on his desk, he took out the pay-as-you-go mobile phone he'd taken with him to Mexico. He checked the credit: still £22.70 remaining. He called the last number dialled and the moment the connection was made spoke two words.

'Target exists.'

'I've told you,' whined the private investigator, 'I'm training Jake up. That's why it's a bargain.'

'He's evidently incompetent,' remarked Raoul. 'How many attempts?'

'Just the one. Intended it to look like an accident – hit and run – but it didn't come off. I've told Jake to snipe him.'

'*Snipe* him?'

'Use a rifle. By the way, he's left The Big Apple, couple of days ago.'

'Waldo?'

'Better to take him out. He's the bigger fish. But it'll cost you.'

'No, no, no.' Raoul felt moisture prickling his brow. 'You do exactly what I tell you. It's the movie man. Otherwise, a blank cheque.'

'Cheque?'

'You know what I mean. Where's Waldo?'

'Geneva. It'll be that village again – Cartigny.'

'Then you'd better head out there.'

Raoul ended the call, returned the phone to the bottom drawer and leaned away from the desk. *Joshua Waldo...* On the surface, he appeared to be an obedient media mogul, and as a consequence Loran had dropped off the radar when it came to the Council. They hadn't even focused for one moment on Waldo's informal relationship with Maqui, a maverick film director if ever there was one. And then there was the old rumour that Waldo's father had several discussions in the early sixties with the then French Foreign Affairs Minister and subsequent 'defector', Hubert Séguy. These elements, coupled with Waldo's failing health, indicated that an assault on the Council was highly probable – and, furthermore, imminent.

Providing his judgement of Waldo was at all valid, and as far as he was concerned it most certainly was, then clearly the man believed he could seize the initiative and expose the Council and its objectives to an otherwise unsuspecting world. In reality, there wasn't the unity available for him to mount a full-blown attack. Nevertheless, Loran

Communications could cause a critical amount of damage and embarrassment, with names and identities undoubtedly being exposed as a consequence.

* * *

Following an earlier than usual consultation with Sarron's most senior editor which, as on most days, amounted to a full half hour, Raoul lunched with Lord Rickenham, a mainstream tabloid proprietor whose correspondence editor was clearly talking to inappropriate economists. He was assured the matter would be looked into. Rickenham's servility was gratifying if unsurprising, since Raoul had personally cleared the way for his lordship to purchase the tabloid.

On his return to Grosvenor Place, the private line that bypassed his secretary buzzed the second Raoul entered his office. Chucking his coat onto a chair, he lifted the receiver, wanting only to wash his hands – more than an hour now having passed since he'd last washed and sanitised them.

'Yes?' he answered briskly.

'Raoul?'

'Erika, I'm leaving at three—'

'Raoul, get up here – *now*. There's been an accident. It's…it's Adam. He's…'

The line crackled, as if someone nearby was rustling paper. 'He's what?' Raoul leaned forward to catch whatever it was she was trying to say, while wondering what the wretched child had gone and done to himself now. 'I can't hear you.'

Suddenly another voice shot across the line.

'Mr Cregan?'

Raoul stood bolt upright. 'Who the hell are you!'

'Sergeant Andrews.'

'Police?'

'Yes, sir—'

'What's happened?' Raoul found himself suddenly short of breath. 'What's happened to my wife?'

'Your wife's extremely upset, sir. I'm afraid I must ask you to return to Ridgeway Hall immediately.'

Raoul caught the desk to support himself. *The police!* 'Where's Adam?'

Silence.

'*Where's Adam?*'

'Sir, it would be improper to discuss what has happened over the—'

'But I'm *telling* you to.'

'Mr Cregan, we need you here. At Ridgeway Hall. As soon as possible.'

'Sergeant, I have an absolute right to know. You're evidently in my home.'

'Mr Cregan, please…'

Raoul hesitated. The sergeant had made an outright plea while standing next to his wife, who was clearly verging on hysteria. But what was this precisely about? A chill crept up his spine to the nape of his neck. Adam… Had he been injured in some way?

'Sir?… Mr Cregan?'

Raoul took a sharp intake of breath and found himself studying his watch, as if his mind were attempting to reboot itself into normality by means of a familiar habit. 'I'm on my way, sergeant. Would you kindly contact Dr Kirkbride to attend to my wife.'

'Dr Kirkbride has been notified, Mr Cregan, and will be arriving shortly. I spoke to him personally.'

Raoul nodded absently at the sergeant's efficient manner, although hearing that Dr Kirkbride had been called upon seemed to confirm that a major incident involving his son had occurred. 'But what has happened to Adam?' he asked again.

'Mr Cregan, I'm sorry, but I would rather speak with you directly, face to face. The line we're using is not secure.'

Raoul noted that the voice had become stricter. He looked out of the window. 'The traffic seems heavier than usual today,' he mentioned. 'It might take me a couple of hours.'

'Not to worry,' said the sergeant, his voice reverting to its softer tone. 'I'll be here when you arrive.'

Raoul replaced the receiver, the turmoil behind his eyes steadily overlapping what was left of his composure. His legs went to nothing and he sank into the chair behind his desk. Erika… She'd sounded in an awful state. Had Adam committed a criminal act of some kind? He couldn't see how; he was barely eight years old. Snatching up the receiver again, he called Scotland Yard and asked to be put through to Sir Alastair Patterson's office.

'Raoul,' acknowledged the Commissioner after a short delay. 'Good to hear from you. How are—?'

'Alastair, I need an escort.'

'An escort? Where to?'

'Oxford.'

'Oxford? You mean Oxford Street?'

'No, the city itself. I have a crisis on my hands. Something's happened to Adam, my son. I think he might be in hospital…' *But why couldn't this Andrews individual have made that clear to him?* 'There's a police sergeant at the house with Erika.'

'Where are you, Raoul? Grosvenor Place?'

'Yes.'

'Five to ten minutes,' confirmed the Commissioner. 'Call me when you have more information.'

'Of course.'

Raoul grabbed his coat, and without saying a word to his secretary, took the elevator to the ground floor, where he found Sarron's chauffeur, Frank Jackson, chatting to the receptionist.

'Frank!' he called across the lobby. 'Follow me.'

Outside, the pavement bustled with people. They left the steps of the building.

'Where's the car?' Raoul asked.

Frank adjusted his spectacles. 'Headfort Place, sir.'

'Get it.'

Frank started to move off, before turning back. 'My cap's in the lobby—'

'Forget about that. Just get the car!'

Raoul thrust his hands into the pockets of his overcoat, the leaden sky crushing him. He paced back and forth, unaware that he was being watched by the now curious receptionist.

There's been an accident. It's Adam.

A hoax? No...a kidnapping.

Sir, it would be improper to discuss what has happened over the phone.

Adam had been kidnapped!

A wailing siren dragged Raoul back to Grosvenor Place. When the patrol car came into view, he stepped off the pavement and raised his arm.

The driver left the beacon flashing. He donned his cap and lowered the window. 'Mr Cregan?'

'My chauffeur will be with us shortly.'

'There's another climate change rally,' the driver explained grimly, his tone suggesting frustration rather than disdain. 'Second one this week. It's over by Lancaster Gate, but we should be able to bypass it.'

Raoul turned towards an emerald-green Bentley stationary in the traffic. 'We're five cars up,' he told the patrolman.

Once inside the Bentley, Raoul flicked a switch to remove the glass partition between himself and his chauffeur. 'Follow the escort, Frank. Shotover's our destination.'

'Shall I use the headlights, sir?'

Raoul agreed and fell back into the seat, oblivious to the precision with which Frank sliced through the afternoon traffic, aided by the patrol car and its siren, the ululating din interrupting his theory of a possible kidnapping: that 'Sergeant Andrews' was in fact a terrorist.

'How's Mrs Jackson, Frank?' he asked abruptly, keen to suppress such conjecture.

'Fine, sir,' Frank replied crisply. His weathered face with its receding hairline glanced at the rear-view mirror. 'She left this morning to visit her sister in Alicante. Coming back Friday.' He swung the Bentley around Hyde Park Corner. 'Never had an escort to Shotover before, sir?'

Raoul dismissed his chauffeur's inquisitive tone, and rather than call his secretary he sent her a brief text, asking her to cancel all his appointments until further notice. Just as he thumbed *send*, the patrol car came to an unexpected halt on Kensington Gore. The driver climbed out and strode towards the Bentley. Raoul lowered the window.

'Mr Cregan, I've instructions to escort you down to Broad Walk. A helicopter's going to land there to take you the rest of the way.'

Raoul nodded and leaned back into the seat, before deliberating whether his arrival at Ridgeway Hall in a police helicopter was such a sensible solution to avoid the traffic after all, taking into account the possibility of 'Sergeant Andrews' being an extremist of some description.

CHAPTER 15

The pilot briefly lost his bearings on reaching Oxford. The helicopter now chattered over Hawksmoor's Gothic twin towers of All Souls College. But Raoul scarcely noticed them, or their ivory sheen. As the drizzle raced off the screen in front of him, he was convinced that Erika couldn't finish her sentence not because Adam had been abducted, but because by some dreadful means he had left this world. He had no confirmation, just a chilling sense of foreboding that was steadily becoming as nauseous as it was overwhelming.

The engine note dropped and Ridgeway Hall swept into view, the Victorian edifice with its lead-grey façade comparatively isolated from other residences interwoven with the woodland across Shotover Hill. The pilot continued with the rapid descent as another police car joined the one already parked on the drive's apron. They brushed over a copse and Raoul's stomach lurched, before a hefty jolt told him they were on terra firma. Ahead of them, in the distance, he saw a uniformed figure climbing over a gate. Raoul disengaged the harness and, with a degree of awkwardness, lowered himself out of the craft. His legs trembled as he struggled against the ferocious downdraft, and he found himself experiencing a sensation akin to that of claustrophobia. He wiped his eyes and steadied himself as the helicopter left the paddock, its banshee whine eventually replaced by the guttural rasp of a crow in a nearby sycamore.

The figure who had climbed over the gate greeted him breathlessly. 'Sergeant Andrews is waiting for you, Mr Cregan.'

Raoul looked at the young constable's florid face and beady gaze and thought at the back of his mind that he resembled a weasel. 'My wife? What about my wife?'

'She's with Dr Kirkbride.'

'And Adam?'

The constable hesitated, and then avoided eye-contact completely.

Raoul started to seethe at his inability to alter the situation he now found himself in, while envisaging all the disruptive tasks, such as comforting his wife, that lay ahead. 'Come on, man, tell me!' he hounded. 'He's dead, isn't he?'

The constable kept his eyes fixed on a wooded area beyond the paddock. 'Sergeant Andrews is waiting for you, sir—'

'Never mind Sergeant Andrews. My son is dead, isn't he?'

The constable fiddled with the sleeve on his jacket, before brushing off an imaginary fleck of dirt. 'RTI,' he mumbled.

'RTI?'

'Road…road traffic incident. I'm truly sorry, Mr Cregan. Sergeant Andrews, he knows more than me. I've just arrived here.'

Raoul folded his arms and kept them tightly at his chest as he marched in silence towards the Hall, knowing now that he was going to have to identify his son.

* * *

He entered the drawing room with its green flock wallpaper and crimson-upholstered four-seater settee and matching tub side chairs. Sergeant Andrews was a burly, freckle-faced man in his early forties, and under different circumstances probably quite a gregarious sort of a fellow. But at this very moment he looked pale and nervous, his eyes gazing for the most part at the parquet floor while he doubtless contemplated how to articulate the tragedy.

They shook hands, and what with having shaken hands earlier first with the pilot and then the constable, Raoul felt his habitual itch to visit the bathroom to rid himself of any possible germs. Back to folding his arms, he went and stood by the picture window. It had been a good year for the delphiniums; their delicate blueness had complimented the spurge, cornflower and Shasta daisies magnificently. Now there was nothing, just a few canes the gardener hadn't bothered to remove. He turned to face the man he was hardly likely to forget. 'The constable here confirmed what I began to suspect. Precisely what happened, sergeant?'

Sergeant Andrews gestured for the constable to leave the room, and as the door closed with barely a sound he said, 'It was instantaneous, Mr Cregan.' His tone was formal, though softened by either genuine or practised sympathy. 'According to the paramedics, Adam never stood a chance; the car in which he was a passenger took a huge impact.'

'Who was driving the car? My wife?'

'Your live-in help, Mr Cregan. It appears Adam went with Miss Birkett to St Clements to collect the groceries, which by all accounts Mrs Cregan phoned through earlier this morning. On the return journey there was an accident in Morrell Avenue. Early indications suggest an ambulance on call from the Churchill Hospital swerved out from a parked car, lost control and collided head-on with Miss Birkett. Regrettably, she too has since died from her injuries. The news came through just as you arrived.'

Raoul took off his overcoat. 'My wife…where is she?'

'In the living room, Mr Cregan. With Dr Kirkbride.'

He started towards the door.

'Mr Cregan?'

Raoul looked over his shoulder.

Andrews visibly braced himself. 'I think perhaps only you should visit the hospital at this stage. There's a staff shortage and the mortuary may not have had the time to…er…well…to have made the body tidy, as it were.'

Raoul shuddered. 'I…I see.' He managed to regain some of his composure. 'I'll be with you in five minutes, sergeant.'

The door to the sitting room was wide open, and without his wife's knowledge Raoul beckoned the man standing by the flaming hearth to join him in the dimly lit corridor of polished oak panelling and family portraits.

Dr Kirkbride, who Raoul likened privately to a Hollywood 'mad scientist' with his scrawny physique and bird-like mannerisms, closed the door behind him. 'A tragedy, Mr Cregan,' he said, his small teeth stained with pipe tobacco. 'Erika is heavily sedated. I had little choice.'

Raoul studied his watch. 'I have to visit the hospital. I'll be away for an hour or so, I imagine. Could you remain with my wife until my return?'

Dr Kirkbride removed his bifocals with a sudden jerk of his hand and slotted them into the top pocket of his Norfolk jacket. 'Certainly, Mr Cregan.'

'I'd rather you refrained from further sedation,' Raoul said, 'unless you consider it to be absolutely necessary. In order to comfort her, I would prefer her to be perfectly coherent.'

* * *

Raoul found himself pacing back and forth down a broad corridor deep inside the John Radcliffe Hospital. At any moment, he expected – *hoped* beyond all measure – to hear the radio alarm, or Erika's voice rousing him. He looked across his shoulder to find that Sergeant

Andrews continued to 'exist' as he repeatedly pressed the bell-push on a door painted in apricot yellow.

'He can't have left,' Andrews muttered, beads of perspiration beginning to appear on his brow. 'I'll have to go and find a porter—'

The door swung open.

'Yes?' enquired the apron-clad figure.

'Ah, Bill,' Andrews responded. 'Thought you'd gone home.'

'Another twenty minutes.' The man's features bore an uncanny resemblance to those of Dr Kirkbride, apart from a rim of fuzzy ginger hair encircling his otherwise shiny crown.

'This is Mr Cregan.' The sergeant's hushed tone conveyed the delicateness of the situation. 'We've come to see the er…little boy, taken in a couple of hours ago.'

They entered an oblong clinical area that contained several refrigerators set into the glacier-white walls. From a distance, Raoul watched in a daze as the mortician pumped a hydraulic lever on a trolley until it was level with the middle shelf on the refrigerator nearest the door. A sickly-sweet odour blended with that of the disinfectant. Feeling its pungency cling to his nostrils, he brought a handkerchief to his nose.

The mortician dragged out a tray until it clattered onto the trolley. Raoul gasped. There was a distinct blotch of blood on the sheet covering the body, its length not dissimilar to Adam's physique and height. He clamped his eyes shut against the hideous sight spread before him. 'I can't go through with this,' he murmured intuitively.

Sergeant Andrews sidled up to Raoul. 'We could go for a short walk first, Mr Cregan… If you prefer?'

Raoul glanced at the sergeant's intrusive expression; then around at the room itself. All of it befitted a horror film, the voice he heard not so much intimate as ethereal. He stepped closer to the trolley. If all this was not some ghastly nightmare his subconscious happened to be fabricating, then perhaps the child beneath the sheet could at least be some other parents' son…

But it was not to be. It was Adam. Raoul saw straight away that his misshapen jaw had been broken or dislocated on impact. As for the once inquisitive brown eyes, they appeared frozen in time, locked inside that final, terrifying moment when death itself had leapt so unexpectedly towards him.

Raoul moved away and experienced a moment of giddiness under the harsh lighting, the contents of the room starting to move. He put a hand on a wall to steady himself, its coldness creeping into his wrist. He nodded and snatched a few deep breaths. 'My son, Adam. Adam Cregan.'

Andrews spared Raoul the upset of seeing his son returned to the refrigerator by putting a restraining hand on the mortician's arm. He turned to Raoul. 'Hardly reasonable of me to ask, I know…but would you mind identifying Miss Birkett? We have yet to contact her parents.'

Raoul nodded and lifted the handkerchief back to his nose as the mortician busily went about his business, pushing a spare trolley to another refrigerator, the body this time extracted from the lowest shelf. Sergeant Andrews raised the sheet and Raoul stepped closer to the waxen face of the girl he had employed for the past six months, her auburn hair and unmarked features seemingly more striking. 'Alison Birkett,' he confirmed.

Andrews produced a small tattered notebook. 'I understand her parents live in Slough. Would this be the correct address?'

Raoul glanced at the page filled with capital letters. 'Yes, to my knowledge. My wife would know better than me.'

Andrews put the notebook away. 'We can leave now.'

Raoul followed the sergeant out of the mortuary, and as he did so he looked back across the corridor, seized by a desire to take his son with him. Just then, however, the yellow door slammed shut, and he thought he heard the mortician whistling to himself.

* * *

The police car, with Sergeant Andrews now sitting in the front passenger seat, drove away from the wrought iron gates, Raoul having requested that he walk up the drive to the Hall alone. He passed an old marl pit filled with water, an avenue of blue cedars ahead of him, planted by all accounts on the day his great-grandmother succumbed to pneumonia after a fall. He thrust his hands into his coat pockets. He needed to think, although he had no idea what about. Adam, of course. And Erika. But what? What was he supposed to think? His mind had just been thrown upside down! He left the driveway and wandered aimlessly into a copse. Remnants of autumn lay scattered like a shattered window into the future, the heir to the Sarron News Agency having been brutally removed from existence in a split second. He should have touched Adam, he now realised. Kissed him, even. It had never occurred to him to do that: the shock of it all too great, presumably. He couldn't get the image of Adam's mashed face out of his head. Why hadn't someone at least closed his eyes? They had looked harsh and…accusing.

He stood under a giant poplar, dusk settling over its naked branches. He remembered the day when he had climbed onto the second bough, his mother fretting below, demanding that he come down at once… *Dear Mama*, he sighed dolefully, perfectly aware that should he shed any tears then it must never be here, at Ridgeway Hall.

CHAPTER 16

Raoul wiped the dirt from his shoes on a mat and entered the dimly lit hall. The oak panelling and grand staircase had been recently polished and the acrid aroma was akin to orchard blossom compared to the oppressive odour of the mortuary. While heading towards the living room, Dr Kirkbride came into the corridor from the kitchen, carrying a glass of water.

'A tragedy, Mr Cregan,' said the doctor.

Raoul reached for the glass. 'For my wife, I presume?'

'Yes.'

'She's awake?'

'Oh, yes. Indeed.' Dr Kirkbride patted the sides of his jacket before delving into an inside pocket to produce an oblong packet, slender in width and pale blue in colour. 'A mild but effective sedative, should she become too distraught. There's an information pamphlet inside regarding dosage, et cetera.'

At the door, Raoul made the handshake as brief as possible – the doctor's palm somewhat clammy, which caused him to almost recoil. He waited for the Mercedes to leave the driveway before joining his wife in the living room.

She was sitting by the open fire, her fragile frame listless, her shoulder-length hair awry.

She looked at him, her cheeks wet with tears. She struggled to get up from the settee. 'Raoul…'

He felt her head suddenly against his shoulder. 'Please, Raoul… Please. I need you to hold me. Something so dreadful has happened. My worst nightmare.'

Raoul leaned away from her to put the glass down on a side table. 'I need to hold you too, Erika.' But the embrace itself, he knew, was awkward on his part and altogether wooden. He gazed over her shoulder at the flames dancing in the hearth. He thought how soft her reddish-blonde hair felt. Months had passed since he had last come into direct contact with it.

He guided her back to the settee and handed her the glass of water. Then he believed he'd found a window of opportunity. 'Erika, I think it's better if you leave it a couple of days before seeing him. They need to do things.'

Erika huddled forward, shivering. 'I don't want them – *anyone* – touching my son.' She left the settee and knelt in front of the fire. 'I must see him, Raoul… I should be there now with him. At his side throughout the night.' She bowed her head and started to sob, her whole body shaking. 'What kind of a mother am I not to be there for him, holding him in my arms?'

Raoul sighed and took the water away before she spilled it. He felt as if everything had been ripped out of him.

Then he remembered he needed to wash his hands.

* * *

Erika stood stock-still at the window in her nightdress, staring as she had done for the past five minutes into the darkness of the night.

Raoul nervously buttoned his pyjama top, sensing her mood about to become volatile. 'Have you taken a pill? Shall I get you one?'

Erika turned and watched him. Her emerald eyes held a wild intensity that to Raoul felt unnervingly coherent.

He lowered his hands, swamped by a sense of awkwardness over what to do with them. 'Erika, did you hear me?'

'I want my son!' she shouted. 'Not a bloody pill. I want my son. Understand me?'

Raoul touched her arm, desperate to avoid harsh words, the atmosphere and the situation between them problematic enough. 'Darling, I was just asking—'

'Have you no sense of loss, Raoul? He's dead. Ten hours ago, he was alive, but now he's *dead*. Why aren't you crying with me? Why aren't you holding me? Where the hell is your grief? You're supposed to be comforting me...comforting each other.'

'I...I am crying, Erika,' Raoul told her helplessly. 'Crying inside. God's sake, I am.'

'Then *show* me.' Erika shook her head. 'You can't, can you? You were never allowed to grieve over your mother. Your father stopped you, and he's stopping you now from showing it over Adam.'

'Erika, that's not true,' Raoul said, as steadily as he could. She could never leave his father out of anything! 'People grieve in different ways.'

Erika turned back to the window and the sickle-shaped moon beyond. 'See out there...Blackthorn Wood. That's where he had his little den. And you know what's inside that den? A photograph – the one we had taken in Mexico City. I caught sight of it the other day, when he showed me around inside. But you're no longer in the photograph, just a serrated edge...' Erika fixed her eyes on him. 'What did you do to him behind my back for him to want to do that? Prepare him for the wretched Sarron News Agency? Like father, like son, yes?'

They stood looking at each other a moment longer before she broke away and went into the bathroom.

Raoul sat on the bed and unconsciously clenched his hands, digging his nails into his palms while regretting the fact that the bond between himself and his son had been at best perfunctory. He'd hardly had the time, his peers demanding so much from him. But as for Erika…

He swallowed and left the bed.

Erika turned from the washbasin, gazing at him with puffy eyes. Raoul quickly manufactured a credible point of view. Anything to keep the peace. He hated it when she accused him of being emotionally retarded.

'This isn't about my father, Erika. Not today, of all days. This is about Adam. About you and me.' He reached out and cleared a wisp of hair from her eyes. 'I know as a couple we're going through a rotten time, but what has happened today will perhaps bring us back together. I want to try and make that happen.' He held her cheek. 'Adam's spirit lives on, Erika – in you more than me, I have to say. He's still inside you. And he will never leave you.'

He hesitated, unsure whether to say something more, before deciding he had been honourable enough. He went back into the bedroom and found himself apologising to his father for dismissing him so rudely.

'Raoul!' Erika called, a measure of urgency in her tone. She rushed from the bathroom into his arms. 'Raoul, please don't give up. Keep trying. If Adam's inside me, then he can be inside you, too.'

Raoul quickly avoided the useless expectation in her eyes. He reached for her hand. 'I hope so,' he agreed as he brought her to the bed, knowing that he was merely stringing pertinent words together.

When she was settled, he switched off the light, only to leave the bed to open the window a fraction. Strange, he thought, as he climbed back into bed, even with all that had happened he still remembered to open the window. He laid his head on the pillow and, for the umpteenth time, recalled the day he climbed the poplar tree. His mother should still be alive, he told himself.

'Raoul?'

'Yes, Erika?' he responded patiently. He wanted her to go to sleep, or at least be quiet, so he could come to some arrangement inside his head. A plan of action, to guide him away from reflecting too intensely on his mainly secluded upbringing.

'I want Adam interred at the church where we took our vows.'

Raoul noticed her hand on top of the blanket and tentatively clasped her wrist. 'Of course, Erika. So poignant.'

'And we can go and visit him.'

'Whenever we want. Clever you, to think of that...'

Raoul heard his wife sobbing quietly. He kissed her hair and she held his arm, and then her agony fell silent as the medication Dr Kirkbride had prescribed mercifully took effect.

He stared wide-eyed at the ceiling, seeing only his father's portrait in his study: the swept-back greying hair; the muscular face with its square jaw; those dark eyes – as dark as his own – that conveyed to the onlooker an awesome presence by way of intellect, wit and intrigue. He saw himself, twenty years younger, sitting at that same desk in his study, staring in reverential wonder back at his father.

In your lifetime, Raoul, the gathering of extraordinary minds to which we belong, this saintly Council that has justly mocked and extinguished all other empires spanning the centuries, will have become the undisputed guardian of the human race. It will have achieved this through the knowledge that on balance intuition is fallible – and therefore, as conduit to the inner mind from where intuition originates, hugely accessible for the purpose of directing information that serves our Agenda.

Raoul wondered again how much longer he would have to wait

before he was invited to attend meetings of the Inner Council. He was forty-two. A favoured age, but as yet there had been no favourable indications cast in his direction.

An hour or so and several upsetting childhood memories later, Raoul visited the bathroom along the corridor rather than use the en suite, so as not to disturb Erika. On his return, he found himself standing in the doorway to his son's bedroom. He stepped inside and felt the hairs across the nape of his neck tingle.

...Ten hours ago, he was alive. But now he's dead.

Raoul looked around. Everything was in its place. A meticulous mind, he had repeatedly told Adam, radiated cleanliness. The kite they'd bought together in Mexico stood upright in the corner. It was a simple affair, consisting of an Aztec motif stretched across strips of bamboo, a multi-coloured streamer adding a touch of gaiety to the contraption. He reached for it and thought of Adam lying in the mortuary, before seeing himself disciplining his son in Chapultepec Park.

I was giving her some of my pocket money. The baby needs food. She kept pointing at the baby's mouth...

WHAT ARE YOU DOING, RAOUL? demanded his father harshly, out of nowhere. *YOU DON'T NEED THIS. GET OUT OF THE ROOM. WHAT IS DONE, IS DONE. YOU HAVE WORK TO DO!*

Raoul wrapped his arms around the kite and sat on the bed.

'You ask too much from me, Father,' he breathed in quiet despair, his head bowed. 'Always, you ask too much from me.'

CHAPTER 17

Rafael finished his coffee and took the green mug he had adopted back to the kitchen. As was now his routine before leaving the apartment, he checked that the threads of cotton were in place across the doorframes leading to the main bedroom, living room and hallway, each secured by minuscule pieces of Sellotape. With the picture of Lena definitely turned away from the window and the gently falling snowflakes out in the square, Rafael reached for his coat and left the apartment.

It had crossed his mind to conceal a camera in the living room, but he simply hadn't found the time to do so. Besides, he now had doubts over whether there had been a break-in after all, the evidence being somewhat flimsy. And as for Upper Park Road, he had more or less reverted to his original theory, that alcohol had been the likely cause. A shocking coincidence, admittedly, that the car should have veered directly towards him, but if he *was* a target then why hadn't there been another attempt on his life? Nine days had passed since the incident.

He left the building and made his way over to the hired Renault which, despite Liam's request, he had failed to exchange but intended to do so after his meeting with Marc Fauré. He tugged up the zip on his coat. Nine days, he reflected. He was more anxious than ever to hear from Liam who, due to some Irish superstition he held, had asked for no contact to be made between them until he arrived in Switzerland. He'd wondered at the time whether it was more to do with Joshua's paranoia, but felt he wasn't in a position to argue the point. Presently, though, he couldn't deny that his anxiety contained a hefty measure of guilt – guilt over the risks he was asking them both to undertake. Senica had surely never faced customs officials before. He knew if she faltered a hostile glare would ensue, further weakening her composure. As sharp as she was, he doubted she'd survive further questioning, the regimented environment itself being for the most part alien to her.

* * *

The Drum and Monkey in Shepherd's Bush was one of those saloon bars that cried out for a refit, while the clientele doubtlessly prayed such a day would never happen; that the walls remained begrimed with a dusty-yellow tint throughout and the faded and scratched utility furniture stayed just so, harking back to an altogether more 'conventional' era.

Rafael nodded recognition to a couple of regulars before joining Marc alongside a window overlooking a concrete yard with empty beer kegs stacked up against a wall. They'd taken to using the bar over the years to discuss current or future filming projects, often over several games of pool.

'Pinewood called just as I came in,' Marc said, taking off his duffel coat. 'They're asking if we wouldn't mind moving to the 007 Stage so that D stage can be used for a series of shorts by novice directors, sponsored by some TV channel. The only problem is we'll have to vacate the premises after seventy-two days instead of our previously allocated seventy-eight.'

Rafael leaned an elbow on the table, which wobbled, his reflexes lifting his glass in the nick of time. 'Should be okay.' He folded a beer mat and wedged it under the table's offending leg. 'Quite beneficial, actually. It's so vast a stage, we can leave some of the sets standing throughout the schedule.' He took a swig of beer. 'Susan's back from Devon?'

'Calling in any moment. She's been looking at a flat to rent in Fulham. Looks like we've sold the house. Any news from Liam?'

'Nothing as yet. I'm quite concerned, to be honest.' Rafael cast an awkward glance at his cameraman. He hadn't been looking forward to this moment. 'Another concern happens to be Senica herself. Fact is, I've taken a risk, Marc. Maybe too much of a risk. As late in the day as it is, I feel I should be on the lookout for an actress. Two come to mind, Jemma Harcourt and Evelina Armstrong, but I've just heard both are under contract.'

Marc shrugged off his concern. 'The last time you went for a non-actor was *Loki's Amendment*. It worked then, so it can work again. What's Senica's English like?'

'Not a single word. I'm fairly certain of that. And no way am I going to dub over her voice.'

'I see...' deliberated Marc, biting his lip while toying with a dog-eared beer mat.

Rafael took another swig of beer. 'I just wasn't in the right frame of mind, Marc, when I made the decision to bring Senica over. I mean, she's pleasant, no question about that, considerate and practical. Put up with a lot in her life. And I don't mind telling you, I miss her. But to make her the female protagonist in this film...' He shook his head. 'I don't know what the hell I was thinking!'

'In the draft you gave me, the female lead talks very little – to begin with. Something of a loner because of what she's been through in the past. Sounds like that could work in our favour.'

'There's that,' nodded Rafael, keenly latching onto Marc's

surprisingly optimistic perspective. 'The character of Nina remains much the same, apart from the change of name. It's now Romina. Oddly, though, I think Senica will identify herself with Romina. Or perhaps the truth is Romina is actually a version of Senica's character – as far as I know her character to be. I only spent a couple of days with her. But you know, Marc, I did detect a screen presence in her, subconsciously to begin with. I think she could hold an audience's attention just with her looks and somewhat rhythmical mannerisms.' He lifted his glass – an abrupt but subtle waft of chic-encapsulating perfume arriving at his nostrils, before two hands covered his eyes.

'And who is this, stranger?'

Rafael chuckled. 'Someone gorgeous and dear,' he said, smiling broadly. He stood to greet Susan, Marc's mobile phone ringing on the table.

Susan leaned over Rafael's chair and gave Marc a peck on the cheek as he took the call, a stylish intricate swirl of green ribbon invisibly pinned to the side of her shoulder-length black hair. She turned to Rafael. 'I've missed you something crazy,' she told him with a lingering embrace. Then, seizing his arms, and with her soft-brown eyes filled with tears, she said, 'Don't you ever leave me like that again.' She reached for a tissue. 'I bloody well mean it, Rafael!'

'That's amazing!' said Marc into his mobile phone. 'We were wondering how you were getting on.' He beckoned Rafael. 'It's Liam…'

Rafael virtually snatched the phone from him. 'Liam, out of ten?' he demanded, the call hardly allowing him to breathe.

'Eleven, from your point of view.'

'From my point of view? What do you mean?'

'It can wait. I tried calling your mobile.'

'I had to replace it, if you remember. I haven't set the new one up yet. Been using the landline.'

'Why don't you meet up with me?' suggested Liam.

Rafael wrestled to focus on a nonchalant approach to the conversation, since evidently Liam wanted it to be that way. 'Sounds fine.'

'What time at the airport?'

'Tomorrow, around noon. I'll be with Marc, but we can only manage a stopover. We're scheduled to hook up with a crew Stateside. Okay?'

'Until noon…' Liam told him.

Susan put away her tissue and sat next to Marc. 'Good news?'

Rafael handed Marc his mobile phone. 'Senica's in Switzerland, thanks to Liam. I bet there's a story there to be told!'

'You must have been worried for them.'

'An understatement. I swear I've lost several kilos.'

'The flat in Fulham's ours?' Marc asked Susan.

'We can move in tomorrow – today, even.' Susan lowered her voice to a whisper while unravelling her scarf. 'Why do you both insist on coming to this place, year after year? It's totally funereal.' She made a point of meeting Rafael's eyes. 'I hope you're not planning to bring Senica here. She must be going through something of a culture shock as it is!'

* * *

Rafael closed the door to the apartment and immediately checked the threads of cotton. He took off his coat. Everything was where it should be, including the photograph of Lena. He went into the kitchen to switch on the kettle before gathering a change of clothes. He knew he could never repay Liam, but the least he could do was to respect his request and move out of Holland Park. He put both laptops into another carrier bag and left everything that he was taking to Hammersmith over by the door, having already paid a deposit on a flat there. The relief that Susan had agreed to teach Senica English and guide her through her lines in the screenplay was still with him. There was a spring in his stride, even. He was certain the two girls would get along just fine.

Back in the kitchen, he rinsed out the green mug and reached for the jar of coffee. He made a mental note to buy some more Marmite while he searched for a spoon, sifting through the contents of the sink as a last resort. He gave up and took another from the drawer when suddenly, from nowhere, a shattering *thwack* filled the kitchen. He threw the coffee away from his chest, the spoon simultaneously spinning wildly across the sideboard.

Silence…

…apart from the kettle coming innocently to the boil. And because the jar of coffee hadn't contained an explosive device and there were no obvious signs of damage, Rafael found himself at a loss as to what had just happened – until he saw slivers of glass where the spoon had fallen onto the floor. He swung around in disbelief; the ferocity of the impact had ejected a chunk of plaster from the wall above the doorframe. He ducked instinctively and tried to think what he should do – whether to call the police. The gunshot could only have come from the square.

Out of safety, he went and stood in the bedroom, and noted the fissure of daylight between the curtains. Despite his traumatised state, he knew he needed to act quickly. With his pulse thudding feverishly in his throat, he moved towards the window in the belief that the gunman would only take another shot providing he could see his quarry in the crosshairs. He swallowed back the pool of saliva that had welled up from under his tongue and peered through the slit. Although the snowstorm had eased, he found it difficult to see beyond the scraggy treetops. But nothing unusual seemed to be happening. The bullet's trajectory led him to focus his attention on the windows on the third floor of the house opposite. All three were closed, one of them curtained.

Then he noticed it. A silver Ford Puma, parked slightly away from the house in question. The same colour and model that had locked onto him in Upper Park Road. He didn't give himself time to consider the danger he was in, just bolted down the stairs and out of the building into the square. Between the railings and a gap in the shrubbery, he saw the Ford leave the kerb, the driver in what looked like a khaki balaclava. He quickened his pace through the snow as the car was about to turn left onto Holland Park Avenue. He raced towards it, touching the passenger door before he slipped and hit the icy pavement, his outstretched arm partially cushioning the fall. He craned his neck, in time to see the car accelerate effortlessly into the distance.

Furious with himself, he hauled himself up onto his feet.

A small, wizened-faced woman appeared at his side. 'Why rush about, young man?'

Rafael brushed the snow from off his trousers, hardly taking in what the grocery-laden stranger was saying.

'And only a shirt, in this weather!' The woman looked up at him and touched his arm in a motherly way. 'I'm eighty-four years old...'

Rafael shook the woman's hand and expressed his surprise. But then, just as he started to turn away from her, he saw that the Ford was caught in traffic. He left the pavement, taking to the road where the snow hadn't had a chance to settle. He sprinted harder and reached the driver's door. Locked. Startled brown eyes framed by the balaclava stared back at him. Rafael tore around the car to the passenger door. Also locked. He struck the glass with his elbow a couple of times – his efforts predictably ineffective. The traffic up ahead was moving away from him. Nearby, a *Big Issue* vendor was trying his luck, a stack of magazines resting on a plastic crate with a stone preventing the breeze from catching hold of them. Rafael grabbed the stone.

'Oi!' yelled the vendor. 'Oi, you! What the—'

Rafael hurled the stone at the Ford's side window. The glass frosted over and he followed through with a high-flying kick to avoid slicing skin off his knuckles. He blindly located the catch, the car all the while shifting forward. The driver leaned across and tried to beat him off, hitting his hand with a solid object, but now Rafael had his thumb behind the catch, whipping open the door – to find a gun with its snub-nosed barrel levelled at his groin.

The man flicked the weapon repeatedly at Rafael, warning him off.

Rafael found his voice. 'Why are you doing this? *Why?*'

The gesticulation became more threatening, the brown eyes darting fiercely in their sockets.

'Who's telling you to do this?' Rafael demanded, gaining confidence. '*Tell me!*'

The Ford jolted forward; the traffic was moving again. Rafael caught sight of a holdall on the backseat. *The rifle.* Another jolt, and his arm was wrenched to the point of dislocation. The gunman attempted an abrupt U-turn. The passenger door swung wildly, flinging Rafael clear moments before a pickup truck travelling in the opposite direction clouted the Ford's rear wing with a jarring smack. The impact made little difference, the Ford screaming back towards Norland Square and beyond.

The driver of the truck stared across the road at Rafael, his right hand clutching a mobile phone. Rafael retreated to the pavement, and guessed there must be a multitude of phones about to call the police, or being readied to take pictures of him – if not having already done so. He slunk off into a side street.

'Oi, you!' bellowed the *Big Issue* vendor. 'My stone. What about my stone? *Oi!*'

Rafael didn't look over his shoulder until he found himself in the narrow confines of Norland Place. He was alone, and only too aware, as he heard a siren drawing closer, that he had made a costly mistake. He should have shattered the glass on the driver's door with the stone. But, Christ…what the hell was going on? The gunman seemed to have an arsenal of weapons. Did that indicate he was a professional assassin?

Rafael reached the square and took a closer look at the house with the burgundy-painted front door. A previously obstructed FOR SALE sign with SOLD slapped across it told him the gunman had likely obtained a set of keys from the relevant estate agent, presumably through deception. Either that, or he was highly adept at picking locks, which seemed likely if he had listened into the message left by Marc on the answer phone.

Rafael walked on, the shock beginning to gnaw into his solar plexus. There were questions, too: who, and why? Mainly, who? If the Council of the Faithful Brethren were responsible, he knew why. Anyone else and he hadn't a clue, beyond thinking a crank may have decided to focus his attention on him – as with Lena. But that by itself would be too coincidental.

Inside the apartment, he spun the cap off a bottle of Bells whisky and circled the living room, pausing briefly at the window. He drew the curtains and switched on the light. The gunman could have killed him on two separate occasions – *three* occasions if he included Holland Park Avenue. So why hadn't he? He took a swig of whisky and surveyed the damage to the kitchen. All it needed to complete the scene was a body thrown across the floor, the expanding pool of blood liquidising the spilt granules of coffee.

Rafael paced the living room again. Hell, this wasn't a movie. This was life. *His* life. He took another swig from the bottle. Senica. Senica was in Europe. And what was he doing? In effect, he was delivering her straight into the hands of a lunatic. What's more, a lunatic armed to the hilt. Senica... He wiped the cold sweat off his brow and, before he could stop himself, threw the bottle at the wall, whisky and glass showering the ceiling and furniture. He dropped his face in his hands. *Senica...* He remembered promising her Uncle José that he would return her to him from San Miguel without a scratch.

Rafael picked up the photograph of Lena and sat at the desk. He touched the glass and felt tears on his cheeks. 'Lena, my dearest, dearest, Lena,' he breathed, 'I miss you so very much. I'm living a nightmare on all fronts, it seems. Perhaps I should just let them take me out. There's always that chance we might be reunited...'

Sitting with the curtains drawn and enveloped by whisky fumes, it dawned on him he needed to warn Marc. He put the photograph down and called his mobile.

'Where are you?' he asked.

'Upper Park Road,' said Marc. 'We're loading the car.'

'Marc, we've got a slight problem. What's the address in Fulham? I'll meet you there.'

Marc gave it him. 'It's right on the corner by Woodlawn Road. What's the problem?'

'I'll explain when I see you. Just get out of the area as quickly as you can.'

Rafael pushed the phone away, put his elbows on the desk and buried his face in his hands. It couldn't be the Council of the Faithful Brethren, he reasserted. It just couldn't be. Surely they wouldn't deploy a hitman who would miss twice. And why hadn't he finished him off on Holland Park Avenue itself, and then made his getaway? Struck by nerves, or what?

A shade upset with himself, he started to pick up the pieces of broken bottle.

CHAPTER 18

Rafael loosened his coat, and with Marc sitting next to him, watched Geneva fade from view, struck by the Christmas-card landscape once they'd left the suburbs. He was still shaken up by the incident in Norland Square, and Marc and Susan likewise. He'd stayed over at their rented flat in Fulham, but all three of them had hardly slept. Susan was now staying with her brother in Battersea. Rafael's immediate concern, however, was how Liam might react, the mystery too distracting not to share it with him. Above all, he wanted Liam to agree, as had Marc, that because of Joshua's decline in health he should not be informed.

Rafael tried to push the gunman to the back of his mind by reminding himself that he would soon be with Senica. That they were about to be reunited felt extraordinary, and he wondered what she made of it all: the snow and the surreal change in culture. He leaned forward slightly to speak to the driver, Michael Ramsey. They had met briefly before, in California, when Lena was alive.

'Michael, how did Joshua react on seeing Senica for the first time?'

'No worries,' replied Michael in a Kansas drawl. He chuckled unexpectedly and removed his sunglasses, his angular 'all-American' face visible in the rear-view mirror. 'The old man looks not so old suddenly. His Spanish is next to useless, but for sure they've taken to each other.'

Minutes later, they arrived at Cartigny, a secluded hamlet swathed in snow, just a couple of kilometres from the river Rhône and the border with France. The winding track Michael turned into brought them to a renovated homestead with a rustic façade. The interior, by contrast, was far from austere and was comfortably furnished throughout – sumptuous but practical.

They followed a beaming Joshua into the living room.

'Hang your coats up in the hall,' he said. 'Liam's taking a nap and Senica's gone for a walk in the lane opposite.' Joshua proffered a hand towards Marc. 'We meet at last.'

Rafael stood by the door. 'I'll join you later,' he said.

* * *

With suitable footwear borrowed from Michael Ramsey, Rafael found the lane Joshua had mentioned. Evidently a tractor had ventured along it, and between the robust tyre tracks was a recent set of footprints.

He knocked the snow off a signpost. AVUSY CHANCY 4km.

Rafael walked on. 'Senica!' he called, using his hands as a megaphone. 'Senica!'

No answer. He breathed the clean air deep into his lungs and kicked up some snow. Memories of his encounter with the sniper in Holland Park floated away from him.

'Senica!' he called again. He put his hands back in his pockets and rounded a sharp bend, only to find himself under attack from a salvo of snowballs.

'Come and get me!'

The moment he heard her melodic Central American Spanish accent, Rafael found himself transported straight from Europe to his homeland. He swung around.

'…If you dare!'

He had to shield his eyes from the sun flaring off the snow to catch her silhouette on the embankment to his right. 'Guess what?' he hollered. 'You're not going to get away with that!' He started towards her.

Senica threw another snowball, skimming his left shoulder. 'You think so, do you?'

'Sure, I do.' Rafael scaled the bank. Senica managed a temporary escape before he caught hold of her waist – both of them tumbling, breathless with laughter, back towards the track.

Senica tried to bury him in snow.

Rafael pulled her down onto himself and gave her a spirited hug, her warm breath on his face entirely wondrous, like that of an angel from a separate universe. He knew in that split second that he had made the right decision to bring her to Europe, if for no other reason than her company.

'It's so good to hold a Salvadorean so far from home,' Senica told him. 'Just so *good*.'

Rafael kissed her cheek, noticing in the midst of all the excitement a vitality about her brown eyes he had not seen before. And as she lay there with him, her heart beating hard against his, he found that the tiny birthmark to the left of her nose still fascinated him. So much so that his desire to kiss it caused images of Lena to spiral down out of the blue sky towards them.

He rubbed her shoulder, conscious that his hesitation over what to do next might have confused her. 'Sorry,' he said. 'Truth is, I'm still somewhat all over the place. Ridiculous, perhaps, but to experience wholehearted happiness feels like I'm being unfaithful to Lena. Aftershocks and their ripple effects, I suppose. I'm sure in time…' He decided he was babbling and bit his tongue.

Senica drew herself up and knelt in front of him. She inclined her head and displayed the same demure smile she had shown him in San Miguel. 'I understand.' For good measure, she picked up some snow and threw it at him. 'See!'

Rafael wiped away the snow and smiled back at her. He felt doubly reassured. It was the Senica he remembered: graceful, intelligent, engaging. And now there was something new for him to be enchanted by: her playful side. 'I can't quite believe it,' he said, 'but thank you for being here.'

'My pleasure. Quite an experience for me, I have to say.'

He helped her to her feet and they brushed the snow off themselves and each other.

'It's so bright,' Senica remarked. 'Crazy stuff. Jorge would be amazed by it.'

He scooped some snow out of Michael's boots. 'And how is that rascal?'

She stood with her head bowed, merriment all at once replaced by solemnity. 'I feel guilty, Rafael. Guilty over leaving him, and guilty for what he did.'

'What did he do?'

'You don't know?'

'No.'

'He took a shot at Liam and hit him in the leg.'

Rafael looked up. 'He did?'

'I've never been so upset.'

Rafael recalled the phone call in the Drum and Monkey and the hint of a hiccup from Liam's perspective. He tried to keep the smile off his face, imagining the scene.

They started to make their way back along the lane to Cartigny. 'It was bravado,' Senica explained simply. 'Jorge's greatest fault. Just like his father. I took Liam to the hills to meet Sancho, Jorge at our side, demanding to know this, demanding to know that. Typical Jorge, really. He gets so protective. Of course, it's endearing in one sense, but an absolute pain in another. When we reached Sancho, Liam explained everything, how he intended to get me out of El Salvador. Jorge immediately pulled a pistol no one knew he had from his waistband, ignored our appeals, and shot Liam.' Senica shook her head and looked at the sky and then at Rafael. 'I fear his mental scars are starting to get the better of him, and that I should never have left.'

Rafael instinctively put his arm around her. To his delight, Senica readily leaned against him. 'What I'm about to say will surely make me sound cruel,' he warned, not wanting to fracture their re-emerging kinship, with all its added charm.

'Tell me.'

'You're going to have to try and put the village to the back of your mind. And that means Jorge, too.'

'I know – and I will.'

'Maybe a way will be found to improve matters for him with the cheque from Joshua.'

Senica shook her head. 'No. I don't want money.' She stopped walking, their loose embrace broken.

Rafael turned to face her. 'What are you suggesting?'

'Before leaving San Miguel, you told me you wanted to spend more time in El Salvador. Is that still the case? Nothing's changed?'

'Absolutely.'

'Then I want you to repay me by offering Jorge some brotherly wisdom. To prove to him that embracing guns and suchlike will not work in his favour. He is interested in technology. If you can help to put him on that path, then I believe there's a chance of diverting his attention from taking revenge on MS-13 for murdering his parents.'

Rafael swallowed. His instinct was to put her off the idea, to maintain his own sanity! 'What about taking the flat in San Miguel, instead? It'll do you just fine. And you could rent it out.'

'I'm tempted, but no deal.'

'There must be something.'

'There isn't. Nothing at all.'

'I haven't a choice, then?'

'No. Another point... I know nothing about acting, filmmaking and the rest of it. If I'm useless and you need to find another person, there must be no disappointment.'

Operation Jorge aside, Rafael breathed an inner sigh of relief, impressed by Senica's reasoning and foresight. He reached for her hand. 'You haven't that many lines,' he said. 'When Romina speaks, she often does so with one-liners. Slightly off the wall, but nevertheless engagingly profound for the most part.' He slowed their pace; the fairy-tale landscape combined with the warmth and the movement of Senica's body brushing against him introduced a measure of idyllic cohesion that he wanted to luxuriate in. 'You managed to get the books back to the village?' he asked.

'Yes. I've read one of them. Sancho has the other.' There was still some snow on his shoulder and she swept it away. 'You must have thought me so naïve.'

'The deception has to be convincing for them to fulfil their Agenda,' said Rafael. 'You know that now. They can't be arrested, Senica, because as far as the law is concerned they haven't done anything wrong. But what they *are* doing is protecting and enhancing a detrimental system that for the most part is shielded by rafts of laws, the majority of which, of course, are perfectly justifiable against the stage-managed unstable setting that we live under. Throw in several dictators to instil fear and trigger migration, accompanied by periodical economic downturns and constant unrest by way of provocation, et cetera, and you're well on the way to creating hell on earth. Once the national governments have been brought to their knees, you'll see the true face of globalisation and its accompanying dictatorship.'

'But it never occurred to me that such a concentrated group of individuals could exist. As Sancho put it, they create situations for the UN to distribute crutches while getting others to kick them away, leaving victims in the target area worse off than ever before.'

'Basically, we're being held hostage by them,' said Rafael. 'All nations, all religions, not to mention the defacement and poisoning of the environment itself out of desperation or greed. The global debt is now more than three times the size of the global economy. Of course, once the coup — or the entrapment, if you like — is secured and we are living under a universal government, then the debt will be erased.'

'It's too depressing, Rafael. Upsetting beyond words. It amounts not only to the demolition of nationhood but the human spirit as well. I mean, nationhood in a sense stimulates innovation, wouldn't you say? A healthy competitiveness between countries.'

'Quite so.' Rafael looked across at her. 'But there's a country in West Africa called Séroulé, and the interim government has announced that it's refusing to pay off the international creditors, feeling they've been robbing the nation for years by backing it up against a wall and applying sky-high interest rates. Séroulé aims to print away its external debt and plough every cent into reversing climate change. When you think about it, the stranglehold of the global debt is nonsensical against the urgency to repair as best we can the environment and the catastrophic decline in wildlife and biodiversity. No comparison — no *argument* — whatsoever. To destroy this planet as a consequence of debt — I mean, how insane is that? But then, of course, these cretinous people and their godforsaken Agenda *are* insane, proven by the fact that fiscal and monetary systems have been designed solely for entrapment, which by its very nature plays on our behavioural outlook, subconsciously or otherwise. And not for the better, obviously.'

'Surely, Séroulé is asking for trouble by not paying off their creditors,' interjected Senica. 'Don't you agree?'

'It's a risk they're prepared to take. If I and others can draw influential figures behind MS-13, preferably with 18th Street onboard, into protecting rather than make vulnerable El Salvador as regards to external detrimental forces then we could be in for interesting times. A virtually impossible task, I know, but I'm going to point out to both gangs via *Agenda Indiscriminate* that they're simply being used to create fear and suffering – because, of course, that's part of the takeover technique by the Council of the Faithful Brethren – create hell on earth and further subvert the national governments.'

Senica looked across him. 'The blood these terrible people have on their hands!'

'An understatement. They're up to their necks in it, Senica. Who knows, perhaps that's how this miserable business will end – that in some way they suffocate in the toxic deception they've created. The deception being that they filter onto the world's stage as our saviours, whilst in truth they remain one thing only…our tormentors. If there is to be an Armageddon, then that's what it will be: the people versus the world government.'

As they left the lane and crossed the salted road that ran through Cartigny, Rafael felt confident he had all the components in place to complete the screenplay. 'Once their Agenda is exposed, Senica,' he said, 'along with their methods of achieving it, the healing process can begin immediately – both for the human race and the environment. And, for sure, nothing like this would ever have a hope of being repeated. The citizens of this world simply would never permit it to happen again.'

* * *

Rafael knocked on the door at the end of the corridor. After he heard a muffled 'I'm awake', he turned the pale-green ceramic knob. He found the man who had saved the day stretched out on a double bed, snow-laden fir trees and a setting sun in the window alongside.

'Have you spoken to Senica?' Liam asked, rubbing the sleep from his eyes.

Rafael closed the door. 'I've left her with Marc.' Careful to avoid the rough-hewn beams supporting the irregular ceiling, he came and stood over Liam with a knowing smile. 'I hear you ran into Jorge.'

'Thanks for warning me.' Liam propped himself up on his elbows. 'As luck would have it, it was just an air pistol. Crazy kid. I find something of myself in him, I have to say.'

'I know what you mean. He's had it tough.' Rafael sat in a wicker chair by the window. 'I don't know how to actually repay you.'

'There'll come a time when I'll need a favour.'

'Don't hesitate to ask. How was it?'

Liam swung his legs off the bed and straightened his shirt. 'It took a couple of days longer than expected because Ricky had to forge a DUI. In the event, it wasn't needed. Senica mislaid the one she was issued with some time ago.'

Rafael felt a private smile on his lips. Bureaucratic requirements such as the possession by law of a Unique Identification Document were at odds with Senica's character. 'But for you personally?' he asked.

'I'll never settle in Guatemala again,' said Liam. 'But the trip did reawaken me to the energy that is…well, that is Central America. I just miss that vibrancy. It's like it's impregnated into the earth, you know? I've been thinking about Costa Rica, a business on the west coast. Boat rental, small time. Something like that.' He reached down to tie his shoelaces. 'All quiet on the London front?'

Rafael shifted awkwardly in the wicker chair. 'Not exactly.'

Liam looked up.

'I'm afraid I just haven't found the time to move out of Holland Park.' Rafael gave a thumbnail sketch of what happened to him the previous day.

Liam stared in dismay. 'He took a shot at you from *across* the square?'

'No question whatsoever.' Rafael handed Liam the bullet he'd dug out of the kitchen wall, having wrapped it in toilet tissue. 'What can you ascertain from that?'

Liam went to the window, where the light was still reasonable, and removed the tissue to reveal a dome of lead partially mushroomed over a copper jacket. 'I'd say we're dealing with a professional, given the nerve of the man to commit the act in broad daylight virtually on Holland Park Avenue itself.'

'How certain?' Rafael privately cursed Liam's opinion. And now, with Senica in Europe…

'Eighty per cent certain,' said Liam. 'The remaining twenty per cent could be an amateur who just so happens to have got his hands on the kind of kit a pro sniper would opt for. I'm guessing you never heard a sonic crack, like a whip, did you?'

'No.'

'Chances are he used a rifle with a suppressor to cut the noise of the shot. Because the slug hasn't fragmented, it reminds me of what we were issued with for a time out in Belize…the 7.62 Ultima Ratio rifle – imperial measurement being .30 calibre. You still think it has nothing to do with the Council?'

'I have my doubts. Their favoured method is to formulate a trumped-up charge to destroy any opponent through the legal system, humiliating that person in the process. In my case, this could potentially be falsified evidence linking me to Lena's murder, or a fabricated pornography-related issue. Being a filmmaker, it wouldn't be too difficult to hang something of that nature on me.' Rafael paused while Liam sat back down on the bed. 'What I can't fathom is why this guy's out to put the frighteners on me rather than silence me outright.'

'Why do you say that?' Liam asked.

'Because he's made three attempts. And you're saying he's likely to be a pro.'

'I could well be wrong on that...' Liam's brow suddenly creased over. '*Three* attempts, you say?'

'By my reckoning,' responded Rafael. 'Upper Park Road? Fine. We can say he screwed up. Norland Square? Before leaving the apartment, I went through the sequence. He fired the shot while I was fixing myself a coffee, but a cupboard partially blocked his view. Besides, the shot came in at least a foot above my head. Holland Park Avenue? He could have dealt with me there and then – and then made his getaway. If the car's not stolen, he would have hired it using fake ID.'

'Hold it there,' interrupted Liam. 'What exactly happened in Holland Park Avenue?'

Rafael explained, adding, 'That's when he pulled the handgun, after I managed to open the passenger door.'

'Hell of a risk, Rafael, to take you out in the street in daylight.'

Rafael shrugged. 'Maybe... I mean, yes, for sure.'

'What did he look like?'

'I don't know. He was wearing a balaclava. Brown eyes, that's about all I got.'

Liam put the bullet on the bedside cabinet and gazed out of the window. Dusk was on its way. 'I'm wondering if any of this is coming from closer to home.'

'The client, you mean? If there is a client.'

'Yes.'

Rafael picked up the bullet. 'Virtually no one knows the project exists, and those who do have been rigorously screened by Joshua himself, which to my knowledge amounts to a few directors on the central board at Loran. Key personnel such as those handling the subtitles will only be informed once we've shot thirty per cent of the schedule. To date, we've shot approximately ten per cent, just a broad spectrum of scenes around London last week, chiefly taking in myself and Marc discussing *Agenda Indiscriminate*.' He shook his head. 'Fact is, I don't know what I'm going to tell Senica.'

'You tell Senica the truth,' said Liam at once. 'She can take it on board. You only have to glance at her background to see that. She's a good kid. You've found a diamond there.'

'I'll talk to her tomorrow,' agreed Rafael. 'Go for a walk with her.'

Liam sat on the bed, pensive once again. 'While you're discussing the film with Joshua, I'll take Michael to a wine bar I've noticed down in the village, see what I can find out about the people closest to Joshua.'

Rafael stood up. 'I'm still unconvinced. But you're right, better to investigate all angles. I should get downstairs. Speak to you later.'

CHAPTER 19

After the meal, Joshua remained seated at the dining-room table. For the first time in months he felt at ease with the project — *relatively* at ease. The girl was a catch, a chance in a million: unknown, capable, and downright pleasing to the eye. He was confident Rafael could project the intriguing reserve of Romina onto the screen through Senica. And he liked Marc; he was clearly Rafael's cinematic anchor, giving technical support and generally keeping the ship steady.

He looked on as Rafael drew up a chair alongside Marc.

'Seems to me Switzerland's just what the doc ordered,' said Rafael. 'You look great, Joshua, believe me. Lots of colour.'

'For the most part a consequence of medication,' said Joshua. 'That said, the fact that we're already rolling, albeit the peripheral scenes, is a tonic in itself.' He folded his chequered napkin. 'Senica's okay?'

'A shade tired. It's been quite an upheaval for her.' Rafael poured himself and Marc Irish whiskey into crystal glass tumblers. 'One extreme to another.'

'Of course,' nodded Joshua. 'You know, I kind of wondered over the meal about a go-between — to keep her informed of events in her village. The person that comes to mind is of Central American origin and wouldn't arouse suspicion. Her name's Juana. She's presently reporting the campesinos' uprising in southern Mexico for Loran News.'

Rafael's eyes lit up. 'She'll love the idea. It'll be of enormous comfort to her.'

Joshua leaned further into his chair as he wondered how close Rafael had become to Senica, and vice versa. He'd noticed how comfortable they looked in each other's company: the little chuckles and almost intimate asides. 'Then I'll have Juana come over to meet her.'

'Much appreciated. Thank you, Joshua.' Rafael took a sip from his tumbler. 'We need to start shooting the scenes involving Romina as soon as possible, to accommodate the flow of retakes that are likely to arise in the initial stages of Senica's appearance in front of the camera. Marc's wife, Susan, has volunteered to teach Senica English and coax her through her lines. Obviously, we've yet to establish those we want to show footage of during the speech. Presumably, we're still unanimous that the individual who makes the speech should be Anthony McCormac. Apart from being identifiable as the current British Foreign Secretary, we know he's a high-ranking operative within the Council. Coincidentally, our production designer, Doug Silberman, bears a slight resemblance to him. Add makeup and I believe we can produce a reasonable lookalike.'

'There's no change on McCormac,' ratified Joshua. 'But apart from the finance minister for Europe, which I mentioned some time back, the other three I have in mind come from the Council's inner sanctum. You'll have footage of them before you leave here.'

Rafael set his tumbler back down on the table. 'Why not let the viewers recognise three out of the five candidates?' he suggested. 'Why not, for example, Raoul Cregan?'

Marc leaned forward, as if on cue. 'But not depicted via Loran News footage on a screen, Joshua. An actual lookalike, sitting next to McCormac.'

Joshua felt he'd been waiting for the name to crop up ever since Rafael mentioned it in New York. 'Why Raoul Cregan?' he asked. He would play along with them both and bide his time.

'Because he's the chairman of the Sarron News Agency,' Rafael said. 'It's arguably the most influential mainstream media outlet in Europe, which probably makes him as senior an operative as McCorm—'

'I don't want Cregan's name mentioned, nor any image of him appearing in the film,' said Joshua, putting an end to the notion, sincere and as rational as it was. 'I've met Cregan on several occasions. My opinion is that his influence within the Council is not as considerable as it might appear. Even he at times might see it that way. That aside, I believe we need three big guns and, as we know, the big guns always remain in the background. The media itself will be obliged to clarify in greater detail our choice of names. It might take time, but it will happen. A case of supply and demand, you might say.'

Rafael glanced at Marc before turning back to Joshua. 'It's been a long day for all of us,' he said, his tone subdued – almost theatrically so. 'I suggest we call a halt until the morning.'

Joshua agreed, suspecting they wanted time together to reinforce their case. But they wouldn't get anywhere with it. As far as Raoul Cregan was concerned, his mind was made up. He was not going to drag his wife through hell and high water. The others and their wives or partners he couldn't give a damn about. But for some inexplicable reason, Erika Cregan reminded him of the woman his daughter might have become had she been allowed to live.

*   *   *

Senica wiped her tears away and drifted over to the window, gazing at the night and her own reflection in the glass. She saw the unhappiness in her eyes, and wished her homesickness would leave her. The fact that she was going to act in a film hardly played on her mind, the subject far too alien for her to comprehend.

Eight to ten weeks, Rafael had said. She supposed that made it an adventure. She might never again be given the opportunity to visit another country, let alone another continent. And she was with good people. Kind people. She would learn from them, become better able to explain things to Jorge so that he might finally realise that his bravado would ultimately put him on the wrong side of decency.

She started to draw the curtains when a knock on the door made her jump. She quickly wiped the tears from her cheeks and went to open it – to find Rafael, his hair tousled, giving him that rugged appeal she remembered from when they'd headed out to San Miguel. She stepped closer to him until he did exactly what she hoped he would do: put his arms lightly around her.

'I'm being pathetic,' she said.

'Hardly.'

'It's the last time you will see me cry this way,' she vowed.

Rafael produced a clean paper serviette from his pocket. 'Here...' he whispered. 'It's difficult being brave, but that's exactly what you are.'

'Bewildered, would be more accurate.'

'Only natural, for heaven's sake. While climbing the stairs, it came to me that if I can borrow the car from Michael, we might head out to St-Cergue tomorrow – just the two of us. The village lies close to the border with France. From there, the view across to the Jura Mountains is breathtaking. I think you'll like it.'

'Then let's do it.'

He closed the door. Reluctantly, she moved away from him, to give him room.

'So, what happens to Romina in the film? She lives happily ever after with Saúl Majano?'

'Not exactly.' Rafael stood awkwardly, hands moving in and out of his pockets, his eyes eventually meeting hers. 'She dies from a bullet meant for him. I could change it so that Saúl is the victim – it's just that an audience usually experiences a greater sense of outrage when the principal female falls victim to the villains. I want people leaving their seats fully aware that an injustice has been committed, not only in the screenplay but against themselves.'

Senica nodded quietly, distracted by his presence. 'I understand.' She sat in the velvet-upholstered chair beside the bed, content just to watch him gaze out of the window through the gap in the curtains. What was the age difference between them? Eight years? Ten? Twelve at the most, perhaps. It didn't matter, she told herself, while trying to prevent her mind from making plans. 'What are you thinking?' she said gently. 'Something to do with the film?'

Rafael dropped his shoulders and visibly relaxed. 'I was thinking about you.'

'About me?' There was that lovely smile of his. 'Something nice, I hope.'

The smile became a chuckle. 'Of course. What else could it be other than something nice?'

Her pulse raced a little and she felt a flush on her cheeks. She tried to think of a witty response, but missed her opportunity.

'Didn't you ever want to go to the city, to study?'

'I lived in San Vicente once – but not to study.' She hesitated; perhaps now was a good time to tell him, get it out of the way. 'I was married.'

'Married?' Rafael cut her a sideways glance. 'What happened? Or shouldn't I ask?'

'It's okay. By the time the end came he was fond of hitting people, me included. A victim of gambling and alcohol, I suppose. One day he just disappeared. A week later his body was found at the side of a road. He'd been hit by a car.'

'I really had no idea...'

'The marriage was a mistake,' she explained quickly. 'Sancho warned me, but I didn't take any notice. I just went ahead with it. It's gone from my life now.'

Rafael left the window. 'Senica, you're certainly full of surprises. And as far as I'm concerned, a soothing influence.' He came and stood over her. 'By the way, Joshua's setting up a go-between to keep you informed of what's going on back home.'

'He is?'

'Yes. I get the feeling he's somewhat paranoid about using mobile phones at this early stage of the production.' He stooped and kissed her brow. 'Anyway, tomorrow we'll have the morning to ourselves, before I have to leave to shoot the scenes at Joshua's apartment in New York. Meantime, pleasant dreams.'

Senica sat quietly in the chair and watched him close the door, the sense of refuge she had experienced in his arms quite beyond anything she could have imagined. She wondered if they would hold hands again when he took her to see the mountains. She'd been so happy when they'd rolled in the snow. There was a playful innocence about them both that reminded her of when – a lifetime ago – she'd sat beside the River Lempa and kissed a boy from a neighbouring village. She closed her eyes and pictured herself introducing Rafael to the ceiba tree over on the ridge behind the cornfield. She hoped one day it would actually happen. It was important to her.

* * *

Rafael retraced his footsteps along the narrow, uneven corridor, finding it difficult to keep Senica out of his thoughts for even a few minutes, his mind repeatedly drifting back to the moment when he'd entered José's primitive store. Mayan intervention, or fate? He still wasn't sure.

Further along the corridor, he saw that Liam's door was slightly open. He gave a knock. Liam was washing his face in the basin over in the corner of the bedroom.

'Find out anything from Michael?' Rafael asked from the doorway.

Liam looked up, took a towel from the copper rail next to him and dried his face. 'It seems Anna Sangster is the closest of all to Joshua, the only one likely to be completely in the loop, but I've been introduced to her and she doesn't strike me as being unhinged.'

'I've met her a couple of times myself,' Rafael said. 'She's good company for Joshua. I noticed it when I last saw them together in New York. So, the threat's unlikely to be from the inner circle as we know it to be?'

'It was a longshot, but I thought it should be checked out.' Liam put the towel back on the rail and looked at Rafael, his face heavy and awkward. 'I'm sorry, but I think I should carry a firearm.'

Rafael felt himself wince, seeing in his mind's eye the Zigana handgun used to murder Lena.

'There's something going on. You simply can't deny it, Rafael.'

With Senica now onboard, perhaps it was the only belt and braces policy open to him. Rafael duly nodded. 'Fine, I agree. And thanks, Liam.' He started to leave. 'You saved the day. No question. Talk to you in the morning.'

He crossed the corridor to his room, still rather piqued by Joshua's outright decision to exclude Raoul Cregan from the film. He would speak to Marc in the morning. Together they would simply have to convince Joshua that Cregan was the right choice and that the viewers would see it that way, too.

CHAPTER 20

Raoul looked up from his desk to find Erika standing by the study door. She had put on her nightgown and seemed ready to turn in. With the funeral now behind them, they were back to sleeping apart. It had been six months since Erika had made the excuse that her insomnia would likely keep him awake. Privately, he was rather relieved. He simply didn't like touching people, and the thought of sweat and other bodily fluids mixing together turned his stomach over to the point of revulsion.

Erika started towards him, and he noticed she'd lost a little weight around her waist and hips. There was a look of determination on her face. He heaved a silent sigh and left his laptop, hardly in the mood for another confrontation.

'Raoul, I want us to leave Ridgeway Hall. I want you to sell it. If you don't, I'm going to leave anyway. I'll move into Eaton Square. I've made up my mind.'

A shade perturbed, Raoul leaned into his chair. He didn't want her in Eaton Square, the apartment set aside solely for his own use. When he spoke his tone was measured, icily so, in order to leave her in no doubt. 'I will never sell Ridgeway Hall, Erika. Never. I thought I had made that clear.'

Erika looked above him at the portrait of his father. 'I'll tell you why I want us both to leave. Neville Cregan was an evil man. Do you know why I think that, Raoul? Because he took the niceness out of you, and now he's taking what's left.'

Raoul felt a ripple of panic. He thought it unlikely, but if she threatened him in taking her version of their fractured marriage to the papers... Of course, nothing would be printed, he knew that, but it would nonetheless be embarrassing for him. Lord Rickenham, for one, would chuckle to himself. Not so much a chuckle, in point of fact, but an effeminate giggle. He closed the laptop. 'That's absolute rot, Erika.'

'No, it's not...' She lurched forward suddenly and snatched the tortoiseshell paperknife off his desk. Then she was alongside him, her arm drawn back. 'I hate him!'

Raoul ejected himself from the chair in a flash and caught her wrist in the nick of time, the knife barely an inch from the canvas. He grappled with her briefly and forced the knife from her hand. 'What's got into you?' he panted.

'He's taking you from me. Can't you see it?' Erika pointed at the portrait of his grandfather alongside, complete with goatee. 'And him. I hate him, too. His eyes... He looks like a pervert.'

'That's enough, Erika!'

'There's something sinister about this place,' she persisted, hands now clenched and a redness coming to her cheeks. 'Your father smoked, right?'

Raoul put the paperknife in his pocket and reached down to the desk to steady himself, altogether shocked. He caught his breath. 'What if he did?'

'On the second floor, sometimes I can smell tobacco. He's still here. His ghost. I haven't seen it, but I know it's here.'

'This is just nonsense, Erika.' Raoul drove a hand through his hair, sweeping it back from his brow. Whenever she attacked his family, especially his father, it put him on edge. He tried to divert her mood. 'You're tired, it's been a traumatic time. Perhaps we'll ask Dr Kirkbride to find you a counsellor.'

Erika pushed him away from her. 'Don't be so stupid. I don't need a bloody shrink. I need you to take me away from here. For you to get rid of it.'

'I've told you, that's out of the question! Just get that into your damn head!' He stormed past her and into the hall, hearing her footsteps behind him. And then her voice.

'Running away again, aren't you? Like you always do. Like a little boy. Well, I'll win you back from them. From Sarron. You wait and see.'

He lifted the latch on the front door, a blast of cold air hitting his face. 'Go to hell!' He strode out onto the drive.

'I don't think so. That's where *they* are.' Erika stood under the pillared porch. 'And how dare you say such a thing to me!'

He felt the key to the Jaguar in his hand. He'd given her everything. *Everything*. The engine caught. He whacked the shift into first gear, rear wheels spinning viciously as the car catapulted itself down the drive. At the slight curve, it drifted wide, its nearside wheels cutting up the grass verge. He braked and the Jaguar slewed, the front wing scraping the iron gates. 'Bitch,' he muttered. He swung the car out into the unlit lane. How could he have married her? His father had warned him she was inappropriate.

He found himself driving into Oxford and wondered whether he should turn back to protect his father's portrait. He took his foot off the accelerator, until he realised that she would likely have already committed the act. His knuckles whitened on the wheel, anger rising again. He swallowed. He'd walk a street or two. Get some air. Calm himself. Why did he always do this? Simply drive off – sometimes all the way to London? He shook his head. He knew why. Of course, he did. Because he was so afraid that he might actually hit her. Better to drive away – not run away, as she saw it.

He parked the car near the city centre and put on the weatherproof jacket he kept in the boot. Cutting through a side street in St Clements, he reminded himself to be on the alert for it was here where the rabble endeavoured to keep body and soul together. Here where people were subjected to constant uncertainty, the fear of being looted or even assaulted never too far away. Nonetheless, depending on his mood, he invariably found the environment therapeutic, a kind of theatre in which he and his peers shaped the players into whatever was required to advance their Agenda.

He stood for a moment on the corner of the street. Two figures were defacing a building directly opposite him. The ground floor appeared oddly windowless. He waited for the figures to scurry into the night before taking a closer look. The white paint had started to trickle: the message, nonetheless, arresting.

THIS SHOP SELLS RAPE!
GOD'S CHILDREN!!!

Raoul turned away and crossed the road. Little had changed since he last visited the area. He still likened it to a deprived ghetto in which a handful of residents gamely fought an endless battle to introduce harmony and nature-related projects for the 'community' to engage in. In time, even these people would give up all hope – a matter of course. Raising his collar to fend off the icy breeze, he came to a derelict telephone box, behind which lay an area of street-lit shabby turf and the occasional bench seat. In the far corner of the clearing sat a group of people huddled around a makeshift fire, post-apocalypse style. Community spirit in any shape or form of no interest to them whatsoever, alcohol and the next fix unquestionably dominant in their deactivated brains.

He chuckled to himself, and felt better for it. Indeed, the subtle promotion of addictive distractions aside, it had always amazed him how so few people had made the connection that fiscal and endless rafts of legislative policies, under the guise of democracy, were nearly always designed to accelerate dissatisfaction and social conflict, a hidden hand all the while financially sapping and undermining the satellite governments.

There was, though, one man who could possibly articulate that connection, via a filmmaker, by taking what appeared to be unrelated fragments of political ineptitude in any number of countries to form a whole. Once achieved, the film could be as effective as taking a brick out of a dam, allowing a remarkable and dangerous truth to flow through the masses.

For three years he had put a question mark against this man. He had even raised the point to his peers at a meeting in Bern back in the spring. But his warnings were dismissed with the comment that Joshua Waldo was a toothless relic, preoccupied with propping up his declining media empire. Raoul knew that such a blasé rejoinder could come back to haunt the Council, for was not Waldo in reality throwing scraps of meat at the wolves whenever they bayed for more? Once the beasts had had their fill, would he not then commit the unexpected – or rather, the *unthinkable* – by broadcasting worldwide the Council's covert Agenda and divulging identities and irrefutable proof in the process? His *own* name included! But would there be enough unity to cause other bricks to fall from the dam? He still had his doubts as he cast a look around himself, again taking in the vagrants huddled around the fire.

More immediate and to the point, perhaps, why all of a sudden had a Latin American girl showed up in Cartigny, going by the name of Maria Fenney? Like hell that was her name. According to his man on the spot, the useful idiot of a private eye, Maria Fenney had *died* in Guatemala. Mystery apart, how spectacularly embarrassing for the president of Loran Communications that he should be found to have been harbouring an illegal immigrant – in Switzerland of all places!

He took the Jaguar's key from his jacket pocket. Yes, it was time to pick up from where he'd left off: to expose the threat to his peers and single-handedly shut it down, destroying Waldo before their very eyes. Surely, by then, with the added bonus of Maqui's imminent termination, he would be guaranteed a seat within the Inner Council? He felt a smile drift onto his lips. There were moments when he wondered whether Erika's pathetic righteousness fuelled the ruthless force that had made him what he was: a ruler of men, of governments – of society and its redesign. Not even Genghis Khan had such far-reaching power!

A movement from an alleyway caused him to swing around, his hands tightly clenched in preparation to defend himself. In the event, he saw only a young girl sitting with her back against a brick wall, much of her face obscured by her dishevelled blonde hair through which her large, childlike eyes peered up at him.

'Leave me,' she warned. 'Let me get on with it!'

Raoul reached the Jaguar, puzzled by what the girl had said. Get on with what, exactly? He fastened his seatbelt and glanced over his shoulder to check for traffic, noticing that the brightly lit street partially illuminated the alleyway. The girl was sitting just outside the shadow cast by its narrow entrance. She seemed to be nodding her head a great deal – as if to music. Then she abruptly stopped doing so and slammed her right hand into her left hand before repeating the action. Fascinated, Raoul pressed the switch to lower the window…

...and then he saw it, the blade glinting momentarily under the streetlight, the sight of it stealing his breath. He turned away to face the windscreen and the night-time traffic – buses, cyclists, coaches to and from London. He released the handbrake. He wasn't going to get involved. Drugged up to the eyeballs, no doubt. She could slash his face or just as easily stick the knife into him. He flicked a switch, the windscreen-wipers sweeping aside some drizzle, like a veil, to reveal an image of Adam's mashed-up face... When was that damned image ever going to leave him!

A muted cry, and his eyes swivelled. The girl was now nodding her head again, only madly so, as if experiencing a fit. He turned to the screen; Adam's eyes glared back at him. Raoul swore under his breath. *Stay away from me!*

I hate you! You hurt Mummy...

Raoul scrambled from the car as if he were breaking out of his son's coffin. A bus rolled by. He sprinted across the road, entered the alley and seized the girl's coat.

'Stop it!' he shouted, lifting her to her feet. 'I'm *telling* you.' The walls of the alley resounded with his panicky voice, just as a dash of blood from her wrist spattered his face. His terror was immediate, the fluid possibly infected with viruses. He should have driven away, goddammit!

The girl abruptly hissed and raised the knife to him. He knocked her hand away. The blade clattered against the wall just as a police car wailed past them. Fleetingly distracted by it, Raoul heard a guttural gasp and looked back at the girl. She had seized the knife and rammed it into herself, blood bubbling out of her already crippled wrist. She stared at him, her expression made all the more macabre by the smudge of grime on her lips. 'You see, I've done it!' Her voice was breathless, her eyes nevertheless ecstatic, glistening and dilated to an astonishing size. 'I've *done* it!'

Raoul dragged her from the alleyway. He was barely functioning. All he could see was her lying ghostly-white and dead on a mortician's slab. He got her into the road. She started to kick and lash out at him, her right fist hitting his face. He hardly felt the blows, his frenzied eyes locked onto the Jaguar. When he reached it, he threw her as if she were a rag doll onto the passenger seat and slammed the door shut. Her gory hands pressed against the window, hectic smears of blood screening by degrees her tortured face from him. Raoul turned away and saw an old man with a stick standing further down the street, before other passers-by joined him, along with waiters from a restaurant – all of them watching. He wondered if he should go and explain to them what had happened, but the girl started to shout and hammer on the window. He climbed into the driver's seat.

'Listen to me!' He gripped her arm and fought to contain her hysteria as blood spurted across the windscreen. 'I'm not going to allow you to—'

'Let me die! I want to die!'

Raoul booted the accelerator, still fighting her off. 'While I'm around that isn't going to happen. Not a chance – so forget it!'

* * *

In a washroom, next to the Accident and Emergency Unit at the John Radcliffe Hospital, Raoul filled a basin and started to rinse the girl's blood from his face and hands. He could even smell the sickly-sweet odour of the mortuary in it, and it was *horrible*. What a thing to have happened, though! His legs were still weak with shock and his hands refused to stop trembling. Perhaps he should call Erika and let her know. He blew his nose into a paper tissue, emptied and refilled the basin and repeated the whole procedure, only more thoroughly. He was beside himself with worry over the possibility that he might have been infected with something: hepatitis, or whatever. He would have to give Dr Kirkbride a call in the morning and ask for a blood test.

With that in mind, he dried his hands, put on his wristwatch and left the washroom. A balding, middle-aged Asian in a blue tunic made a beeline for him.

'I'm Doctor Ashraf. And you must be Mr Cregan? I understand you brought Sabrina Prescott to us? I thought you might have already left.'

'I went to the washroom,' Raoul explained. Reluctant to find himself entangled in an investigation, police-related or otherwise, he continued on his way. 'You have my address and telephone number, so if you don't mind—'

'There's no need for concern.' The doctor's easy smile revealed neat rows of small white teeth, not unlike Dr Kirkbride's only without the tobacco stains. 'She's calmed down quite a bit now. We've seen to that. We're going to be taking her into theatre. Would you like to have a word with her?'

Raoul shrugged. 'I don't know…' He was nonetheless a shade curious as to why the girl should have done such a thing to herself. He nodded. 'All right.'

'I have to say, Mr Cregan, had you not intervened we would have lost her. She was obviously determined to see it through.'

'Have you tested her blood?' Raoul asked, checking the time on his watch. 11:20. He hadn't realised it was so late. He wondered again whether he should call Erika. 'I'm rather concerned. It's all over my car.'

'I understand your concern, Mr Cregan.' Doctor Ashraf escorted Raoul into an area with curtained-off cubicles. 'We should have the results by nine o'clock tomorrow.' The easy smile resurfaced. 'But be assured that contamination is most unlikely.' They arrived at the last but one cubicle. 'She's right here. Inform the staff nurse, should you need me.'

When the doctor left, Raoul paused. He wished the strength would return to his legs. It felt as if he was having to identify Adam all over again: the harsh lighting, the building itself, the people around him. After all, Adam must have been brought to this same department. Or had they taken him straight to the morgue? *It was instantaneous, Mr Cregan. According to the paramedics, Adam never stood a chance.* He needed to get out of the place and utterly regretted agreeing to Dr Ashraf's proposal.

In spite of everything, he drew back the curtain. To his immense relief he found the girl lying quietly on a stretcher, her heavily bandaged hand and forearm resting on a pillow across her waist. She opened her eyes. He was unsure what to say or do. Finally, he decided to move the plastic bag containing her clothes from the chair alongside her. When he sat down, the chaotic silence between them directed his gaze to the tears on her lightly freckled cheeks.

She yawned unexpectedly. 'You should have left me to get on with it,' she said without turning her head. Her remark was an accusation. 'I would be with him now.' Another tear meandered down her cheek. 'With Matthew...'

'Matthew?' Raoul asked. 'Who is Mathew?'

'My world ended eleven days ago. A drunken idiot walking into the road took Mathew off his motorbike.'

Raoul looked at her right hand, a part of him wanting to clasp it. But he hadn't liked it when Dr Ashraf shook his hand.

'I'm tired,' mumbled the girl quite suddenly. 'Go away and leave me.'

He went to the tiny washbasin and refilled her beaker, then looked over his shoulder. 'Sabrina?' he called softly. She seemed to have fallen asleep. Without a second thought, he slipped the Silberstein wristwatch over his hand and deposited it into a side-pocket of her jeans in the bag. He stepped out of the cubicle, told a nurse he was leaving and asked her to check on the girl.

* * *

Raoul thought about the girl constantly during the drive back to Ridgeway Hall and couldn't get Doctor Ashraf's words out of his head. He had saved a life. If he hadn't intervened, her heart would definitely have stopped beating at some point, leaving her slumped against the alleyway's brick wall. Passers-by, not realising they were in fact seeing a corpse, would have regarded her as just another down-and-out and perhaps pitied her.

Once inside the Hall, he felt completely exhausted, his legs like lead weights. He hauled himself up the broad staircase and noticed Erika's door was ajar. She had fallen asleep with the reading lamp on, her blonde hair curled angelically across her cheek. For the briefest of moments, he wanted to kiss her, to wake her and tell her about his unexpected achievement. How would she react?

He flicked the switch on the lamp and crossed the corridor to his room. He pulled off his sweater, preoccupied suddenly by a bedroom over on the east-wing. Half undressed, he followed the corridor down to it, switched on the light and stood for a moment in the doorway. The watercolour alongside the dresser had been painted by a distant uncle who fancied himself as an artist. Raoul took the painting off the wall and sat on the bed. The cancer had already taken hold, but his uncle had been kind with his brushstrokes and she looked lovely, standing by the rockery in a turquoise silk dress. And there he was, sitting cross-legged in front of her, something of a puckish smile on his round face.

Raoul brought his gaze back to his mother, her hair reddish blonde. Like Erika's.

'I saved a life tonight, dear Mama...' His eyes welled up, taking him by surprise. As if embarrassed, he turned from the painting and started to wipe his tears away, before seizing the frame with both hands. 'Oh, dear Mama, I can't ever remember you smiling. I just can't remember!' He stood up and realised he was shaking. Still clutching the painting, he sat on the chair in the corner of the room and, hiding his tear-stained face from the world around him, sobbed quietly – as he had done throughout much of his childhood, until he discovered the art of malice.

CHAPTER 21

Senica stood stock-still in the entrance to the apartment in Norland Square: T-shirt, jeans and sea-green suede pixie boots. Rafael figured her distinctly intimate smile was going to fix itself in his mind for eternity.

She brushed a wisp of hair from her cheek. 'Hi.'

He held out his arms. 'Senica, you look terrific.'

'Liam's on his way up.'

She came into his arms and they hugged. Rafael's pulse thumped like a jackhammer.

She gave him another kiss on his cheek, eyes glistening. 'Feels like weeks!'

'Say, are we filming?' jested Liam from behind them. He took off his coat. 'Coming across as high drama.'

They laughed and Senica put her canvas shoulder bag against an armchair. 'What time did you arrive back from New York?' she asked.

'In the early hours,' said Rafael. 'Marc called earlier. He's seen some of the rushes. Reckons we've done a decent job. Joshua played the part of himself like a pro.'

Senica stood back from Rafael and straightened herself. 'What do you think to my Roque Dalton T-shirt? Liam had it made for me as a welcome gift to England.'

Rafael glanced at the words printed on the T-shirt below a sketch of the Salvadorean poet. '*Creo que el mundo es bello,*' he read aloud, '*que la poesía es como el pan, de todos*. Liam translated it into English for you?'

'Yes. It's a quote, you must know it. Here goes: *I believe the world is beautiful, and poetry, like bread, is for everyone.*'

Rafael grinned. '*Bravo. Perfecto.*' He turned to Liam. 'Can you stay for a beer?'

'Sure I can.'

'How's the flat in Chiswick?' he asked, maintaining the conversation in Spanish for Senica's benefit.

'No complaints,' shrugged Liam. 'Reasonable rent, taking in the area.'

Rafael headed towards the kitchen. 'Senica, you're having a beer?'

'Please.'

Rafael searched for and then found the opener. He took the tops off the Budweisers and went back into the living room.

'…She mentioned her son to me the other day,' Senica was telling Liam. 'He stays with her mother in Nicaragua when she's on assignments.'

'Who's this?' Rafael interrupted. He handed them their beers. 'Sorry, no glasses.'

'Juana, my go-between. The journalist from Loran Joshua set up for me to get news from my village. Incidentally, do you think it is a risk using cell phones as Joshua seems to think so?'

'I have to go along with what he says, to be honest,' admitted Rafael. 'You're not exactly legal.'

'It's true, Senica,' pitched in Liam. 'It might seem extreme, but anyone if they wanted to could listen in.'

'Okay, I get that. Anyway, Juana's from San Carlos, close to the border with Costa Rica. She's been staying over here with her cousin the last couple of days.'

'In Edinburgh.' Liam lifted his sleeve to glance at his wristwatch. 'Flying back in this evening. I said I'd collect her from Heathrow. And then the day after tomorrow, she's off to Salvador for the first update.'

'She's so pretty,' Senica added. 'Sort of cute-pretty. Don't you agree, Liam?'

Liam raised the Budweiser to his lips. 'Can't say I've noticed.'

'Come on, Liam!' pushed Senica. 'I mean, there's pretty and there's knockout pretty, and she's right up there.'

Liam coloured. 'Well, all right…yes. She is quite attractive, to be sure.'

'She showed me a photograph of her son, Andrés.' Senica went to a shelf with several CDs. 'You can see he's going to be very handsome, but she's having to bring him up on her own.'

'What is she?' Rafael asked. 'Divorced?'

'In the process of,' Liam chipped in.

Rafael left the settee's armrest. 'It's not all that warm in here. I'll turn the heating up.'

Liam casually trailed behind him into the kitchen, leaving Senica looking through the CDs.

'When are you going to make the move over to Hammersmith?' he whispered as he partially closed the door behind them.

'I haven't had the time, Liam.' Rafael turned the dial on the thermostat. 'I'll do it tomorrow.'

'Relieved to hear it.'

'I'm keeping the curtains drawn and the blind down in here.'

'And Senica?' Liam persisted.

'Oh, Rafael!' Senica called from the living room. 'You've got León Gieco! And Lhasa de Sela. Can we listen to Lhasa? I haven't heard *La Frontera* for ages. Probably make me cry.'

'I'll put it on in a minute,' Rafael said over Liam's shoulder. He came back to Liam's enquiring eyes. 'What about Senica?'

'You haven't told her about the gunman, have you?' fretted Liam. 'She has to be told. It's only fair.'

'The opportunity hasn't exactly arisen, has it?' Rafael pointed out. 'Last time I set eyes on her she'd only just arrived in Europe. I will tell her though, obviously. I'll tell her—'

'Tomorrow?' Liam straightened. 'I've noticed that about you, Rafael, it's always tomorrow. You've still got the Renault parked out there in the square!'

'I've been up against it.' Rafael tried to keep his voice down while being somewhat surprised by the abrupt onslaught. He couldn't quite fathom why Liam seemed so on edge. 'I only arrived back here in the early hours.'

Liam looked down at his shoes and then gave a barely discernible nod. 'You have a point, I suppose.' His big frame heaved a sigh. 'But you must tell her.'

'Of course I will. This evening. She's staying with me now, so there'll be plenty of time to find a suitable moment.' They left the kitchen.

Senica turned from the CDs. 'Rafael, while you were filming in New York, I've been learning more about them – about the vile people we're going to expose in the film. When you think about it, it's the height of barbaric stupidity what they're doing to us. It cannot possibly be interpreted as an act of supreme intelligence.' She looked at Liam and then back to Rafael. 'These operatives, or whatever they like to call themselves, are completely twisted. Disgusting, don't you think?'

'No question.' Rafael took a swig of beer. 'They know how to put the world on an even keel. They have to know, to stop it from happening. And it's that fact that makes them so evil. Instead of dismantling the system that's so detrimental to the planet in its entirety, they enhance it to maintain their grip – their lousy global Agenda.'

'Destabilising governments while tripling surveillance in the process?' interjected Liam.

'The prerequisite for a world government to exist is to demolish nationhood,' said Rafael. 'The surveillance aspect, for the most part, is voted in by the public because of the volatile landscape that we're surrounded by.'

'That's quite interesting,' said Senica, leaning into the settee, 'because when I lived in San Vicente, the odd street camera started to appear. Some of us protested, saying it was an absolute intrusion. Then came a reduction in the local police force and a crimewave followed. And before long people were asking not for fewer cameras but for more.'

Liam's mobile sounded in his coat pocket. 'Hopefully not an issue,' he muttered, leaving them for a corner in the room.

'Rafael, I want to watch all the films you and Marc have made together,' Senica said. 'Each in turn, starting with the shorts. *The Fisherman* – I'm intrigued by the title. Sounds biblical. Tell me about it, the story.'

Rafael sat on the arm of the chair opposite. 'Very briefly, the film concerned the smuggling of Algerians into Marseilles and how a fisherman's act of humanity gave way to exploitation fuelled by greed, followed by revenge from a victim, forgiveness, and ultimately friendship.'

'A kind of full circle, then?'

'Yes, definitely.'

'Which directors inspire you? Not that I would know them.'

'I'm what's called a minimalist director,' explained Rafael. 'Focusing on intimate studies of the human condition, rather than shootouts and car chases. So, for me, Robert Bresson and without question Chantal Akerman are the directors I most admire. *Agenda Indiscriminate* is an exception. We're seeking the widest possible audience.'

Liam came back to them. 'Juana's flight's just landed, ahead of schedule.'

Senica left the settee and gave Liam a hug. 'Give Juana my love.'

'Will do.' Liam fastened his coat.

'I'll see you down the stairs, Liam,' said Rafael.

When they reached the main door on the ground floor, Liam turned to Rafael. 'Do me a favour.'

'Like what?'

'Use a wedge of some description as well as the lock on the apartment. I mean it, Rafael. We know someone's been inside.' Liam gave him a hard look. 'What I'm saying is, play it very safe. There's a settlement in El Salvador that would never forgive us if anything happened to Senica.'

'I'll wedge the door,' said Rafael.

'And tell Senica…' Liam glanced at the square. '…Tell her what happened.'

'This evening, Liam. I'll catch you tomorrow. We'll come over to Chiswick. I'll get to meet Juana then.'

CHAPTER 22

True to his word, Rafael started to figure out how he could fortify the hallway.

Senica hurried over to him from the living room. 'They're in love,' she said impishly, glowing with excitement.

Rafael looked up from the door. 'Pardon?'

'They're in love. Definitely in love. I can't believe it!'

'Who are you talking about? Am I missing something, here?'

'Liam and Juana. They're in love with each other but they just will not admit it.'

'Hold on, hold on...' Rafael went into the living room to retrieve his beer. 'If you want some wine, then you're out of luck. Just beer. Sorry.'

'Beer's fine for me,' said Senica. 'Wine leaves my mouth dry.'

'I'll get you another bottle.'

She followed him into the kitchen. 'José tried his hand at making wine once. Poisoned half the village. Put everyone out of action for just about a whole week.'

Rafael laughed. 'I envisage the roof blowing off that store of his one day.'

'Sancho jokes that José's *aguardiente* is close to jet-fighter fuel.'

'He has a point.' He handed her a beer. 'Incidentally, your room's at the end of the corridor, away from the square. Should be quieter for you, not that there's much in way of noise,' he added. 'Back to Liam and Juana... I can't see anything happening between them myself. Liam's still very much cut-up about Maria and what happened in Guatemala. Although, I have to say, he did seem a shade tense this eve—'

'They've been playing husband and wife.'

'Husband and wife?'

'Yes. Liam's been going around the flat with his toolbox – *new* toolbox, making sure everything's just right. There was a broken cupboard in her room. He's fixed it. Things like that. And Juana's taken to making sure his clothes are nicely ironed. We've been watching them.'

'We?'

'Susan's been with me. I didn't realise her mother's Burmese. How long has she been married to Marc?'

'About eight years. By the way, how are the English lessons going with Susan?'

Senica twisted her mouth. 'Something of a snail's pace, I'm afraid. But I'm growing in confidence, and Susan makes it fun.'

'I'm proud of you. No question. Main thing is not to panic, or to get upset with yourself. Progress will happen, almost without you realising.' Back in the living room, Rafael sat in an armchair while Senica settled on the settee opposite before stretching, raising her arms. Just then, as she stretched herself, he found himself to be hooked more than ever before on her rather adorable elf-like mannerisms.

'So, what do you think about Liam and Juana?' Senica asked.

Rafael dragged his eyes away from her T-shirt. 'What do I think?'

'Yes.'

He shrugged. 'Time will tell, I guess.' Refocussing, he put down his beer. 'I've been meaning to ask you...how come you never got into a college? I understand the financial aspect, but you're smart enough to find a way around that.'

'It's not that simple, Rafael. There's a different problem. Although it's wrong of me to regard it as a problem. Disrespectful, really.'

'What's the problem?'

'Uncle José. There'd be no one there for him. I know there's Sancho, but he spends most of his time up in the hills. I mean, when I lived in San Vicente, José all but fell apart. He basically lost interest in the store and life itself. But if I could find a cure for the condition he's got, I think it would help. He gets so distressed by it.'

'By what?'

Senica glanced at the floor. 'Well... Well, he finds it difficult to pee properly. He's had the problem for years. I've tried all sorts of herbs. Sancho knows this man in the next village who has some medical knowledge when it comes to pigs and goats. We had him over to examine José—'

'A pig farmer?'

'Yes. He has a few pigs, I think.'

Rafael sat up straight. 'Are you saying he *examined* José?'

'Yes.'

'Were you there?'

'No. I was busy that day. I had to take Jorge to Father Rodríquez for new shoes. It's quite a trek. It's a side-line for Father Rodríquez, and the shoes he makes are cheaper than anywhere in Chalatenango.'

'Returning to José...' prompted Rafael.

'The man came over. I didn't like the idea myself. José was desperate, though. And Sancho thought he was doing him a favour.'

'What was the result of this 'examination'?'

'The man said he couldn't find anything wrong. It cost us two chickens, and José couldn't sit down for a week. I think he picked up an infection. Put him in a terrible mood. In the end, I managed to get hold of some antibiotics. They cost a fortune, but they did the trick.'

'He shouldn't have been examined by a pig farmer, for God's sake.'

'Well, like I said, I wasn't keen on the idea. I've been saving the best I can for him to see a doctor.'

'That, I can assure you, will happen. In fact, I'll ask Juana to get things moving as quickly as possible. You should have told me about this sooner.' Rafael stood up. 'Want another beer?'

'I still have some left... But thank you, Rafael. Thank you so much. That would be wonderful.'

'One way or another, we'll get José sorted out. I'm not surprised he's feeling lousy for much of the time.' He went into the kitchen to get himself a beer, remembering he'd promised Liam he would fortify the door.

Senica handed him a CD as he came back into the living room. 'This has an interesting cover,' she said. 'What's the music like?'

'Manu Dibango? It's good. He came from Africa – Cameroon.' Rafael took the CD from her. 'Here's a track you might like.' He selected *Poinciana*. 'Listen to this... I'll be back in a moment. I've just got to fix something.'

* * *

Senica watched him disappear into the hallway. Taking her hands from her jeans, she dropped back onto the settee, closed her eyes and listened to the silky rhythm of *Poinciana*, with its seductive saxophone swaying back and forth. But it was hopeless. She couldn't settle. She recalled the moments they'd shared in San Miguel and Cartigny. They had seemed so cosy, so...private. She got up and paced the room, hands clenched. What could she do? What were his feelings towards her? Little more than cordial, she supposed miserably. She simply wasn't sophisticated enough for him. How could she be?

She reached the desk and the framed picture of Lena, fresh-faced, capable and flawlessly beautiful...

Then suddenly she found herself standing in the hallway.

'Rafael, what are you doing? I'm missing your company!'

Rafael gave her a quizzical look over his shoulder. 'You okay?'

'Yes, of course.' Senica became curious. 'Why do you ask?'

'You sounded sharp.'

'Sharp?'

'Well, flustered.'

His observation made her realise the emotional state she'd unconsciously drifted into. She tossed her hair, folded her arms and leaned against the wall in an effort to suggest he was mistaken. 'No, I'm fine. Far from flustered. What are you doing?'

'Liam wanted me to make everything a shade more secure.'

She watched him increase the thickness of a piece of cardboard and wedge it under the door.

'Rafael, I don't want to point out the obvious, but the door has a lock.'

'I know...'

* * *

Rafael straightened and looked back at her, and felt his heart melt, for she seemed even lovelier. And still not a trace of makeup, despite finding herself financially secure and immersed in the glossy texture of Western consumerism. He imagined her to have been something of a tomboy in her teens, but now, standing before him, she positively glowed with femininity. And as for her pert-looking—

Senica unfolded her arms. 'You really like it, don't you?'

Rafael looked up.

'My T-shirt. You really like it, I can tell.'

'Oh... Yes. Totally suits you.' He lifted his shoulders to smile apologetically. 'Liam's put me to shame. I should have bought you something to welcome you to England, too.'

'I have your company.' She glanced down at the chunk of cardboard jutting out from under the door. 'So, why does Liam want you to do all that?'

'We've a slight problem.' Rafael brought the ornamental chair that stood under the mirror over to the door and found that the back of it slotted neatly under the handle with its front legs only fractionally off the ground. Satisfied with his handiwork, he took Senica into the living room.

'What's the problem?' she asked.

Rafael reached for his beer, trying to find the right words. 'I was going to tell you tomorrow. Liam wanted me to tell you in Cartigny, but the right moment never seemed to come along. I should have done; I realise that now. He had a go at me in the kitchen this evening about it, for not having told you—'

'Rafael, please tell me. What exactly did Liam have a go at you about.'

'There's a gunman, he's been kind of hanging around—'

'A gunman?'

'Well, first of all he tried – or so it seemed at the time – to run me over in his car. I'd just left the Underground, was on my way to visiting Marc. Then the day before I met up with you in Cartigny, he took a shot at me from across the square. I was in the kitchen when it happened. The bullet just missed me.' He told her what had happened on Holland Park Avenue, when the gunman had become wedged in traffic.

Senica sat on the edge of the settee, wide-eyed and legs tucked back. 'Is this coming from the Council-thing? The Brethren?'

'No. I don't think so. If it were character assassination via the media, yes – probably. Besides, if they'd opted for a hitman, he wouldn't miss twice. In other words, he'd be highly professional. No mess, no nonsense.'

'So, what are you doing about it – about the gunman?'

'We're moving to Hammersmith tomorrow, a couple of miles down the road.'

'What about the police? A waste of time?'

'It would likely find its way into the newspapers, bearing in mind what happened to Lena. Something we don't particularly want at this stage in the production. We're keeping it from Joshua because of his health.'

'Of course.'

'I've had to fortify the door because we think whoever it is has taken a look around at some point.' Rafael met her eyes and felt another pang of guilt claw at his conscience. 'Perhaps you should have stayed over a while longer with Liam.'

'It's come as a shock to me, I have to say,' she said. 'Nothing's happened since, has it?'

'No, nothing at all. I've been out of the country, mind you.'

'Like home from home, really... The gunman-thing. I mean, it wouldn't be MS-13 or anything like that onto you, would it?'

'I can't see it. I've given them no just cause.' He finished his beer. 'I guess we'd better turn in. I'm pretty whacked, to be honest.'

Senica stood up. 'Sorry to ask... Have you a T-shirt, or any kind of shirt, really, that I can sleep in? I've been wearing this a few hours now. I need something clean.'

* * *

Rafael straightened the pillow, leaned back and cursed where his mind seemed hell-bent on taking him. He felt both ashamed of himself and disloyal to Lena, and tried again to conjure images of all the recent global horrors to divert his errant deviation – but it was useless. He still pictured Senica naked from the waist up before him. It went deeper, of course. He knew that. Her courage, her decency, had touched his soul in some magical way, perhaps going as far as initiating a process of healing. He recalled the moment when they'd touched hands in San Miguel. He'd noticed then that she had long, slender fingers with short nails. Despite knowing toil, her hands had retained their elegance. He imagined them gliding down his torso to take hold of him.

Rafael threw himself onto his back, and in a final fit of anguish flung the duvet across the room. He shut his eyes, only to find that he now pictured her without a stitch on. She looked magnificent, like a Mayan goddess, silken hair way down past her shoulders as the radiant tone of her dusky skin directed him to those vibrant, self-assured dark brown eyes. He simply wanted to take her in his arms and experience the scent and the movement of her body.

He rubbed a clenched hand across his brow and stared at the ceiling. What was he doing? What was he *thinking*? Lena, for God's sake. Dearest Lena!

He left the bed to retrieve the duvet, only to stub his toe on a chair. That sorted out his inappropriate desires, but left him hobbling around the room. He managed to curse under his breath, so as not to wake her, no doubt sleeping soundly in the spare room next door – oblivious to his torment. What would she make of his pathetic yearning for her while barely four months had passed since the day Lena had been brutally taken from him? He sat on the bed and clutched his foot...

...until the sound of a creaking floorboard from somewhere down the corridor made him sit bolt upright. A moment passed, and then it happened again. He grabbed the towel from the chair and threw it around his waist. Surely, he had sufficiently secured the door in the hallway… Could be Senica, of course, using the bathroom. He opened the door as silently as the night itself and saw a light on in the kitchen.

He found her filling a cup with water.

'Are you okay?' he asked. Although he'd detected little evidence during the evening to suggest otherwise, it dawned on him that she might be homesick.

Senica remained facing the sink. 'I couldn't sleep.'

The shirt he had given her had somehow caught under itself, revealing much of her thigh. Rafael found himself adjusting his towel. 'You're thinking of Sancho?' he asked. 'Jorge?'

'No.'

*

Senica kept her back to him. She was certain her hair looked a mess. Oh, why did this have to happen? Why did he have to come out of his room at this moment?

'You're not homesick, then?' said Rafael.

'No.' She shut her eyes. Why hadn't she said *yes*? Idiot! She wanted to leave the apartment and disappear; it was all she could think about doing – to disappear from him, from herself, from everything. If he saw the look on her face… 'I mean, yes. I am a little homesick. To be expected, I suppose.' She drank some water and realised he was talking to her.

'…You're going to feel upset from time to time, but I think you're handling it superbly, Senica.'

And then his hand touched her shoulder, catching her off guard. She turned instinctively, a tear on her cheek. She couldn't help herself.

*

Rafael was shocked. He'd never seen such sorrow in her eyes before and wondered if she blamed him for the way she felt, that he'd mistaken her near matter-of-fact reaction after he'd mentioned the gunman. 'I'm sorry, but I had to mention what happened out there in the square—'

'It's not that.'

'What is it then? I mean… Please, don't cry – it crucifies me to see tears on you. You've no idea.'

She brushed the tear away with her wrist. 'I'm not usually like this. I think I'm starting to come down with something.'

Rafael moved closer. He wanted to kiss her lips. He simply *had* to. And that birthmark – he needed to kiss that, too. Another tear spilled down her cheek, and this time he touched it. His heart was racing. 'My God, Senica… What's happening inside us both? It feels like more than words can ever express.'

*

'Rafael…'

She felt sudden shame, picturing the photograph of Lena on the desk by the window in the living room.

'I…I shouldn't be here. I must leave, now. I can get a taxi. You're going to be so cross with me. I'll get out of your life. You'll easily find someone better than me for the film. I'll be useless, I know it—'

*

He silenced her, his fingers lingering over her lips. Again, their eyes met, silent longing rather than sorrow. The decision was made for him.

'I love you, Senica. Truly. Believe me, you're not going anywhere. This is where you belong – where *we* belong. Wrapped up in each other's arms. It's as pure as that. I know it is. I've thought it through as much as I can about Lena. I know it's only been a matter of months and not years. But I can't let you go, there's too much for us to lose.'

*

Senica gasped. She simply hadn't anticipated such a sweeping declaration from him.

'Rafael…' Her mouth was bone dry. 'I really don't want to say it, but I have to… Maybe you just want to hold onto someone – to ease the pain. And perhaps because I'm Salvadorean, that might also comfort you in some way.'

She placed her hands on his broad shoulders, her heartbeat so fervent it was making her chest ache.

'I have a point, don't I, Rafael?'

*

He took her in his arms, the fragrance of her hair fresh and liberating – like spring blossom. He settled his cheek against it. 'Not really. But I understand why you raised it.' He met her eyes again. 'Hey, having you around has been fantastic for me, no exaggeration. I want it to be permanent. I really do. This is the right thing for us. What's the alternative? That you just walk out of this apartment and my life, leaving us both miserable. That would be insane.'

Senica held him tightly, as if fearful that he would vanish from sight. 'I love you, too, my dear Rafael.' She pecked his cheek. 'I haven't been able to think straight!' She smiled broadly. 'This is going to help my English. I'll be able to concentrate – finally.'

He leaned closer, conscious now of the warmth of her breasts. A tentative kiss on the lips, but it was enough for his groin to tingle with expectation.

'I'm kind of nervous,' she said. 'I'm telling you!'

He lifted her hands onto his shoulders. 'It'll go away in a

moment.'

'And afterwards? You might blame me. Be angry with me. I couldn't bear that.'

'Not in the least. I promise.' And then he brought her up into his arms, carrying her into the corridor.

'Wait!'

Rafael looked at her. Her face seemed severe and his heart sank. 'What is it? What's happened? A change of mind?'

Senica brought her hand across and stroked his eyebrows, each in turn.

'What are you doing?'

'They're gorgeous, Rafael. I've been dying to do this since San Miguel.'

He kissed her out of relief. 'Senica…putting it mildly, I'm keen to get you into the bedroom.'

'It's just… Well, I've got this thing about eyebrows.'

He smiled with her, entranced. 'I so needed to hear that!'

* * *

Rafael leaned on her, utterly spent. And as his body came to calm itself there steadily developed feelings of loss and of gain, the divide between himself and Lena wider than before. But there was no sense of actual shame or guilt, no demon intent on persecution. He even found himself searching for guilt, yet the overriding perception remained as much as it had begun: wondrous and true.

Senica basked in his virility, protective and soothing. She gazed at the ceiling as blissful sensations of wellbeing drifted through her. And as she lay with Rafael's now restful pulse against her breast, she found she wanted to keep the warmth of his semen forever inside her, in the same way a person might keep a love letter next to their heart… Life. This life. An hour or so ago she'd been wretchedly miserable, and now she wanted to embrace life as never before, to run with Rafael up into the hills towards the ceiba tree and then throw herself to the ground to lie with him under its majestic canopy and explain to him its importance to the Maya in connecting the Underworld with the sky – a moment that only they would share and treasure into the future.

Gathering herself, Senica brought her hands up to his shoulders, angled her neck and gave him the smudge of a kiss on his cheek.

Rafael raised himself to look at her and saw the silky glow of contentment in those brown eyes. It gave him a sense of elation knowing he had put that there, that it had worked out for her. For them both.

'Nothing has changed,' he said aloud, by way of reassurance.

She stroked his hair. 'Thank God. I felt it hadn't, but to hear you say it…'

Rafael kissed her brow and carefully left her. He felt the shirt she had borrowed from him under his hand and used it to wipe the sweat off himself. Struck by a thought, he looked across at her. 'Shall we go to sleep to the mellow sound of Manu Dibango? Would you like that?'

'What a romantic!' She sighed, her fingertips meandering over his chest. 'Perfect timing, Rafael.' She reached up to him. 'Don't leave me for too long.'

'As if…' He leaned over to kiss her and then dragged himself off the bed.

In the living room, Rafael switched on the light to search for the CD on the shelf, before he remembered it was still inside the portable player. He cut across the room, towards the desk – and froze: Lena gazed directly at him from the photograph he'd taken in Cornwall.

It seemed ridiculous, but for a moment he was unsure what to do over his nakedness. He shook his head, almost in horror. Wasn't she still inside his heart of hearts? Love and death, past and present, intertwined. Why not? How could it be anything other than that for him?

He watched himself pick up the frame and touch her smile.

I've been on a rollercoaster of a journey since you were taken from me. He wanted to embrace her. *There've been days when I believed I'd lost my mind...* He quietly kissed the photograph. *In this world I have found Senica. Please, I beg you Lena, be happy for me.*

Respectfully, he tucked in the hinged stave to lay the frame down on the desk.

'No, Rafael!'

He turned sharply, startled.

'You must *never* do such a thing.' Tears glistened on Senica's cheeks. She came closer, her hands on her shoulders so that her arms covered her breasts. 'I'm perfectly happy to have a picture of Lena in the room – in any room, wherever we live. I want that to happen.'

Stunned by the generosity of her reaction, Rafael left the photograph as he had found it. 'I wasn't sure what I should do.'

Senica kept her gaze. 'I feel I'm starting to know Lena. It's like I'm getting to know a sister I never knew I had.'

Rafael felt himself shake his head in wonder, a moment of moisture in his eyes. 'Senica, what can I say? I'm so proud to have you in my life. That's how it feels to me, and how it's always going to feel.'

He took her hand, and in silence led the way back to the bedroom, the past decade measured for the most part by joyful memories, the future to be greeted with conviction, the present memorable.

CHAPTER 23

Framed by the dawn light that came through the curtains, Rafael watched Senica walk naked towards him, having taken a shower, her sensuality enhanced by the rhythm of her hips. A lithe, exotic creature, and a sight he altogether appreciated after the horrific dream from which he had just awoken.

Senica knelt beside the bed, her eyes clear and inviting. 'I feel so cosy and happy inside,' she said in a near whisper, as though she were telling him a secret. Her fingertips journeyed along his jaw and then over his lips. 'I like touching you.'

Her words, her presence, made his heartbeat resonate as he fell in love with her eyes all over again. They always seemed to physically express her thoughts and actions – a transparent corridor to her inner being, exclusively for those whom she chose to trust. 'Come back to bed,' he said.

'My hair's still wet.'

'Doesn't matter.'

She climbed over him, presenting him with another kiss that included a playful tickle with the tip of her tongue in his ear, before giggling.

If it hadn't been for the recurring nightmare, Rafael imagined he would have been more than ready for her. But when she lay on her front and tucked her forearms under herself, he couldn't resist idly straightening her hair between her raised shoulder blades.

'That's nice,' she sighed. 'I like you doing that. It's like you're preening me.'

He ran his hand from her neck down her back and over her rump to her thighs. 'Senica…these curves…just fabulous.' He went back to straightening her hair. 'You know, if I were a sculptor, I would insist on getting to work on you – immediately.'

She studied him, an impish look about her. 'You don't have to be a sculptor.'

Rafael smiled with her and lay on his back, bringing her hand to his lips. He gazed at the ceiling, feeling relaxed, liking her pillow-talk. For some reason, his mind conjured a rural stream coursing peacefully through a rising dawn.

'Do you think Liam and Juana have slept together?' Senica asked suddenly.

'If they have, then my life seems to be running parallel with Liam's.' He looked across his shoulder at her. 'It would be quite remarkable.'

'I think they have. I have this feeling they wanted me out of the way.'

He adjusted the duvet. 'Hope Liam's okay.'

'Why wouldn't he be?' There was a flicker of uncertainty in her eyes. 'Because of Guatemala?'

'Yes.'

'He mustn't blame himself for what happened. He was in a warzone, not of his making.' Her earlier mood now seemed supplanted by concern. 'Rafael, you're fine, yes? I mean…'

He gave her hand a reassuring squeeze. 'I was never going to let you go, Senica. Not after I saw the look in your eyes.'

She kissed his shoulder, and curled up alongside him. 'I want it to be like this for ever and ever.'

Rafael tucked his arm around her. 'Amen,' he breathed tenderly, perfectly aware that Hammersmith alone wasn't going to fix the gunman. How could he avoid Pinewood Studios, the Underground, moving from location to location whenever required? Liam was right, he was without question a soft target. And, as a consequence, so too now was Senica.

He held her instinctively. Perhaps he should fix himself up with a gun? And Senica...maybe she should have a gun, too. He shut his eyes. What was he thinking? If she was caught in possession of false papers *and* a firearm, they'd lock her up and throw the key away. How could he ever explain himself to José and the rest of the villagers?

She is my treasure. The child I never had. You understand what I'm saying?

He opened his eyes, his vision blurred. He turned his head away from her, and moments later felt her hand on his arm.

'Oh, Rafael,' she gasped. 'What's happened to you?' She touched his shoulder. 'Is it...is it, Lena? You must tell me!'

He wiped the tears off his face, knowing it would hardly be fair to try and dismiss her dread, for it was obvious that was what it amounted to. 'I keep experiencing these dreams, Senica,' he explained. 'Lena's in hospital. She's all right, not badly injured. So, I get ready to visit her, but the moment I leave the house I wake up and realise she's dead. It's a hell of a shock.' He swallowed, and held her closer to himself, each breath she breathed reminding him of the dawn that had filtered through the curtains and across the room. 'After waking from that dream this morning, watching you walk into the room, it was like an angel had come to visit me. Only it's better than that, because I can touch you, feel you. Be in love with you. It's not a question of me attempting to interpret you as a surrogate for

Lena. I see only Senica. Beautiful, considerate Senica.'

She laid her head on the pillow and gently massaged his temple. 'Considerate or not, it was thoughtless of me to have kissed you earlier in the way that I did. I should have taken a moment to reflect. I was just so happy when I opened my eyes and found you next to me. I wanted to wake you.'

He lifted his hand to her shoulder, her sense of regret like a wound to him. 'Senica, the last thing I want you to feel is that you're having to tread on eggshells.' He kissed her brow. 'Promise me you're not going to feel that.'

'I promise.'

'Really?'

She presented him with the perkiest of smiles. 'Cross my heart.'

'It was the perfect kick-start to my day,' insisted Rafael. 'Delicious, no two ways about it. Fact is, it's not Lena that's upsetting me. It's the gunman. Now that I have you at my side, he absolutely terrifies me.' He lifted a hand in a gesture of frustration. 'But where is it all coming from? That's what I want to – *need* to know. If it's not linked to the Council of the Faithful Brethren – and I'm certain it isn't – then why is all this happening? The man who killed Lena is dead.'

'Remind me again the name of this place we're moving to?' Senica asked directly.

'Hammersmith.'

'In London?'

'Yes.' Rafael rolled onto his back. 'A few miles away.'

Senica leaned on his chest. 'We'll move to Hammersmith, and we'll be on our guard. We can even move out of London, if necessary. And we have Liam, Juana, Marc and Susan. We're not alone.' She held his shoulders and kissed him. 'But the best of it is, he's up against Salvadoreans. Mayas. What does he know about

Mayan ingenuity and our history of survival? Absolutely nothing!'

Rafael touched her lips. Talk about a perfect match. 'Crazy, I know...' He ran his hands through her hair. '...But I keep wondering if Javier had something to do with us getting together.'

She stared at him, a small furrow between her eyebrows. 'Javier?'

'When he died, I asked the spirit world to guide me. I said it was my only wish. An hour or so later, I walked into José's store.'

'And what did I do?' beamed Senica. 'I slapped your face. Quite a welcome!'

'It was worth it.' Rafael brought her back into his arms. 'I promise you, Senica, I would give up everything to have this moment with you.'

* * *

Rafael had made a start on filling a cardboard box with his belongings when his newly purchased mobile phone rang on the desk. He went over to answer the call, Senica sitting there writing letters to José and Sancho for Juana to take with her to El Salvador. It was his old friend, Lazaro, likely contacting him from the warehouse where they'd last met.

'*Oye, mi querido amigo!*' responded Rafael. 'Coffee business good?'

'Fair to moderate, you could say, given the day-to-day frictions. Started filming yet?'

'We get to grips with several major scenes this coming week. Tight schedule, to say the least. Any news?'

'Sure. I can't quite believe it, actually, Rafael. He's going to talk to you.'

'Who?'

'Joaquín Hernández.'

'You're kidding!' Rafael noticed Senica had stopped writing and was looking at him. *Joaquín Hernández*, he mouthed. She promptly pulled a face. 'When, exactly?' he asked.

'In about five minutes, on this number.'

'I'll let you know how it goes, Lazaro.' Rafael put down his phone. Senica was still looking at him, her expression heavy with disdain. 'I know, I know... Joaquín Hernández is evil. I have to take this opportunity, though. With both MS-13 and 18th Street having – so it appears – joined forces how will the Salvadorean government deal with such an onslaught?'

'I can't bear to think about it, Rafael,' said Senica. 'All that's happening to my beloved country. This nightmare came from Washington in the first place, because of its constant bullying and interference. If there hadn't been a Civil War then there wouldn't have been any refugees returning from north of the border, and their offspring wouldn't have brought with them the whole gang culture scene.'

'You're not alone in thinking that. But, of course, it does go deeper, as you now know.'

'I don't believe they are working together, MS-13 and 18th Street. I've never believed it. They hate each other. But I agree, both gangs want to take control of Salvador.'

'I'll ask Hernández about 18th Street—'

Rafael's mobile phone sounded again. 'Here goes...' He made the connection while leaning back into the settee. 'Joaquín Hernández?'

'Rafael Maqui, I'm presuming.'

Rafael was surprised that Hernández's voice sounded different to how he'd imagined in that it came across as being moderately cultured. 'Thanks for your time—'

'As you know, Maqui,' cut in Hernández, 'we're thinking of involving ourselves more in the movie industry. Thought you could give us some insight and leads.'

'As things stand, Joaquín, no chance whatsoever.'

'Oh, yeah? Where are your manners, Maqui?'

'Why would I want to assist a criminal – a criminal whose motto is *Kill, steal, rape, control?*'

'Well, let me see now. I figure we could always take you off the streets, as it were – do it that way. Extract all that's useful and then blow you out.'

'There's another way,' said Rafael, 'but first, put my curiosity to bed. Are you and 18th Street working together?'

'Hey, enough of the wisecracks!'

'Okay, okay. So, MS-13 wants to bring down the government and make Salvador the drug capital of the Americas without 18th Street. Correct?'

'Yeah, why not? Want to join the party? But I was under the impression we'd be discussing MS-13's involvement in the movie industry?'

'We can do that at some point. First, I want to outline something to you.' Rafael gestured for Senica to join him on the settee. 'What I want to share with you, Joaquín, is a straightforward, unarguable fact…that you're being used by higher forces. A ruling elite, if you will. I grant you, you and your MS-13 cronies have power, but nothing like these bastards – who can crush you overnight whenever they choose. When you've served your purpose. Understand me?'

'It's not going to happen in my lifetime. I'm riding high—'

'Sure. In a wholly repulsive fashion—'

'Hey, I can cut this call.'

'No question. But you can make yourself many times greater than you are now – if it's greatness you desire. The procedure is very simple. The worldwide ruling elite need you to cause as much despair and fear as possible, using up resources and generating debt in the process. Governments around the world are falling into disarray, mainly as a consequence of rising debt.' Rafael put his arm around Senica, bringing her closer to himself. 'That's the global stranglehold…insurmountable debt. We're hostages to it – and so is the environment. Nations have basically been conquered by it, including El Salvador. Got me?'

'I got you,' said Hernández. And then an audible chuckle. 'But I tell you, Maqui, this has to be the dumbest phone call I've had in my lifetime.'

'Stay with me. Heard of a country called Séroulé, in West Africa?'

'Just about. There was a coup there a year or so ago.'

'Correct. The interim government is now refusing to pay off its external debt to the creditors, who have basically been robbing the nation for the past six decades. Furthermore, they are going to print that debt and throw every cent at cleaning up the country after the multinationals screwed it for minerals. From what I've heard, three other West African countries are now following suit. So, my question to you is what is so difficult about you no longer attacking the government, but joining forces and *protecting* El Salvador against the absolute evil in this world – debt, and its instigators? No reason to suggest why the policy couldn't spread throughout Central America, with no more bullying tactics from Washington because you'll be a united front, united by social cohesion and by rejuvenating the environment, and in so doing addressing the two thirds decline in wildlife that's arisen over the past fifty years.'

'Shit. You're insane—'

'What makes me insane? I'm telling you, in three months' time a film will be released with the title *Agenda Indiscriminate*. I insist you watch it, then I will talk movies with you. I'll give you contacts, everything you want within my power. I'll give you the release date when it's in the can.'

'It's so insane, I'm intrigued.'

'And I'm guessing you're educated – and somewhere down the line you just got messed up and hooked in. So, do El Salvador a favour, Joaquín…put right the wrong in your life and—'

'Call me with the release date, Maqui. Use the number on your screen.'

The call ended as abruptly as it had begun. Rafael kept his arm around Senica and leaned back into the settee, surprised that he felt so exhausted from the call. 'I think it went better than I thought it would. He actually listened.'

'You did your best,' said Senica. 'In fact, you were very impressive.'

'He's a criminal. A vile one at that.'

'Then it's down to the film. You just have to make it so good. Imagine if both gangs did actually unite, but in a positive way – to safeguard El Salvador alongside the government?'

'Too much to hope for, I think. If Hernández did as we want him to do, the problem then would be a division in MS-13. Some would follow him…others would turn against him. I've no idea what that percentage might be. Imagine if you had no chance of gaining a legitimate livelihood, that all you had been brought up to do was to steal by any means, rape whenever the desire hit you, and so on. Are those people ever likely to change?'

'It's not impossible, Rafael. The film, and hopefully a positive response from viewers, could generate movement in the right direction.'

Rafael stood to stretch his legs. 'The card we have above all others is the environment, because ultimately that's what it'll come down to. The Council's forefathers could never have envisaged the environmental damage their Agenda would generate by corrupting the human spirit for their own gain – as dumb and as absurd as that is.' He noticed the letters she had written on the desk. 'You've been very productive.' He picked up a folded piece of paper that resembled a bird. 'What's this?'

'It's for Jorge. He likes me to make them for him. It's supposed to be a crane. I can't say for sure, but I think in Japanese folklore a thousand paper cranes represents a thousand years of happiness.' Senica took the crane from him, carefully opened its wings and, holding its belly, made it fly towards him until its beak touched his nose.

He smiled with her. 'Will you make me one?'

'We each have to make one, and pass them over.'

Rafael pulled up a chair and sat next to her. 'Before we head over to Hammersmith, teach me how to make a crane. Between us, let's make a start with two years of happiness – not that I feel we need the assistance of paper cranes for that to happen.'

CHAPTER 24

Raoul watched the shaft of light move across the ceiling and then hover almost directly above him. He threw the sheet aside and went to the window. The car below left the apron and sped down the driveway, its tail-lights diminishing into the night. Pensively, he rubbed his hand over his lips. Now that it had happened, he wasn't at all sure whether being left alone was what he wanted.

He had to admit he didn't feel so good these days. It had crossed his mind that his apathy might be the consequence of a virus or an allergy in its infancy. In the morning he would have to ask Dr Kirkbride to drive over, his only concern being that the surgery had a waiting room, and he certainly didn't want the man to bring any germs with him. It had given him scant comfort when the blood test after the incident with the girl had proved negative, since there was always the risk of a mix-up, that her sample might have accidentally been switched with another that was clean of viruses. He hadn't driven the Jaguar since, opting to use his chauffeur or taking Erika's car.

Erika... Why had she gone to such extreme measures? It was ridiculous.

He switched on the bedside lamp and found the remote for the television. Movement, sound, distractions of various kinds floating in on the ether – the Agenda itself hard at work. He flicked through the networks and chanced upon the headlines on a 24-7 news channel, ironically a subsidiary of Loran Communications. Two bombs had been detonated simultaneously in central Paris, killing five people and injuring scores more. Unconfirmed reports were coming in of a massacre in Burkina Faso, while Syria intended to lodge a formal complaint with the United Nations over a border 'misdemeanour' involving three Israeli soldiers.

He left the bedroom and drifted along the corridor, the news channel fading behind him. He tightened his pyjama cord, and for no particular reason made his way down the grand staircase and into the hall, its dark oak panelling portraying lacklustre landscapes by run-of-the-mill Victorian artists. Looking around forlornly, he muttered, 'Here I am, Mama, all alone…' A slight echo rolled away from him, as if his voice sought a response. More than his voice, he supposed: his actual being – or soul, however precisely that could be defined: the hub of his being, presumably. He sat down on a chair, conscious of his apathy and muddled mind. 'A stranger even unto myself, Mama.'

He reached for the note Erika had left for him beside the telephone.

GONE TO LONDON. UNABLE TO LIVE INSIDE THIS SHRINE TO YOUR FATHER A MOMENT LONGER. CALL ME. PLEASE!

Far from her usual eloquent style, the words appeared jagged, each capital letter screaming off the paper at him. He hardly relished the prospect, an untimely disruption from his perspective, but he wondered again whether another child would present Erika with a sense of purpose – fill in the blank, so to speak. And, more importantly, diminish the threat of her becoming the melodramatic loose cannon he so feared.

Raoul looked at the note a while longer. Perhaps ten minutes, perhaps half an hour. But somewhere during that expanse of time he found himself asking whether he was cracking up. Had the persecutor become the victim of his own…duplicity?

Drivel! contradicted his father, his thunderous voice like a detonation inside his skull. *Without guidance and foresight on our part, society would have reverted to barbarism long ago!*

The girl, Sabrina, dove into his mind and, more jarringly, the confrontation with Erika before leaving the Hall that same night.

Neville Cregan was an evil man. Do you know why I think that, Raoul? Because he took the niceness out of you, and now he's taking what's left.

Raoul closed his eyes and recalled what Erika had told him the day Adam died. Had his son really severed him from the photograph they'd had taken in Mexico?

The grandfather clock to his left chimed dutifully, the abrupt commotion jerking him forward as if he were awakening from a hideous dream. It was 2 am. The note slid off his knee, swaying momentarily in mid-air before sweeping to the floor.

Mexico… For sure, nothing had gone right for him since then. Nothing at all.

He left the hall to change quickly out of his pyjamas, consumed by an indefinable compulsion to find the photograph. He went into the kitchen and searched impatiently through the cupboards for a torch but found only a faded packet of candles. He took a box of matches from the same drawer and headed down the back lawn and into Blackthorn Wood. The moonlight came and went with the clouds, and on occasion filtered through the leafless canopy above him. He tried to remember the last time he'd visited the wood. He'd never found it particularly enticing, even as a child, for it seemed to have something of a funereal tone, what with the sycamores and poplars having suffocated the Scots firs, leaving them looking skeletal and apocalyptic. Erika had once said that his father should have planted bluebells and primroses to give the wood some cheer.

Raoul lit a candle to reveal the beginnings of a path to his right. The twigs beneath him fractured loudly, creating eerie echoes that made him catch his breath. He took a handkerchief from his coat pocket to protect his hand from the melting wax, before he came to what he took at first to be a heap of rubbish. Surprised he'd found it with such ease, he looked around the den, positioned against two trees. The roof was Perspex, and the structure itself – made from sacking and lengths of wood – formed a crude rectangle. He should have shown an interest, he realised now. He brushed a cold tear from his eye. A fox screeched nearby. Then a distant reply, after which came a dense silence that crawled over the back of his neck. He stooped and entered the den. There were several tins of fruit and baked beans in a cardboard box, presumably donated by Erika.

What appeared to be a cross – two sticks neatly bound with twine – stood on top of a biscuit tin in the far corner. He leaned towards it – only to recoil in shock, the candle illuminating the remains of a rabbit with a hollow eye socket. His heart thudded and his mouth became bone-dry. He wondered if Adam's intention had been to try to resurrect the animal. Children contemplated and attempted the oddest of endeavours. He reached over the carcass for the biscuit tin, his nerves more jittery than ever, unsure of what he might find next. The lid came cleanly away, to reveal a single item: the photograph taken in Mexico City. Sure enough, he had been torn from it; his son held only his mother's hand.

Raoul left the den and lit another candle to examine the photograph. He'd never noticed before but Adam had an interesting smile, sort of wistful and altogether mature for his age. And Erika looked enchanting, downright attractive, in fact, with those high cheekbones and heart-stopping emerald eyes.

He shivered suddenly against the cold, against the oppressive desolation that now occupied his every waking moment.

'A life broken,' he breathed. He gazed through the wood, towards the Hall…

And then came a thought. A thought altogether shocking, but by the same token so perfectly logical in the way of decency. Or was the truth of the matter that he had now crossed over the border into irreversible insanity?

He brought the candle closer to the photograph. 'Whatever's happening to me, we'll do something together,' he said aloud. 'Something we should have done a long time ago. Just the two of us. Father and son. And we're going do it for your Mother.'

He tucked the photograph in his pocket and made his way out of the wood. The sizable shed he arrived at was hidden from the Hall by a beech hedge. With the shed's windows too narrow for him to climb through, he slammed his foot against the door. Splinters of wood erupted around the padlock, and after two more high-flying kicks the door swung violently inwards. He found the light switch and walked over to a pair of lawnmowers, struck by the fact he no longer felt lethargic. And he wasn't bothered by the dirt on his hands. Indeed, a series of tasks now lay ahead of him, culminating in a make-or-break situation; the repercussions, should he ultimately fail, insufferable beyond words.

He struggled to heave the jerry cans across the lawn and into the laundry room, and from there along a corridor, where the cans banged against the walls. He sat, breathless, on the Windsor chair next to the grandfather clock and stretched his fingers. His arms felt as if they'd been wrenched from their sockets and then rammed back in. Wiping the sweat from his brow, he looked around and recalled how as a child he'd always crossed the hall without a sound, fearful of his father's temper.

The catch on the smaller of the cans showed signs of rust and it took brute force to release it. Paraffin. He hadn't expected this and could only presume it was used to heat the greenhouse. He tipped the fuel onto the parquet floor and watched it surge towards a Caucasus rug. *A healthy reaction against a previous madness*, Raoul told himself rationally – although it did little to stop him from trembling with trepidation. He entered his study, and found he wanted to tear into shreds the portraits of his father and grandfather. He sensed now the absolute trickery with which he'd been alienated from his browbeaten mother, and the vileness of the journey they had set him on, having blinded him with a heady mixture of power and prestige by way of a substructure to instil and nurture mockery and hatred. But as of this moment, he would not permit them to reverse or contaminate the auspicious transition within his grasp. He promptly pulled the catch on the second can which contained petrol and drenched the carpet before sloshing the remainder of the fuel around the drawing room, where just a few months earlier Sergeant Andrews had given him an account of how Adam had died.

Inside the kitchen, away from the inflammable stench and with both empty cans at his side, ready to be removed off-site, he screwed Erika's message into a ball and tried to light it, but his hands shook so much that he had to strike another two matches. When the paper did finally ignite, he tossed it onto the trail of petrol, staring transfixed as the flame bolted like a spirit possessed down the corridor towards his study and from there to the drawing room. A fire sensor began to ping, evolving moments later into an intermittent ear-splitting screech, the manic flames starting to roar, obliterating the area with a stack of smoke in seconds.

He made his exit via the laundry room and walked quickly along the rear of the Hall, desperate to leave before someone called the emergency services. He came out onto the driveway and wondered if he might just be striding through a chaotic dream, accompanied by a cocktail of emotions: exhilaration that he'd kept his courage, seesawing to fear that he'd lost his mind and that the forces of madness were now stalking his inner landscape; his thudding heart, as if in a bid to escape, seemed set to leap from his throat.

He threw the cans into the boot of the Jaguar. With any luck, Ridgeway Hall would be nothing more than smouldering rubble by the time the head gardener arrived. Insurance investigators would be unable to identify the actual cause of the fire, though defective wiring couldn't be ruled out. There again, perhaps he wouldn't bother putting in a claim. On reflection, the head gardener would likely report to the police that two cans of fuel were missing. Because the Hall – surprisingly – wasn't listed, he might just admit he'd disliked it so much that he'd razed it to the ground and intended to donate the land to some just cause... He nodded to himself. The decision to do precisely that prompted a wry smile as he reversed up to the garage – and the metallic-green Peugeot parked inside it.

What the... Raoul's blood froze in horror. He scrambled out of the Jaguar. Sprinting along a path that took him to the heather garden, he looked up. Her bedroom light was definitely on, the window a brightly lit rectangle against an otherwise monolithic black edifice. *But the note...* he reminded himself. *The car disappearing down the drive...*

He tried to think. Petrol down the length of the corridor to the kitchen and laundry room: fast and furious. Paraffin across the hall... Didn't paraffin have a higher flashpoint than petrol, thus initially proving less volatile?

Raoul reached the porch, fumbling with his keys. Their revenge, he told himself above the dread sweeping through him. This was *their* revenge – their wretched souls now on the rampage. He pushed against the studded front door, a wall of acrid smoke virtually flattening him. But he hadn't a choice, he knew that. To die with her was preferable to a future crippled by remorse. He moved inside, goading himself through the clamour of alarms and crackling wood. He lifted the collar on his coat and guessed a minimum of twelve paces to the staircase – which proved to be a miscalculation because, on reaching the ninth, he struck the bottom step, the back of his hand and face catching the blazing balustrade as he stumbled. A sharp explosion over on his right side from the direction of the kitchen suggested a gas pipe had burst. The roar of the flames duly intensified, propelling him through sheer terror towards the landing.

His eyes stinging viciously, he staggered like a drunk into Erika's bedroom.

Erika swung around, both hands clutching a telephone. 'Raoul, there's no connection!' Throwing the phone onto the bed: 'Where the hell have you been? I tried to find you. Have you called the fire service?'

'No—'

'Why not, for God's sake? My mobile – where's my mobile?'

Raoul swayed and tried to steady himself, eyes streaming. 'Forget your mobile...' He started coughing, badly – his lungs barely functioning, as if they'd had cement pumped into them. He struggled to strip the sheets from her bed and gestured for Erika to tie them together. Then he left her for the corridor. For whatever reason, she must have returned to the Hall while he was taking a look at the den... *Don't think about it*, interrupted a separate voice. *She's alive, keep it that way!* Tossing duvets aside in guest rooms, he gathered several more sheets from off the mattresses, when suddenly the lights fused. He swore aloud, the corridor as black as ink. He endured another coughing fit, all the while shifting towards what he took to be moonlight spilling through a doorway.

'Raoul!' Erika cried out.

Raoul reached her and found she'd put on a knitted sweater. 'It's going to be okay,' he told her. He stayed focused on their escape, certain the room was on the verge of collapsing into the inferno below. He closed the door as a defence against the advancing smoke, the noise horrendous, comparable to an ocean liner breaking up in a squall. 'How many sheets?' he asked.

'I took some from a drawer,' Erika shouted above the racket. 'Raoul, this is terrifying! What have we done to deserve all *this*? How could it have started?'

Raoul used a leg on the bed for an anchor and hurled the knotted sheets out of the window, before taking her in his arms. Almost oblivious to the fire, he feverishly ran his lips across her cheek to her ear. 'You're everything to me, Erika. I promise you. Whatever happens to us, never forget that!'

She swept her hair from her eyes. 'What is this? What are you telling me?'

Another thunderous crash, followed by a hefty thump that shook the floorboards. 'Be brave, Erika,' he told her. 'Climb up onto the sill.'

She turned to the window. 'I need a chair, for God's sake.'

Raoul dropped to his knees. 'Use my shoulders.' He felt her struggle, seeing her engagement ring glint briefly against the moonlight when he turned his head, and then she was gone. He found what looked to be a cotton dress on the floor in front of the wardrobe and flung it past her, followed by a pair of shoes, Erika screaming for him to hurry.

His knuckles scraped against the ledge as he came out of the window, fearful that the sheets wouldn't take his weight. He kept himself away from the masonry with his feet and began a controlled descent, until he reached the ground floor, when a fireball burst through the living room's mullioned windows, tossing him into the air and onto a shale path. He rolled over in the shards of glass, dazed, watching Erika move towards him, her screams lost in the clamour around them. He waved her away, and struggled against being winded to escape the burning embers.

'I...I thought you'd left for London?' he told her. He doubled over and caught his breath. 'I noticed the Peugeot...'

'There was an accident on the bypass,' Erika explained in a rush. 'The tailback went for miles.' She gripped his arm with both her hands. 'Raoul, look at the Hall, your grandfather's—'

'To hell with him.'

'What?'

Raoul straightened. 'Later, Erika. We'll talk later. I don't want to be here when the emergency services arrive.' He guided her over to the Jaguar and opened the passenger door.

'What's all this mess across the upholstery?' Erika asked.

'It's blood,' Raoul explained without any thought. 'I should have had it cleaned. I'll cover it over.'

His reply brought a gasp from Erika, before she stepped back from him.

Still catching his breath, Raoul called after her, mystified.

Erika started to bolt. 'What the hell have you gone and *done*?' she screamed. 'Don't... Don't come near me.'

'Erika...' He started towards her.

She wasn't quick enough for him, both of them stumbling onto the grass verge. Raoul was forced to seize her arms.

'Blood,' fought Erika. 'There's *blood*.'

'You don't understand, Erika! A girl tried to kill herself in St Clements. I took her to the hospital—'

A prolonged, strident crackle made them look up at the Hall. Flames were now rocketing through the windows on the first floor, twisting fiercely upwards into the night sky. The Hall seemed ready to implode on itself, like a monster with its back broken and only its death throes to be heard.

'A stunning sight, Erika.' Raoul helped her to her feet. Whatever protests she might have wanted to make were undoubtedly suppressed by the ferocity of the destruction they were now witnessing. 'Awesome. You have to admit that. Completely awesome.'

Erika found her voice. 'We've lost everything. Don't you understand? *Everything!* Trembling, she put her face in her hands. 'I'm so frightened!' But then, by degrees, she lowered her hands, eyes now wide open. 'Raoul… Oh my God, Raoul. You did this, didn't you?'

He brought her back to the car. 'Yes,' he replied simply. 'For us. You and me.' He covered the blood with his coat. 'Somewhat theatrical, maybe. But we're now rid of the place. You can't deny it's what you wanted.'

Erika left the dress on her lap and fell into the seat, exhausted. 'I can't take all this in. I want to, but I just can't!'

'To be honest, Erika, I'm much the same.' Raoul closed the door and glanced back at the Hall. Flames had now fought their way through to the second floor, but had yet to shatter and spiral out of the majority of the windows. It could only be a matter of minutes. Savouring his decisiveness, Raoul walked around the Jaguar to the driver's door. 'We'll take to the minor roads. The motorway might still be blocked.'

* * *

While Raoul drove through the suburbs, Erika put her face back in her hands. He reached across and rubbed her shoulder gently. 'I repeat, Ridgeway Hall's out of our lives for good. I know we haven't Adam with us...'

Tears spilled between her fingers.

Raoul pulled over and parked the car. Taking her in his arms, he said, 'Listen to me, Erika... I need you. All of you. I need to learn from you, from your strength...for you to show me that life is a gift and not something to tear you into a thousand pieces.' He kissed her lips, tasted her salty tears, and then felt himself cast the very essence of his being at the stillness in her eyes. 'I know you're going to have to dig deep to forgive me.'

Erika wiped away her tears with the sleeve of her jumper. 'This is just too bloody surreal, Raoul. I nearly died back there. You nearly *killed* me! And now it's a ruin...'

'But you loathed the place, didn't you?'

'Raoul, I more than loathed living there. It's just that I'm having difficulty taking in all that's happening between us. I mean, what *is* going on? Yesterday I had no reason to exist so far as you were concerned, but now you shower me with these words and gestures of...of affection. You're saying this is genuine?'

'That's exactly what I'm saying. It came to a head when you drove away. I felt just wretched inside...confused, frightened – humbled, I suppose.'

He glanced in the rear-view mirror, saw lights flashing: the driver of a coach wanting him to pull away. He took his hand from her and left the slip road.

Erika ran her fingertips over his blistered jaw. 'I've just noticed. Painful?'

'It's not a problem.' He pulled up at a set of lights.

She looked back at him. 'Tell me about this girl, the girl who tried to kill herself. When did it happen?'

'A couple of weeks ago. After we had that argument. She cut her wrist and I took her to the hospital.'

'Why didn't you say anything about it to me?'

'I've hardly seen you. Seems like we've been avoiding each other. I can't blame you for that.' The lights changed. Raoul came off the bypass to avoid any delays due to the accident, instead taking a countrified route via Wheatley to join the M40. 'I've been so confused,' he said.

'*You're* confused?'

'I've made such a mess of everything. You can't imagine, Erika.' He reached across to her, her willingness to clasp his hand giving him a sense of relief – of hope. But no sooner had he decided on that than an appalling remorse crept over him as he watched himself pull Adam away from the peasant in Chapultepec Park.

I was giving her some of my pocket money. The baby needs food. She kept pointing at the baby's mouth.

You don't give these people money. You don't give anyone *money. Do I make myself clear?*

I hate you. Hate you! You hurt Mummy. You upset her. I really hate *you!*

'Raoul!' shrieked Erika.

The Jaguar slewed across a corner in the lane, his reflexes catching the skid, the offside a hair's breadth from slamming into the bank. The car coasted to a standstill, tears blurring his vision. His hands fell from the wheel, the self-loathing having finally crippled him.

Erika looked at him in dismay. 'Raoul...what's happening? Tell me!'

He rubbed a hand over his brow, his head feeling as if it were about to explode: from guilt over the way he had treated Erika and Adam to fear over the Council of the goddamned Faithful Brethren and the manner of their reaction against him – the punishment to be served for betrayal. 'I've been an unforgivable fool, Erika,' he said. 'Greedy, deceitful, arrogant, a bully to everyone. You deserve a life, and you're not going to get that with me. God's sake, I wish I could say something different to that. But if I'm honest, I can't.'

She caught his wrist. 'Raoul, what exactly has been going on? Are you in some sort of trouble? With the police? Or is it that you've been having…' She looked down at the dress on her lap, her voice barely above a whisper. '…Having an affair? Tell me that's not true.'

He shook his head. 'It might have been easier for you if I had had an affair, but it's none of those things. In a sense, it's far worse.'

Erika's eyes started to blaze. 'Look, you've just demolished Ridgeway Hall single-handedly. You nearly killed me. I *need* an explanation—'

'It's to do with a brotherhood, you could say,' Raoul blurted. He switched off the engine. 'The Council of the Faithful Brethren…'

* * *

They sat in silence, only the breeze to be heard as it toyed with the hedgerow. Raoul looked across at Erika, watching her stare into the night, stunned by what he had told her. 'To say I'm sorry feels absurdly inadequate.'

Her eyes didn't move from the screen. 'I've always been right about your father, haven't I?' she said coldly.

'Yes.'

'When you think about it, it's just revolting.'

'I know it is.

'The suffering…'

'Of course. But what of us, Erika,' urged Raoul. He was now quite afraid, and a part of him regretted planting the idea that he was unfit to be her husband – although it was perfectly obvious after what he had just told her. 'We need to start with us,' he nevertheless persisted, trying to build a case for them to remain together. 'You can have as much time as you need. I meant what I said before we got out of that godawful place…you're everything to me.'

Erika took a deep breath and looked at him. 'I'm not going to leave you, but I can't make that a promise. I just feel…' She turned back to the screen. 'I feel I've been trampled over. That I'm worthless. Been used. Abused. Touched… Touched by an unbelievable evil.' She clenched her hands and there were tears in her wounded eyes. 'Why couldn't I have done something? *Seen* it in some way.'

Raoul cleared his throat, choked up inside at her sense of marital duty to shoulder some of the blame. 'You couldn't possibly have, Erika. In your eyes, I was a successful businessman. Aside, of course, from being a rotten husband, not to mention an inadequate father to Adam.' He risked bringing her hand to his lips. She didn't take it away. 'I came across the photograph. In his den. Adam wanted to protect you from me, Erika. Can you imagine how ashamed that makes me feel? He was eight years old.'

Erika took her hand from him and with shaky fingers wiped the remaining tears off her cheeks. 'Whatever future we do have, Raoul, I think I'd rather you didn't bring that shame into it. That you have recognised and felt it is enough…' She settled back into the seat. 'Please, can we go to London. I'm exhausted, not to mention traumatised.'

Raoul released the handbrake, and only now, as the Jaguar purred forward, could he see the full extent of the unholy mess of a labyrinth that was his soul. He cursed his father and grandfather, wanting to tear them out of his mind, though at least managing to leave their presence behind him in the ashes of Ridgeway Hall and the darkness of the night itself.

CHAPTER 25

Rafael sat by himself with a cup of coffee in the bar at the Rockford Arms, waiting for Marc. They'd used the Buckinghamshire inn on various occasions in the past; it was handy for Pinewood Studios and the Irish landlord, himself a part-time actor, was always the perfect host. Rafael put down his cup and cast another anxious glance at the Guinness clock above the brick fireplace. 7:35, and a challenging day ahead. On the plus side, there was now a tangible sense of relief across both crew and cast that several major scenes had reached the cutting room, including the tricky Underground incident when Saúl Majano rescued Romina from a racist assault on meeting her for the first time. Transport for London had been particularly helpful, allowing them to film at Golders Green from 12:30 a.m. for four hours over two consecutive nights. However, one of the most rewarding aspects of shooting *Agenda Indiscriminate* had come when he'd realised the character of Romina worked best when he allowed her to become synonymous with Senica herself. Predictably enough, when it came to Senica, the overriding difficulty he had was that if a scene went beyond three takes she would invariably begin to 'act' – disastrously so. But with little effort other than the care she was taking to learn and pronounce her lines, she had won the respect of everyone on the set. Moreover, filming the shorter scenes at the outset meant that any retakes caused little disruption to the shooting schedule.

Rafael gazed out of the window with a degree of concern; a distant truck with its hazard lights ablaze was scattering salt onto the snow that had fallen in the night. The wintry weather was something he could have done without, with a bunch of technicians travelling up from London for the day's shoot. He turned from the worrying sight just as his principal cameraman came into the bar.

'I don't believe this weather,' muttered Marc Fauré as he buttoned his duffle coat. 'I tell you, Rafael, when it's like this I'm quite tempted by Central America, despite the machete-wielding crazies! Where's Senica?'

'Liam's bringing her to the studio later on.' Rafael finished his coffee. 'We'd better get going.'

They left the Rockford Arms and headed out towards the village of Iver Heath and Pinewood Studios, Rafael at the wheel. He flicked on the wipers to take some sleet off the screen and smiled as he recalled a particular evening after he and Senica had moved to Hammersmith. While lying in each other's arms on a threadbare settee, listening to Lhasa de Sela and reflecting on the singer's tragic and premature passing, Senica had started to talk of an 'ethereal bond' she had with a ceiba tree that stood behind the cornfield. Between them, they'd come to realise that it was this same tree, with its enormous buttress roots, against which he and Javier had leaned after the makeshift sled had failed them. The revelation had caused Senica to spring to her feet, doubly convinced their union had been initiated by the spirit world of the Maya.

'You know, Marc,' he said aloud, 'it means everything to me, and to Senica, that you and Susan have accepted our relationship.'

'We find her adorable. We're happy for you, *mon ami*. And that is the truth.'

'Even now I find myself pinching myself. But I confess there are occasions when I feel I'm being unfaithful to Lena.'

'Lena's in a different world to this one,' reacted Marc. 'Her generous nature convinces me she would be happy for you, Rafael.'

'It just happened so unexpectedly – and so naturally. Neither of us were looking for a relationship. I certainly wasn't. But then you can't organise fate, can you?'

'Precisely.'

Rafael flicked the wiper switch again and glanced at the rear-view mirror. A blue BMW had caught his eye, throwing up slews of slush in the country lane as it rapidly closed in on them, only to overtake moments before a blind bend.

Marc flinched. '*Merde*, that guy's going to an early grave.'

Rafael felt something stir at the back of his mind. It couldn't be...surely? 'Know what? I reckon I've seen that car before. This same road, perhaps. Last week.'

'Must be a local guy,' said Marc. 'Seems he knows these lanes.'

'Maybe...' Rafael felt threatened suddenly, the overtaking manoeuvre wholly aggressive, as if the driver wanted to force him into a mistake on the treacherous lane; to launch him into a ditch, perhaps, or head-on into a tree. He leaned into the seat, but try as he might he couldn't defuse the tension in his muscles.

* * *

While Rafael and Marc headed out to Pinewood Studios, Raoul Cregan drove through Salzburg towards the Austrian ski resort of Bad Gastein. After some uncertainty, a meeting had finally been arranged with Joshua Waldo. He suspected the delay was not entirely due to the old man's failing health, but more to do with overseeing what would prove itself to be a resourceful assault on the Council of the Faithful Brethren, to which he still belonged. If it weren't for having to protect Waldo, he would have cut his ties by now –

although how the Council might react once he did so was something of a concern to him. Nevertheless, information gathered by the private eye he'd employed suggested Rafael Maqui was unquestionably making a feature film, *not* a series of commercials for a fashionable brand of Latin American coffee, as was being put about in the world of commercial film making. As luck would have it, Jake the assassin was evidently incompetent and had failed on two occasions. *But it'll be third time lucky*, he was reassured before he announced that he wanted the contract on the filmmaker cancelled. The private investigator immediately tried to squeeze another ten thousand pounds out of him by threatening to go ahead and snuff out Maqui's life. He'd cut the call, there and then, after telling the once useful idiot that he wouldn't be receiving a cent more from him. He wasn't going to fall victim to extortion.

Raoul located the partially white-washed Hotel Steinberger and turned into the car park, the snow having been cleared into a mound several metres high at the far end. He parked the rented Saab and, with time to spare, took the opportunity to stretch his legs. Wandering over to a bridge adjacent to the main road, he joined a group of tourists, their cameras and mobile phones focused on the Gasteiner Ache, thundering against giant rocks as it hurtled down the valley. It was an enthralling place to hang out, Raoul decided. Dramatic, for sure. He smiled quietly to himself and left the group. Very Joshua Waldo, in fact.

Inside the hotel's majestic foyer, a series of impeccable watercolours of the valley drew his attention, several of which included skiers as they competed in the Alpen Cup. Engrossed, he started to remove his coat when a voice called his name.

'Mr Cregan?'

Raoul looked over his shoulder.

'I'm Anna Sangster, a close acquaintance of Joshua's.'

Raoul shook the proffered hand. Struck by Anna's perfect poise and the vibrancy she radiated, he imagined how attractive she must have looked in her younger years.

'I was daydreaming,' Raoul explained. He tilted his head at the watercolours. 'Skiing right alongside them.'

Anna smiled. 'It's such a pleasure to meet you at last, Mr Cregan.'

'Thank you. And do call me Raoul.'

'Kind of you to say. Actually, we nearly met around six months ago. I was out of town at the time, visiting an old friend. You lunched with Joshua at Picardi's on East 63rd, as I recall. I remember making the reservation.'

'Indeed. Joshua was typically buoyant, despite the health scare. How is he?'

'Untameable,' said Anna, as though she were complaining to a parent about a rascally child. 'Refuses to slow down.' She took a phone from her suede handbag. 'I'll call him to let him know you've arrived. He's over at the Elisabeth Promenade.'

'How far away is that? If it's not too far, I'd rather like to take in more of the scenery.'

'Of course. Joshua will be delighted.' Anna guided him towards a framed map next to the softly lit receptionist's desk. 'It's just a couple of kilometres. Instead of heading towards Salzburg, turn left at the Mozartplatz and continue along the Kaiser-Franz-Joseph road toward the rail station. You'll see a turning on your right, which leads to the promenade.' She returned the phone to her handbag. 'You're staying over?'

'My schedule's become somewhat inflexible, regrettably,' Raoul explained, putting his coat back on. 'I need to head straight back to London.'

They shook hands. 'Then I wish you a safe and comfortable journey, Raoul,' said Anna.

As Raoul left the foyer, Anna's tender smile lingered with him. He wondered how close Joshua actually was to her, knowing that he'd been a widower for the past fifteen or so years.

* * *

The moment Raoul left, Anna headed for the elevator. Taking a small bottle of sanitizer from her bag, she rubbed the gel vigorously over her hands and felt better for doing so. She'd dreaded shaking Cregan's hand and didn't quite know how she'd gone through with it without retching.

The room that she'd booked herself into was on the third floor, directly opposite Joshua's suite. Though Joshua insisted that she should take a suite whenever they travelled abroad, she saw it as a needless expense. So long as her room had its own bathroom, she was quite content. Closing the door, she opened her travelling case and from a side pouch extracted a brown envelope. The black-and-white photographs it contained were mostly creased and dogeared. The same two people, a man and a woman, appeared in all of them. In one of the photographs the woman held a baby, garbed in linen and lace. The man's eyes and expression showed wholehearted affection for the woman and the baby. Anna turned over this particular photograph, and on the back was written in German:

1936 – The last photograph before Sachsenhausen

Anna wiped away a tear and returned the photographs carefully to the envelope. Taking her cell phone from her handbag, she tapped in a number rather than scrolling through her contacts. Her call was answered almost instantly.

'I still don't have a date,' she said. 'I'm guessing a month to six weeks. You have the money?'

'I asked for an even supply of both dollars and euros,' reacted the male voice, his muffled accent slightly nasal.

'I couldn't get the amount you requested in euros in time.' Though Anna suspected the man was disguising his voice by some means, she thought she detected a trace of Irish and wondered if his roots were in South Boston. 'Sixty-forty is still a reasonable ratio, don't you think?' She was somewhat irritated that he should complain. 'Is Switzerland complete?'

'Complete.'

'Santa Monica?'

'Complete. Text me when you have the date. We will not speak again.'

The line was cut. Anna returned the cell phone to her handbag. So, now she had a gun in California and another in Geneva. Just New York to go. Better to cover all fronts, despite the outrageous cost involved.

Raoul Cregan, though? She headed back down the corridor to the elevator. That had been an unexpected intrusion. Why in all the world would Joshua want to talk to that monster of a being? It made no sense – no sense at all!

* * *

Raoul pulled up next to a taxi in an otherwise deserted car park. The driver looked briefly across at him before putting his head back against the seat. Raoul left the Saab and fastened his overcoat, noticing the Gasteiner's current to be more leisurely than it was lower down the valley. He cast his gaze beyond the river and imagined the summer months here, with an array of wild flowers, the skiers replaced by cattle grazing on the foothills, the cerulean sky unchanged. Perhaps he might even bring Erika here for a short vacation. She hadn't left him, as he had feared she might. Indeed, he felt the issue of them still sleeping apart would shortly be resolved, perhaps by nothing more than a cosy fireside meal.

He eyed the snow-compacted path that followed the river with a degree of caution, not least because of the figure sitting on a bench up ahead of him gazing into the middle distance. He realised now how his relationship with Joshua Waldo had really been: that he had loathed him out of envy – envy of his strength and ability to remain a decent man within what was generally considered to be a ruthless, power-crazed environment. He couldn't resist a private smile. What a dance the old fox had led the Council!

'Joshua,' he said, arriving at the bench, doubting his host was at all pleased to see him. He had likely felt obliged to go through with it to maintain his cover with his 'European counterpart'.

Joshua adjusted his alpaca scarf, drawing it up to his fleshy chin, and reached for his cane. He started to leave the rough-hewn bench, quick to dismiss with a flick of his hand Raoul's plea for him to remain seated.

'Good trip?' Joshua asked, his voice typically guttural – gruffly so, to those who were not used to it.

'Very.' Contrary to his hunch, Raoul found the handshake to be enthusiastic.

Joshua swung the cane with militaristic precision at an imposing, distinctly angular mountain. 'Hoher Stuhl…two thousand three hundred metres in height. While to our left stands Graukogel. And behind us…right there, Stubnerkogel. She broke my leg in three places and taught me never to play to the gallery while on skis.' He picked up his phone from the bench and sat down, beckoning Raoul to join him.

'Erika sends her best,' Raoul said.

'She's coping?'

'More or less. Day at a time, you know? Barely four months have passed since Adam was taken from us.'

'Yes, indeed.'

'They were very close.'

'I can imagine…' Joshua's remark hung in the air, but not in a judgemental or barbed way. A spontaneous reaction, laden with characteristic solicitude. He settled his cane against the seat. 'So, Raoul, what brings you to Bad Gastein?'

Raoul leaned forward, and reminded himself to choose his words wisely. 'I happened to be more or less passing through, so I took the opportunity to make the detour to see you. I know your health isn't up to scratch. God's sake, I wish it were.' He found he needed to stand up. Putting his hands in his pockets, he started to pace back and forth on the compacted snow. It dawned on him that he'd scarcely prepared himself for how to bring the topic of Rafael Maqui into the conversation. Some peripheral gestures first, perhaps.

'Truth is,' he ventured, 'this might well be the last occasion we get to see each other. Right now, I'm up to my neck in it, and as for yourself…well, undoubtedly you have issues that need to be…resolved, shall we say.'

Joshua patted the bench. 'Raoul, your pacing – it's making me giddy!' Raoul settled once again beside him. 'I'm touched,' Joshua said finally. 'Touched by your words and that you found time to make the detour.' Almost imperceptibly, his lips quivered, as if he were struggling to contain the wryest of smiles. 'And as for business?'

'Business?'

'There's always something.'

Raoul nodded. 'Business…' he repeated warily, for it felt as if Joshua had started to circle him, waiting for the moment to take him apart. He needed to be careful and, above all, subtle – ambiguous, even. 'Nothing that comes specifically to mind.' Then by chance he recalled an authorisation he'd signed earlier in the year. 'Unless, that is, you're interested in a five-part series that Sarron recently purchased from a crew we occasionally deal with. It simply highlights whether the United Nations should directly intervene to try and quell the campesinos' uprising in southern Mexico. Also, this ongoing miserable disruption across the Middle East with its tiresome conflicts. The UN evidently requires more troops, particularly in view of the fact people are starting to talk of the organisation as having lost its way.'

Joshua chuckled dryly, and when he spoke his tone was just as derisive. 'The age-old ploy to gain more power – eh, Raoul? The UN's hardly a lame duck at all.' He swung around to meet Raoul's bemused expression. 'You're welcome to send it to Loran, but enough of this charade. You've come here to ask me about Rafael Maqui, haven't you?'

Raoul turned away, unable to tolerate Joshua's chilling gaze, which seemed to penetrate the intimate depths of his being and strip his psyche naked – leaving him standing, as it were, with his trunks off and the tide having rolled out. 'Okay…' he sighed. He suspected the crafty devil had been ten paces ahead of him all along. 'You've disarmed me. But as hard as it might be for you to believe, I come to you as an ally, not as your enemy.'

'I'm quite aware of that,' Joshua remarked. And then the knowing smile finally showed itself. 'Do you think I would have bothered to have seen you? Or that I would have mentioned Maqui in the way that I just did? Of course not. Ridgeway Hall in Oxfordshire reduced to ashes a couple of months or so after the tragic loss of your son. Hardly a coincidence – particularly when I know, even if you haven't yet admitted it to yourself, that you've been struggling with your conscience for years.'

Raoul hunched forward and clasped his hands together, an almost greater sense of liberation welling up through him than he'd experienced with Erika, for he was admitting his guilt to a man who already knew he was – or had been – complicit in perpetrating hell on earth to make absolute the Agenda, mocking all satellite governments while promoting the expansion of the United Nations into a Universal Government. 'Is there anything you don't know about me, Joshua?' he asked with a submissive shake of his head.

'I think you've come here to deliver me a warning,' Joshua prompted out of the blue. 'But I don't know its exact nature. I'm interested, obviously.'

Raoul straightened and cleared the emotion from his throat, seeing suddenly that Joshua had definitely lost weight, his cheeks having something of a pinched look. He put his hands back in his pockets. 'Make of it what you will, but there's a meeting of the Inner Council on the twelfth of April, which I might be asked to attend. Although I congratulate you on the game you've played, maintaining the deception in your newsrooms, and never expressing in-depth alarm over fiscal procedures, et cetera, questions concerning Loran Communications could be raised – and not for the first time. You're an outsider, and naturally the Council's paranoia knows no bounds when it comes to outsiders.'

Joshua made another adjustment to his scarf, drawing it tighter to himself. 'How I would like to be a fly on the wall for that get-together. As a matter of interest, how did *you* get onto me?'

'You overdid it,' shrugged Raoul. 'You accepted, without question, the Council's unwritten code of conduct regarding trends and so-called free speech, promoting detrimental aspects of both in subliminal formats, shaped on the whole for the younger generations to adhere to, and in so doing activate rallies and flare-ups of anarchy. My peers reacted in exactly the way you wanted them to react. So comfortable with you were they that you slipped off the radar.' He turned to face his host. 'But I suspected you might be protecting something, protecting an objective of sorts. Not forgetting, of course, your father's rumoured meetings with the French Foreign Affairs Minister and turncoat, Hubert Séguy. So, I started to dig, and came across Maqui, for starters.'

'I see. It was you who put that private investigator into an apartment on East 81st?'

'How did you find out?'

'His lens kept catching the sun.'

'I never met him.' Raoul tried instinctively to salvage some credibility until he realised that in this instance it was a pointless exercise. 'Something of an amateur, I've since discovered.'

'What's happening with Sarron?'

'I'm there to protect you, that's all.' Raoul started to speak earnestly. 'So, I'm asking you to make the date of release no later than the eleventh. It would be in both our interests. I really don't relish attending that meeting on the twelfth.'

Joshua gave no direct reply, just a moment's apparent thought in the form of a gaze in the direction of several skiers sweeping down Graukogel. He reached for his cane. 'Are you staying overnight?'

Raoul studied his watch. 'Unfortunately not. I'm needed back in London, which means I must make a move.'

'A lift back to the hotel?'

'Certainly.'

Joshua hauled himself up from the seat. 'In that case, I'll pay off the taxi.'

* * *

Several minutes after he'd dropped Joshua off at the Hotel Steinberger, Raoul parked the Saab on the road leading to Salzburg. He climbed out and walked over to the verge. With dusk set to fall, the town of Bad Gastein and its spirited river far below him resembled a jewel-encrusted ornament set in cotton wool.

He lifted his gaze towards the mountain introduced to him as Graukogel, as silent in appearance as it was formidable. He now believed, with absolute clarity, that if Joshua Waldo succeeded in exposing the Council of the Faithful Brethren and its programme to enslave the people of the world, then such a state of affairs would never be repeated, the lesson to humankind learnt once and for all.

He returned to the Saab. What to do with the Sarron News Agency, though? Once the organisation had exhaustively promoted Rafael Maqui's screenplay, it could rot in a ditch, as far as he was concerned. In truth, though, he would likely break it up into segments, a comprehensive contract forbidding the subdivisions from reforming, and then leave London for a more agreeable climate, a viewpoint he instinctively knew Erika wouldn't be averse to realising.

Raoul turned the ignition key, appalled with himself for even contemplating the idea of having Maqui assassinated. If only he'd had a father like Joshua Waldo. That said, at least he was driving away from Bad Gastein with a slightly lighter conscience.

CHAPTER 26

Rafael climbed out of the passenger seat, Marc having on this occasion taken the wheel on the journey from the Rockford Arms to Pinewood Studios. They walked between two medium-sized stages, past the Stanley Kubrick Building, towards the monolithic Albert R. Broccoli 007 Stage – twice resurrected, on both occasions as a consequence of fire.

'You've spoken to Joshua about Cregan?' Marc asked, putting the Mazda's key in his coat pocket.

'Last night. He's adamant. So, definitely no Raoul Cregan lookalike.' Rafael checked his mobile phone for incoming texts. 'I just don't get it, Marc. The wretched man's a purveyor of fear and misery – and far worse. But the fact is, when you think back, Joshua's been against the idea all along.'

'What about this date of release – eleventh of April. A fortnight ahead of schedule? It's going to cause bedlam with post-production.'

'Don't remind me.' Rafael grimaced at the thought. 'If I had the time, I'd go to Austria and assess Joshua's state of mind. For the last week, he's done little more than talk in riddles—'

From behind them came the abrupt squeal of rubber on asphalt. They turned together, instinctively.

'The BMW!' Rafael breathed.

'Again!' Marc threw himself against the wall of the 007 Stage.

Rafael did likewise, the entrance yards from them.

The blue BMW continued its charge, all but grazing Rafael as it departed Broccoli Road for 007 Drive and a maze of TV studios, workshops and office buildings.

Marc had the Mazda's key in his hand. 'He's heading for the gatehouse.'

'Marc, wait!' Rafael scrabbled to enter the BMW's registration number into his mobile phone. 'I'll call the gatehouse. What's the number?'

'Hell, no idea. We need to get after him!'

'No. Wait a sec.' Rafael called Pinewood Studios directly with a view to being patched through to the gatehouse. He was greeted by a pre-recorded announcement informing him that reception opened at 8:00 a.m. He looked at his watch: 7:50.

Marc had reached the Mazda. 'We're wasting time!'

'Forget it.' Rafael put the phone away in his pocket. 'It's our last day – and the most crucial. If we trigger a car chase around these buildings the police will investigate and we'll have to deal with their enquiries.'

Marc looked in the direction of the gatehouse. He heaved a sigh and slammed the car door shut. 'He's probably already out of here.'

'I'll call Liam,' Rafael said. 'Greg was on duty at the gatehouse when we came through. Ask him what excuse this maniac gave to get inside the place.'

'They'll have him on CCTV.' Marc set off towards the gatehouse to interrogate the duty keeper.

Rafael scrolled for Liam's number before looking up from his phone. 'Marc!' he called. 'Tell Greg we've got a stalker, or something. We need security. Outside the stage, not inside. We can't have anyone inside during the take.'

Liam answered the call.

'Liam, where are you?'

'With Senica, waiting to hear from Juana… You okay? Anything the matter?'

'It's happened again.'

'What's happened again?'

'The blue BMW.' Rafael made his way to the stage door. 'Inside the studios.'

'*Inside?*'

'He was waiting for us. Just missed me. I can't work out whether he's trying to unnerve me, or actually kill me.'

'Is he still inside the complex?'

'Doubt it. Marc's gone to speak to the gatehouse keeper. Point is, you need to be vigilant when you bring Senica in. Have her lie down across the rear seats the moment you leave the Rockford Arms.'

'Did you get a clear view of him?'

'No. It happened so quickly. Everything was just a blur.'

'Registration number?'

'Yes.' Rafael uploaded it from his phone's notebook. 'Not a hundred per cent sure whether the last letter was C or D. I think is was D.'

'I'll check it out.'

'How, exactly?'

'Friend of a friend, et cetera.' Liam paused for a second. 'Ironic, isn't it?'

'What is?'

'You, housed up in the 007 Stage. If Bond was there, he'd be in a 'copter by now, chasing down the guy—'

'Liam, no wisecracks.' Rafael pushed on a side door and entered the stage, dwarfed by its vastness. 'Bad timing, okay?'

'I'll do the plate check,' confirmed Liam. 'Senica wants a word.'

'Put her on…'

'Rafael!' came Senica's voice in a rush. 'Oh, Rafael, what does this crazy man *want* with us?'

'I don't know, Senica.' He walked past a dummy Arriflex camera that was to feature in the upcoming scene. 'It makes no sense. Look…I need to speak to Doug right now. We'll talk when Liam brings you in.'

He silenced his phone. James Bond, indeed. Although there was no denying that Liam's quip had given him a moment's respite from the drama. But *could* it really be the case? That the driver wanted to kill him rather than unnerve him for whatever reason? Either way, it just didn't add up. *Four* attempts now!

* * *

Rafael closed the door to the trailer parked up in a corner of the stage. He forced the morning's bizarre incident to the back of his mind and greeted Doug Silberman, production designer turned actor for the day, set to portray the British Foreign Secretary, Anthony McCormac. While a makeup artist deftly highlighted Doug's eyebrows, Rafael pulled up a chair and quietly discussed the speech 'McCormac' was to deliver to the Inner Council of the Faithful Brethren, a speech penned by Joshua Waldo himself.

'Since the rehearsal, Doug, I've come up with something a shade different for the opening sequence. As it stands, I feel the transition from filming the crew to filming the speech is too abrupt. The audience will take fifteen or more seconds to adjust, so the first paragraph will be effectively wasted.'

'A drift-in, as it were,' Doug mused out of the corner of his mouth, unable to move, the makeup artist continuing to work her magic. 'In retrospect it felt to be quite a jolt at the rehearsal.

Presumably you're after a single take?'

'Ideally. But going back to the switch. Imagine the camera decides there's something more "entertaining" going on than watching myself and Marc talking shop. With Lena's bass guitarist, Jeff Layton, responsible for the score, I'm going to have him create an eerie inhalation throughout the transition…starting faint, coming on strong, and then fading as the lens finds itself drawn into the speech you're delivering.'

The makeup artist reached for a comb, allowing Doug to glance at Rafael. 'Let's go for that. It's a wrap in my head already, for Christ's sake.'

'That's how I see it, too.' Rafael went over to the door. 'Speak to you on the set.' Bolstered by Doug's approval, he left the trailer and followed a rivulet of cables that meandered towards Marc, who was quietly discussing a point with his boyish-faced assistant, Gerald Davey.

'Doug's in agreement,' Rafael interrupted. 'Gerald, excuse us both for a moment.'

He walked with Marc back towards the trailer. 'What did Greg have to say?' he asked.

'You're not going to believe it,' said Marc.

'Try me.'

'Andy was on duty yesterday at the gatehouse.'

'I remember.'

'Greg said you left a message with Andy, to tell him – Greg, that is – that a blue BMW would arrive around seven o'clock to deliver a Taylor Hobson lens for today's take. The name of the driver you gave Andy was Laurence Peterson. Greg phoned Andy at home, and Andy confirmed that he did receive such a message from your PA.'

'My PA?' Rafael grew incredulous. 'But I don't have a personal assistant. Neither of us do. This guy has to be working for a total screwball!'

'That's if he has a client,' said Marc. 'We have a description, if you can call it that.'

Rafael raised an eyebrow. 'A description?'

'Black hair, late-twenties and, according to Greg, a well-to-do accent.' Marc glanced at Gerald, who continued to run checks on the lead Arriflex camera. Turning back to Rafael, his brown eyes showed an even deeper concern. 'I don't want to say this…'

'Say what, exactly?' asked Rafael.

'Is this some kind of an elaborate set-up by Joshua? You know how paranoid he is.'

'I don't follow…'

'What have we just done? What have we been doing all along, ever since this psycho arrived on the scene?'

'I still don't follow,' Rafael insisted, impatient.

'We've intensified security, haven't we? Greg's going to speak to his supervisor to fix us up with more personnel, positioning them around this stage throughout what happens to be the final and most crucial – not to mention politically scandalous – take in the entire production.'

'But if you're saying that,' argued Rafael, 'then you might just as well be saying Liam could be a part of it, too.' He shook his head, his conscience swamped with remorse for even giving the theory a moment's thought. 'Joshua would be straight with us. Besides, on the first two occasions this individual came within a hair's breadth of wiping me out. Too risky, by far.'

Marc shrugged. 'Maybe. I just don't get what this guy is trying to achieve.'

'To kill me, by the looks of things,' Rafael interjected bluntly.

'Rather than Joshua being involved, I'm wondering if there's a connection here with Lena.'

'Stephen Briggs was obsessed with her,' countered Marc. 'A loner – a loner who took his own life, and so no longer exists.'

'Okay,' shrugged Rafael. 'So, not Lena.' He looked at his cameraman. 'Marc, I'm going for a short walk to try and clear my head.'

He set off to walk the length of the stage, a distance of over a hundred metres. Senica was now his main concern. If anything happened to her, his life would more or less be over. He'd become a recluse, perhaps… No, not perhaps. Very likely. Life just wouldn't be worth living. There was a chance he'd wind up permanently in Central America, little more than a drifter. He found himself nodding, which shocked him.

He about-turned. The walk wasn't working!

* * *

Later that same morning, Raoul entered the Sarron News Agency on Grosvenor Place. He raised a cordial hand to the receptionist before subconsciously casting a glance at the portraits of his father and grandfather above her desk. Maintaining the fitness routine he had followed for the past sixteen years, he avoided the elevator and took the stairs. As he approached the second flight, the two portraits refused to shift from his mind's eye, as did the foyer itself. It had never struck him before, but there was something Stalinesque about its starkness, emphasised further by the size and centre-stage positioning of the rather surly-looking portraits. Before Adam's death, he'd revered his father and grandfather, privately envious of their unequivocal influence in the City and way beyond – which, from taking ownership of the Sarron News Agency, he'd never quite managed to emulate, much less have any hope of surpassing. But there was not a morsel of envy in him today, and neither would there ever be in the future!

He reached his office and the mobile phone in his desk that he'd used solely to contact the private investigator. It had occurred to him on the journey in to get rid of it. Taking it from the bottom drawer, he discovered it still had £20.57 credit. After deleting all personal data, which amounted to virtually nothing, he would perhaps hand the Samsung over to his chauffeur, Frank Jackson, who would surely welcome both the phone and its remaining credit... Raoul abruptly leaned forward to take a closer look at the screen: there appeared to be a message, sent barely an hour ago. Curious, he opened it, the agreeable mood he found himself to be in rapidly diminishing.

25K OR HE GETS IT!

Raoul swallowed. There was an attachment – a video. At first, as he ran it, he couldn't see the significance. A camera had evidently been fixed to the car's dashboard as it raced between warehouse-styled buildings, similar to an industrial estate. Then two men had to dash for their lives as the car skimmed past them. Seconds later, the video came to an abrupt end.

Raoul leaned back, taking the mobile phone with him. *The little shit!* he told himself. More to the point, how was he going to play this? If he handed over the twenty-five thousand pounds, it would simply encourage the wretched man to keep coming after him for more money. He could, he supposed, put some money in a bag and adopt the same procedure as before by buying a bicycle with panniers, heavily camouflage himself with a cap, scarf and overcoat, then park the bike in some street, wait for the cretin to collect it and physically challenge him. But that could end badly, what with street cameras and witnesses all over the place.

An idea came to him that might possibly work, the only flaw being the off-chance of the man asking him what he happened to be wearing on the day he collected the first payment – because, of course, he'd stupidly left the scene the moment he'd parked the bike without waiting to gather any information about him, such as taking a discreet photograph of him with his phone.

Raoul took a deep breath and dialled the number. He was going to have to take the risk.

'Yeah?'

Despite the sloppy attitude that he was now perfectly familiar with, Raoul found himself to be more than relieved that contact had been made. 'So…I've received your message.'

'Oh, got to say, nice and prompt call-back.' The private investigator's voice brimmed with confidence.

'You don't recall me telling you to terminate the contract?'

'Yeah, but come on – you've got lots of dosh, haven't you? Share and share alike, you know? A little generosity…'

The investigator's chirpy tone with its menacing undercurrent effectively intensified Raoul's already anxious state. He wasn't used to handling this kind of an individual. Nevertheless, he still went for the bluff. That was all he *could* do. 'Listen carefully… You remember the day you collected the first instalment from the bicycle pannier on Shelton Street?'

'We can do it that way again—'

'You don't think I was foolish enough not to have taken some footage of you, do you?'

'Bullshit!'

'Well, you're going to be taking a hell of a risk if you start messing me around or threatening me. You're right, I am certainly wealthy. Wealthier than you could ever imagine. I should also inform you that as well as knowing people in high places, both in government and in industry, I'm actually in the mainstream media business. With the police no doubt keen to interview you for past crimes, I can have a picture of you, while maintaining my anonymity, on the front page of any national newspaper I so wish within hours—'

'Hey…hey, can't you take a joke? Just a bit of fun, that's all it—'

'Anything happens to Maqui and you're on the front page.' The bluff, he felt, was working beautifully. 'And if by chance it wasn't you collecting the money, then it will be your co-conspirator who ends up on the front page.'

With that, Raoul cut the call. He was confident that Rafael Maqui was now safe, certainly from the fortunately incompetent 'Jake the assassin'.

CHAPTER 27

As the time approached midday, those technicians over at Pinewood Studios who had volunteered to put on suits and be in the forthcoming scene assembled in the vicinity of a sizeable conference table, its light shade of beech set against a backdrop of jade and moss-green flock wallpaper. Standing back from them, Rafael ran his eye quietly over the four separate LED-lit screens that flanked the table; each screen was primed to show muted Loran News footage of a heavyweight from within the Council of the Faithful Brethren.

Rafael compared the photograph of the current UK Foreign Secretary he'd downloaded from the Commonwealth Office website against that of his production designer, Doug Silberman, seated at the head of the table. The transformation was remarkable, uncanny to the point that he felt the back of his neck tingle – the emergence of Silberman's double chin identical with the portrait he was holding. He moved closer to the table to speak to the Spanish makeup artist directly involved, her T-shirt causing him to smile:

I speak Basque
What's your Superpower?

'Itziar, I want you on my next picture. The location will be far from Basque Country and might well be Central America, so apologies in advance.'

The heads-up made Itziar laugh. 'Anything to get away from this weather!' she said, plainly delighted that her morning's work was considered a triumph.

Rafael turned to his principal actor for the scene. 'So, Doug, keep me up to speed on what's running through your mind?'

'Nervous as a cat in a room full of rocking chairs, I'd say,' answered Doug with a blunt shake of his head. 'Or a whore in a church. Take your pick!'

'Don't worry. We'll capture more than enough material off the remote cameras to splice, should the need arise. Just remember to stare in a rather hostile way, blinking as little as possible.'

Doug tapped the script. 'Where did the bare bones of this demented material come from? Lucifer himself, by the looks of it! I remember you mentioning something about our producer having received it in some form or another.'

Rafael saw no harm in Doug knowing the facts as he knew them, as limited as they were. 'According to our producer, a B-25 Mitchell bomber came down in Romania towards the end of the Second World War. The producer penned the speech using material taken from a folder discovered in the wreckage...' He caught sight of Senica and Liam, and breathed a sigh of relief that they'd arrived without apparent incident. 'I'll be back with you in a moment, Doug,' he said, leaving the platform.

Liam came towards him. 'The registration number tallies with a BMW, but not the BMW in question.'

'How reliable is your source?' Rafael asked, standing next to Senica.

'Inside the Met.'

'Okay, tell me more.'

'The number originates from a green BMW written off in a fatal accident on the M5 last February.'

Rafael nodded. 'I figure it doesn't get us anywhere, but Marc would appreciate the update. I need to talk Senica through the take.' With that he guided her away from the growing activity around the set.

'This is so disturbing, Rafael.' Senica's voice was a frantic whisper.

'I know, but we're just going to have to block it from our minds.' And in an attempt to achieve precisely that, and to divert her thoughts, Rafael said, 'I've come up with a solution to mend fences with Jorge, for taking you away from him.'

'I'm intrigued. Tell me more.'

'It's something I dreamed of doing as a child, had my father been there for me. Simply, to take Jorge into the bush for a week or two – fishing, outdoor craft, et cetera.'

Senica looked across at him and seized his arm. 'He'll love it!'

'Let's hope it does the trick.' They drifted past an Arriflex camera that was to feature as a prop. 'As for now, to business,' Rafael said. 'This is how it goes… When I show the photographs of the key players inside the Council to Marc, you say: "Let me look." Our remarks make you curious. Okay?'

'Yes.' She tucked her hands into her jeans. 'And this is the scene where Liam puts in another appearance?'

'He's going to bring me the photographs. That's all. Remember, the speech is your dream. Or more precisely, daydream. So, the last shot will be a close-up of you holding the photograph of the British Foreign Secretary before the lens focuses on Doug – or rather, Anthony McCormac.'

Marc joined them. 'The remote cameras are live. Gerald's in position on the lead – the individual footage for each of the four ancillary screens set to roll.'

* * *

Rafael gazed through the diffused lighting at the platform. His eight volunteers were now seated at the table, immersed in a dusky wrap-around shadow, their heads turned towards the ninth volunteer, Doug Silberman, the arrangement in effect masking their identities.

'Doug?' he called.

'Go for it,' Doug hollered back. 'Before I fall apart at the ruddy seams.'

'On your feet, then.' His pulse thumping with adrenaline, Rafael swung around. 'Gerald, it's with you.'

'Stand ready,' instructed Marc's assistant. The absolute hush that fell across the stage seemed to last an age, until punctuated by Gerald with the familiar words: 'Three...two...one... Turning over.'

Marc faked an adjustment to the lens on the prop camera. 'I reckon a medium close-up on both yourself and Romina would suffice, before receding into the hallway.'

'I see it that way, too.' Rafael folded his arms: a cue for Liam to join them on the set.

'The courier's delivered the photographs,' Liam notified briskly. 'All five.'

Marc left the Arriflex camera and waited for Rafael to open the envelope – and in so doing, to reveal the identities of those who were set to occupy, by way of muted Loran News footage, the ancillary screens presently off-camera.

'Carl Dürrenmatt,' announced Rafael, holding a photograph of a man with close-set eyes whose dour expression suggested he was perpetually in a foul mood. He handed the picture to Marc. 'The Council of the Faithful Brethren's central warlord, you could say. He sits between the eight who chose him – according to our producer.'

Senica came and stood alongside Marc. 'Let me look.'

'Frederick Weiss,' continued Rafael, taking all the photographs from the envelope. 'Best described as the Council's media guru. Here, we have Luciano Corsi, Italy's Defence Minister before he became Finance Minister for Europe. And this one's Pierre Dumas, strategist – rarely seen but nevertheless a key figure within the Council.' He presented his cameraman with the final photograph. 'Anthony McCormac, currently the British Foreign Secretary.'

Out of view behind the operational Arriflex camera, Gerald Davey lifted his right hand, informing Rafael he was ready to focus directly on Senica and the launch of Romina's daydream.

'Imagine them shown for what they are,' said Marc as he passed the photograph of McCormac to Senica and quietly slipped away from her, moving with Rafael in the direction of the prop camera. 'Their depravity,' he continued, 'measured by the extent to which they have perverted the gift of life itself...'

'...Though our destiny is assured,' proclaimed Anthony McCormac, putting a half-filled glass of water down on the table, 'it will be achieved in a more expedient way if the people themselves demand our intervention. Even the most unobservant eye can hardly fail to notice they are worn down, and division coupled with fear and perpetual misery has not unnaturally directed the people into criticising their governments. Before long, these same people will be saying, "We need a world authority to prevent this constant ineptitude!" And that world authority, of course, is now in place – for have we not finally taken control of the United Nations? Indeed, we have!

'Apart from struggling to pay their debts, the resources of the governments will be further strained by their vain attempts to quell the violence we have nurtured into a living nightmare. Not until they fall to their knees, pleading for a universal government to put an end to the misery, will we say to the people: "What dreadful happenings. Such discontent! We will sweep aside all borders, outlaw alcohol, gambling and pornography in any shape or form, erase all state debts: indeed, we

will rid you of all that has caused you anguish." From that moment, we will slay where necessary – and, most importantly, without mercy. Should any sect rise up against us it will make the fundamental error of doing so with violence, and will be no match against our troops and weaponry. Unless useful for the purpose of propaganda, such insurrections will go unreported, thereby preventing a coordinated response from those who dare to obstruct us.

"There are, of course, those who know and those who think they know why the world is in turmoil. The latter are only too keen to spout forth their fanciful remedies, while those who know our every move, a fraction in comparison, find themselves unable to make any impression, since the former group, in tandem with the governments, have so demoralised the people with their dreary, repetitive sermons that such an individual will invariably witness his words falling on deaf ears.

'Thus, by creating bewilderment, division and fear, we will cause the total destruction of the present world order, and by distortion and deceit tear out the roots from which that order grew, leaving a clear field in which to plant our own ideology, which we shall maintain and sustain with the iron grip of brutal force.

'In summary, I remind you that our central strategy requires immediate and significant adjustments. Our forefathers could never have predicted the warming of the planet and the advancement of climate change. Our scientists have now proven beyond doubt that it is a troublesome reality. Needless to say, we must maintain our control on credit, global debt being the ultimate lever that will present us with our prize. This comprehensive debt, which we have wisely nurtured from the moment we acquired the Templars crude blueprint, will remain in place until the entire power of every nation has been vanquished. To reverse the issue of climate change will require a programme of depopulation, by all means possible – whether it be as a consequence of conventional warfare, tenacious virus mutations, or indeed multiple nuclear strikes with retaliatory responses – the ramifications of which will have the added advantage of shocking the global population into accepting a World Government with open arms. In addition, by instilling precise targets laid down by science, we can calibrate

debt payments solely for the purpose of reversing climate change. By introducing severe penalties if a government should deviate from our instructions, we will thus remain in supreme control of our destiny.

"*Understandably, those few and far between economists who talk of a fiscal dividend interdisciplinary and distributive policy, and how it could ultimately cure both societal and environmental concerns, must remain side-lined from discussing their opinions in the media – whether mainstream, or otherwise.*'

* * *

While the screens continued to run silent footage of those named in the photographs, Rafael slipped away from the set, the applause fading as he walked down the stage towards a pair of elephant doors. There would be no second take. Doug Silberman's performance had outstripped the acceptable target he had set himself.

Some fifty yards away from the vociferous relief over a successful afternoon's work, Rafael sat on the doorstep of the Victorian house where Romina had lived, its hallway, staircase with threadbare carpet and the first-floor bedsit propped up by scaffolding. He reached for his mobile phone and made the call he was expected to make.

'Hi there, Anna. How's it going with you?'

'Rafael, my dear, we're okay. We're heading back out to Switzerland tomorrow.'

'He'll like that, Anna. The air seems to do him wonders.'

'He's right beside me – champing at the bit, as they say. I'll hand you over.'

Moments later, and after what Rafael presumed to be a slight coughing fit from Joshua: 'Rafael?'

'Hi, Joshua. You okay?'

'A sip of water went the wrong way.'

'Oh, right. Anyway, we're done, Joshua. Just the wrap-up in post-production.'

'You don't think the speech is too short?'

'Not at all.' Rafael looked back at the set. Marc and Gerald were packing away the Arriflex cameras. 'As I've mentioned to you before, it's not only what Anthony McCormac is saying that's relevant, but the images on the four screens flanking him are just so arresting. When it comes to Dumas and Dürrenmatt in particular, the media will have no option but to scrutinise their every move from the moment the film is screened. As you, yourself, once mentioned: a case of supply and demand.'

'This is my hope, Rafael.'

'It's guaranteed, taking into account the conversations relating to the Brethren and their Agenda between the characters throughout much of the screenplay. Incidentally, the makeup artist did a terrific job on my production designer in transforming him into McCormac. You wouldn't know the difference.'

'And that's a fact? It's just so vital…'

'I'll get the rushes over to you as soon as I can. Anyway, Joshua, I'll leave you in peace. Just wanted you to know, nothing could be better.'

Rafael ended the call and started to make his way back to the set.

Nothing could be better.

Fact was, with the driver in the blue BMW still on the loose, he felt for the most part downright lousy, knowing that his life was still in danger. And very likely Senica's life, too.

His blood chilled at the thought.

PART 3

RETRIBUTION

CHAPTER 28

Senica shivered on leaving the bed to answer the phone. She put on the nearest thing she could find – Rafael's green sweater – and went into the living room. Another day nearer El Salvador, she noted keenly. Unlike the people themselves, the British weather seemed forever hostile.

She lifted the receiver and waited, as instructed from the day she arrived in Europe, for the caller to introduce themselves.

'Rafael?'

'It is Senica, Joshua. How are you this morning?' she asked, using her English.

'Oh, mustn't grumble. I'm good. The sun's...the sun's just breaking through.'

To Senica, he sounded frail – and she thought she heard a rasp, as if he was straining to fill his lungs properly.

'At a guess it'll be with us all day,' added Joshua. 'And

Anna…Anna's going to prepare a heaven-sent meal for this evening. Yourself?'

'Not good for me. No sunlight.'

'We're nearly there. Not long to wait.'

'I tell myself this. Joshua, I go now and bring him.'

* * *

Rafael snapped out of a dream he couldn't quite remember to find Senica standing over him. 'What is it?'

'Joshua. He's on the phone.'

He rubbed the sleep from his eyes and peered at the luminous dial on his wristwatch. 'It's not even seven o'clock.'

'Hurry, he's waiting for you. He sounded a bit breathless.'

Rafael dragged himself off the bed and pulled on a pair of boxer shorts before clipping his elbow on the doorframe.

'Oooh, careful,' reacted Senica, following him into the living room. 'I felt that, Rafael.'

'I'm half asleep.' Rafael rubbed his arm and picked up the receiver. 'Joshua…' he acknowledged warily, sensing some sort of a crisis.

'Screening's going to be Central Europe, Rafael. 21:00…21:00 hours.'

Rafael heard for himself Joshua's shortness of breath. 'Are you okay? I can hear you wheezing.'

'I'm good. Went to take some dawn air, to the end of the drive and back.'

'And Anna and Michael, are they with you?'

'Certainly are. Where can I reach you this evening?'

Rafael sat on the arm of the settee. 'We're taking a meal out, with Marc and Susan.'

'Thought you'd be…having popcorn.'

'With each frame engraved on my mind for life?'

'You'll take your cell phone? I know you hardly carry the damn thing. What's the number of the restaurant…in case I can't get you directly?'

Rafael gave it to him while idly watching Senica drink a glass of water. 'It's called Lukács. They know me there.'

'I'll call you.'

'Later, then.' Rafael cradled the receiver.

'What did he want?' asked Senica.

'To say it's being screened tonight.'

'Do you think he's all right?'

'Told me he went for a stroll. Got him a bit out of breath. Anna and Michael are with him.'

In the bathroom, Rafael threw some water over his face. He considered Joshua's move to go for primetime in Europe rather than the States or the Far East to be a shade symbolic – a stake through the monster's heart, since according to Joshua the Council's get-togethers were invariably held in either Bern or London.

He came back into the bedroom. 'I need to call Joaquín Hernández, MS-13. Tell him it's going to be screened. Want some coffee?'

'Just water.' Senica sat cross-legged on the bed and held out her glass. 'The weather might be all bad here, but the water I do like.'

Rafael started to leave the room, until what she'd said struck a chord. He went and sat next to her. 'My concern when you came over to Europe had little to do with you taking on the part, but more to do with trusting you didn't fall victim to a certain way of life. An absurd thought, now that I truly know you.'

Senica hitched his sweater over her shoulder and leaned into the pillows. 'In a park in San Salvador there's a statue of Christ with his arms outstretched, standing on the globe. Gringos, I've been told, refer to it as "Christ on the Ball". There's an epic poem by one of our greatest poets, Oswaldo Escobar Velado, that mentions the statue. It's called *Exact Homeland*. Do you know this poem?'

'Yes, I do.' Rafael was intrigued about the point she clearly wanted to make to him. 'The section I think you might be referring to starts... *Under the shadow of El Salvador del Mundo*. Right?'

'Can you remember all of that section?'

'I'm sure I can.' Rafael reached for her hand. 'Here goes...

'Under the shadow of El Salvador del Mundo
One sees the face of the exploiters.
Their grand residences
With windows that sing the night
Illuminated
To kiss a blonde in a Cadillac.

There, in the rest of the country,
A great pain
Nightly:
There are the exploited
And I with them.
Those of us that have nothing
Except a scream,
Universal and loud
To frighten the night.'

Rafael smiled with her. 'How did I do?'

'You said it perfectly.' Senica squeezed his fingers. 'This is what I want to tell you... When I lived in San Vicente, glossy out-of-date magazines that came my way filled my everyday thoughts. Pictures of beautiful women wearing beautiful clothes living beautiful lives – or so I believed. But the truth is, how can I ever turn my back on those who sacrificed food so that I would not go hungry? And Jorge…how can I dismiss my duty to watch over him? His mother had the patience to be there for me throughout my childhood. She, in effect, became my surrogate mother.'

Rafael kissed her cheek, and found himself thinking about the question that had started to haunt him. She had given him no indication to suggest otherwise, but he couldn't quite see how she could not be reminded of it. 'Tell me, Senica, with honesty…when they took Jorge's parents away, do you think of the MS-13 thug who hurt you when we make love? Does he invade our love-making?'

Senica inclined her head and toyed with a loose thread on Rafael's sweater. 'As with the body, the mind has healing qualities, too. The scars are there, but you find ways, methods, to go around them. Of course, some people are not so fortunate, their lives completely ruined with open wounds that can never heal. Every day, I say a prayer for them. And whenever I pass a church, I always light a candle for Lil Milagro Ramírez, because she suffered so badly at the murderous hands of the National Guard all those years ago.'

Rafael felt tears in his eyes and brought her closer to himself. 'I know she did.'

'A person can't get rid of such a thing entirely, Rafael.' With a calm smile, Senica lightly touched his lips. 'But don't worry. It doesn't put me off, because you are too strong for him. Too refined, in so many ways. As brutal as he was, he was a pathetic creature – and a coward, probably. I'm sure they usually are.'

Rafael kissed her hand, her answer perhaps as pragmatic as he could have hoped for. He wiped his eyes and got up to go to the kitchen to replenish her glass. While running the tap, he took a coffee cup for himself from a shelf – the gunman in Norland Square all at once leaping from his subconscious.

He spun on his heel to face the sash window. The layout of the neighbourhood was virtually identical to Norland Square, only without the railings and tennis court. Nothing unusual appeared to be happening, apart from the primeval tingle on his spine. The weather was the same: grey and dreary, as it had been for the entire past fortnight. He sighed over his stupid paranoia. Something out of nothing. Had to be. Little more than the movement of a pigeon on the ledge opposite, perhaps.

Nevertheless, he lowered the blind.

'What are you doing?' asked Senica from behind him.

He swung away from the window, believing she was still in the bedroom.

'You're worrying again, aren't you?' she remarked, a little sharply.

'I thought someone was watching us. I think it was just a pigeon, to be honest.'

'A pigeon?' Senica hesitated, as if she was about to fall into a heap of laughter before changing her mind. 'Rafael, I'm honestly grateful you're protecting us both. But it…well, it just unnerves me when you start doing things like this…' She indicated at the blind. 'I mean nothing's happened now for weeks, has it? Since our last day at Pinewood.'

'It's only for a couple of more days.' He reached for her hands. 'I don't know where I'd be without you, Senica. I can't imagine. It terrifies me so much. You can understand that, can't you? With what happened to Lena?'

'Of course…' A tenderness came to her brown eyes. 'I didn't think.'

He held her face, and then brought her into his arms. 'You're just going to have to put up with me in this frame of mind until we're out of the country.'

CHAPTER 29

Keen to avoid Erika from being identified and logged by secret servicemen housed opposite the building he was expected to visit, Raoul left the car in Mayfair's Charles Street. He turned into Hay's Mews, the streetlamps illuminating a surprisingly spacious alley flanked by orderly mews cottages, several of which were painted while others retained the colour of their bricks and mortar. It was at such a cottage that he was greeted by an individual of similar age and height, although not as broad as himself.

Carl Dürrenmatt had been everywhere and yet nowhere. Hardly mentioned in the chronicles of history, he was nonetheless more influential than any president or prime minister or the more obvious puppets – the psychotic dictators and generals whose thirst for power guaranteed outrageous mayhem and suffering. To all intents and purposes, Dürrenmatt was a ghost, a ghost nevertheless feared by those who sought to shake his hand, each and every one of them pre-stained by irrefutable allegations of inappropriate behaviour in preparation for immediate removal should they dare to disrupt the Agenda.

But there was another side to Dürrenmatt, a side that spurned opulence. Ushered into the living room with hardly a greeting of any kind, Raoul noticed several armchairs haphazardly facing each other as though a meeting had just broken up. The remaining pieces of furniture consisted of a plain table with a reading lamp next to a television set. Unlike the lamp, the television set was switched on with the sound muted. *Agenda Indiscriminate*'s principal characters appeared to be under attack from a gunman across the street from where, Raoul presumed, they were now living, having watched the film's opening scenes before the anticipated call came through from Dürrenmatt demanding that he 'drop everything' and visit Hay's Mews.

Dürrenmatt removed his spectacles and pointed vaguely towards the television set. 'This…this Maqui – Rafael Maqui, I understand the director's name to be – is greatly mistaken if he sees himself as a folk hero,' he insisted, before emitting a barely audible snort. 'He will be loathed for what he has done. Should the people need prompting, then we will prompt them, rigorously so, until they realise that only a supranational government can save their miserable lives.' He strolled to the table, turning his back to Raoul. 'For how long have you been aware of Loran Communications' duplicity?' he asked, his French accent having dropped an octave, its pitch palpably ominous.

In the past, such chilling tones from Dürrenmatt would have made Raoul quiver to the core of his being. But having predicted the question, he decided to play along with the man, fascinated by how he intended to handle a defective operative standing in his midst. It had surely never happened this way before.

'I stated that Waldo was capable of developing into a threat over a year ago.' As he spoke, all he could actually think of was the rhyme *I'm the king of the castle, and you're the dirty rascal* spilling out of Dürrenmatt's nasty, virtually lipless mouth. 'No action was taken.'

Dürrenmatt swung away from the table, the chubby face that seemed at odds with its rigid mouth redder than before. He folded his spectacles and slotted them firmly into the top pocket of his nondescript charcoal suit. 'He was serving us well. But that is irrelevant. At some point you became aware of his intention, since you would have had him under surveillance in your quest to prove to your peers that he needed to be dislodged.' With eyebrows raised, Dürrenmatt beckoned Raoul to be more specific. 'So, when did this…this shabby *volte-face* occur? I'm curious to know.'

Raoul was barely listening; his chest felt as if it had been struck by a sledge-hammer as he stared in disbelief at the television. 'That actor's meant to be Anthony McCormac,' he uttered, as much to himself as to Dürrenmatt. 'And the newsreel footage…it's a close-up of you standing in the background – at the last World Trade Biennial Conference, I'd hazard a guess.'

Dürrenmatt glanced at the screen. His jaw twitched. 'Pitiful,' he rebuffed. 'They haven't a hope. Unlike the mob, we have troops. We can quash any protest, any upris—'

'I wouldn't be so confident.'

'Oh, and why is that?' Dürrenmatt's tone was sarcastic rather than curious.

Raoul spoke effortlessly, a life of deception to him now characterised by stupidity and self-inflicted oppression against one of fundamental truth and liberty. 'After today, the troops you speak of must realise they're protecting a system that believes it can govern the world by orchestrating hell on earth.'

Dürrenmatt chuckled, but there was hatred in his beady eyes. 'And if we advance the crash? Permit a more potent virus than the last one to traverse the continents? The mob will resemble wave after wave of headless chickens! Soldiers will be deployed to quell the chaos, their sense of duty and that of their generals hardly likely to fail them.' Dürrenmatt steadily clenched his left hand in front of himself. 'You see, both the mob and the troops are like clay in my hands, moulded and motivated to whatever action, or *re*action, our strategies dictate. The people will be left with no alternative than to howl for mercy.

Understand me...*no* alternative.'

Unnerved by a glimpse of his past amid the manic contempt in Dürrenmatt's eyes, Raoul set the seal on his departure from the Council of the Faithful Brethren – or, as he now referred to it in his mind, *The Council of the Damned*. 'The Agenda has never before been so exposed, and with it, the Council's abhorrent doctr—'

'Listen to me, Cregan! You were never one of us. You were regarded by the Council as little more than a politician. In other words, a mere foot-soldier.' Dürrenmatt swaggered about the room, his left hand clasping his right wrist behind his back. 'The mob will bungle it. Your observations overlook the unarguable fact that as a force it is divided and thus ineffectual – comically so, I might add. When did you ever witness headless chickens organise themselves?'

Without a moment's thought, Raoul went for him and seized Dürrenmatt by his lapels. 'Chickens? You're talking about my people! People I've loved. My wife...my Mother...and yes, my son!' He glared into a pair of now uncertain if not scared, though certainly soulless, eyes. He pushed Dürrenmatt up against a wall. 'Make no mistake, it is the people who are and always will be the true victors, their courage measured by everything that is thrown at them. And you will *never* conquer courage of that kind, because it is inherently founded on love and not hatred.' He thrust Dürrenmatt aside, watching him stumble awkwardly into an armchair. 'You haven't a hope, Dürrenmatt. The dogma you indulge in is as flawed as it is grotesque. That's what my observations have taught me!'

Raoul left the cottage. The best was yet to come, he told himself. He picked up his pace, breathing the night air deep into his lungs, the rain itself sanitising. The moment he turned into Charles Street, Erika climbed out of the Jaguar and ran towards him. He caught her in his arms, his lips against the lobe of her ear.

'Yes, Erika. Thank God for Erika!'

She held his face and kissed him, taking her time. 'I love you. I just *love* you.'

When she finally pulled back, Raoul chuckled. 'You're an amazing woman. I can't compare you with anything, damn it!' He put his arm around her. 'Something I've been meaning to tell you…rural France. A flight, right now. What do you say?'

Erika walked with him back to the Jaguar, and then kissed him again. 'It can be anywhere, Raoul. I'm telling you!'

He bowed theatrically and swept open the passenger door for her.

She laughed, throwing her head back, eyes glistening. 'Thank you, my good man.'

'Much appreciated, Ma'am.' Raoul suddenly pictured Ridgeway Hall engulfed in flames. His journey had been like no other. He walked around the car and slid into the driver's seat. At the back of his mind he wondered what form McCormac's reaction to the film would take.

He turned the ignition key. What did he care? He was nothing to do with them anymore. He looked across at Erika and touched her cheek. 'Thank you,' he said to her. 'For everything about you, Erika… I'm so grateful.'

He smiled with her, and simply couldn't resist bringing her back into his arms.

* * *

Dürrenmatt shook his suit into shape. It was not the first time an operative had turned court jester, nor would it be the last.

That aside, an opportunity had clearly arisen to replace the remaining strands of nationhood with the Agenda's *inauguration absolute*, an opportunity resulting from Joshua Waldo's absurd oversight! He leaned back into the armchair to watch the tail end of the speech, taking with him the tonic water he had poured earlier.

The mention of 'climate change' caused him to smile. No matter what anyone thought or tried to do, the financial resources to modify it were solely in the Council's hands.

The phone rang. Annoyed at the interruption, he reached across to a side table. 'Yes?'

'I've...I've got a gun in my hand.'

Dürrenmatt sighed. He'd half expected the call. 'So?'

'The way we're doing it,' Anthony McCormac murmured, his voice heavy and patently distraught. 'We're going to be looking at an uninhabitable wasteland. We were warned—'

'You imagine for one minute I have the time to listen—'

'Glory binds itself to creation, not destruction. Integrity, as opposed to narcissistic hindrance. It's goddamned obvious!'

Dürrenmatt sat back in the chair, reminding himself that fate always found a way to weed out the weaklings, and today was no exception. 'Say, Anthony...'

'What?'

'You're no good for us. Why don't you just go off some place?'

'After this film? With me, the Foreign Secretary, giving the speech? Go off some place? I've got the media camped out down by the lodge. A daughter in Cambridge wants to know what the hell—'

'Anthony...use it. Just use it.'

'I'm going to. Right...*now*!'

Dürrenmatt heard a detonation – loud enough for him to jerk his head away from the receiver. He looked at it, half surprised, but that was all.

He left the phone off the hook, not wanting to be disturbed – his own words drifting reassuringly back to him as he reached for his glass.

The mob will bungle it.

CHAPTER 30

Cartigny – Switzerland

The shot panned from the horror on the faces of those gathering in the street to focus on Romina. The fatal wound inflicted by the gunman before he was seized showed itself as a crimson patch below her left shoulder. Oblivious to the clamour around him, Saúl Majano fell to his knees and reached for her hand. The final frame morphed by degrees into exquisite sculpture, their clasped hands epitomising humanity's defiance against repression.

The symbolic image became a backcloth for the silent roll of credits, pseudonyms for the most part. Joshua settled himself in the armchair, an impression that his life was now complete dawning slowly on him. It was not so much a sense of irresistible euphoria, as one might have expected, as a modest ripple of contentment. If he were allowed a private wish, it would be that his wife, Sarah, and his daughter, Jemima, had watched the screenplay at his side.

He looked at Michael Ramsey, and in particular his ever-supportive confidante, Anna Sangster. 'You're not going to deny me a cheroot, are you?'

Anna tut-tutted and shook her head, but smiled warmly. 'Your darn charm, Joshua Waldo!' She left the settee and massaged the small of her back with her fingertips. 'I suppose on this occasion we can overlook the misdemeanour.' She crossed the glowing hearth and brushed her lips against his cheek. 'Rafael's done you proud. He's captured everything that we know to be true.'

Joshua reached for her hand. 'I can't argue with that. We were fortunate to have had his artistry on board.'

'So, what happens now?' Michael asked in his Kansas drawl.

'It'll be repeated over twenty-four hours,' Joshua explained, 'covering peak viewing across all time zones.'

'And the net?'

'About an hour ago.' Joshua took the slender cigar and lighter from Anna. 'Michael, there's a bottle of Krug in the compartment alongside the icebox. Would you do the honours?'

'I sure will.' Michael got to his feet to go to the kitchen.

Joshua called the number Rafael had given him earlier in the day. Speaking by chance to the restaurant's manager against a background of chitchat and the clink of glass and china, he was soon talking to Marc Fauré.

'What have you decided on eating in that place?' Joshua asked. 'Long time since I've savoured Hungarian.'

'*Lecsó*, and we're drinking *Kadarka*,' Marc said. 'Haven't touched a red like it in a while. Heavy and not at all rough. Rafael's on his way over. Has it finished?'

'A minute ago. I'll try and get my hands on a Palme d'Or.'

'Don't leave yourself off the credits. Rafael's right here.'

Joshua leaned into the armchair and smiled at Anna.

It was the briefest smile in his life, broken by the sight of a pistol levelled at his head.

Without speaking, Anna took the receiver from an open-mouthed Joshua and severed the connection with London, just as Michael entered the room.

'Hey, what the—'

'Stay where you are, Michael.'

Michael blindly left the bottle of champagne on a side table. 'Anna...' Though his face was ghost-white, he nevertheless stepped towards her. 'Anna, give me the gun.'

He barely covered two paces before the room was hit by a shattering report, the bullet piercing the vibrant Kilim rug centimetres from him.

'Down on the floor, Michael!' Anna kept the gun trained directly on him. 'Your hands behind your back. Now!'

Joshua fought for breath, and with Anna's voice ringing in his ears he found himself craving the oxygen bottle next to his wheelchair. His eyes must have shown it.

'You're not going to be needing any of that,' Anna said, as if she were conducting a business matter with a subordinate. 'Our work is done.'

Sensing cold sweat breaking out over his face and chest, Joshua looked up to see the frightening intensity in her eyes. 'Anna...I don't underst—'

'It's very simple, Joshua. You see, my grandparents on my mother's side perished in Sachsenhausen. You know all about Sachsenhausen, *don't* you?'

Joshua clamped his eyes shut, as if to banish her words and the awful horror they embodied as described to him by his father, a war correspondent and photographer assigned to the Polish Army's 2nd Infantry Division, the camp's liberators alongside the Red Army. *They were living skeletons as a consequence of disease and malnutrition. Three thousand of them. The remaining thirty-three thousand were sent on a death march as the Soviet Army closed in on the camp. The SS intended to put them on boats and then sink those boats...*

Anna started to wave the gun about, pointing it loosely at Michael, face down on the carpet, then back at Joshua. 'Neighbours risked their lives to help smuggle my mother out of the country. *That's* courage. Decency. Humanity. And, of course, beginnings have endings, Joshua, just as endings have beginnings!'

Joshua glanced at Michael, stock still and likely to be shaken – if not terrified. Despite the band of pain tightening ominously around his chest, he realised he needed to stall for time – and so asked the first question that surfaced in his fear-ridden mind.

'You planted that microphone in the living room in New York, didn't you?'

'And in your study.' Anna threw up her hands. 'God's sake, Joshua, I had to keep up to date with the schedule.'

'And now…now I'm presuming you intend to maximise the hit by taking me out?'

'And have the world believe the order came from the monstrous ruling elite – the likes of Carl Dürrenmatt? Yes, precisely that.' Anna shrugged her slender shoulders. 'It's logical, really. Of course, it is.' She fixed her eyes squarely on him. 'But what is far from plain to see, Joshua, is who financed Hitler and the Nazi regime – don't you think? Germany was a wreck of a country, ravaged by the First World War. So, where did the finance come from to construct such an effective war machine in a few short years? Industrialists hell-bent on promoting anti-Semitism? Their donations were trivial in comparison! And tell me this…were there any prosecutions? Hardly. So, *where* did the bulk of the finance come from? What channels were used, aside from the Bank of England's role on behalf of the Reichsbank in the transfer and selling of Czechoslovakian gold looted by the Nazis? Without such channels opening up as if by magic, there would have been no camps, no goddamned Hitler…no carving up of Europe…no Cold War…'

As Anna spouted forth, Joshua struggled to wipe the icy sweat off his face, convinced his deteriorating condition was on the verge of eliminating any hope of a preventative outcome. Time, it seemed, was now evaporating into mere seconds.

'You know, just as I know,' continued Anna, 'that anti-Semitism wasn't created by people who hated Jews…it was orchestrated by people who despised *humanity* in its entirety, as a line of defence for the ignorant and clueless to soak up, to deflect from themselves – from their greed and vile scheme to enslave us all under a World Government.' She abruptly redirected the gun. 'Keep your hands together, Michael. I've shown you I'm capable of using this.' Her steely eyes darted back to Joshua. 'And so Rafael, as decent as he is, has to be sacrificed, too.'

The shock of her words detonated with the force of a grenade inside Joshua's petrified mind. He gripped the armrests on his chair, wanting only to catapult himself into her and extract every detail of information in the hope of preventing such an atrocity.

'Anna, what the hell are you saying?' he heaved. 'You've actually got someone to murder Rafael?'

Anna shrugged. 'I had to get myself a specialist. I'm sorry about the Ming dynasty pieces that I took in Santa Monica to pay for his services. These professional hitmen seem to charge an absolute fortune. You've no idea—'

'No, Anna!' Joshua's inner screen was invaded by a grotesque image of Senica kneeling with her face buried in her hands. 'Absolutely, *no*! Do what you feel you must do to me, but stop this person from killing Rafael!'

'He has to die,' countered Anna fiercely. 'Surely you can damn well see that? He just *has* to. Don't you dare tell me what to do! You can't imagine the effort I've put into all this. I've examined every option…' She paused, as if to prevent herself from hyperventilating, and as her breathing settled there came an awful sadness in her eyes. She shook her head. 'Dear, dear Joshua, I don't want it to end this way. But it has to. Please understand. The suffering has to stop. If we allow it to continue there will be more Holocausts, genocides, more famines—'

'How is this man going to kill Rafael?' demanded Joshua. He tried to stay focused, away from the dread that at any moment he was going to black out. 'By what means?'

'I told him to make it spectacular, at the restaurant. He's a wizard with Semtex, apparently. By tomorrow morning people of all nations and faiths will be pointing a finger straight at—'

'I'm begging you, Anna!' cried Joshua. 'Call off this hitman. *Please!*'

She reached for the notepad next to the telephone that bore the number for Lukács restaurant. 'I think it would be foolish to leave information around for the police to analyse. Don't you?'

In his peripheral vision, Joshua noticed that Michael had parted his hands. He avoided the temptation to turn his head to take a closer look, seeing instead the need to create a diversion. 'Tell me, Anna…are you going to end your own life after you've dealt with me?'

She tossed the notepad to the back of the fire. 'Of course I am. What's the point in—'

Michael leapt from the floor and slammed his weight into her, the blow flinging the pistol from Anna's grasp. She tried to make a grab for it, but when he pushed her she stumbled across the hearth and hit her head, the stunned glaze in her eyes sliding swiftly into unconsciousness.

Michael wasted little time. He separated the ammunition clip from the pistol before firing the single bullet left in the chamber into a basket of logs. After a glance at Joshua, he strapped the oxygen mask into position. 'I'll be a moment – no more,' he said. 'The case is in the kitchen.'

'No!' Joshua dragged the mask from his face to make himself understood. 'No time for drugs, Michael. Warn them!'

Michael hesitated. 'I have to make sure you're...'

Joshua jabbed his finger at the phone.

'What's Rafael's cell phone number?' Michael stepped away from the door. 'Can you remember it?'

Joshua repositioned the mask, now fighting not only for his own life but for Rafael's, too. 'He...he doesn't carry it much. The restaurant... Lukács – Hungarian.'

Michael seized the phone.

'It'll be the last number I dialled in when...when you were in the kitchen.'

'It has to be a bomb,' insisted Michael while retrieving the number for the restaurant. 'A wizard with Semtex, she said. And that he had to make it spectacular.'

As Michael began to speak into the phone, Joshua sank deeper into the armchair. The atrocious vice-like grip started to melt away from his chest – and he had the idea he was recovering as an avenue of sacred memories materialised directly in front of him.

CHAPTER 31

'It'll be a fault on the line at his end,' Marc interjected, making a minor adjustment to his attire by running his thumbs under a stellar pair of braces depicting planets and shooting stars. He glanced back at Rafael as he replenished Susan's glass at a packed-out Lukács, the West Ealing restaurant renowned across the city for its traditional Hungarian cuisine and assured bonhomie. 'I can't see it being anything to worry about. Besides, Anna and Michael are with him.'

Rafael sipped his coffee, convinced that the sound he'd heard had been that of someone replacing the receiver rather than an untimely fault. And now there was no response at all from either Joshua's mobile phone or the landline, just a constant engaged signal from the latter. He turned to Senica. 'Why don't we finish off here and call Juana?' he said, making an effort, conscious of the change in mood around the table. 'Speak to José or Sancho if they're around. Liam should arrive any minute.'

Senica took her hand from Rafael's and stood up. 'Give me a moment,' she said, and left them for the cloakroom.

Susan tucked in her arms and gave herself an excited shake.

'What?' asked Rafael.

'She's lovely, Rafael. So caring.'

'I know she is.' Rafael was touched by Susan's growing affection for Senica.

Marc put down his glass. 'Nothing short of a miracle, *mon ami*.'

'Tell me about it. And that you've both taken to her means the world.'

'How couldn't we?' Susan remarked.

Rafael watched Senica with a sense of pride as she moved across the restaurant – a couple of gentlemen diners, he noticed, distracted by her presence. Over the past couple of weeks, he'd privately wondered whether they might marry and have this Father Rodríquez character she kept mentioning conduct the ceremony under the ceiba tree behind the cornfield – with the villagers in attendance and Marc as his best man. Even Javier might drift by in some ethereal form or another!

Senica disappeared into the cloakroom just as the robust manager swept into view and rapped a spoon loudly against a side-plate. Everyone looked up. The manager cleared his throat. 'A call's come through to say there might be a device – an explosive device – left on these premises…'

The statement struck Rafael with the ferocity of a thunderbolt in some bizarre dream. Except this was no dream! He grabbed Senica's jacket as the manager launched into an animated modus operandi on how to calmly evacuate the restaurant, pointing initially at the tables on his left.

'Join you outside,' Rafael told Marc.

He shouldered his way through the barrage of people scrambling for the main entrance in a state of near panic, having all but cast aside the manager's procedure. With five bombs having been detonated in the city by extremists in the previous week, no one was taking any chances. Arriving at the cloakroom, Rafael found Senica checking herself in the mirror.

Her eyes widened. 'Rafael, what are you—?'

'Someone's put through a call claiming to have left a bomb in the restaurant.'

'A bomb?' She stared back at him, her hand moving to her breastbone. 'Rafael, it's happening. They're going to try and take us out!'

He handed over her cotton jacket and whipped open the door. 'It's not connected with us. The film's already been screened, so how can it be? A hoax, hopefully.'

Senica glanced back at him as they emerged from the cloakroom, hair swishing around her shoulders as if to emphasise her sense of alarm. 'But this morning, when you thought we were being watched…'

He guided her through an emergency exit and into an alley littered with plastic crates. 'Just me being paranoid, with any luck.'

They joined Marc and Susan and the rest of the diners on the pavement. The manager stood with his waiters and kitchen staff further down the street on the other side of the restaurant.

Rafael turned to Marc. 'I've got some cash on me. Should be enough to cover the cost of the meal. We can then head out of here.' He set off down the street towards the manager.

* * *

Senica reached for Susan's hand. Nothing added up, as far as she was concerned. Why put a bomb in a restaurant if Rafael was the target? *Unless* the killer's strategy was to make such a call, empty the restaurant as a consequence and simply wait for the target to appear in plain sight. She scanned the street again. And then…

She saw a restless-looking figure in a white car several metres from the entrance to Lukács. The driver had the sidelights on, and perhaps had the engine running, too – *ready*.

She took her hand back from Susan and moved away. 'Rafael!

Rafael, the car!' She started down the street. 'The car *next* to you!'

* * *

Rafael turned to see Senica sprinting towards him, just as a bulbous object emerged over a car's side-window alongside him. Without a second thought he threw himself against the rear door to trim down the gunman's line of vision, his right hand seizing the weapon's silencer – which coughed, the bullet skimming past him. Then came a rapid second shot that barely missed his foot, throwing up cement shards from the pavement. He tried to force the gun from the gloved hand. Two more shots, again ricocheting millimetres from where he was standing, the silencer on the verge of scorching his hand. Should he chance his luck and make a dash for cover – for the van parked directly behind? But just as Marc reached him, he caught hold of some hair and gave it a fierce yank. There was a yelp from inside the car and the Sauer pistol with its smoking silencer clattered onto the kerb.

Unsteady with shock, Rafael caught his breath, seeing people flee the area just as Marc dragged a blond male from the car. Vaguely aware he needed to interrogate the man, Rafael watched helplessly as Marc swung the dazed assassin around and rammed him into and through a shop window – the pavement suddenly awash with glass.

'Come on!' Marc shouted across at Rafael. He kicked the gun away from the car. 'Before the law gets here!'

Rafael seized Senica's arm and sprinted with her down Northfield Avenue, Marc and Susan several paces in front. 'Marc!' he called out after they'd covered forty or so yards. 'Wait a moment!'

From the corner of a side road, Rafael looked over his shoulder. The manager had evidently found the gun and was shouting some kind of warning while aiming it at the white Mercedes.

'He's getting back into the car,' Rafael told them. 'That was quick.'

An ominous crack rang out and the manager simultaneously collapsed without a sound.

Marc gasped and looked at Rafael. 'He's shot him! *Merde*, he must have had another gun in the car.'

Rafael headed back up the street towards the restaurant.

'Rafael!' screamed Senica. 'What are you doing?'

'He's shot the manager. He was out to get us…'

Senica fought to pull him back. 'He's got a gun, for God's sake!'

'We can't let him get away, Senica.'

'He'll kill you. That's what he's been instructed to do!' She lifted a hand to his shoulder and made him meet her eyes. '*Don't* do this to me, Rafael.' She held his face. 'You'll finish me inside. And what of Jorge? You know he's never going to admit how much he adores you. But he does. You know he does!'

Rafael could see the Mercedes moving, the manager curled up on the pavement — sirens in the background drawing closer. He had seconds to act. 'But who's his client? He has to be doing this for someone. He just has to be.'

Susan put her arm around Senica. 'Rafael, listen to me!' she snapped. '*Listen* to yourself. What of dear Senica, right here.'

'Susan's right, Rafael,' said Marc. 'Besides, if you go back, we're going to get caught up with the police. Senica's not exactly legal, is she?' He drew himself up suddenly. 'And if you want another reason, she's just saved your goddamned life.'

The Mercedes made an abrupt U-turn, rear wheels squealing.

Rafael glanced down the street. 'He's coming towards us!'

They darted into a side-street, Rafael turning his head before reaching the hired Mazda.

'Rafael, open the bloody car,' demanded Marc.

'I think he's gone past.'

'He could have taken a side road to cut across into this one,' suggested Susan.

'You could be right...' Glancing at her, Rafael did a double-take, horrified. 'Susan, there's blood all over you.'

She looked down at herself. 'Oh, my God!'

Marc stepped back from her. 'It's...it's me,' he said. He lifted a hand under a streetlight. 'It's coming from me. I must have caught it on the window.'

'Rafael, can we please leave,' insisted Senica sharply in her native tongue. 'I don't feel safe.'

Rafael unlocked the Mazda. 'You're right, let's get out of here.' He waited for everyone to settle. 'How bad is it?' he asked Marc, before pulling away from the kerb.

'Nothing a plaster can't fix,' Marc said.

Susan wrapped her silk scarf over his wound. 'We should call in on Alec, ask his opinion. He's a GP, after all.'

Rafael took the road to central London. 'That bad?'

'It's going to need stitches,' Susan predicted. 'It's still bleeding.'

Rafael made an adjustment to the mirror, offering a better view of the road behind. 'Your brother it is, then. Use Marc's phone to call Liam, tell him we're okay. He'll be at the restaurant at any minute.'

Senica put her hand on Rafael's shoulder. 'Do you think it's the same person who aimed a gun at you in Norland Square?'

'I'm not sure. The one who visited Pinewood Studios had black hair, according to the gatehouse. This one is blond.' Rafael looked at her; her brown eyes were laced with concern. 'I lost it back there,' he confessed. 'So sorry.'

She rubbed his shoulder gently. 'You want answers. I understand that. But I can't bear to think what this person is capable of doing. Everything you've been through.'

'Liam's engaged,' Susan interrupted.

Rafael came up to a set of red lights on the Uxbridge Road. 'Keep trying him.' He stared back into the rear-view mirror, searching, knowing that somewhere nearby was a gunman who just wasn't going to give up. He wondered if the restaurant manager was still breathing. The thought of the trauma he was going through, *if* he was still alive, turned his stomach over.

CHAPTER 32

Rafael swung the car out of the traffic on the carriageway and parked in a bus lane.

'I can hardly hear you, Liam,' he said into Marc's phone.

A moment passed. 'That better?'

'A bit. Are you still with your sister or at the restaurant?'

'Rafael, listen to me. Yes, I'm at Lukács. Get out of the car. Just do that, *now*. He's injured, but he's out there – and he's armed. He got the manager in the shoulder.'

'We saw it happen. What do you mean, he's injured?'

'One of you pushed him through a shop window, right?'

'Yes.'

'The glass cut his neck. He might be tracking the Mazda…but it could be that he's stuck some putty to it.'

'"Putty"?'

'Semtex. I've had a call—'

'Are you kidding me? *Semtex?*'

'I've had a call from Switzerland. From Michael. Where are you heading?'

'To visit Alec, Susan's brother in Anhalt Road.'

'A short distance from Albert Bridge?'

'You have it.' Rafael gave Liam the house number, his pulse starting to thud in his chest. 'Why did Michael call you?'

'I'll explain later. Just do as I say, Rafael. Get out of that car. You hear me?'

'I hear you.'

Rafael handed the phone back to Susan and reached for the doorlatch. 'We have to abandon the car,' he told his passengers. 'Liam thinks we might be sitting on a chunk of explosive.'

'I should have throttled the wretch,' declared Marc.

'It's weird...' Rafael moved his hand back to the doorlatch. 'But it seems Liam's received information about what's going on here from Switzerland...'

Senica was staring over his shoulder. Everything about her looked different, her eyes frozen in horror. And then he realised why: there was the reflection of a person in the passenger window alongside her. Blond hair. The gunman. He seemed to be grinning.

'I can see him,' murmured Rafael against the rumble of the heavy traffic. 'Marc, don't do anything. Act like you're unaware he's right beside me. Talk to Susan or something.'

His eyes came back to Senica. Inexplicably, given the immediate crisis, Sancho and the cornfield flashed across his mind's eye, and then the ceiba tree with its buttress roots...

While looking for advantages over your opponent, barged in Javier, *remember to breathe – and as sweetly as a crocodile!*

Rafael shifted his focus back to the vile image in the passenger window. It struck him then that the man was probably sadistic, so at a guess he was waiting for him to turn around, to feast on the fear in his eyes before putting a bullet between them. But in the midst of that rising fear, a fear that had all but jellified his limbs, he remembered that the door was already off its latch. One less manoeuvre to make, he told himself.

He touched Senica's hand, running his fingers lightly over its graceful form, detecting a trace of puzzlement now in her eyes but all the while remembering to breathe deeply, so deeply, sweetly as a crocodile…

…before unleashing himself against the door, the frame connecting satisfactorily with the man's face. A truck blasted its horn feet away, followed by a car skidding to avoid them as they fell together onto the road. The assassin writhed under Rafael's weight, the air filled with the din of squealing rubber and the clash of steel as vehicles careered into one another. Two shots left the man's gun in quick succession. The first evidently struck either a fuel line or the fuel pump itself on the Mazda, the flicker of a flame visible below the engine bay. The mounting danger didn't register with Rafael; blind rage had taken over. His hand scraped across the asphalt as he grappled to gain possession of the gun.

Then, out of nowhere, a green pixie boot came flying in to kick the man's face, and Rafael realised Senica was with him. A guttural groan switched to a wail as the suede boot stamped on the assassin's right shoulder-blade – and in that moment, Rafael tore the handgun from his grasp.

'You bastard!' he heaved, and seized a fistful of the assassin's blond hair. 'Who hired you? How do you make contact? *Tell me!*'

Blood was flowing freely from the gash on the killer's neck. 'No contact,' he moaned. 'I can't contact.'

Rafael slammed his head down onto the road. 'You're going to have to do better than that.' Onlookers had started to gather around them. Rafael discreetly jabbed the gun into the man's groin. 'A whole lot better! You have a client?'

The man flinched and clamped his eyes shut. 'Yes.'

'What does he look like? Describe him.'

'Never seen her.'

'You mean it's a *woman?*'

'My neck, damn it!'

'Why the attempts before tonight? Tell me!'

A look of bewilderment emerged across the bloodied face. 'Attempts?'

Rafael felt a hand grip his shoulder.

'The girls are getting into his car!' Marc shouted, taking his hand away. 'He's left the keys in it.'

The man held onto Rafael's jacket. 'I need a hospital. My neck…it's bad…'

Rafael stared in disgust. 'A comic, as well as a murderous piece of shit!'

He slipped the gun into his coat pocket, shocked by the state of the Mazda as he stood up, flames already licking ravenously at its front tyres.

'Help me move him away,' Rafael told Marc. 'He's evidence.'

Those drivers who weren't arguing amongst themselves gave assistance. A big man with a lantern jaw lifted the right arm and asked what had happened, but the question went unanswered. They reached the central reservation. Rafael dropped the leg he was holding, Marc the left arm.

'You need to be more careful,' said the big man.

With the assassin clear of the Mazda, Rafael looked desperately at Marc. 'I want more time with him.'

'You can't have it!' Marc's face glistened with sweat. 'We've got to go. There's going to be 'copters in the sky – the works. I repeat, Senica's not legal. Right?'

Rafael started back down the carriageway with Marc, heading for the white Mercedes. He pulled the gun from his coat pocket. 'Marc!'

Marc swung around. 'What?'

'This is unfinished business. I've got to hospitalise him, so I can visit him.'

Marc snatched the gun from Rafael and chucked it towards the Mazda – its flames now beginning to soar into the night sky. 'How the hell are you going to talk to him while you're locked up in a cell! All these witnesses? Answer me that!'

They reached the Mercedes; Senica was sitting in the front seat. He hesitated, and felt the words *Dios mío!* on his lips. He was spellbound by her dark brown Mayan eyes as she looked desperately back at him.

'Marc, let's get the hell out of here,' he said.

Marc opened the rear passenger door to sit next to Susan. '*Cent pour cent, mon ami.*'

The moment Rafael sat behind the wheel, Senica presented him with an object that resembled a Sat Nav, which she cradled in her hands as if she were showing him a little bird. 'It was on the seat. What shall I do with it?'

Rafael took the gadget from her and briefly examined it. 'Most likely a tracking device.' He threw it out of the window. 'That's how he knew precisely where we were all evening.'

The explosion came just as they moved off. The Mazda's ruptured petrol tank sent a fireball into the sky, illuminating the carnage across the carriageway amid bewildered travellers doubtlessly debating the cause of the pile-up.

Susan dragged her eyes away from the rear window and took another look at Marc's injured hand. 'I'm shaking all over,' she said. 'Did you get anything out of him?' she asked Rafael.

Rafael settled into the seat. A hell of a day! he told himself. 'Not as much as I wanted.' He quickly familiarised himself with the Mercedes' facia. 'Odd in a way, but he seemed puzzled when I mentioned the previous attempts. He said his client was a woman.'

'A woman? Did he meet her?' asked Susan, leaning forward. 'Do you have a description?'

'No.' Rafael reached for Senica's hand, bringing it to his cheek before kissing her fingers. He glanced back at the rear-view mirror. 'He said he never met her. He sounded American. I don't know about any of you, but everything feels disjointed. I can't get a grip on any of this!'

* * *

They pulled up outside a Victorian terraced house in Anhalt Road, Battersea. Apart from the porch light, the building was in darkness. 'Perhaps they're asleep,' suggested Marc.

They left the car and Susan strode up the path to her brother's house, where she pressed the bell push repeatedly. No lights came on. Nothing.

'It's no use.' Rafael went over to her, his arm around Senica. 'They're out for the evening.'

While Susan kept trying the bell, Marc peered through the opaque pane of glass above the brass knocker.

'Your hand, Marc…hurting?' asked Senica in English.

Marc stepped back and adjusted Susan's ruined silk scarf. 'No, not hurting. A few shots of whisky would be welcome, though. My nerves are in shreds!'

Senica touched his arm. 'When you come to my village, we will have… How do you say…like fun, you know? Lots of people.'

'Party? Celebration?'

'Yes. Celebration. Uncle José's *aguardiente*. Very good for nerves.'

Rafael turned away from peering through the letterbox. 'I've tried it,' he told Marc with a note of pride, as if he'd survived a trauma of sorts. 'Volcanic in every sense of the word!'

Susan finally gave up with the bell push. 'I know where they keep the spare key. Under a flowerpot or something, somewhere back here. Rafael, help me find it.'

In the event, it wasn't a flowerpot but an ornamental stone. Rafael gave Susan the key. 'The alarm?'

'I know what to do.' Susan put the key in the lock and pushed the door open.

'I should call Juana,' Senica reminded Rafael. 'You said it would be safe to do so now the film's been released.'

Rafael turned to Marc. 'Can we use your mobile…?' The intruder alarm bleeped menacingly as it approached full-blown activation. 'I don't want to leave Juana's number on Alec's phone bill.'

'The alarm's off,' Susan announced. 'Rafael, give Senica a beer and whisky for ourselves. I'll be in the kitchen with Marc. You know where Alec keeps everything.'

Rafael took the phone from Marc and went into the living room. He chose a bottle of Pilsner for Senica. Handing her the glass, he was about to make the connection on Marc's phone for her to speak to Juana when a call came through on it – number withheld.

'Hello?'

'Maqui! Mother of God, Maqui, I've been sifting through your contacts trying to locate you.'

Rafael was bewildered. 'Is…is this Joaquín Hernández, by any chance?'

'Sure is.'

'What do you mean you've been going through my contacts?'

'Had to hack your phone. Precaution, you know?'

Rafael couldn't believe what he was hearing. 'When did you hack into it, exactly?'

'Not long after we last spoke. You don't use it much, do you?'

'Bloody good job I don't!' Rafael feverishly tried to recap whether the MS-13 commander might have picked up anything sensitive during the past couple of months. Fortunately, the majority of his calls to Joshua had been conducted over landlines – not that he supposed it mattered now.

'I've watched it – the movie,' said Hernández. 'I thought I was scum, but these bastards are something else. Top drawer, yeah?'

'Definitely,' said Rafael, sitting with Senica on the settee. 'And?'

'I think we could have some fun with this, but the government has to play out its part.'

'Fun? In what way?'

'Try and screw these *cretinos* back into the slimy hole they crawled out from. Nice if MS-13 switched to protecting Salvador from the crap that's certain to hit the fan – via the Pentagon, obviously.'

'You think there's a chance you can influence MS-13?'

'Segments, that's all. Don't hold out any hope. Get your man in San Miguel… What's his name?'

'Lazaro Dueñas.'

'Get him to set up a meet with the government minister he's in contact with. Before I consider anything, I need it documented that I will be exempt from prosecution. You got that, Maqui?'

'Point taken. Going to take some persuading, for sure.'

There was a snort of amusement from Hernández. 'Tell me, Maqui…you think there's a chance the government will join up with those West African countries and choke off the external debt – printing it instead?'

'If they're keen on repairing the environment and want to implement an acceptable standard of living for everyone, then there's no alternative. The debt amounts to extortion. Thirty-five per cent of the population are now below the poverty line. All it's doing is fuelling MS-13 and 18th Street. You know that. And what with the brain-drain thanks to Washington's recent policy on the border—'

'I'll call you, Maqui.'

Rafael put down the phone and glanced at Senica. 'I know I shouldn't say this, given the vile criminal he is, but Hernández can be quite amusing.' He checked the charge left on the Samsung. Sixty-eight per cent.

'I heard some of it,' said Senica. 'How can he get inside your phone without physically touching it?'

'There are ways. I'm not familiar with them myself, but I suppose, thinking about it, he would need to know how to hack into or clone everything to maintain his freedom against double-crossers informing the law.'

Rafael put Juana's number into the phone, then left Senica to join Marc and Susan in the kitchen, bringing with him a bottle of Glenmorangie. 'I need to get Senica out of the country,' he told them, searching the cupboards for glasses. 'Are you two ready to leave, whenever?'

'There's nothing preventing us.' Susan filled the sink with tepid water and gently began to remove her scarf from the congealed mess on Marc's hand. 'What about you?'

'I wanted to pay the gunman a visit at whichever hospital he might have been taken to, but I think that's out of the question now.' Rafael set three tumblers down on the table. 'The point is, I suggest we head for Madrid and board the first available flight. Belize, Honduras...wherever. That way we'll avoid Miami and stricter security.' He poured the whisky.

'You're saying we're still in danger, over here, that is?' said Susan. 'From another gunman?'

'I have to admit, I'm totally baffled where the hell the other one came from – unless the same client was using him separately. Or maybe the client wasn't satisfied with the first one, after he'd missed so many times. Whatever. The point right now is the restaurant's certain to mention our names to the police. They'll want to question us, and like hell am I in the mood for that.'

The doorbell chimed. And again, continuously.

Susan looked up, startled. 'Who could that be?'

'It'll be Liam,' Marc said. 'Hopefully.'

Rafael put down his tumbler. 'Just our luck if a neighbour's called the police.' He went into the hallway and looked through the spyglass: Liam stood there, larger than life, with his arm extended and his finger on the bell push. Rafael swung the door open. 'We heard you the first time,' he said.

Liam didn't speak but jerked his head for Rafael to follow him out onto the path.

'What is it? What's happened?' Rafael couldn't be specific about what made him think it but as they stood together in the pool of light that spilled out from the living room, Liam looked as if he'd aged ten years. 'How's your sister?' Rafael asked. 'Nothing's happened to her, has it?'

'Michael's been trying to reach you on your mobile,' Liam snapped.

'It's back at the apartment,' Rafael replied defensively, unable to quite gauge Liam's mood, realising now that he looked pale and hunched, as if some invisible parasite was sapping the strength out of him. 'You know I hardly ever bother to—'

'Anna Sangster.'

'Anna? What about her?'

'She's the one who hired the hitman.'

Rafael fixed his eyes on Liam. '*What?*'

'I'm telling you.'

'That Anna Sangster organised everything?' Rafael shook his head and chuckled. 'Don't be bloody ridiculous, Liam! Where the hell did you get this nonsen—?'

'As for the previous attempts on your life,' interjected Liam, 'no one knows where they came from. But Michael assures me that Anna Sangster was the cause of what occurred this evening. She stole part of Joshua's Ming collection to pay for it. But that's not all...'

'Anna Sangster,' murmured Rafael, trying his utmost to picture her as a cold-blooded murderer – before again shaking his head. He looked straight back at Liam. 'It's a mistake. You know yourself it has to be. Anna could never do such a thing. Who said all this to you?'

'Michael. He witnessed everything.'

'What do you mean *everything*?'

'Rafael, listen to me... Something bloody awful has happened.' Liam kicked a loose stone on the path, clearly struggling. 'Joshua... Well, Joshua's passed away, for Christ's sake. He's no longer with us.'

Rafael stood still, incredulous, a numbness spreading through him just as it had when Marc had given him the news about Lena.

'I'm gutted,' carried on Liam. 'He probably saved my life, putting me in that clinic after Guatemala.'

'Died? But...but he can't have...not now. Not today of all days!' His strength having left him, Rafael sat down on a low wall that separated the neighbour's front garden. 'No, Liam.' He looked beyond the pool of light spilling out from the living room; Senica was still chatting away to Juana on Marc's mobile phone.

Liam sat next to him.

'How?' asked Rafael, seeing himself leaning over the gunman on the dual-carriageway.

What does he look like? Describe him.

Never seen her.

You mean it's a woman?

He glanced at Liam. 'How did Joshua die? I mean, Anna didn't—'

'Michael believes the shock of it all brought on a heart attack. It probably did.'

The name *Anna Sangster* began to slice through Rafael like cold steel, skewering him. 'But why should Anna behave in this insane way? What possible motive could she have harboured to have done so?'

'Michael said her grandparents perished in Sachsenhausen.'

Rafael glanced up in shock. 'Sachsenhausen? As in the concentration camp?'

'Yes.'

Rafael slowly nodded to himself. 'Okay…I get it now. I can't fail but to see the convoluted logic that fuelled her line of attack against the ruling elite.'

'Joshua's strategy – the making of a film – likely made it irresistible for her to take her revenge,' remarked Liam. 'And not just for her grandparents.'

'I'm guessing Michael overpowered her?' Rafael asked.

'He did.'

'Had he not done so, and had Joshua not had the heart-attack,' considered Rafael aloud, 'she would have murdered him, and Michael, before committing suicide. Coupled with my death, people would be waking up to some dramatic headlines, to say the least. Yes?'

'As I see it, yes,' agreed Liam. 'The accusations directed at the Council, regardless of what forensic tests came up with in Cartigny.' He straightened himself. 'The point right now, Rafael, is that you're going to have to make a decision. Michael needs to know.'

Rafael looked up from his hands. 'Needs to know what?'

'Whether you want her taken into custody. I mean, we presume you do.'

Rafael shook his head again, his mind all at once littered with random images pitching into one another. 'A few minutes,' he managed to say. 'To myself.'

'Of course.' Liam got to his feet. 'Are you going to be okay?'

'Just go to the others, Liam.' Rafael stood and drifted aimlessly down the path, away from the house. Then another recollection surfaced, jagged and brutal: Anna greeting him with her crocodile tears in Manhattan.

We've been thinking of you.

But how could she have done this to him? To dear Joshua? He wondered how Joshua had felt before he died. Overwhelmed by a sense of guilt that he had been harbouring someone preparing to slaughter them both? He prayed not. How could he have known?

Rafael came to the end of the path, the path that he had walked along so many times with Lena when visiting the house for parties and get-togethers. He looked up, vaguely aware of the traffic passing by. Dearest Lena…

A hand caught his arm. His eyes left the velvety glow of Albert Bridge to see the present collide with the past.

'Would you prefer I left you alone?' Senica asked.

Rafael let his arms fall to his sides. 'No, absolutely not.'

She clasped his hand between hers and held it to her chest.

'But I'm in a mess,' he confessed.

'Liam told us about Anna. It's so hard to believe. What are you going to do?'

'I just don't know, Senica.' He shrugged, sighed and wiped his face. 'What am I supposed to do? I've had this uncanny feeling right inside me, ever since I've known her, that Anna had some kind of a link or connection with the Holocaust. Most Jews do. And now I know it to be a fact. She's evidently suffered over the years. It's unlikely she will ever find peace of mind. On that basis, how can taking her to court help her?'

He gently swept back the wisps of hair blowing across Senica's anxious face. 'But as I stand here, looking at you, I find it's the future I want to embrace, Senica. Wholeheartedly so.' He took hold of her waist and kissed her lips, and then her brow, conscious more than ever before his sheer fortuity to have such a gracious soul as this in his life. 'I think I've been wanting to say that out loud to you for some time. It feels very much that way.'

Senica reached up to him and kissed him back. 'Thank you.' She made him keep his hands on her waist. 'Juana told me Jorge's been busy making a cross for Javier's grave in the cornfield. I really can't imagine what it's going to look like. I'm hoping Sancho's had some input in the project.'

Rafael nodded quietly, before a spontaneous smile took him by surprise. 'I never thought I'd hear myself say this, but Jorge has a certain charm. Hurts like hell to admit it!'

'I wish I could have met Javier,' Senica said. 'I've always imagined him to have been a brave man, a good man.'

'He was all of that.'

Rafael found himself back in the cornfield, kneeling beside Javier while he tried to comfort him as best he could. Or had it, he came to wonder all at once, been the other way around...?

'It's chilly out here, don't you think?' he said aloud, and put his arm around Senica as they passed a fragrant flowerbed. 'Javier? Well, on occasion he could be demanding.' He rubbed Senica's shoulder and she settled her head against him. 'Quarrelsome even, in a mischievous sort of a way. But, yes, for sure, Javier was a hugely decent soul.'

It's about faith, Rafael heard Javier telling him moments before his guide left this life. *Live each day with faith, and liberty will grace this world. This miracle.*

THE END

Printed in Great Britain
by Amazon